BEWITCHED BY PASSION

Henri's strong arms pulled her close. "My wife!" His voice hoarsened, his words sounding more like a whispered prayer.

Maddie drew in a shuddering breath as she raised wide, wondering eyes to his. All the strength had ebbed from her. In its place, desire pulsed through her veins. She waited for him to take her, to possess her. "Make me a woman, Henri," she whispered. "Teach me to be everything you want me to be, and I shall obey."

His arms encircled her. His face, lean, ardent and handsome, moved closer to hers. His lips pressed upon her mouth, caught her up in a thrill of unfamiliar emotion. Her heart raced, and she could feel that his beat in pace with her own.

His lips lingered on hers, drinking in her passion, her warmth, her tremulous eagerness to please him. She clung to him with hands and arms hungry to savor the heat and strength of his body. She writhed, hardly understanding the sensations that consumed her now. "I loved you," she whispered, "from the moment I first saw you."

Bright Glows the Dawn

SANTANA ARROYO

Book Margins, Inc.

A BMI Edition

Published by special arrangement with Dorchester Publishing

Printed in the United States of America.

Chapter One

Maddie Bradshaw glanced to the pew directly adjoining her own family seat in the stately Salem Village church where she had come with her father to worship. Her heart fluttered in nervous apprehension as she thought of the one sitting hidden just behind their shared privacy wall. Andrew Mathias, second cousin by marriage to the Reverend Cotton Mather of Boston, and her own father's business partner, retained that space for himself and his ward, a pallid, sickly boy of thirteen years whom illness had recently kept bound at home.

The man's behavior had alarmed her that morning. As she filed with her father into the sanctuary, she had noticed Andrew Mathias staring at her with a peculiar glint in his eyes. A little later, before services actually began, she had seen him again, still watching. She felt grateful for the high wooden partitions that separated each family pew and served to block his view of her. These closed the worshippers off on three sides so that they might better concentrate on their Puritan God, instead of each other. She knew, however, that his dark, slightly bulging eyes were probably fixed toward her just then—for whatever reason he might have. The very thought made Maddie shudder. In order to attend his ailing nephew, he had come recently from the colonies far south. Some said he had been overseer at a sugar refining factory. Others held he had run slaves from Senegal through the King's West Indian colonies, to ports further north in Virginia and Maryland. If so, Maddie knew he himself would not have done the running, for he was a sedentary man by nature, and weak looking. He would have sat behind a desk indoors, and hired others to face the dangers and discomforts of the open sea.

Andrew Mathias was a tall, gaunt man who held his face in a habitually mournful expression. The grayish yellow of his compexion resembled tallow. Traces of heavy beard badly shaved always shadowed his long, narrow jaw. He had cropped his brown hair short, but then so did all the other men of Salem, for the Puritan Commonwealth of Massachussets had banned cavalier locks. His own, however, looked as if he had clamped a bowl over his skull to trim the edges. Although lace, ribbon, bright color, and fancy ornaments were forbidden here for both women and men as frivolous, Andrew Mathias carried sobriety in dress to an extreme. He wore only black, and the funereal effect he created in so doing repelled Maddie.

Because of his business dealings with her father, he had often visited her at home. Even so, Maddie had never gotten to know him well. Nor did she particularly want to. Joy and humor were as totally alien to his soul as they were necessary to her own. She had once asked him, playfully, what it was that had made him so sad. To her surprise, he had answered that the sins of Mankind burdened his spirit. Maddie, who detested pomposity, tried hard to hide her scornful mirth.

Since coming here a year ago, he had collaborated with her father on certain business ventures here in Salem Village, and in the town itself a few miles away. Both had prospered from the association, but Maddie knew that Andrew Mathias wanted more.

Only yesterday he had approached her father to ask her own hand in marriage. Maddie thanked God the old dear had evaded him, replying that the decision must be her own. She could not see herself bound for life to one so passionless and somber. Maddie had refused, of course, and when she did, she had witnessed another ugly side to the man's nature. He had turned from her in sullen silence. Without even so much as bidding her "good day," he had slammed out of the house.

When they stood to sing a hymn, his face showed clearly over the partition's top molding. His eyes, fixed on her again, glittered. Maddie wondered with a chill what he wanted. What was he thinking of just then? His attention riveted so intensely upon herself made her nervous. She sighed with relief as the congregation reseated itself.

The minister droned on and on. Maddie licked her lips and tried to swallow. Her mouth had dried out long ago. Air inside the meeting house had staled from the swelter of August heat and the crowding. She would have given anything to be out of there, perhaps galloping across her father's fields on the back of her horse Farrow. How she loved the wind they made, and its feel roaring past her cheeks. The sound of Farrow's hooves, thundering on the furrowed soil, lifted her with a rush of power. Dressed in boy's clothes, she always rode astride, free and wild like an Indian. She didn't even mind when the sun burned her face, and speed tangled her hair into knots impossible to comb. Other girls she knew were not so lucky. They lived bleak lives; always spinning or weaving, cooking, sewing, or tending garden. She blessed luck for having such a kind, indulgent father. However, like all good Puritans, he insisted she accompany him to church. In any case, keeping the Sabbath was law for all but the ailing.

Church in summertime was always a trial and tribulation, but in the green season of 1692, it had turned into a horror. The taste and smell of fear hung everywhere. A sense of foreboding had oppressed the congregation. Some wondered who else was guilty. Others merely dreaded who might be taken next. The sermon, warning them to beware the Imps of Satan, cut close to them all. It had started early last spring with Mr. Samuel Parris's eleven-year-old ward, Abigail Williams. Maddie had met the girl once and didn't much like her. Abigail and her friend Ann Putnam had fallen prey to bewitchment, or so they claimed. Maddie herself had never seen them in this sorry state, nor did she want to, but she had heard it described in lurid, rather nauseating detail. As for how it had happened, how it had gotten started—everyone knew *that*.

Mr. Parris, a minister, had kept a slave in his house, a strapping black wench named Tituba. She was the one who had hexed the girls first, although why, nobody seemed to know or care. As a result of her bewitchment, they had fallen into fits, writhing on the floor and screaming. Through dry cracked lips, they had moaned aloud, whimpered, and screamed. Then they began crying out the accusations that had sent Salem Village into turmoil.

Worse, other children too had fallen prey to that same unholy enchantment, whatever it really was. The people, previously proud of their community's wholesomeness, had learned to their horror that Tituba was only one of many witches, Others too, some even neighbors, had joined with the negress in their allegiance to the Devil for the powers He would bestow on them. They had forsaken God and were damned.

Everyone agreed that the horror must be cut out by its roots and destroyed. Satan would not be allowed to spread His night black wings over this stronghold of God. The light they had carried with them all the way from England was too precious to suffer extinction. They had endured too much hardship, risked too much danger to see it blotted out now. Drastic measures were called for, and strong ones were taken. Sir William Phips, the Governor, called for a special investigation.

He had appointed judges who sat not in Salem Village, where friends and relatives of the accused might try to influence a verdict, but in the City nearby, and those taken faced trial for their lives.

Abigail and Ann would fall into fits wherever they felt Evil Ones lurking nearby. Even Andover, their sister town, had invited them to come and sniff out any local witches they might detect. As a result, those two were responsible for the arrests of several local women there too. In Salem, they sat in the courtroom and judged the accused along with the magistrates.

But Maddie didn't trust them. Abby had impressed her as a silly girl given to flights of fancy. Worse, she seemed spoiled, demanding always to be the center of attention. If mistress Ann was anything like her friend, Maddie feared murder rather than justice was being committed. She cared not a whit about the fate of their two souls, should their accusations be false, but pitied the others arrested. Worse, she chilled to think what those two had started. Crying "bewitched" had become a fad which had spread to other children. Since they could name their tormenters and did, each day the gaol filled. Sixteen so far had writhed away their lives at the end of a hangman's rope. At least one hundred more awaited trial, and others their execution. Maddie wondered how long these arrests would go on. Terror, accusation, and death spread like a plague.

Sweat trickled down her forehead. She raised her hand to brush it away. When she and her father had walked along the path from home to church earlier that morning, the sun had barely risen above the eastern horizon. It blared now through the clear glass windows right into Maddie's eyes. From its position, she knew it must be almost noon.

The veil of finely spun white muslin she wore felt hot against her head. She longed to tear it off. Propriety and custom, however, dictated that women of her congregation hide their hair in church. Maddie's own was indeed her crowning glory. When she allowed her hair to hang free, it cascaded almost to her waist. As a child she had worn braids that reached down her back like two thick ropes. Now that she had grown into a young lady, Maddie caught those plaits into a bun that she fastened to her head. Unruly strands always managed to wisp free, however, so that tendrils curled around her oval face to frame it. Right then, however, they were plastered wet and limp to her forehead and cheeks.

Her frock that morning had been woven of cream-colored linen, spun from flax cut in her father's own fields. A rounded collar and plain starched cuffs provided its only trim. She was vain enough to notice how its cut flattered her slim but rounded figure. Its stark simplicity provided the perfect foil for her own rosy, translucent coloring. As she stifled in church, however, Maddie longed to tear it off and run naked through the dandelions, tall grass, and wild mustard growing in her father's fallow back acres.

Just then, the congregation arose to sing its final hymn, a song unadorned by the Papist trappings of instrumental music. As she stood, Maddie sighed in relief. She had been sitting with her father close to the pulpit, in a pew designated as a place of honor. He was one of the village's richest and most respected citizens, and even in the house of God, they sat by caste. Less wealthy families worshipped further back in the church, while servants, slaves, and Christianized Indians had to content themselves with the balcony. Occupying seats assigned to those of a higher social set was a misdemeanor punishable by a heavy fine. Each seat in that church, however, was as hard and narrow as any other. Each resembled a shelf inside a cupboard more than a proper chair. Maddie suspected they had been designed that way on purpose, to keep the congregation awake during those interminable sermons.

As she stood, she felt Andrew Mathias' eyes upon her again. To avoid meeting them with her own, she glanced around. Five rows back, she stopped with a jolt, then turned away. A chill ran up and down her spine. She had seen the pale, desolated faces of Susanna Martin's family.

When the constables had arrested her, their route had taken the woman past Maddie's house. She had watched, because the spectacle had been impossible to ignore. Goodwife Martin had protested her innocence all the way to the gaol. Her screams had shattered the early evening calm. Maddie had stared in horror. She saw that the guards had tied their prisoner's hands behind her back with hemp rope, then fastened its loose ends to a wooden crossbar on the wagon, as if they feared that the devil himself might rescue her from death by hanging. Maddie had known the woman, not well, but as an acquaintance. Nevertheless, she found it hard to believe that the woman was a witch. Whenever she thought about Susanna Martin's fate, Maddie found herself desperately frightened. Why, exactly, she couldn't really say. Finally, the minister's benediction put an end to services.

Maddie looked forward to enjoying a pleasant afternoon out in the back garden with her father. As she stood with the others to file outdoors, however, Andrew Mathias leaned to her over the partition. "Mistress Bradshaw," he whispered, "I must speak to you about a matter of utmost urgency."

Maddie drew back. She found merely speaking to him distasteful. "What for?" She glanced to her father and saw him talking with the Widow Kellogg. "If you're going to ask me to reconsider your proposal—"

"No," he interrupted her, "I know better than that.

11

What I have to tell you though, it's about your father."
He spoke very softly, as if he didn't want her father to
hear.

As Maddie glanced to him, her eyes narrowed. For
some reason she couldn't explain, she had always
distrusted him. The pitying concern she read in his face
at that moment, however, reassured her of his sincerity.
She felt a pang of apprehension. Was her father ill, and
unwilling to burden her with it? Had his business fallen
into rough waters? "What is it?" she whispered.

"Not here." He glanced beyond Maddie. "Come
around the back of the church where we can be alone.
I'll wait for you in the cemetary."

"I'll be there." Ordinarily she wouldn't have gone
off alone with him like that, but her father's welfare
meant more to her than her own feelings about Andrew
Mathias. She accompanied her father and Anne Kellogg
outside. Maddie normally enjoyed socializing after services had ended, but today she wanted only to escape
and find out what Andrew had to tell her. She maintained vigil for the opportunity to slip away unnoticed.
Finally, as her father and Widow Kellogg wandered off
to greet friends from the other side of the village, Maddie hung behind, then edged toward the side yard. A
narrow walkway stretched from the church's front
facade to its rear wall. Bushes grew along its founda-
tion, and a whitewashed fence marked the south boun-
dary between its own and the adjoining property. Sunshine beat hot and bright upon the cemetery's long,
sinewy grasses. A lone bird twittered from the branches
of an aged gnarled maple by the gate, nourished by
those who slept under its roots.

Maddie slipped inside, then glanced around. The
stone wall encircling these graves, and the trees and
bushes growing beyond, obscured her view of the congregation milling in front, and theirs of her.

The air hung unmoving in the dusty afternoon's heat. The smell of freshly-turned earth rankled her nostrils. She fancied that the dead were lying awake, listening to her footsteps past their graves. At first, she believed herself to be quite alone. Silence and the appearance of solitude had convinced her. The stones among which she wandered had risen only recently. Their lettering, carved into rock, stood out in sharp relief.

She even recognized some of the names, like old Katty McGrew, who had died last winter of the ague at age sixty, and beyond her Jon Henry Peterson, 1655-1690, who had been Salem Village's best blacksmith until a horse's hoof had crushed in his skull. He had lingered for almost a week, fighting for his life until the Lord, losing patience, had taken him.

Just below to her right slumbered the child Aaron Michael Swift, son of Nathanial and Rosemary, who had come into daylight colored blue and had died the same afternoon of his birth. A scar of fresh dirt raked outside from his headstone revealed how recently the baby had been lowered to its final cradle.

With a sudden flush of impatience, Maddie wondered what had happened to Andrew. She glanced around, looking for him. She wanted to find out what he had to say, then get out of here. The dead, and their tombstones, inscribed with poems and proverbs of human mortality, oppressed her spirit.

Suddenly she saw him standing by the back fence in among the oldest graves of the churchyard. These had already begun to lean, as their foundations sank into the loam on which Salem Village's older settlers had planted them. Their faces had softened. Wind, rain, and cold had blurred the inscriptions etched into their granite. Weathering had all but obliterated the names and proverbs carved on the gaunt wooden markers of the village's earliest and poorest settlers.

"Well, Mister Mathias!" Maddie greeted him with little friendliness.

He stood unmoving like a statue as he waited for her to approach. A hot breeze, blowing from the south, lifted the hem of his coat. It ruffled the clipped edges of his hair.

"I've been waiting, Mistress Bradshaw," he said.

"Not long," Maddie retorted. "Anyway, I came as soon as I could. What is it? What do you want?"

His lips curled into a curious grin. His eyes glittered with cold superiority.

"What do you want?" As Maddie stared at him, a queasy sense of alarm tugged at the outer edges of her mind. "Is anything wrong? What about my father? You said you had something to tell me about him."

"No, girl," he replied. "I had to say that to get you out here. In fact, your own self is what I wish to speak about."

"You lied?" Maddie drew back.

"Goodwife Jameson is angry with you." He ignored her own anger. "She claims you enticed her husband. I was in Mistress Coney's penny shop yesterday when I heard her talking."

"It is not true!" Maddie stared at him in outraged disbelief. John Jameson had followed her last week as she crossed the commons. When he had caught up to her, he had shown the audacity to reach for her shoulders. She had pulled away before he actually touched her, and she had harangued him with sharp words of reproach. Instead of slinking off as he should have, however, the man had persisted. He had plied her with improper compliments and would not stop. Finally, she had run from his presence, angry at his indecent boldness but unable to stop him.

"He inflicted his attentions upon me," she cried. "I would never have encouraged such behavior, and surely

14

you know it."

As Andrew moved closer, Maddie saw that the smile had frozen upon his lips. "No, I daresay you did indeed reject him, and all with a fine display of righteous anger. After all, you are, as you protest, a virtuous maid." Sarcasm mingled with cold amusement in his voice.

He moved closer. "But a beauty like yourself, full-breasted, ripe and golden, needs to be more than merely virtuous to escape slander." His breathing quickened. He reached for her arm. Maddie, sensing danger, recoiled. With a frightened cry, she stumbled forward into a run.

Within an instant, he caught up. He proved stronger than she had ever imagined. With one arm only, he yanked her back to him, then clasped her to his body. For the first time, she noticed his hands. They were cadaverous; thin and pale, with pronounced veins running up their backs, and he had permitted his fingernails to grow indecently long. They curved in toward the fingerpads, then yellowed. They suggested to her the talons of a predatory bird.

His arm, encircling her with one hand clamped over her breast, imprisoned her. His other slid up under her veil to clutch at a wad of hair. Maddie cried out as his fist clenched, pulling at its roots. Tears streamed out of her eyes. "Let me go, or I'll scream." She fought to catch her breath.

"Go ahead," he laughed, "and everybody will know what you are—a harlot who brazenly thrust herself at me."

"Liar!" Maddie's eyes widened. "You dare to—"

"Who will they believe, you or me?" His smile, cruel and triumphant, mocked her. "Who will suffer the destruction of a reputation? Who might be sentenced to suffer the stocks? Or forced to wear the brand of a fornicator embroidered upon her bodice? Not I, surely, because I live far enough from here for my own convenience. Only my words need remain here in Salem Village. My words—burned into everybody's mind." He smashed a kiss upon her lips.

"How dare you!" Maddie lurched, then bit him hard upon the wrist. Even as he cried out in pain from her teeth, his grasp remained tight around her. Desperate, Maddie kicked at his shin. His grip loosened. She yanked herself away, then slapped his face. Anger must have given him fresh strength. He muttered a curse. He swung around to grab a fresh hold on her hair. Maddie, to defend herself, jammed one knee upward between his legs where she knew it would cause pain.

He choked out a shriek and doubled over. He stumbled forward until his foot tangled in a clump of roots. Caught off balance, he crashed to the ground. He sprawled in a heap, then retched.

Maddie's eyes fixed on him with horror and loathing as she backed away. "You pretend to be so godly, yet look at you!" she whispered. "You've not only defiled the Sabbath with your indecent lust, but this—" She gestured to the surrounding land. "This is consecrated ground!" Maddie struggled to regain her breath. Its short, painful gasps interfered with her ability to speak, or even to move. "You sicken me, sir," she cried. "You sicken me."

"You'll be sorry," His voice resembled the snarl of a dog. He could hardly speak, but his hatred of her, kindled at first by her refusal to marry him, and now fanned alive by the way she had so painfully thwarted his attempt to rape her, had given him strength.

Horrified by the venom she saw in his eyes, Maddie backed away. "God help you, Andrew Mathias," she whispered. "May He forgive what you've done, because I cannot."

16

Her voice broke. She whirled, then fled the cemetary, knowing with sinking heart that Andrew Mathias had become her enemy. An instinct warned her, even then, that he would do anything he could to hurt her.

Maddie's heart pounded in wild fear as she ran toward the congregation milling in front. As she drew closer, however, she stopped. She knew she could not let anyone see her just then, not while she still trembled in such a frenzied state of disarray.

Under the church building's front side window grew a thick berry-laden bush. She stepped behind it. The leaves and branches, heavy with bird fruit, blocked her from view. She waited there in hiding until her breathing had slowed almost to normal.

She felt safe in its shelter. She knew that Andrew would not dare to approach her so close to the others, so she took time to check herself over. To her relief, her dress was intact. Although he had tried, Andrew had failed to tear the sturdy linen off her shoulders. As she reached to straighten her veil, however, Maddie's eyes widened in horror. *She was bareheaded!* She must have lost her church veil when he had reached up and grabbed her hair.

She glanced back toward the cemetery and saw that he remained where she had left him leaning against the stone. On the ground a few yards away, she spotted something white, crumpled and gleaming in the sun. *Her headcovering.* With sinking heart, Maddie knew she would have to abandon it. Andrew remained too dangerously close. Even later on she'd be too afraid to go back in there alone. Perhaps she could send a servant.

Luckily she spied her father just then, standing alone at her own edge of the crowd. The Widow Kellogg had abandoned him to go off and chat with Dame Blaze. Without drawing too much attention to herself, Maddie

17

caught his eye and motioned for him to join her.

Her father was a lean, strong man still in his prime, with graying blond hair and blue eyes like her own. Seeing her, he approached as fast as he dared. His expression revealed worried concern. As he drew up, he scrutinized her. "Maddie, girl, what is it?" he whispered.

"Papa, I feel unwell. I should like to go home now."

"I asked you a question," he confronted her sternly. He knew his only daughter too well to be put off by an evasion.

"Papa, I—" Her voice broke.

"Where were you? Where did you go? I was looking for you."

"This is not the place to talk about it, Papa," she replied. "Please trust me enough to believe that." She turned away so that he would not see her tears.

"Let me take you home then. I want you calm. We will be receiving a visitor this afternoon, a guest who will remain with us for about a week. He and Mister Mathias will be joining us for supper." Maddie recoiled. "Papa, no! Not Mister Mathias. I will not stay if he joins us."

"Maddie, are you defying me?" He seemed more bewildered than angry. He had no way of knowing that his business partner had attempted to rape his only daughter.

"No, Papa," she replied. "When I tell you what happened, you will understand."

Her father took her arm. "Then I want to know. You must have some reason for your strange behavior." Without bidding anyone farewell, he walked with her toward home.

As she described what had happened in the cemetary, Maddie struggled to hold back her tears. She had to remain calm. She knew that if she allowed herself to cry, she would succumb to hysterical sobbing and make a public spectacle of herself. When she finished, her father fell ominously silent. Finally, he turned to her. "You were right to fend him off as you did, Maddie, but tell me—why did you consent to meet him there in the first place?"

"He lied to me, Papa. He told me he wanted to speak to me about you. He had led me to believe that something was seriously wrong. I thought you might be ill, or in some kind of financial difficulty, and I was worried."

"You are a good daughter—dutiful and virtuous, but like all of us, you have a flaw. Maddie, you are too careless when it comes to outward appearance. I have always worried—" His voice trailed off. "And the way things are now, I believe I had just cause."

"What do you mean?"

"You are too fair to be so free and lighthearted in your ways, so merry. I am afraid you've made enemies."

"Who have I hurt?" Maddie's eyes widened in hurt surprise. Her father patted her arm. "No one, except Andrew, who deserved it. I know you are too good and gentle for that, but still, people talk. Try as we might to be Godly, we are all afflicted with human flaws, and for some, unfortunately, the curse is jealousy. It gnaws at their innards and makes them hate anyone more fortunate."

"Like Goodwife Jameson?" Maddie scowled.

He nodded. "Yes, like her. She was never a beauty, God knows, not even as a girl. I think she considered herself lucky to have found any kind of a husband at all and now, believing that her man has gone and letched after you—"

"I never encouraged him!" cried Maddie

"I know, and I think she does too, but who else can

she blame?''

"Herself, for growing fat," Maddie pouted, "or her husband for being such a lout. But why me? Anyway, I know plenty of women just as homely who have devoted husbands. A woman doesn't have to be pretty; only sweet-natured, dutiful in a wifely way, and a good cook.''

Her father's lips twitched in an amused smile. "You are only seventeen, Maddie," he said. "When I was your age, I too believed I had all the answers. I know you'll outgrow it, but meanwhile, try to keep such pearls of worldly wisdom to yourself.''

"What will you do about Mister Mathias?" Maddie turned to him.

"First, I will cancel his invitation to supper," replied her father. "In any case, I'm sure he knows now that he is no longer welcome in my house or on my land. I shall furthermore sever all business relations with him.''

Maddie's eyes widened. "Is that all?" She had no desire for revenge, but felt that people at least should be warned. How many more unsuspecting girls would he try to lure to lonely spots? How many had he assaulted already? She herself didn't know whether it had been luck, Providence, or fierce fighting that had saved her own virtue. "Why not denounce him?''

"What good would it do?" her father sighed. "To broadcast what he did would only besmirch your own reputation.''

"But I am innocent!" Her eyes blazed.

"People talk, Maddie. They ask questions. Why had you consented to meet him under secretive circumstances, if not for some forbidden tryst? They would lack the imagination, or the inclination, to consider any other possibility. You met him on the Sabbath, the holy day of rest and prayer. And why, for Lord's sake, did it have to happen on consecrated ground? People like to gossip, you know, and these details would all provide a tasty morsel indeed—especially since you've aroused such envy among certain women."

"It's not fair, Papa!"

"I never said it was." He shrugged, then led her up the front walk into their house.

Home was a haven she loved. The three peaks of its roof reached toward the sky. Its sturdy shingles and wooden walls had always sheltered them from the weather's fury. During winter, logs crackled in the great fireplaces to heat each white-plastered room. Its chimneys were good and solid, built of brick and kept in good repair. When the weather turned icy, smoke billowed up from them to be swept away by freezing winds. Right then, however, only the August sun warmed their walls. The fireplaces lay swept and cool, waiting for autumn to revive them.

The front yard as they entered it smelled of the roses that tangled there, among violets and lilies in sweet profusion. The pink ones climbing a whitewashed arbor under the south window were Maddie's favorite. When their petals opened from buds, they reminded her of shallow cups painted pale pink on the inside with golden hearts, and they smelled like Heaven. The afternoon was a gift of beauty, but Maddie was still too upset to appreciate it. She wanted to be alone with her thoughts, tears, and anger.

Her father could not help but sense her mood. "Take comfort in the scriptures, child," he said. "They will console you. Meanwhile, you have my promise that I'll do whatever I can to discredit him without involving you."

Maddie squeezed his arm. "Thank you, Papa."

"And Maddie—" Once they were inside, he turned to her. "You look a fright. Wash your face and try to put on a cheerful expression. I think the visitor I'm expecting will improve your mood. To judge by his letters to me, he is most well-educated, worthy, and congenial. I myself am looking forward to meeting him."

"W-who is it?" The last thing Maddie wanted right then was to entertain a guest.

"His name is Henri August de Rohan. I'm thinking of entering into a business venture with him. He'll be coming here to explain his ideas more thoroughly."

Maddie's eyes widened. "Is he a Frenchman?"

Her father, a strict Calvinist, had never shown himself inclined to tolerate any but his own kind. Although she herself entertained no strong feelings one way or the other, she knew that most citizens of Salem, like those everywhere in Massachussets, considered even the Church of England too corrupted by vestiges of Papism to be tolerated in their cities and towns. That he should consider going into business with a Frenchman, probably a Roman Catholic, startled her.

As if reading her thoughts, her father smiled. "French, yes, but a Huguenot—a Protestant. I know very little of his background yet, but I will, soon enough. Now please, go and make yourself pretty again." Upstairs, Maddie paused a few moments to stand at her bedroom window. Her room faced out over the back yard, and its neatly tended rows of flowers, vegetables, and kitchen herbs. The fields beyond all belonged to her father. He had been a farmer at first, toiling in a small plot of land, but his aptitude for business had prospered him.

Eventually, her mood lightened. Suddenly, as she sat combing her hair in front of her mirror, she heard voices downstairs. Her father's description had aroused her curiosity. Wondering now what this mysterious Frenchman was like, she arose from her pillow-tufted seat, turned, and headed through her boudoir door.

22

She heard her father's voice first, followed by the obedient murmur of George, one of their indentured servants. Unlike many men of comfortable circumstances here in Salem, her father kept no slaves. He considered it indecent that one child of God should bind another to himself in lifelong servitude. His servants, brought mostly from England, tilled his soil, kept his house and gardens for seven years. At that time, they became free, to pursue their own futures in the new land they had chosen.

Suddenly, another sound reached her ears, words spoken softly in a resonant, clear baritone. Even though she could barely hear the words, she caught the accent. She had dreaded meeting him, but now she found herself curiously eager to fly downstairs and make his acquaintance.

The staircase spiraled. Its shape obscured anyone standing below. As she stepped onto it, her hand slid against its polished oak bannister. As she descended, Maddie savored as she always did the feel of its cool wood and hard sheen under her fingertips. She rounded its curve into view of the landing below.

Suddenly, she spied him standing alone. She had expected a man her father's age, but she knew now that she had guessed wrong. Indeed, she had never seen anyone like him. Of its own, her pulse quickened.

He was about thirty-five years old. He could not be called handsome, but he exuded an animal magnetism that took her very breath away. His hair was black with reddish glints that caught even the oblique rays of the sun streaming in through the room's north window. It curled thickly on his head and tumbled down his neck. His face was thin—aristocratic, even, with high angular cheekbones, aquiline nose and good, strong chin. His thin-lipped mouth was hard, with a hint, perhaps, of cruelty, and his green, clear eyes reminded her of a hawk's. They studied her as she approached with wary interest. Drawing closer, she saw in them fire, spirit, and alert curiosity, mingled together in an expression that fascinated her. His clothes of sober color and simple cut seemed wrong for him somehow. Maddie could hardly tear her own eyes away. "You must be Monsieur de Rohan," she said.

The smile he bestowed upon her was pensive, as if only half of his consciousness took notice of the social amenities he returned. His mouth opened to reveal white, strong teeth, while his eyes, lingering on her, sent chills down Maddie's spine. "Mister Bradshaw never told me he had such a beautiful daughter. You *are* his daughter, aren't you?" Those eyes held her in willing capture.

Maddie's heart raced. "My name is Maddie," she whispered. She glanced to her father and saw the slightly bewildered, mildly alarmed expression on his face. "Papa mentioned going into partnership with you. What is it you do in business, sir?"

A slight pause. "I have a fleet of ships," he replied. "Small but growing as my fortune does. At one time I had many more, and of a different sort." His voice trailed off.

"Did you lose some in a storm?"

His mouth flattened into a grim line. "A storm, yes, but not of God's design."

"What do you mean?" Maddie stared.

"Ninety-six years," he replied. "For ninety-six years we all lived in peace, all of France in harmony and everyone was free at last to worship as he believed, but then...." He sighed. "Just seven years ago, it all changed, and to this day I ask myself why. Why did our king revoke the Edict of Nantes and forbid my faith once again?" He shook his head. "I should have left right then, but I did not. It seemed proper at the time to stay and fight for my beliefs. In any case, I had too much property to dispose of without a loss. I assumed, wrongly, it turned out, that my social position would hold me exempt from all persecutions. It did not."

"Oh, I'm sorry!" Maddie found herself at a loss for words.

He shrugged. "You did nothing to be sorry about."

Maddie fell into an uncomfortable silence. She could think of nothing else to say. Her eyes lingered on him to savor the clean, trim lines of his body. She wondered idly if he had bought that sober gray linen suit especially to wear when doing business in the Puritan colonies. She had always believed Frenchmen dressed flamboyantly, in laces, ribbon, and shiny cloth. In France, would he do so too?

"All that horror, and just because you're a—" She couldn't finish the question.

"Yes, Maddie, a Huguenot." Her father's voice jolted her. "He has suffered for his beliefs, just as our own people have. He too has been forced from his motherland."

"I have made the best of it," replied Rohan stiffly.

Her father smiled. "So have we. As you see, Monsieur de Rohan, our renegade colony has prospered."

Rohan smiled. "I hope to help it prosper more." As he spoke, his eyes remained fixed on Maddie, as if he too found what he saw fascinating. "Salem possesses a fine natural harbor, and the people of New England seem above all practical. I need a place, you see—a home port where the people hold a sensible attitude about their paying guests and do not ask troublesome questions. If you agree, then we will grow rich together, while Salem herself could increase in greatness to become a jewel in the crown of your Commonwealth. If you refuse, then I will find my harbor somewhere else."

"Would you—Would you be settling down here

then?'' When she spoke, Maddie found herself strangely breathless.

"I settle nowhere," he replied curtly. "The seas are my home, and not one small plot of land upon them."

Maddie's heart plummeted. The very floor itself felt as if someone had yanked it out from under her.

"What are the troublesome questions you fear we might ask?" he father interrupted.

Rohan smiled. He glanced to Maddie once again, then back to her father. "We will discuss those at a later time, sir," he said, "and in private."

"Very well," replied her father. "For now then, freshen yourself upstairs, then meet us back downstairs. We'll discuss no business on the Sabbath, but we can all enjoy a glass of good port and get to know one another better." He turned to Maddie. "Show him to the guest room please, dear." With that, he left them alone.

In his presence, Maddie's heart pounded. The yearning she felt toward him was like nothing she had ever before known, yet disappointment crushed her. He would be here awhile, then take himself to the seas once again, leaving her desolated. To hide her feelings, Maddie glanced to the carpet. What did it matter that she might never learn how she wanted him? Obviously, he didn't care.

As if sensing her turmoil, Rohan spoke to her now in a gentler voice. "I am a nomad, Mistress Bradshaw, by choice, by nature, and perhaps by God's will. I must wander the earth. It's my fate."

Maddie put up a cheerful front. "Well, we are both sorry to hear that. As for myself, I bid you welcome, and I shall endeavor to make your stay here as pleasant as possible."

His eyes burned into her, melting her. "Your very presence is a delight to me, Mistress Bradshaw," he said. As he reached for her hand and kissed it, Maddie nearly fainted with delight.

Chapter Two

For the next few days, Henri and her father spent most of their time shut inside the study. As she passed by attending to her own chores, Maddie glanced with longing toward that closed door. At night alone in her bed, she found herself preoccupied with thoughts of him. Desire smoldered inside her, and in his presence at meals or during chance meetings in the hall, the dull ache of longing flared into something Maddie hardly understood.

She found herself ill-prepared to deal with the strength of her own emotions. She no longer trusted herself to behave like a lady, and so grew very shy around him as a result. She took to avoiding him whenever possible, and only looked upon him when she felt sure he would not notice her presence.

One day, her father presented himself in her room. At his bidding, she put down her needlework to listen. "You care for him, do you not?" His eyes fixed on her face.

"What difference does it make?" Maddie shrugged. "If you are worried that I will make a fool of myself and embarrass you, rest assured that it will never happen. You raised me to be a lady, and a lady I am. I am quite capable of controlling my behavior."

"I never doubted that you would behave yourself," he replied.

"Then why confront me?"

He squeezed her arm. "Because I am concerned. I have seen the way you look at him. The way he looks at you. Frankly, I know now who and what he is, and I don't want to see you hurt. By that, I mean that I don't want you to involve yourself with him."

Maddie started in surprise. Her father had never taken such a strong stand before. She stared at him in bewilderment. "Just what do you mean, Papa? I thought you liked him." They had seemed to grow closer in the past few days, becoming great comrades. If anything, she would have expected her father to encourage such an alliance.

Her father sighed. "I do, and that's the damnable part. I understand what he is, and even sympathise, but you are my daughter. I don't want you to even *think* of marrying him."

Maddie stared at him. She was too surprised still to do otherwise. "Then tell me please; what in Heaven's name *is* he?" Not that it would make any difference. She already knew she loved him. Her greatest sorrow was that he'd go off, and she'd never see him again.

Her father sighed. He studied her for a moment, then said, "Maddie, I'd rather you did not know. In any case, I'm not entirely sure. It's only a suspicion I have."

"Of *what*?" Maddie stared at him in exasperation.

"I told you. I have no wish to discuss it with you." His voice hardened. "I've indulged you in the past, but I'm your father, and I stand now on my rights. Don't get involved with him. In fact, I forbid you." He added, "Trust me...*please*."

"I hardly have much of a choice anyway," Maddie sighed. "He plans to leave all too soon, I fear."

"Thank Providence for *that*!" her father replied with heartfelt sincerity, then turned to leave.

Maddie called after him, "Father?"

He stopped, then faced her again. "Yes?"

"If he's so terrible, why do you allow him to stay?"

"He's not an evil man, Maddie, but a good man gone wild—far too wild for me to want as a son-in-law. In any case, I like his idea well enough that I'm tempted to accept it in spite of what I know. We're working out details right now." Her father sighed. "He is all too right, I fear, about the sensible attitude we New Englanders hold toward money, and I am as bad as the worst of us. For that reason especially," he added, "I don't want you asking any more questions. Just trust me enough to hold your heart."

Her father's warning had unsettled her. Unable to bear remaining where she was, stitching a pillow case, Maddie prepared herself to go out. For lack of anything better to do, she went to Mistress Coney's penny shop to buy some candies her father especially liked.

Goodwife Jameson, accompanied by her eleven-year-old daughter Prudence, followed her inside. Almost immediately, the woman's eyes fixed on Maddie, following her every move. Maddie, glancing once in her direction, recoiled with horror at the sight of naked hatred in the woman's expression.

Maddie wanted to confront her, to remind her that gossip and the slander of an innocent person was not only cruel, but morally wrong. She held back, however, because Goodwife Jameson was known to have a nasty way with words, a shrill voice, and vindictive spirit. Since Maddie had no desire to become embroiled in a public scene, she tried to ignore the woman as best she could and go about her own business.

Both she and Goodwife Jameson completed their transactions about the same time. Maddie followed her out the door. Suddenly Prudence, whose hand was entwined inside her mother's, stumbled and fell.

"Prudence, are you all right? What is it?" Her mother, Goodwife Jameson, kneeled beside her daughter.

"Mama, I'm sick. My stomach hurts." The girl began to cry.

Forgetting her dislike of the woman and desiring only to help the stricken child, Maddie bent to her. "Can I be of assistance.?"

Goodwife Jameson whirled on her with fire in her eyes. "Stay out of this! You've done enough by turning my husband against me."

Horrified, Maddie recoiled. She hadn't deserved that insult, but the woman apparently believed what she had accused. Goodwife Jameson continued, "And now you are the one behind my child's illness. You are a witch, Mistress Bradshaw. I've suspected it all along, and now everyone else thinks so too. They've found your church veil, you know—right where you dropped it, in the coven field they discovered." She spoke with malicious relish. "Right near what was left of a Devil's altar."

Maddie's eyes widened in horror. What was the woman saying? How had her veil come to be near some unholy site? She chilled—she already knew the answer.

The girl began to moan. Maddie saw that the woman's face, lifting toward her, had frozen into a mask of horror and loathing. "You did it to her," she whispered, pointing a finger. "You plan to destroy my children, one by one, just to hurt me. As if you hadn't harmed me enough already!"

Overwhelmed, Maddie could only back away. She whirled, lifted her skirts, and ran toward home. She flung open her front door, not caring if it clattered into the wall directly adjoining it. Breathless now, she stumbled toward her father's study, calling out to him, screaming for him in a voice gone as shrill as a child's.

Out into the hallway stepped Monsieur Rohan. Maddie stopped short in confused despair. She felt the same pang of longing, of desire unfulfilled that she always experienced in his presence. The feeling fought now with the constraint of her father's warning, and the threat that drove her half wild with terror. "Where is my

father?'' Her breath tore in short gasps. ''Where is he?''
Tears streamed down her cheeks.

The man stared at her in bewilderment. ''Your father
is not here,'' he replied. ''He has gone out.''

Maddie wanted to run to him, to fling herself into his
arms. At news of her father's absence, Maddie flung
hands over her mouth. ''Oh no!'' She turned from him
on trembling legs and began to weep. ''Now I know I
am lost.''

She felt rather than heard him moving toward her.
''Mistress Bradshaw, what is it?'' He placed a comfort-
ing hand on her shoulder. ''Perhaps I can help.'' His
voice had gone very soft and tender.

''No, you can't. Nobody can, except maybe my
father.'' She choked on the words. ''And I doubt that
even he—''

''Let me try. Your father received an urgent message
concerning business, and won't be back until quite late
this evening. At least those are his plans, so let me hear
what it is that is troubling you.''

''Oh, you wouldn't understand.'' Maddie drew in a
great, shuddering breath.

''I can try. Certainly I have the *will* to help you.''

''I guess it can't hurt.'' Maddie forced herself to calm
down a little. Finally, the sobbing convulsions subsided.
''What happened is that Goodwife Jameson, who hates
me, has accused me of being a witch.'' Images of
women and men hanged for the sin of witchcraft
haunted her mind. She wondered again as before, how
many of them had stood falsely accused, merely because
someone hated them. How many had been innocent
when they had gone to their death on the gallows? ''You
know what that means, don't you?'' Her voice had
fallen to a whisper. She had lost the strength to speak
aloud.

''Yes, I know exactly what it means.'' His own voice

fell very soft. "If the accusation is officially made, they will arrest you, submit you to a farce of a trial, then kill you."

Maddie nodded, too horrified by what might be her fate to speak.

"On what grounds does she accuse you?"

"Her child fell ill on the street today. Collapsed to the ground and began moaning. Her mother accused me of having sickened the child on purpose, and that I did so by witchcraft."

"That is all? Because some half-hysterical woman points her finger and accuses?" His tone revealed misbelief.

"It is *not* all," she replied, miserably. She explained how she had lost her church veil while fleeing the obscene advances of Andrew Mathias. How that same veil ended up discovered at some unholy site. "I know he put it there," she added, "but how can I prove it is *I* telling the truth, and not he? And who do you think they'll believe?" She turned to him with hands clasped in agony. "Oh, Monsieur Rohan, what am I to do?"

"I think your father might say to wait and see what happens, and to trust the wisdom and mercy of God to protect you."

"It would be easy enough for him to say," retorted Maddie. "He's not the one they're likely to come and arrest."

Rohan chided her. "Do not speak scornfully of him like that. You are of his flesh, of his blood, and of his lineage, and I know he loves you."

"I love him too," replied Maddie. "When I was a child, I used to worry, because I loved my father, whom I knew, so much more than God, who was invisible. But Monsieur de Rohan, what would my father tell me to do? I want to run away and hide, but what would he say to that?"

"I think if it were necessary he would approve," he replied. "Your father is a wise, intelligent man. Many times this past few days, we have discussed the troubles plaguing Salem Village. We do not agree on everything, but we both concur that these months of fear will eventually pass, and when peace returns to the village, its citizens will realize that they have made a horrible mistake. He would not want to see you hanged as a witch."

"You think then that all the accused and convicted witches were innocent?" Maddie stared at him with horror-widened eyes. He had expressed the unthinkable, and the implications of his words frightened her.

"Look at whom they have accused, Mistress Bradshaw. Old women with no friends or family. People like yourself, who have made enemies." His hand stroked her cheek. At his touch, a thrill of pleasure warmed her flesh. She wondered again why her father had forbidden her to love him. He was wise and kind—a perfect husband and son-in-law. "What is happening now," he continued, "it is a sickness. A tragic delusion. Your father dares not speak out against it—not because he is a coward, but because denouncing it now would be suicidal. Look at what they did to John Willard. Your father was telling me about him only yesterday. When he refused to arrest more people, they arrested and hanged him. How could anyone but a fool go against such a tide?"

"Oh, Monsieur de Rohan, are you saying that I am likely to be swept away in spite of my innocence?"

He nodded. "Tell me, does your father have a house or property away from the village?"

"Other than some business holdings in Salem and Plymouth, he owns some land down the coast. There's a small cottage on it, I recall. A shack, actually."

"What about kin? Have you any relatives far away

33

from here?''

Maddie shook her head. ''No, my mother came from England, but she was an orphan. Papa's family down in Boston got taken by smallpox three years ago.

''Is this property on the coast far away from Salem then?''

Maddie nodded. ''Inconveniently so.''

''Well, you must go there to hide until the air clears, and I think you must leave tonight. Sundown should be soon enough, I think,'' he added. ''Your father's position should protect you until then...I hope. If your father has not returned by sundown, I will take you myself. As I said, I think they will not act until then.''

''Thank you.'' she whispered. What was so wild, so dangerous about him? Right then, he seemed nothing less than the greatest haven of safety to her.

''Do not thank me.'' His voice grew soft. As he stroked her cheek, his physical presence overwhelmed her. She longed for him to take her in his arms and kiss her. She would return such a gift with all the tenderness and passion now awakening in her soul.

''Be ready then, and just in case we must leave before your father returns, write a note. Explain everything so that he understands why you've gone. God willing, I will return and bring him to you myself.''

''Oh, Monsieur de Rohan, it has all gotten so ugly!''

''That is why I think you should be on your guard!'' he replied. ''Dress in traveling clothes, and keep a wrap and some money within reach at all times. Most importantly, keep that horse of yours saddled. Maintain vigil, so that if they come for you this afternoon, you can leap upon your animal and get out.'' He continued, holding her hand in his own. ''If you must flee before I get back, elude them, and if you can, go to the wild chestnut grove beyond your father's fields. If you are gone from here, I shall assume the worst and go looking for you

34

there. If nothing has happened by the time I get back, we'll ride together peacefully to your father's other property."

He bent to kiss her gently on the hand. "Take heart, beloved," he whispered. "I must leave you alone for now to complete some arrangements. Pray to God for justice and hope for the best. I will come back for you after dark, when night will hide our plans from the prying eyes of your enemies."

"Henri!" As he turned to leave, Maddie called out to him. For the first time, she used his Christian name. At her cry, he faced her again. He gazed upon her with strangely tender eyes.

She ran toward him, hardly understanding why, yet knowing that every atom in her body ached for him. She could not bear to tear her gaze from his face. In spite of her father's warning, her heart throbbed with newly-aroused love.

He caught her in his arms. Her own slid around his back to hold him. Her hands lingered below his shoulders. She felt as if she had melted in all the tenderness welling up inside of her. She knew now, as she had never realized before, that he loved her, too.

"Oh, Henri, I—" Her voice broke. She wanted to beg him never to leave her. She longed to confess her love. It had been unfolding inside her like a rare, beautiful flower ever since he had first arrived, and its secret existence had become a burden she could no longer bear. "Oh, Henri!"

He seemed to understand. The skin around his eyes crinkled as he smiled at her. Without speaking, he pressed her so close that she could feel his own heart racing like her own. Then he bent and touched his lips to hers. "Remember what I told you." He pulled away from her gently. His voice, as he spoke, had grown strangely hoarse. "Time is critical, my love, I'll be back just after dusk. Be ready for me.''

And then he was gone.

Chapter Three

Maddie counted the hours until his return. She waited, glancing impatiently toward a sky that remained stubbornly light. In keeping with his advice to maintain vigil, she sat by the front window, not daring to sew or do anything else that might pass the time but take her attention away from the approach of unwanted visitors. As the minutes dragged by, she glanced in dread toward the street below.

Finally the sky's color fractured into the streaks of purple and pink that heralded oncoming darkness. Half an hour passed, and these deepened to a somber blue-gray.

As the sky turned to night's black, Maddie stood and began to pace in darkness. Henri said he would be back by nightfall. Where was he? She had to fight down a choking sensation of panic.

In the early hours of afternoon, she had written her father a note and hidden it in his desk. It waited for him now, should she have to leave before he returned.

Maddie tried to sit back down and wait calmly for Henri, but found she jumped up again within seconds.

Suddenly she heard footsteps outside growing louder. Thinking it might be Henri, but dreading someone else, she leaned out the open window to catch a better look. To her horror, three men turned onto the walk leading to her father's front door. Her eyes were used to the darkness and she could see them clearly, since the flickering fire of their lanterns highlighted their features. She recognized two of them as neighbors sworn to duty as citizen-constables. Her horror mounted when she realized that the third man accompanying them was none other than her sworn enemy, Andrew Mathias. She knew then that she had fallen into mortal danger.

Maddie grabbed her hooded cape, its pockets full with money, then fled in darkness toward the back of the house. She flung open the sewing room door and raced for its window.

Trembling in terror, Maddie flung open the shutters. As she scrambled into its sill, she felt as if she would faint. From out front she heard them pounding on the door. Only minutes would pass before they would lose patience, break it down, and search for her inside. Those few minutes would be her only head start. As she slipped through into darkness outside, Maddie prayed that her father would not be punished for her escape. She thanked God that he had left home for the day.

Her feet sank into the shrubbery growing below. Its branches tore at her stockings, but she hardly noticed. Terrified for her life, she struggled free and lifted her skirts to run. Even as she stumbled through the nighttime mists toward the uncertain safety of her father's fields and the forests beyond, Maddie heard the door splintering as her pursuers kicked it down.

She took one last look at the house where she had grown up, then turned away forever. As she fled, she blessed the darkness that stood between her and certain death. She prayed, her lips moving without voice, that Henri had kept his promise and would come for her. Dressed in boy's clothes and carrying a dress wrapped up in a bundle, Maddie flung herself on Farrow's back. The creature whinnied questioningly as she kicked at its sides with her heels. At that signal, he broke into a canter, then a gallop.

Fear blotted out all thoughts except the urge to escape. She hardly saw her surroundings, as she rode on her horse through cultivated fields toward the woods beyond. She choked back tears of rage at the unfairness of her circumstances.

This was not gentle land, but hard like the people who had settled here. Icebergs and ocean winds had been its primeval builders, and they had shaped the soil in the image of their own power. In its space existed the feeling of suspended life. While walking here at earlier, happier times, Maddie fancied that the great brooding stones must speak to each other, when all else fell silent in the nights.

By the time she reached the forest itself, Maddie's horse had grown breathless. To her dismay, she saw no one waiting for her in the wild chestnut grove. With a pang, she thought that Henri might have forgotten, or worse, purposely betrayed her. She had no time to grieve, however. She glanced one last time toward the village, then plunged into the forest's refuge.

Suddenly, from behind, Maddie heard shouting. Andrew and the others were still following. Worse, they seemed to be gaining, riding on horses that thundered like the worst sky-flashing storm. Maddie prodded Farrow, praying that he had a little strength left. Upon the exhausted creature she lurched forward, then cried out as he almost fell over a half-rotted log. The trees, spreading out their leaf-covered branches like a canopy, blocked out light from the moon and stars. Not knowing what else to do, Maddie guided her animal off the path. Something, a small animal perhaps, moved in the undergrowth directly below its hooves. Farrow reared, and she, already weak with terror, felt her body twist with the momentum of his movements. Her foot slipped from the stirrup. A jolt hurtled her through air. She landed with a cry of pain on her belly, and there she lay motionless until her wind returned.

When she lifted herself up, she saw at once that Farrow had run off, leaving her alone, stranded on foot in the middle of the forest. Most of her other attackers had fallen back, but Andrew Mathias still pursued her. She heard him even now crashing through the summer green brambles; fallen branches crackled under his heels. He kicked water-sodden logs out of his way with the toes of his boots. From where she cowered, hidden still by darkness and forest green, she heard him cursing aloud.

Glancing back, Maddie stifled a sob. She forced herself to stand, then fell forward into a run. Her legs trembled as she stumbled ever onward, like a fox harassed by dogs and hunters.

She fled until at last almost too exhausted to move, her body craved only to fall to the ground and sleep. She knew that if she did, however, Andrew and the others would surely capture her. They would arrest her in the name of the King, and take her back to Salem Village as an accused witch. They would imprison her, shave all her hair, then examine her for witchmarks—warts, pimples, or growths on the body, from which a demon might suckle. They would find one; they always did. Its existence would prove her guilt.

From behind, she heard boots now, as well as horses' hooves. Men shouted and a dog barked, a hunting spaniel trained to follow the scent of witches. Her pursuers were much better equipped for capture than she was for flight. Exhausted, she crouched behind a boulder to catch her breath. She wished she had her horse.

Men's voices and the barking dogs grew louder as her pursuers closed in. Maddie sobbed aloud as she ran from them. Numb now with despair, she fought the nettles clawing at her face. The smell of damp, of rotting logs and wild fungus, mingled into a sweet-sickening stink that nauseated her. She fought down sickness as she struggled forward, ever forward.

The dogs were almost upon her. She heard boots crashing, hooves pounding, and always the voices shouting, growing louder with each passing minute.

Finally, Maddie could go no further. As her enemies drew closer, she crumpled to the ground. Lying face down, too weak to move, she moaned like a wounded animal. Helpless, exhausted, and paralyzed with despair, she waited to meet her fate.

Chapter Four

Suddenly, a clump of evergreens parted. Whispered words startled her. "Get up! We have no time to waste. They're closing in fast now."

She raised her face from its bed of undergrowth. "Henri!" She saw only his eyes glittering out of darkness, but she knew it was he. He bent down and helped her to stand up. She tried to walk, but her legs refused to stop shaking. When he realized her plight, he took her up in his arms and carried her.

"Where were you?" she whispered.

"Never mind that for now." He too spoke in a whisper, but rapidly. "A forest path starts just a few yards beyond here, and I've tethered the horse by its side."

"Where were you? I thought you'd have come for me before."

"I did," he replied, "but too late. I was almost to your house when I saw men streaming out of the back toward the fields beyond, and I knew that I should have gotten back earlier. Worst of all, I had left you in peril.

I took a shortcut back into the woods, and prayed that I might find you before they did. God must be on our side, darling."

Maddie knew that she could face the danger now. Her terror had diminished. She was no longer alone.

They reached his horse. He helped her mount, then climbed on behind. After guiding it out onto the road, he goaded the beast into a gallop. Behind, the voices of their pursuers grew fainter. Distance separated them from her. They had met their match in Henri Rohan.

A wind blowing from the east caressed her cheeks. The clattering of his horse's hooves comforted her with its calm, sure rhythm. Clouds drifted past the moon.

Suddenly, from behind, Maddie heard hooves pounding after them again. The shouting of men, their voices carried on the wind, chilled her. Despite Henri's best efforts, she had not yet escaped danger. Neither of them had. "I fear we are in for a merry chase," he whispered. With a cry, he urged his horse to greater speed. Maddie glanced behind in fear. Their horse, burdened by their combined weight and slogging through mud, snorted with exhaustion. It had slowed to a shaky trot. "They seem most determined to catch up," he said, and shouted more words of encouragement to his beast. "And I fear they might almost succeed."

Suddenly, Maddie heard a cracking noise. The animal screamed in tones of pain and fear that distorted its neighing, then lurched forward. Its falling catapulted her into space. As she fell, she realized with horror that their mount had caught its hoof in a pothole. Their only chance for escape had broken its leg.

Chapter Five

Maddie had fallen face down onto rain-softened mud. There she lay, startled and immobile, as the great beast crashed over her. Even as it fell, Henri slid from his saddle and bent to help her. She stared at him in dread. "What now, Henri?"

She glanced back toward their pursuers. As she struggled to recover, she heard galloping hooves goaded by fanatic men. They were catching up. "If we are captured now," she whispered, "the whole town will call the intervention of God the reason, and no one at all will doubt my guilt. No one!" Despair froze her soul, now that their flight seemed hopeless.

"Take heart. Earlier today I noticed a farm very close to here, with horses grazing in its fields." He pulled a pistol from his coat, then lowered its muzzle to the creature's head. "If I had a knife on me," he said, "I'd slit his throat. It'd be quieter." A blast exploded the nighttime silence. Maddie glanced uneasily over her shoulder. She feared that the din would herald their location to the constables and Andrew Mathias.

"Now run!" He grabbed one arm and yanked her forward. They fled as from death itself, as they stumbled from the woods into a natural clearing. To the south, a field of corn stood silhouetted against the moonlit sky. Their feet sank ankle-deep into vegetation, grasses, and weeds; it was a fallow field, for grazing and resting of soil. A few yards to the north, Maddie saw a pumpkin patch, and what looked like berry canes.

"How far is the barn?" Breathless now, Maddie threaded between rocks that seemed to grow from the sparse New England soil.

"Just beyond *that*." He pointed to a copse of trees. Suddenly, a building forty feet long loomed up ahead of them. The structure had been solidly built, with logs dovetailed one on top of the other to form its walls. Only its corners revealed how it had been put together, for planking covered most of its sides. Its roof, rising in a steep grade toward the sky, lay hidden under wood shingles.

While Maddie waited, leaning against a rock, too exhausted to move any further, Henri ran to it, pulled open its heavy lumber doors, and disappeared inside. Within seconds, he rode out of the stable, his heels goading a stallion already bridled but unsaddled. As he thundered toward her, galloping bareback at full speed, Henri bent at the waist and swept Maddie into his arms. She felt herself go weightless, yanked through air, then wedged in front of him against the creature's neck.

She felt his breath upon her right ear, and savored his body warmth as he encircled her with his embrace. "The horse you chose looks like a fiery steed!" she commented, with more than a little trepidation. She was unused to sharing a horse with someone, and her lack of control frightened her.

"He is," replied Henri. "I chose him for his energy and strength. He was the best of them."

"Oh Henri, what will that poor farmer say when he finds his horse is gone?"

"He will discover in its place a bag of Spanish gold equal in value or surpassing that of his missing animal. I would rather not steal from an honest yeoman."

"Nor I," replied Maddie.

Their mount, at full gallop, carried them back through the woods to a road heading south. Maddie felt as if she were flying.

"We will go to your father's lands first. If, as you

say, the place is utterly desolate, then we'll have to make other arrangements. Perhaps I can find you someone to stay with in Rhode Island, where minds seem to be free of this contagion afflicting Massachussets. If all else fails, I have contacts down in the Carolinas, if we can only get there. Friends of mine on Ocracoke Island who will take care of you. You could wait down there until this all clears.''

Maddie's eyes widened. "The Carolinas? Why, that's so far away!"

"And perhaps not necessary, but if so, we can reach it by ship. My own, the *Genvieve*, is waiting in dock at the Boston town harbor. The coastal winds could take us there in no time."

Maddie thrilled at the opportunity to spend so much time with him. The thought of traveling over open sea, however frightened her. "Are there not privateers at sea, and even pirates?" she whispered.

Henri laughed grimly. "We have no need to worry about pirates, my dear," he replied. "Indeed, none are safer from them than we."

A well-armed ship to take them safely wherever they needed to go, yet for some reason, Maddie felt a chill. They had ridden beyond reach of Andrew Mathias and the others for the time being. Their mount now descended toward the ocean. Huge boulders, left behind by some ancient movement of earth, jutted from soil, to which dead grass and bushes still clung by withered roots. Beyond, to the east, the ocean glittered dark, silent and vast, while above, clouds covered the moon. Now that the noise of barking dogs and shouting men had faded into silence, this wilderness seemed all the more vast and empty. "So quiet," she whispered, "it deafens me."

Maddie stroked Henri's hand. His arms were a haven and she savored riding there, warm and safe under his protection. "You risked your life to rescue me. Why?" She turned to him. She longed to hear him confess that he did it out of love for her. Now that fear had subsided, desire flooded back to take its place. Her thoughts fixed again on how much she loved him.

"Even if they had taken you to the gaol, I would have tried to free you—you, and all the others as well." His voice grew suddenly hard. "I will not stand by and do nothing, if I can stop any part of this carnage."

Even as he spoke, denying any love, any emotion save revulsion for the Salem witch trials, Henri clung to her. His hand pressed against her. His strength held her gently.

"Henri..." His name was like a one-word prayer to her. "Virginia, Rhode Island, or even in the wilds, I can think of no one I would rather be with than you. No matter where you take me."

"Maddie, you must not!" His voice broke. "It is wrong to say such things." His voice revealed fear.

"I am not playing with your heart when I say it, Henri," she said. "Nor am I merely expressing gratitude. I really mean it. I've felt this way ever since I met you, and I sensed the same feeling in you this afternoon."

"Mistress Bradshaw, you do not know me." Suddenly he became formal, and almost distant in his politeness. "I'm little more than a stranger to you and it's best that I remain so."

Her father's words exactly, but echoed in another's voice. "But I mean it, Henri," she persisted. "I really do. I know now that my home is with you."

"Maddie, I forbid it! You are too young, too innocent to know what you would suffer if I allowed myself...." His voice trailed off. When he resumed speaking, it had turned stilted and formal. "I am not like other men, Mistress Bradshaw. You see only the aspect of me that I wish to show—a middling-attractive man with excellent manners." As he spoke, his voice trembled slightly. "But it is a facade, and your father guessed it almost from the start. I am not what I seem, and you would be horrified to learn the truth."

"Liar!" she whispered, and she vowed to herself that she would prove him wrong. "Nothing about you would horrify me."

From then on, they rode in silence down the coast. Minutes passed into hours. Finally, Maddie raised one hand and pointed south. "My father's place is very close by here. Once there, we can rest."

"I see nothing."

She pointed again. "It's just beyond those rocks at the mouth of a cave still hidden from view. But I must warn you—the place is miserable. It might have been an Indian hut, or a shack for some poor fisherman that its builder constructed out of scrap wood."

"I care not, so long as it is shelter, where we can sleep." He sighed as he continued, "I would have preferred that we spend the night in a warm inn, where food and brandy would revive us, but there seems to be none around. Not even a farm house."

Maddie dared not say aloud the thought that she would rather be his companion in a hovel, or in a damp and chilly cave, than lie alone upon some warm feather bed. She snuggled close to him, and her heart raced at the prospect of spending the rest of the night in his company.

Suddenly, she saw it. She pointed toward a formation of boulders down the beach. "There it is!"

A wind, rising from the north through air crackling with energy, reminded her that the shelter built there, however rude, would save them from the chill and rains of a thunderstorm. "It looks even poorer than I remember." Maddie frowned in dismay.

"It is a blessing nevertheless," he replied.

The shack was little more than driftwood piled into a hut and lashed together with rope. A mere shanty to keep out the worst of nighttime chill and storm, but its existence meant shelter. The rising tide of Maddie's own yearning had turned this hut into a mansion. She turned to him and smiled as he pulled their horse to a halt.

He slid off, tied the beast to a post, then half carried her into the shack. "Wait here," he said, "while I look around. I am a man of the sea and distrust land to the very bones of my soul. I want to look at what we have here; where the dangers lie—and the opportunities." Without waiting for her reply, he strode out into the night.

Left alone, Maddie looked around. She found a pallet of straw set down by some recent traveler who, like them, had found temporary shelter here. Little else, not even a table, graced the crude interior. When Henri returned, he threw his cloak down on it. He motioned for Maddie to lower herself down. She obeyed, then looked to him with a smile. "Was your walk interesting, Henri?"

"Land is never interesting to me," he replied. "Except as an adversary to be endured and conquered. However, I learned well enough its lay. It will serve us well, if we have to leave in a hurry."

"God forbid!" she whispered, horrified at the thought that their adversaries would pursue them so far.

"I agree." He kneeled by the hut's crude hearth and piled a few pieces of dried wood into it. While Maddie watched, he pulled out a flint and struck it near the kindling. Its spark reached to the nearest dry twigs. It became flame, which grew into a fire. Once it caught hold, Henri remained where he was, crouched in front of it.

Maddie gazed at him longingly. She ached for him to

join her on the mat. "And where will you sleep, Henri?" she whispered.

"Never mind about me. I shall manage. I'm more used to traveling under uncomfortable circumstances than you are, and I am less fatigued."

The air here by the ocean had grown chilly in the small hours of night. Maddie, kneeling now on his cloak, saw him shiver. With concerned tenderness, she reached to him. "Oh Henri, don't be so proud. I can see how cold you are. Come lie by me and keep warm. My own cloak will provide for us a blanket."

"No, I cannot!"

When she saw the stricken expression in his eyes, Maddie's own widened in surprised disbelief. What did it mean, this sudden hesitation in a man normally so bold and hard? She could see that he was at war within himself, and did not totally understand why. In response to the bewildering mix of feelings she sensed from him, Maddie faced him boldly. "Are you afraid of me, Monsieur de Rohan?" Her words were meant to taunt him.

"Not you." His voice broke. "It is myself whom I distrust. You are not like other women I know, and I hesitate to risk hurting you."

Her heart soared. She knew then that she had not been wrong this afternoon in the upstairs hall. If he did not love her, he at least wanted her the way man should a woman. "What you desire will not hurt me, sir," she replied. "The feeling is entirely natural, and often sacred. It is all in what we make of it."

She stretched her hand to him and continued in a coaxing voice. "I was taught that solitude is an unwholesome state, so come sit by me, Henri," she whispered. "I will do nothing to alarm you, I promise. It is only that when I see you shiver as you do, I too feel cold. When I see pain or sadness on your face, my own soul darkens with those same unwelcome sufferings."

He moved toward her. He stared at her a moment with longing eyes, then dropped on one knee beside the pallet where she sat waiting for him. "Oh, Henri, you might have succeeded in hiding what you feel from yourself, but your eyes reveal the truth. Why even my father, who hardly knew you, could read your thoughts from the way you looked at me. In fact, he was the one who first showed me the truth." She chuckled. "Ironically, he did so by warning me away."

"Your father was right to do so," he replied. "I am not like other men. Even my love is a curse. Better to crush it in its early stages, before it can do you any harm."

Maddie's heart pounded exultantly. "Then you do indeed love me, Henri!" she cried. When she saw the look on his face, read the longing in his eyes, she needed no answer from him to confirm the truth.

He took her in his arms. "Maddie," he whispered. "Oh, Maddie, it is wrong of me to love you, and yet I do." He held her close. "But for your sake, I must stop myself. I would only ruin your life. Try to understand."

In spite of his words, she felt the longing pulsing through his very body as he clung to her. Fate had brought them together in a strange and turbulent way, and Maddie knew she must fight for her own happiness. "Well, Henri," she whispered, "it's not as if my life is running a smooth course now anyway. Being branded a witch and driven from my home—some would say my life is already ruined." Her arms slipped around him. "Oh, my darling, I love you." Her arms drew him to her, and he did not resist until at last they lay very close, their bodies pressed against one another on his cloak.

"Oh, Maddie," he whispered. "I cannot fight it any longer. God help me, I love you. Indeed, I would even die for you."

49

"I would rather have you alive." Maddie's heart pounded. She had never experienced such joy, such wild, abandoned happiness mingled with desire. Her flesh felt as if it had caught fire and melted from the heat.

His fingers buried themselves in her hair. His lips pressed again and again upon hers, in deep kisses that revealed in their intensity his long pent-up yearnings of love.

He pulled away for a moment, and allowed his eyes to linger on her face. "Your hair smells fresh, like a flower," he whispered, then smiled.

His fingers slid across her cheek, stroking it. "Maddie, when I look at you, my heart gladdens. To be lying here, touching you as I am—it is more joy than I think I can endure."

"Nonsense!" she whispered and raised herself to kiss him. "You can stand as much joy as I can dish out."

Henri laughed in a way that cheered her. Maddie's fingers explored, as they never dared before, the warm, tangled jungle of his hair. They skimmed across the soft skin of his neck hidden underneath. Her hands pressed into his shoulders, savoring through her palms his rippling strength. She nearly fainted with delight as they slid hard against the curve of his back, and their pressure squeezed him closer to her. "I love you," she whispered. "Do with me what you will!"

"I want only honest love, my angel," he replied. His voice had grown suddenly serious.

"Then teach me!" she cried. "I want to learn. To be a woman, instead of a maiden, to be the kind of woman you want, so that you will love me always, just as I love you."

Henri drew back, suddenly sobered.

Maddie sensed his change of mood. Alarmed, she leaned on one elbow to face him. "What is it?"

"This is wrong. I cannot dishonor you like this. I love you, and I know your father, whom I respect as I would my own." He turned away from her and buried his face in his hands.

"Oh, Henri, no!" He had awakened yearnings in her that Maddie had never felt before. She was aflame with desire for him now. She longed for his embrace and his passion.

"It is wrong, this way," he replied. "We would be taking our love, which is sacred, and turning it into something less."

Maddie shook her head. "No, Henri, it's not true. If our love is truly sacred, as I believe, then nothing can profane it. What is profanity anyway, except unsavory thoughts? If our hearts are pure, then why shouldn't our love be too?"

Henri took her hand. "Nevertheless, we must marry first. It is the only way I could ever face your father. I know now that I love you beyond all life, but our consummation must wait until the time is right."

Maddie could not hide her tears from him. They glistened in her eyes and overflowed down her cheeks. His smile was tender as he bent to kiss them away.

Suddenly, he took her hand. He whispered with sudden fervor, "I, Henri August de Rohan, take thee, Maddie Bradshaw, to have and to hold from this day forward. For better or for worse, in sickness and in health, until death us do part!"

Maddie thrilled to hear him recite that vow of marriage. In her heart, she knew how she would respond. "I, too, Henri," she whispered. She realized with a shock that her hand, held inside his, had begun to tremble.

"I, Madeline Elizabeth Virginia Bradshaw, take thee, Henri August de Rohan, to be my lawful wedded husband. To have and to hold from this day forward, in spite of all adversity. I love you Henri, and I promise to honor and obey you, until God takes either of us to Himself in eternity.''

His arms enveloped her, buried her in their warmth and loving tenderness. ''Maddie, my darling!'' He reached for her hand and slid onto her finger a ring. A ruby, red as his own heart's blood, glittered amid a nest of tiny diamonds. Maddie's eyes widened. She hadn't seen this ring before, and its magnificence stunned her.

''I'll wear it always,'' she said, ''as proof that I am your wife.'' She raised her face to kiss him.

''I believe that in the eyes of God, we are truly married, and when we can, we will find someone to make it so in the eyes of men, as well.'' His hands raised to clasp her shoulders. His strong arms pulled her close. ''My wife!'' His voice hoarsened. His words sounded more like a whispered prayer. His eyes had melted in tenderness.

Maddie drew in a shuddering breath as she raised wide, wondering eyes to him. All the strength had ebbed from her. In its place, desire pulsed through her veins. She waited for him to take her, to possess her. ''Make me a woman, Henri,'' she whispered. ''Teach me to be everything you want me to be, and I shall obey.''

His arms encircled her. His face, lean, ardent and handsome, moved closer to hers. His lips pressed upon her mouth, caught her up in a thrill of unfamiliar emotion. Her heart raced, and through Henri's clothes she could feel that his beat in pace with her own.

His lips lingered upon hers, drinking in her passion, her warmth, her tremulous eagerness to please him. Finally, he raised from her mouth to savor the rest of her face. Her cheeks heated at his touch, turning a rich, rosy red. A thrill rippled down her spine, as he nestled against her shoulder to kiss behind one ear. She clung to him with hands and arms hungry to savor the heat and strength of his body. She writhed, hardly understanding the sensations that consumed her now. "I loved you," she whispered, "from the moment I first saw you."

"Oh, my angel!" Very gently, he freed the buttons that locked Maddie inside her dress. Impending storm had turned the night chilly, but in the rising heat of her own passion, Maddie felt no cold. Sheltering her under his cloak, Henri opened wide her bodice. "So beautiful, my darling," he whispered.

No one had ever seen her this way before. Even though he was her husband and she loved him, Maddie rolled her head away, suddenly embarrassed at his eyes upon her nakedness, but as his hands caressed what his gaze must have savored, a thrill of yearning swept away her maidenly scruples. She felt as if she was afire. "Oh Henri, take me!" She feared she'd go mad if he teased her this way much longer.

Henry took her hand in his own, then kissed her on the palm. Still kneeling over her, he guided Maddie to the outward edges of her reach. With his hand still clamped around hers, he closed her fingers around what had been, until now, a mystery for her.

Maddie's eyes closed in bliss, as she felt the throbbing pace of his hunger. He was a man, all right—hard and strong, and ready to conquer her in the only way he would ever care to, with love and passion and tenderness. A rushing torrent swept away her reserve. A curious, yet pleasant tingle warned her of mysterious delights to come. She clung to his back and pulled him hard against her. She moaned in lush pleasure at the feel of his weight crushing down upon her.

His breath, hard and frenzied now, blew against her. Its wind rustled a few loose locks of hair. Close to her, he smelled of soap, for he was clean by habit, but sweat and horse and leather had mingled with it to create a rich and manly perfume.

His fingers explored secret parts of her that no one had ever known, and his touch thrilled her. Spasms of almost unbearable need pulsed through her. Maddie writhed underneath him. With head thrown back and tears in her eyes, she begged for him to take her.

Suddenly, with one mighty thrust, he pressed himself inside her. Flesh joined flesh, soul met soul, two becoming one. A cry of pain forced itself from Maddie's parted lips as Henri tore away her maidenhead.

He caressed her. He whispered words of love and comfort into her ear. Finally, the pain subsided. Desire returned. Her body, awkward at first from inexperience, but helped along by Henri's tender patience, soon learned to move in time with his own. "Oh, Henri!" she cried, "I love you. *I love you!*"

Like a comet, sensation burst into a thousand stars to light the night-black sky.

And then it was over. Holding her, Henri lay spent and exhausted at her side. "You are everything a man could want in a wife, my love," he whispered.

"And you, Henri—I cannot imagine life without you. It would be too dark and bleak for words." Feeling happy and serene, she stroked his face. She smiled as the stubble of the beard he hadn't had the chance to shave scraped across her palm. On any other man, its existence would have proven distasteful, but to her, everything about Henri was perfect.

"You are so gentle, darling," she murmured. "I cannot understand why my father was so afraid of you."

Henri smiled in amusement. "Your father wasn't afraid of me, Maddie. I know when a man is afraid, but from him, I felt no such emotion."

In his arms, Maddie shrugged. "Not for himself, I think; but he believed somehow that you were wrong for me. As I told you before, he warned me against you."

Henri stroked her cheeks. "He was right to say what

he did."

"That's the odd part. He said so little. Usually when he wants me to do something, or not to do something, he'll give me good reason. This time, he did not. He only kept repeating how I should obey him and hold my heart aloof." She gazed upon him. "What was it about you that alarmed him so? What did you tell him?"

"I can't imagine." Henri smiled, as he pulled himself up from her. Instead of explaining what he meant, he drew Maddie's frock over her. While Maddie stared, dissatisfied at this reply, he dressed her. His fingers lingered as he fastened each button back into place once again, then smoothed the skirt over her legs. "It breaks my heart to hide such beauty from my view, but we must be ready to travel at a moment's notice."

"I thought we were safe," Maddie stated, still annoyed at his evasion, yet at the same time alarmed.

"I pray to God that it be so, but keep in mind that our foes are determined. Andrew Mathias hates you for humiliating his manhood. I believe he will stop at nothing to see you hanged."

A bleak chill running through her soul blighted Maddie's mood. Suddenly, from beyond the road where Henri had tied their mount, came a horse's neighing. Carried by the wind, it was a distant sound, barely audible, yet one threatening trouble and unwelcome visitors. Henri pushed from the floor and scrambled over to the crude window.

"What—who is it?" Horrified, Maddie joined him. She too strained to peer through darkness.

"Damn!" Henri started in alarm, as a second whinneying shattered their peaceful silence. From far away, galloping hooves pounded toward them. "We have to get out of here," he cried.

"Then untie the horse!" cried Maddie.

"No, we're no faster than they on land, and indeed

much handicapped by the fact that we must ride together."

"Well then, how?" cried Maddie. "How shall we escape?"

Chapter Six

"When I was out walking, I noticed a boat beached upon some rocks below. It is a small, miserable vessel. Probably sat there for years, but it's been protected from the elements by an overhang of rocks. In any case, we must flee by water, or not at all."

"Oh, Henri!" Maddie stared at him with wide, horrified eyes. Her hands, clasped together, felt wet on the palms. "I've seen that little boat when my father brought me down on a holiday. I cannot see how—

"We have no choice," he said grimly. "It won't get us to Boston, but I think it will still float well enough to send us out of their reach. Once we are safe, then we can worry about how to travel onward."

He sighed. "I regret leaving my horse behind, but I will set him free, so that at least *they* will not lay hands on him as their reward." As Henri grabbed her hand, Maddie glanced fearfully toward the door.

"What if they're lying in wait for us?" She stared with terror into the darkness outside.

"Do you think they would be so subtle?" Henri's jaw was set. The expression of his face hardened, becoming like a grim mask of tragedy. "They would storm this shack, for the greater glory of God, and murder us both. At best, they would play us a farce of a trial, then have us hung." He glanced to her, as he spoke through clenched teeth, "Be prepared to run—as fast as you can." As they stood in the door, Henri gripped her arm. In the intensity of his feelings, his fingers dug into her flesh, hurting it. "We have no time to waste." He pointed south. "Run fast as you can. In the cove just below, you'll see the boat. When you find it, hide near-by. Keep watch until I join you."

"What about you, Henri?" Maddie's eyes were wide as they stared up at him. Her heart pounded wildly in fear.

"I want to free that horse. When I come running, calling for you, join me, and we can both shove away to safety. If others come first, then you know I was taken."

"Oh, Henri!" Her voice trembled.

He continued, "If that should be, then hide and make your way to Rhode Island. It's the closest safe harbor, and if necessary, you can always hire out as a servant, until the people of Salem come to their senses." He grabbed the back of her arm and shoved. "Now run. *Run!*"

Terrified, Maddie stumbled out and into the night, praying he'd follow right behind. She clutched her skirts with trembling hands. She lifted them so that their hems hung high above her feet as she half-ran, half-stumbled down the rough terrain. On legs jellied with fear, she scrambled as fast as she could toward the cove below.

The night crackled with electrical static as a storm broke over the clouds above. Even the frothing heads of waves crashing on rocks glowed with unearthly brightness. Maddie sobbed aloud as she fled. Suddenly, she stumbled over a rock. She caught herself, however and struggled forward. Some dunes stood between her and the cove below. When she stepped into them, her feet bogged in the soft, deep sand. She fought her way across it to the rocks guarding land from sea at its outer rim.

The way down those rocks was steep. Lit only now and then by distant flashes of lightning, Maddie struggled to keep from falling from the erosion-rutted path of the granite cliff's face. A wind had come up, and it whipped at her hair, tearing it free from the pins and ties that held it in place.

Ahead, a great boulder glistened from the waves crashing over it. Its edge jutted far into the ocean. More boulders rising behind on shore merged to form a small mountain, a jagged wall that blocked access to the cove beyond, and to the boat just out of reach.

Maddie stared at it in dismay. Her eyes searched the enormity of that rock barrier, but found nothing other than wind-carved holes barely large enough to fit a fist into. Too desperate to linger, however, Maddie tried to forget all the dangers its slippery surface presented. Death by a broken neck was far preferable to death by hanging. She gripped at the rock with both hands then forced the toe of her shoe into a fissure. Sobbing with terror, she kicked herself higher, ever higher, each moment more certain that she would fall and dash herself against the rocks below.

"Keep going, darling!" From behind, Henri shouted out encouragement. She heard him running closer and closer, and then the scraping of his boots, as he too mounted the rock. Following them, however, shouting voices warned that their pursuers trailed close behind.

"Oh, how can we ever escape?" Maddie stifled a sob as she scrambled over the top.

"We've come this far, darling, so be brave," he cried. "God must be on our side." From above, atop the rocks, he held her arm, using his own strength to steady her descent as she struggled downward to the cove below.

From where she clung, Maddie got a closer look at the boat. When she did, her heart plummeted. She had forgotten in the months since she had been here with her father how tiny it actually was. The thing measured barely five feet long—the smallest of specks, next to the ocean's mighty power. "Oh, how can we ever escape in *that*?" It looked dangerously unseaworthy; particularly now that a storm was coming up.

"We have no choice, darling, I'm afraid." Henri lowered himself down behind Maddie, as she stepped into ankle-deep brine. She splashed through water to the boat. Together they struggled, standing in waves as they pulled it from its shelter atop an outcrop of rocks. Its landing created a small tidal wave that nearly knocked Maddie off her feet. They began pulling it further out to sea.

Gradually, forever it seemed, the water rose higher. The breakers crashing against shore seemed less troublesome, once the water reached past their waists. At that depth, Henri helped lift her into the boat. He himself stayed outside, however, to push from behind into ever-deepening water. Finally, out where the breakers became merely swells that lifted them up and down gently, Henri stopped pushing. While Maddie held the craft as steady as she could with oars, he swam around to one side.

As Henri joined her in the boat, his weight nearly capsized them. With skill, he studied their lurching, then reached for the oars Maddie clutched so tightly in her hands. She was only too glad to relinquish them to him.

Suddenly, Maddie saw the night-darkened outline of a man shoving to the summit of that boulder. She screamed and pointed. Her eyes widened in horror, as three others joined the first. Standing there with the wind wipping at their clothes, the men shouted at them to halt, to surrender in the name of God and the King.

"Why do they keep on hounding us?" Maddie's voice trembled. She moaned aloud as she saw one of them raise a musket.

"Theirs is a merciless God." Henri spoke through clenched teeth, as he struggled to row with his oars against the perilous surf.

From high atop that boulder, two shots blasted. To her relief, the bullets splashed harmlessly into the water just behind. Again and again Henri raised the oars, lifted them into an arc, then lowered them to the resisting waters. Their movement was painfully slow, but by his exertion, he sent their boat to flight.

When Maddie saw how he struggled, she longed to help. Sweat poured down his face. His shirt matted to his back and chest. In and pull, up and push, he rowed until their craft glided from the range of Mathias and his cronies, who still stood on the rock shaking their fists.

Suddenly, she heard her enemy's voice booming out over the roiling waters. "You will not escape me, Witch! I will follow you, even if your travels take you all the way to China! Your accomplice too, be he man or devil, he too shall taste my wrath!"

Maddie remembered his face all too well. It was the bony, intense visage of a fanatic. The image of his eyes, burning with hatred, would always chill her. She had little doubt now that Andrew Mathias would indeed follow her, even if she were to flee to the far side of earth. Shivering, Maddie turned back again to Henri. He had straightened now, and was rowing at a more even pace. Seeing her fear, he smiled. "No matter what his threats," he said, "Andrew Mathias will not be able to touch you."

Maddie's eyes widened. "They came awfully close, sir," she replied. "It could be nothing else but a miracle, that we did not die by their bullets just then."

"Not a miracle," replied Henri. "Those men are so busy hunting witches, instead of game, that they have lost their eye for shooting.''

"Whatever the reason, I am grateful.''

The night glowed again with life and promise. A streak of lightning crackling across the sky illuminated them both, so that she could look upon him and adore what she saw. As Maddie gazed on the man who had saved her, who would live forever in her love, she smiled, and he returned one of his own.

Suddenly, chilly moisture soaked into her stockings. As she glanced to see its source, Maddie cried out in alarm. An ever-deepening puddle spread across the bottom of their craft. They were sinking!

Chapter Seven

Horrified, Maddie cried out. She pointed to the water spurting up from the bottom. Until that moment, he had been too busy rowing to notice anything but his own exertions. At hearing the horror in her voice, he glanced to her face, then followed her eyes downward. He too groaned at what he saw.

From shore, their pursuers still waited with muskets ready, just in case Henri's rickety craft might wander within range one last time before escaping forever.

"Take that jar!'' He pointed suddenly to a receptacle rolling around the bottom of their boat. "Scoop out as much water as you can.'' Blown of a thickish green glass, it had probably held rum to warm some chilly fisherman. As Maddie grabbed it, she saw that salty mud half filled it. She lowered its mouth to the leak. As water flowed inside, bubbles of air gurgled to the surface. When they silenced, she lifted the jar with shaking hands and poured its contents into the sea where it belonged. She bent again to scoop a second load.

Maddie saw Henri glance to where the constables and Andrew Mathias waited. Beyond, from somewhere in the night-blackened sky, a wind had risen. Blessedly, it came from the north, from behind, to blow them southward and out to sea. In the distance, Maddie heard the rumble of thunder.

She leaned forward to toss another jarful overboard. The waves had risen higher now. As they crashed into shoreline rocks, foam splattered upward and into air. Their craft lurched with violent suddenness that made Maddie sick.

Feeling the water rising to her ankles again, she applied herself more vigorously to scooping more of it into the sea. Wind had blown waves into swells of crashing power, that raised their boat to dizzying heights, then hurtled them down again. Great walls of water surged up on either side, until their momentum swept them once again to its crest.

They forgot about the water rising past their ankles. Sea crashing over them from above posed a far greater threat. Henri grabbed a rope and thrust it at her. "Tie yourself down with this!" he cried, then coiled a second length around his own waist. As Maddie knotted it in place, she raised her eyes to him.

"What if the boat capsizes?"

Henri handed her his knife. "Then cut yourself free." She reached, grabbed it, and dropped it into her pocket.

Lightning followed thunder. Each jagged bolt sizzled overhead to crackle the nighttime darkness. At the instant of their flashing, black night exploded into cold brilliance.

Maddie's stomach seemed to slip away as a breaker swept them upward. She screamed aloud as it hurtled them off its crest into empty air. The water stinging against her face felt like ice. It froze her hands. "Dear

God, save us!'' she breathed, in prayer to the Diety who seemed to have abandoned her. She did not want to die at sea, lost for all time in an unmarked grave of water.

Suddenly, out of the darkness, she spotted a shape. It too tossed and rolled in the storm, but its weight was greater. Instead of flying and falling like a floating scrap of wood, it rode deeply in the water. A ship!

Lashed to its mast flickered one lone lantern. In its light, she saw men bundled in thick clothes struggling with a sail. Along its side, the name *Anna Marie* spread in wood-carved shadows to proclaim the ship's identity. Suddenly, one of the sailors pointed. Two more joined the first. They stared in darkness and storm to where she and Henri struggled in their tiny boat.

A whistle's shrieking penetrated the din of wind and waves. Its noise, faint above the storm, reassured Maddie that the men on board had seen them. A rope hurtled through darkness. It splashed into the water just within her reach. Straining against the knots that lashed her down, Maddie grabbed for it. Her fingers closed around the inch-thick coil and pulled it into their boat.

''Toss it here.'' At Henri's shout, she handed the rope to him. She watched as he tied it to a rusted ring fitted through the prow.

When seamen of the *Anna Marie* had pulled them close, someone on deck uncoiled a rope ladder. It uncurled, then dangled from deck, while its bottom end splashed into the water between them and the ship.

''Cut yourself loose!'' Henri had already freed himself. Clutching at the side of their boat, he leaned into the water and grabbed the lifeline. Maddie followed his example. She sliced through her own rope, then dropped his knife back into her pocket.

A second rope, looped by some strange knot into a large noose, lowered to them next. Clutching the ladder with one hand, Henri reached for the second line and

63

handed it to Maddie. "Pull it over your head, then draw it up under your arms!" He had to shout to make himself heard over the wind. "It will save you if a wave should knock you off your footing."

As she obeyed, draping it around her back and under her arms, Maddie turned to him. "Henri," she whispered. "I fear we may not live through the night." Her eyes filled with tears.

"Even so, is it not better than hanging as a witch?" Without letting her speak again, he shoved her gently onto the cross-tied passage. Maddie grasped it with both hands to begin the endless climb toward deck. Her legs trembled. Her feet hung from a tie while her fingers clutched the ropes just above her face. The ladder was a slender link between life and oblivion. As it swung outward, then crashed back against the side of that ship, she held tight for her very life.

"Climb!" Henri shouted at her from behind. Terrified, but knowing that this hazardous passage was her only chance of survival, she raised one foot to a higher rung, then one of her hands. Moaning aloud, she hauled herself up, struggling skyward toward the deck above.

If only she were a man, instead of a maid burdened by skirts! The wind whipped at them. Spray and rain had soaked the fabric, until its entire limp mass clung to her legs like icy, leaden weights. As she raised herself to yet another rung, a tugging from below told her that Henri too had begun to mount the ropes.

From above, voices shouted out encouragement. She peered upward at their source and saw faces. Reaching hands could almost touch her now, but not quite. She had climbed to a dizzying height, but their rescuers still seemed so far away.

Suddenly, a wave of monstrous size crashed over them. The prow of the *Anna Marie* lurched forward and submerged for an instant into crashing sea. When it

64

sprang upward again, the shock sent Maddie reeling outward. The cross-tied ladder slipped from her grasp, her ankles and feet twisted free. As she found her self dangling in mid-air above the hostile, storm-roaring ocean, Maddie screamed in soul-deep terror.

Chapter 8

She dangled like a fish hooked on a line. The rope! Maddie blessed it. Even though its hempen coil seared her armpits with pain, it had saved her from certain death in the waves below. She clutched her arms tight to her sides and prayed for strength to hold fast until they pulled her aboard.

From above, she felt a lurch. A fresh spasm of pain tore into her torso as sailors hauled her in. The wind, grown stronger, whirled her like a top. It battered her against the ship's wooden sides.

Clinging to the ladder, Henri hung beside her now. No rope tied him to safety. If he let go, he would fall into the sea and drown.

"Hang on!" he cried. "They almost have you now. Be brave, my dear Maddie!" But she could only sob aloud in terror. Every bone and muscle in her body ached. Hands grabbed under her arms. Men's voices reassured Maddie, as they lifted her up, up and over the railing. As they lowered her to deck, however, one thought alone dominated her mind, one fear. "Henri?" She glanced around. "Is he still in danger?"

"Calm down." A voice cut into her anguish. A youth of eighteen, with hair the color of cornsilk, pointed to where Henri clambered over the side and onto deck. "See, your man is safe."

"Henri!" Maddie cried out. She ran to him and threw herself into his arms.

Propelled by the rising storm, their savior ship flew like the wind, heading south ever southward down the Massachussets coast. Through the rain that had begun to fall, Maddie could see how the cliffs of black gray rock stood higher, like great steep walls holding back sea from land. High tide and storm buried the tiny beaches now under tons of swirling, angry water. She had never seen this cape before, but had heard it to be treacherous. She understood now how true those stories had been.

The storm grew worse—so bad indeed, that the ship's lurching flung her down. To her dismay, she sprawled across deck, skidding toward the railing. She might have hurtled overboard and into the sea, had not another young sailor grabbed her arm. "Hang on tight," he cried, "or would you rather we lash you to a timber?"

Maddie shook her head. She dreaded being held prisoner by ropes. "I'll hold tight," she promised, and clutched the railing with all her strength. Hanging there, she watched as Henri struggled toward her through a wall of rain.

"Get below!" He reached for her arm. "I'll help you down."

"No!" She pulled free.

"I said, get below!"

"I will not!" She had no wish to be hidden away in a room where she would be left to wonder what was happening above. "I will stay right here where I can see everything that goes on." Her eyes met his. This one time she would not obey her husband.

"You'll freeze." Henri seemed dismayed by her sudden stubbornness.

Maddie knew he was right about the cold. Even now, she shivered, and saltwater spray stung her skin. Her hands had long ago numbed. She tried to warm them in her cape.

"Over here, hurry!" Suddenly, one of the shipmen shouted at Henri. "We need you, man!"

After glancing to her one last time, Henri turned. He hurried to join the crew in pulling down the last of rigging and sails. Beyond, through darkness and rain loomed the dim silhouette of coastline and forest. Wind screamed as the ship hurtled southward at a terrifying speed. The rain whipped at her. Even when she turned from it, stinging drops pelted her through the thick, brine-soaked clothes clinging to her body.

Even the ship itself seemed to suffer aloud. Its wood fittings, its mast, and joinings creaked and groaned from the force of wind and the weight of water crashing into it. Salem Village seemed so far away now, and Andrew Mathias like some half-forgotten nightmare. Even the love between her and Henri had turned into a dream that had long ago faded into ugly wakefulness.

Nearby a man struggled to fold a huge stretch of canvas. She saw his face contort with effort. Over the din, she heard him cursing as one end wrenched free to flap violently in the wind.

Beyond rain, the sky flashed alive with lightning. Thunder boomed so loud that she recoiled. It vibrated the boards on which she stood. Suddenly, a bolt of hot white power crackled out of the electricity-saturated darkness. It sizzled into the ship's main mast. A white, unnatural fire spit and crackled down its timber. Wood, shattered from the force of the bolt's attack, flew in all directions. Maddie watched in horror at flames rippling outward from it.

"Fire!" A voice shouted out the alarm. Men grabbed buckets and anything else that would hold water, as they tried to douse the conflagration. Rope that lay coiled below added fuel to it. Maddie screamed as she saw Henri struggle against the storm to grab the flaming rope and fling it overboard.

From a distance, light played out over the water, man-made light from shore. It flashed to them, moved away, then returned. Still fighting the fire on board, and the storm too, men began to look to that beacon with hope. Maddie sensed that all hands on board had believed, until now, that their ship was doomed.

"Thank God!" Someone near her seemed ready to collapse to his knees and offer thanks.

"That cannot be!" Henri hurried to the railing. He leaned out as far as he could to peer at their savior beacon, then frowned in consternation.

"Why not?" Maddie stared at him surprised at his reaction.

"I know of no lighthouse on this stretch of coast."

"Then it is a Heavenly sign," said one of the sailors who had joined them at the railing.

"No!" Henri shook his head. "This coast is lethal. Do not obey its summons."

A third, who carried himself with such authority that Maddie took him to be Master of this ship, joined Henri and the other. He turned to his own man, who saluted. "What is it? Why are we not heading toward that light, as I commanded?"

"No!" Henri whirled to him. "There is no lighthouse out there. I promise you, that beam comes from some other source."

"The storm has driven us many miles further than we first thought," replied the captain. "Perhaps you are mistaken."

"No!" Henri shook his head. "I have made no mistake."

"I say you're wrong. What else could it be but a lighthouse? In any case, we have no choice. We're taking water fast. The ship is sinking.''

Henri shook his head. ''I swear, you'll find not refuge there, but death. Let the winds drive you further, where only the land itself can hurt you.''

The captain stalked away. Maddie heard him shout orders to his men. The ship turned toward shore. ''What are we going to do?''

''I hope to God I am wrong, and if I am, we can wait out the storm in shelter. When it is over, I will accompany you to Carolina where I have friends.'' Henri kissed her on the forehead. ''If we become separated somehow—''

''Oh no!'' Maddie clutched his hand. ''We must not!''

He continued, disregarding her interruption. ''If we become separated, go first to Boston and ask about the ship *Genvieve*. He paused, as if thinking. ''If the *Genvieve* should already be gone, and if you can make your way somehow to Ocracoke Island, just off the Carolina coast, ask for my friend there, Pierre Dumont. He owns a tavern, but don't be alarmed by that. He's a good man and a true friend. Identify yourself to him and ask that he give you shelter until I return. I go there often for supplies.''

''But why should this man believe I have any connection with you?''

Henri embraced her. ''By my ring—always by my ring. It was cut off the finger of a dead Mogul, and there is only one like it in all the world. He knows that ring, and will recognize it when he sees you wearing it.''

Maddie's eyes widened. She stared at the ring with sudden revulsion. ''Off a dead Mogul? How—how did you come by this ring, Henri?'' And why would he have kept and given her such a gruesome souvenier?

He fixed a steady gaze on her. ''Maddie, do you remember your father's warning? When I told you that

69

knowing the truth about me would only horrify you, you laughed and playfully called me a liar. I can see now that I was right. You should have listened to your father's words, while I—'' he sighed, his breath joining with the wind that screamed past them now as the shore lurched dangerously close. He held her in his arms to steady her, as he continued, ''I took that ring from Ibraham Akbar al Devi when I siezed his ship.''

Maddie's eyes widened. A chill clutched her heart as she began to understand. In peacetime, only one sort of man took ships belonging to other men. She stared now at her husband with horrified awe. ''But—but did my father know? My God, he was going to do business with you. Surely he never would have....have done business with a common pirate?'' Henri's eyes grew steely. His voice hardened, as he interrupted her, ''Your father is a New Englander, Maddie, and like all his kind, he has a healthy respect for money, whether it be in the form of ducats, sovereigns or doubloons. Oh, he pretended not to know, but he guessed. The mere fact of his having warned you proves that to me.'' Seeing her confusion, her dismay, Henri took her into his arms. ''Maddie, forgive me. I may never have the chance to say it again, but I love you. You *must* believe that. I should have told you before, and I tried in other ways to prepare you, but I lacked the heart to say it right out.''

Perhaps the threat of death, hanging dark and thick over what might be the last few minutes of their lives, drew her own thoughts into such sharp focus. That he could be what he was and do what he did, horrified her to her very bones, yet at the same time, Maddie was able to look deep into her own soul as she had never done before. Mirrored back, like some bright reflection from the purest, sunlit pond, she saw the love she would always feel for Henri. It mattered not that he was a pirate, a predator of the open seas, who seized and plundered and killed for the sake of stolen riches. God help her soul, she loved him, needed him even, to give her life the brightness and splendor she had never known until that first moment their eyes had met, and their flesh touched in a secret, stolen promise of a kiss that would linger forever in her future. Fate and chance had brought them together, and love would bind their intertwining lives in the strongest of all possible chains. Understanding now, as she never could have before, Maddie raised her eyes to him, then smiled. "An accused witch and a pirate stripped of his ship—what a couple we make, darling!"

Suddenly, a man's cry jolted both of them; Maddie whirled to see its cause, then moaned in horror. The shoreline loomed ahead—a wall of rocks and shoals rising skyward from below. As their ship hurtled landward, at speed too great to break, Maddie screamed. She saw what awaited them. The lights came not from a tower that beamed troubled ships to safety, but from the lanterns of men standing at the water's edge. Men who seemed to be cheering at their disaster.

"Hold tight!" cried Henri, and then he left her alone to help the sailors in one last, vain effort to turn their ship aside. He had been right! Wicked men who wanted to plunder had led them toward doom. Moving too fast to stop, the ship plowed into the wall of rock. The force of impact tore Maddie loose and hurtled her toward Hell.

Chapter Nine

That stretch of coastline became a trap. Jagged outjuttings of rock chewed like teeth into their hull. The impact flung Maddie down, breathless, onto deck. Wood splintered. It exploded in all directions as breakers crushed the ship. She heard beams splitting asunder, saw water boiling upward into the rift with spray-laden fury. Maddie screamed as her half of the ship suddenly tilted. Six men, and Henri among them, slid off the broken hull to disappear under waves.

"Oh no!" She began to sob aloud. He was gone. Had she become a widow, even before properly consummating their marriage? Her own half of the ship remained upright, but she didn't know for how long. Even now, it rocked and trembled under this onslaught of waves, rain, and gale. Maddie's eyes filled with horror, as she glanced again to the rolling waters below, to the place where she had last seen the only man she ever cared about. How could he survive even a few moments in water like that? How could any of them?

But she had no time right then to mourn. Her end of the ship had begun to tilt. As she felt herself slipping, losing control, she screamed. Her arms failed to grasp at something solid, but sea, rushing in and over the deck, swept her outward. She stared in horror at that surface of black, glittering beyond.

A rope dangled within reach. Hoping it was tied to something solid, she grabbed for it. She screamed as it pulled loose under the stress of her weight. She clawed the wooden deck with her fingernails, but could not stop herself from hurtling toward water. She fell sobbing into the sea.

The relentless storm showed no mercy. Icy water froze her to the bones. Its spray nearly blinded her and the smell of wet salt nauseated her. She struggled to stay afloat. Against her will, she inhaled water and choked on it. She coughed to drive it from her lungs, but more splashed in. As Maddie vomited salt, she knew she would surely drown.

She glanced again toward the sinking ship and saw with horror a great wave. It had risen in a crest, moving swiftly, and even now towered above her like a dark and powerful moving wall. White foam, like that on a glass of ale, rippled across its crest. Before she could move, or even think, gallons of water crashed over her.

Maddie held her breath as it sucked her under. Its force battered her against the ocean bed. In the next instant, it spat her upward. Its movement twisted her like a limp and broken rag doll.

As the wave crashed against the rocks beyond, Maddie bobbed to the surface. Gratefully, she filled her lungs with air. She realized now that she could touch bottom with the tip of her toe. Relieved, she struggled toward shore. But the wave, retreating from where it came, swept her into deeper water once again.

She cried aloud with dismay and frustration. She shivered as its whirlpool swirled around her. Yet another wave, rising behind, threatened to buffet her again. This time she ducked underneath and learned one of the sea's precious secrets: turmoil happens only on the surface. Deeper water remains calm. Maddie used its gentle motion to carry her forward to shore. When her feet touched bottom again, she wasted no time, but thrashed into shallow water as fast as she could.

A tall, jagged boulder loomed ahead that even in darkness glistened with sea water. Maddie reached to hold herself steady against its weight and stability. Shivering so hard that her teeth chattered, she searched the empty beach for signs of her missing Henri. What had become of him? The question tormented her. It drove her nearly mad with anxiety and fear. In her fight to stay alive, she had drifted past the wreck. Down the beach, where the *Anna Marie* lay disintegrating just off shore, she saw lights bobbing along the sand. In their illumination, she was able to spy on the ship's deceivers searching for plunder. Maddie slipped to another rock closer in, and then another. She wanted a better look at them. She saw that they clutched lanterns, as they scrambled over slippery stones and sand to examine anything that caught their eye. She counted five of them. She would have hesitated to call them men, preferring to think of them as animals.

The flickering glow of their lights cast eerie shadows across their faces. In the highlights, Maddie discerned a family resemblance in all of them. Each had similar wide jaws, bulbous upturned snouts, and wide, thin-lipped mouths that opened to reveal teeth in various stages of decay. The hairs bristling out of their cheeks and chins discolored the entire lower halves of their faces. Their voices grew audible as they moved closer. She could hear them cursing a worthless haul.

Suddenly one of the bodies washed ashore struggled to move. The injured man raised himself up and begged for help. Maddie had to restrain herself from crying out in horror. Instead of showing mercy, the bandits fell on him. One raised a club, while the others grabbed rocks, and with these makeshift weapons, they battered their victim's brains out.

"Dear God, no!" Maddie could not take her eyes off the monstrous action she was witnessing, even though the sight of his blood splattering and brains flying made her sick. She stood frozen and watched in horror with eyes that refused to close.

Other survivors struggled too, only to be slaughtered in the end, living men battered into eternity. Horrified, and knowing too well that Henri must surely be dead by now, Maddie wanted only to flee. Anywhere she ran would be better than this blood-soaked stretch of beach.

From where she crouched, her eyes scanned dead faces as she searched for the features she dreaded to find. She saw, however, only mask-like countenances of sailors who moments ago had been healthy, breathing men. Although terrified at her own peril, Maddie breathed a prayer of thanks that her beloved was not among the corpses within her view. She would not have been able to bear it. She probably would have thrown herself sobbing upon his body.

"Oh God, help me!" she whispered. She backed from her hiding place, intending to slip into the shadows beyond. If she could remove herself from their presence, she might make it to the nearest village and there report the atrocity she had witnessed. Escape was her only chance. They would certainly kill her too, if they knew she was alive.

Suddenly, from behind, hands grabbed her. Stifling a scream, she struggled to fight free, but clutching fingers dug deeper into her flesh. One arm flung around her waist. She felt herself hauled back against a man and pinned to his body.

"I got me the winnin' prize, boys!" a whiskey-coarsened brogue shouted out from behind her.

"What did ye bag, Pat, some gold?"

"Some golden hair and soft, pink skin is what I found. I bagged me a maid!"

"Alive?" Running feet pounded on the water-packed sand, as three others joined her captor.

"Let me go!" Maddie screamed. She kicked him in the shin and struggled to get away as she heard him cursing.

"The little bitch is alive and kicking!" one of them laughed aloud. "We'll have some fun with her, we will. Ye can bet on that." The others joined in the snickering that followed.

"A toothsome little piece, ain't she?" The largest of them scanned her with his eye. His only eye, for the other appeared to have been gouged out. As he drew close, she smelled his unwashed body and filthy clothes.

To her horror, she saw the swelling in his trousers.

"Leave me alone!" She tried to kick him too. She writhed in her captor's arms, but his strength clamped her like a vise.

"She be a reg'lar little wildcat, ain't she?" The larger suddenly grabbed Maddie away and flung her over one shoulder.

"Let me go!" she screamed. "You have no right!" She tried to kick, but his arms held her legs tight against him. Her fists pounded impotently at his spine.

"The fiery ones are best, they say," cried one of the brothers. As impudent hands patted her on the backside, Maddie shrieked in fury and tried to squirm free.

She could not see the two-room shack in which they lived until they carried her almost to the door. Built of stone, it nestled among a formation of boulders forming a cliff just behind the tide line. Inside, a fire burning told her that this was what these creatures called home. The room was suffocatingly hot, and reeked of sweat and excrement.

"Fling her on the hay, Mack!" The one who had first captured her cried out in group invitation, as he himself reached for a jug resting on the table. Maddie saw him raise it to his lips and gulp.

"Well, me little pretty, are ye ready for a night's frolic with five hot-blooded men?" The man's single eye leered at her.

"Five hot-blooded *pigs*, I should call them!" Maddie glared at them. She sensed they would kill her once they had their fun, so she made little effort to ingratiate herself. She wished that she had slipped Henri's ring into the secret pocket of her cloak, where it might remain safely hidden.

"Well, pigs or men, yer sweet meat'll ache from their stingers all the same." As the man spoke, he squatted beside her. His fingers fumbled to unbutton the bodice of her dress. His weight pinned her down, as his hands made free upon her. "So firm," he murmured. "I be used to older wenches, girlies past their peak of ripeness."

"What're we waitin' for, boys?" cried another.

"How'll we do it without gettin' kicked where it'll really hurt?" The one who appeared youngest glanced to her with trepidation.

"Tie her down." The man's ugly face grinned at her. "That way we be havin' an easy playground."

"How can you be so vile?" cried Maddie. Until this night, she had never guessed such depravity existed.

Coarse laughter drowned her cries as they tied her up with rope. As they did, one of them, the youngest, noticed her ring. He yanked it off and dropped it into his own pocket.

"No!" cried Maddie, "please...that is my wedding ring."

"Ye'll have little need of it now," retorted the thief. "If yer husband were aboard that ship, it's sure'n that he be dead by now."

"He left behind a pretty enough widow though as our reward," added the one-eyed brother.

When they had finished tying her, the eldest, his eye glittering in anticipation, straddled her. "I go first," he cried, then squatted. Maddie squirmed under his weight.

"But it was me as found her," cried the other. "Without me, she might have escaped."

His brother laughed. "Tough! I came to light six years before ye, and I say, respect yer elders."

His hand gripped at her open dress, then ripped it off. She cried out in pain at the sudden friction against her skin. When he had finished, he crumpled its remains. He threw her fine linen gown across the room, as if it

77

were nothing but a worthless rag.

And then he turned to her, making ready for the moment she had been dreading. His eye, fixed on her, was gleaming unnaturally bright. His lips, spread wide in a grin, glistened from his own saliva.

"Get away from me!" Maddie screamed. "I want none of your loathsome touch polluting me!"

"Too bad," he replied, then lowered himself to her.

"No!" She tried to struggle, but the ropes and his strength overpowered her. Maddie knew she had no choice but to submit.

Chapter Ten

"No—stop. *Please!*" Maddie's throat closed. She squeezed her eyelids shut to block off the view of his approach. His breath panted hot and foul-smelling upon her. She turned her head away, sickened. He was an animal. No, less than an animal, for not one of God's dumb creatures would ever have dared to inflict upon her what he intended. His hand, calloused and unwashed, pressed upon her now. It roamed at will upon her. Maddie's flesh crawled with revulsion at his very touch.

An eternity passed under his hated caresses until, unable to stand it any longer, she faced him with searing eyes. "Your soul shall burn for all eternity in Hell!" she whispered. She struggled again to pull away from him.

The man laughed a short, harsh bray. "Since when is God a juicy wench who can damn me?" he retorted. "More likely, He sent you to all of us as His reward." All the brothers joined his mirth, giggling aloud at Maddie's plight.

As Maddie lay there, bound and hating her very existence right then, her senses heightened until she could see, taste, hear, and smell almost painfully clearly. The surf, pounding onto beach, pulsed up from the ground through the floor itself, and into her back. The light from their single lamp flickered. As the flame inside devoured its fuel, it sent mad, wildly-moving shadows against the ceiling. Another, larger fire burned in the hearth. Instead of pitch, it fed off driftwood washed from the sea. Deep-water weeds had clung to the wood, and stranded along with it on shore, had dried under the sun. The smell of it burning mingled with the stink of rum and tobacco-laden breaths, and with the sweet-acrid scent of blood from all those murdered sailors, still splashed on the bodies crowded around her. Maddie knew she would never forget this night as long as she lived.

His full weight crushed her now, so that she could hardly breathe. She gasped for life-giving air, yet choked as it streamed into her lungs. Its chill and the odor of that hut permeated even through her pores. Pain, fear, and revulsion slashed into her sensibilities like a knife.

Maddie groaned aloud. Her head rolled from side to side, as she writhed with loathing. The flesh seemed to crawl off her very bones. She struggled against her attacker, but she was powerless. The ropes digging into her wrists and ankles prevented her from pushing away and fleeing.

And still his passion mounted. He had begun to moan. Sweat, streaming along with dirt out of his pores, coated her with a clammy chill. Suddenly his lust seared into her. His fingers against her shoulders dug now into her flesh. So great was his force that each forward stab of his fury-heightened lust seemed to rip apart her very being. Tears streamed from her eyes, as she fought to keep from suffocating under his weight and brutality.

Unable to bear it any longer, Maddie screamed. The momentary release comforted her for as long as the sound streamed from her mouth, but as her cry subsided, the horror returned. Still overwhelmed, she screamed again, then gasped for breath as a dirty, calloused hand slammed across her cheek and jaw. The blow blinded her with stinging pain. Its force wrenched her head painfully to the side. Maddie's screams subsided into a whimper.

Through it all, the others watched. Their attention focused upon her with waiting eagerness. They stared at the forced mating inflicted by their eldest, and in their eyes and faces, Maddie could read all that each intended to do, when it came his turn to take her for his own pleasure.

In the face of the youngest, she saw only simple, unreflecting lust. He would be easiest to endure. In another, she detected a certain calculating shrewdness. He would be cold, yet demanding. From the third brother, however, she sensed cruelty. He had relished the sight of his elder brother slapping her. He gloried in her suffering, and in his eyes gleamed a wild, unholy fire, far worse than any of the others. His turn was next, and she dreaded him most of all.

Suddenly from the window behind them all, Maddie saw movement. Her eyes widened. Her heart pounded now in sudden hope. She had seen someone out there, a figure moving close enough that she could recognize the outlines of a man.

"Henri!" she whispered. She prayed to God it would be he, back from death to rescue her. If not Henri, then an honest stranger who, revulsed by what he saw, would come to her aid for the sake of decency. She prayed to be spared the touch of yet another one of these tainted brothers.

"Y' can squeal to him all y'want, my pretty, but yer husband's dead,"

"No, damn you!" Defiant now, Maddie cried out. She rolled her head away so that she wouldn't have to look at him. Almost at once, she felt his paw close around her jaw. He forced her face toward him once again and shoved a kiss onto her lips. But not before she caught yet another glimpse of the outsider.

This time he stood close enough for her to see his face. He was not one of these wreckers, but his features dashed all hopes that it might be Henri. Before the eldest brother had pulled her face to him, she had seen the man's signal: two fingers to his mouth, as a warning to remain silent. Maddie obeyed, stifling her cry of relief, but her heart surged with exultant joy.

Even as he signaled her, the man stepped back, moving, Maddie hoped, toward the door. She knew that at least one person would help. She prayed silently and with all her heart that he had not come alone or unarmed. After all, how could one man alone defeat such an unholy quartet as these? His only advantage would be surprise, for none of these inside knew he waited beyond their walls.

The outsider's presence, however, had emboldened her. The brother, confident in his own superior strength, bent down. He rammed his lips into hers, then thrust his tongue into her mouth.

Maddie bit down hard, clamping her teeth upon his flesh with all the strength her jaws could muster. With a strangled cry, he writhed away. His hands clawed frantically against her shoulders.

Maddie's eyes had frozen opened. They saw, with a sharpness bordering on unreality, how his face had drained of all color. Beyond, his three remaining brothers, stared at the two of them with mounting bewilderment, but he, trapped by his own victim, could not signal to them for help. He writhed helplessly as her teeth cut through his tongue.

Her thoughts churned wild and incomprehensible. She had no idea what she was doing, but an instinct pulsing upward from the smoky depths of her mind compelled her to hang on for the sake of life itself. She held, crushing the only part vulnerable to her helpless, fettered desperation. Suddenly, he broke free. With a gurgling cry, he fell from her body.

To her horror, something foreign, soft, and suddenly loathsome remained behind in Maddie's mouth. Revulsion nearly overwhelmed her. To free herself of this last remaining part of him, Maddie lifted her head. She turned as far as she could and spat it out. The metallic taste of his blood remained behind, however. Writhing on the floor beyond, her former assailant clutched himself. As he clawed at his face, streamlets of blood gushed through his fingers.

His brother peered at him, then whirled at Maddie. His eyes narrowed with a sudden violent hatred that portended violence. The look on his face promised all the unspeakable cruelties he would inflict upon her as his revenge. "Why, you-!" He moved toward her with fists clenched and legs wide. Just as he reached her, just as he raised his hand to deliver the first of many blows, the hut's door clattered open.

"Stop right there, please!" A man's voice, calm yet forceful, arrested her attacker's movements.

With wild rising hopes, Maddie lifted her head again and saw him—the one who had signaled to her from the window. He stood tall and strong, dressed in a gray linen suit, a hat placed squarely upon his head, and a cloak. Behind him stood four others, all armed with muskets and poised for whatever confrontation they might encounter at the hands of these four depraved wreckers. Maddie sighed in relief. Five against three. It would be easy now. Surely the remaining brothers, knowing they were outnumbered, would simply surrender to these superior forces and be done with it. They could see they'd get no help from their eldest, who lay moaning on the floor. Half-conscious from pain and blood loss, he barely lived.

But she should have known that men so depraved as to lure a ship up onto the rocks, then ravage the sole woman survivor, would fight like madmen. At hearing the voice of a stranger, the second brother whirled. With a low, animal growl, he grabbed a gnarled stick of driftwood from the pile beside the hearth. With a cry, he hurled it at her rescuers.

He moved so suddenly, and with such swift and deadly accuracy, that he took them by surprise. Before her saviors could divert the blow, the stick hurtled against the barrel of the leader's pointed musket, forcing it outward. A shot exploded. Molten lead propelled by fire tore into the roof above.

Unable to reload so fast and realizing now how these criminals would fight, the stranger resorted to using his weapon like a cudgel. His hands clutched tight, and his shoulders knotted as he swung it around. Just then, the second brother lunged, knocking him off balance.

Maddie screamed, horrified that her rescuers would be doing so badly. Straining against the ropes still binding her, she stared, then moaned in relief, as the outsider caught himself from falling. In the struggle, he dropped his musket and fought hand-to-hand with the one who even now had lunged for his throat.

As the stranger fought, his friends came to his aid. They streamed inside, one of them ducking as a rock hurtled toward his head. His partner meanwhile threw himself onto the youngest brother. Maddie saw the third remaining wrecker draw a knife from his belt. Her eyes followed his movement as he concealed it behind his back. They widened in horror, as he crept toward one of those who had intruded on their evening's fun of rape, murder, and plunder.

Maddie screamed to warn the intended victim. The man whirled ready to fight with bare hands, until he saw the knife glitter in the firelight. Its owner lunged.

One of the other strangers yanked around, slamming the side of his musket into that brother, but too late. The hopeless rescuer cried out, doubling over and crumpling to the floor, as a knife thrust into his shoulder.

The first man she had seen, the man she had come to look upon as the leader, glanced over. He saw what was happening, just as the wrecker grabbed a fallen musket. The stranger kicked. Like a miracle, the musket skidded from the wrecker's grasp. One of his men immediately gathered it up in his safe-keeping.

Her rescuer turned back around, just as the youngest grabbed a chair to send it crashing down upon his head. He wrested it away, then rammed it toward the attacker himself. Flung off balance, the brother stumbled and crashed against the cabin's only table. The back of his head cracked on its edge. He fell unconscious into a heap on the floor.

Two brothers were left, and three of her rescuers; the others having fallen in the fighting. Whether wounded or killed, Maddie couldn't be sure. Suddenly, in the middle of the fray, one of the remaining brothers turned to her. From somewhere, he had materialized another knife. As he crept toward her, his eyes glittered.

Maddie's own widened with horror. She knew beyond doubt what he intended, and the very thought congealed her blood. Killing her would be too quick for him, and too easy. He wanted to taste and savor the sweet blood of revenge. As his eyes flitted from her face, to her breasts, than down her belly, he betrayed his thoughts.

Panic overwhelmed Maddie's mind. She screamed. All her consciousness focused on the sound that welled up from inside, carrying upon its vibrations all the pain and fear she had collected. Its shriek tore from her throat to overpower the din of fighting and the ocean's pounding, so close beyond. Nearly faint from terror, she screwed her eyes shut, so that she would not have to witness her own doom.

From close by, a scuffle. She opened her eyes again, just in time to see that same noble stranger grab her attacker from behind. He twisted one wrist until the hand loosened its grip. The knife intended for her clattered to the floor.

Maddie silently cheered as he pinned both the wrecker's arms behind. Once accomplished, he jammed a knee in his prisoner's back, forcing him to the floor. With a swift, sure movement, he pulled a cord from his inside pocket. Maddie watched as he tied the man's wrists securely behind, while from the corner of her eye she saw those other two men overpower the last remaining wrecker. They bound him hand and foot, then tied those who still lay unconscious on the floor.

"Oh, thank God you came when you did!" Maddie stared at her rescuer with gratitude. She saw that he could never be called handsome, yet, right then, he seemed so to her. His nose jutted too prominantly for true beauty, however; it gave his entire face a craggy appearance. His thin lips stretched taut and grim, as he looked from her to the four men bound by ropes upon the floor. His stubborn chin had a cleft in it so deep it appeared to have been cut by a knife. His square jaw had tensed, so that a vein pulsed directly under his ear. His wide-set gray eyes radiated intelligence, and more importantly, kindness. At that moment, however, they lingered upon her nakedness.

Maddie's cheeks burned as she averted her eyes.

"Please, sir—" Though grateful for his rescuing, she felt now painful shame. The expression on his face intimidated her.

Suddenly embarrassed, he tore his gaze away. "I'm sorry," he said, with a shortness of breath that hardly surprised Maddie. After all the exertions of fighting, she wondered that he could talk at all. "Here, let me cut you loose." In obvious confusion, he bent to pick up the knife that had clattered to the floor during that last, frightening combat. His hand held the rope away from her flesh as he hacked through it. His touch lingered upon her a fraction of a second, but, catching himself, he drew back with sudden movement. He finished cutting her free as fast as he could and flung the ropes away. As she struggled to sit up, fighting against her numbed limbs, she saw him fumble with the fastenings of his travel cloak. Once undone, he swirled it from his shoulders and lowered it upon hers. Its folds of gray linen fell across her body. Its volume buried Maddie underneath to hide her from view.

Once he had covered her nakedness, the stranger visibly relaxed. "My name is Nathan Dundee," he said, introducing himself. "I'm sheriff of Providencetown, just a short way from here." He nodded to the others. "And these are my deputies." His fallen man had begun to revive, groaning in pain. His comrades, the other three deputies, turned from Sheriff Dundee and Maddie. Both kneeled and tried to comfort the fallen man. Nobody, however, bothered with the ones who lay bound by ropes upon the floor. Not one of them cared about the well-being of such criminals as these.

"We saw lights where none should have been, and it aroused my suspicions," he continued, speaking alone to her. "So I gathered four able men and we rode out here to see." He sighed. "Unfortunately, we were too far away to stop the carnage, but we intended to make sure it never happened again. We were merely going to take a leisurely time arresting them—until we heard your scream."

Maddie shuddered. "It was awful. If I live to be a hundred...."

"You were on that ship, then?" The sheriff of Providencetown glanced around. Even as he questioned her, he strode to a pitcher set on the floor in one corner. He carried it back and set it down next to her. She saw that brackish water filled it to overflowing, and wondered what he intended doing with it. In answer to his question, however, she nodded. "Yes," she replied. "The storm itself probably would have destroyed us. The ship started falling apart. Things collapsed and started leaking, but then we saw those lights on shore, and it sealed our doom." She watched him pull a handkerchief from his pocket. He dipped it in water, then began very gently to wipe the dampened cloth across her mouth and chin. Seeing the surprised expression on her face, he answered her unspoken question. "You bear traces of your struggle, mistress," he said softly, rinsing the now-stained cloth in the water. "I couldn't bear to see a face as lovely as yours so polluted."

Maddie stopped short, embarrassed again. She had forgotten about the blood that must have dried on her face. She glanced almost involuntarily toward the man she had wounded, now motionless, and probably dead, upon the floor.

He continued interrogating her. "And you believed what you wanted to believe—that those lights were some kind of beacon."

"Not I," she replied, "but the captain. My husband even warned him—"

The man drew back. "Your husband?" he asked, with surprising and ill-concealed dismay.

Maddie nodded, then added miserably, "He was with

87

me on that ship, and he knows this shoreline. I don't know how he does, but he knows." She raised wide, pleading eyes to him. "Oh, sir, is it possible he survived? I did somehow. Maybe he did, too."

The man looked upon her sadly, yet with a certain wistful tenderness, as he took her hand. "Would God grant more than one miracle in so short a time?" he whispered. "I cannot know, but frankly...." He glanced out the window and sighed. "The sea has been so vicious tonight, madam, and the rocks along this shore are large and sharp. This stretch of beach is known to be a boneyard of ships—even without the likes of *them*." He nodded scornfully toward the prisoners.

Maddie lacked the strength to reply. Instead, she remained motionless. She stared into the void she imagined as her future.

"Exactly what happened?" The man spoke gently now as he leaned to her. "We saw the ship, but barely—only because of the lights down by the rocks below. We figured out almost at once what had caused those lights, and *who*." He glanced again with loathing toward his prisoners. "But what happened afterward? You were a witness. We'll need your testimony when we take them back."

Maddie shuddered. "Most died at sea," she replied. "All around me, I heard their screams, but their voices were barely louder than the waves. It was awful!" She drew in a great shuddering breath. "A few made it to the rocks on shore without being smashed against them. I could never guess how, but we did."

Maddie fell into a pensive silence, as she relived the horror of those moments. The sheriff of Providencetown urged her to continue.

Maddie sighed. "I had barely pulled myself onto the rocks and out of water's reach, when I saw what was happening—how those, those four *animals* fell upon anyone who moved and killed them.'' Her eyes burned as she glanced toward the prisoners. "I tried to hide,'' she continued, "but this beach is unfamiliar to me.''

"So one of them saw and captured you,'' the sheriff finished off what she had been saying.

Maddie shuddered. "Aye, they did not kill me as they had the others, although—'' Her voice trailed off for a moment. If Henri were dead, she wished they had ended her life, too. "Although I feel certain they would have—eventually,'' she sighed.

The others went outside to search for any bodies still scattered upon the rocks below. When she and the sheriff were alone, he reached to take her hand. "What you went through was horrible,'' he said, "utterly horrible, but thank God you, at least, survived.'' That he meant it sincerely, Maddie had no doubt. To her, however, life remained only a horrible burden. At his words, she turned her gaze away. "You must forgive me, but I am not feeling all that glad to be alive right now.'' If Henri were gone, then she had nothing to live for. She had no home, the people there having branded her as a witch, and now no husband. Fate had left her completely alone in the world. Not even her father dared come to her now. She had no friends any more. No money, nor even clothes. At best, she would become an object of charity. At worst, sell herself into indentured servitude. Worse still, her memory of this night's ravaging still tormented her almost unbearably. She doubted that time would heal this particular wound.

The man reached to take her hand. "I know it seems very black to you right now,'' he said, "but you have friends.''

"I have no friends.'' Maddie's lips quivered. Her eyes swam with tears.

"I am your friend,'' he replied, "if you'll allow me.''

"Nobody gives anything to a stranger, without wanting something in return," Maddie said harshly, bitterly.

To her surprise, he replied in a soft and gentle voice, "Do you really believe that?"

Despair had flooded Maddie like a giant, fast-moving tide. "I no longer know what I believe in, sir," she replied. "But if my Henri is dead, then I wish I were, too."

He squeezed her hand. "Every life has a purpose, a reason for being." As he spoke, however, he glanced to the prisoners. "Even theirs, although for the life of me, I fail to understand what it might be."

The three surviving brothers cast evil looks at them both as they lay, still bound, upon the floor. Maddie returned their glares with loathing. She too wondered why such men as these had been allowed to be born.

"Now you'll excuse me, please," he said, speaking with obvious reluctance. "I have to join my men below. The tide is going out, so we should be able to recover some more of the bodies."

"I'm going with you." Suddenly energized, Maddie leaped to her feet. She wanted to see with her own eyes what might have happened to Henri.

The man started in surprise. "What are you talking about? You can't go out there. It's too gruesome for a maid."

"My husband may be out there. I want to view the bodies."

He recoiled at the very idea. "No!" He seemed genuinely horrified.

Maddie fixed wide, stubborn eyes on him and spoke calmly. "I *must*."

He stared at her. Even in the dim and smoking glow of the wrecker's tallow lamp, she saw how he had paled. "I will not hear of it!" When he spoke, his voice came out hoarse. "I'm sorry," he added, softening. Averting his eyes, he lifted her hand from his arm. "I know it's difficult for you, but I must insist. *Now stay here!*"

He left her alone in the hut, with only the prisoners for company. He had ordered her to remain, but she could not obey. Those three lay on their bellies. Only their heads were free to raise and look at her, and their voices unmuffled to curse at her, which they did, using fouler language than Maddie ever thought possible. She could not stand to remain. As she ran past them to the door, one of them spat. As a vicious wad hit her ankle and slid into her shoe, Maddie's throat closed in revulsion. She flinched inwardly, but would not give them the satisfaction of seeing her revulsed or angry. "You know, you're going to pay for what you've done," she said, forcing herself to speak calmly. She turned from them, burst outside, and slammed the door behind her. The rain, she saw, had slowed to a light drizzle that misted the fibres of Sheriff Dundee's cloak. An occasional shaft of lightning still lit the sky, but the clouds had already begun to drift away, herded by the warm, gentle wind that had replaced the howling gale. She picked her way gingerly over rock-strewn dune wasteland to the men searching with torches right where surf swirled against land over the rocks below. She remembered from before how the narrow cleft had widened into a footpath down the face of a bluff. She found it again, and struggled to keep from falling as she slid, half-stumbling down the steep incline. Torches bobbled below. In their dim glow, she saw one man pull a corpse from a rock-bound pool left by retreating tide. Clouds glided past and away from the moon, leaving the great pale disk exposed. Under its light, water-washed rocks glistened like jewels, crystalized in a matrix of sand. Crumbled like dark clots of half-jellied blood, however, lay the corpses—the pitiful shells of men who would never again walk among the living. Maddie saw how hard the sheriff and his deputies worked, gathering the victims together, so that later they could send a wagon back from their village to pick them up before the tide rose again. Maddie knew they intended bringing all these into town for Christian burial. Their mood as Maddie approached was somber, their voices muted. What they saw had horrified them. Even in the pale flicker of their torches, she could see how close they were to tears.

At hearing the rustle of her cape in the storm-dampened wind, her friend the sheriff whirled. When he saw who was standing so close, he scowled. "What are you doing out here? I thought I told you—"

"I want to view the bodies," Maddie said with quiet determination.

"I already told you." The man moved toward her, genuinely horrified at her resolve. "I am sorry, madam, but I cannot allow it. You are but a young woman, too young, surely, and too tender to withstand such a sight as this."

Maddie stared back at him defiantly. "Sir, I saw those crimes committed. If my eyes could stand the sight of *that* without driving me mad, then surely they can endure looking upon the pitiful remains."

"But why? Why should you be so intent on it?" He frowned at her in bewilderment.

"I already told you," she replied. "My husband was among those on board. How am I to know, unless I see for myself, whether I am a widow, or still a wife?" As she spoke, her voice broke. She could hardly bear the thought of losing Henri before she had even the chance to know him well as a husband. Tears sprang to her eyes.

The man moved toward her. His hands reached to her shoulders and rested there. He held her gently for a moment. As a tear rolled down her cheek, he wiped it away, tenderly, with the back of his hand. Finally, he said, "If he is among...those who lie here forever sleeping...." He chose his words delicately to spare her feelings. "Do you realize how painful it will be for you to witness? Now I know you've seen men being killed tonight, but obviously not your husband." He continued, "The corpse of a stranger is unpleasant enough, Lord knows. What if you should come upon...?" The man sighed. "If you should come upon him, you'll suffer tremendous pain. Most likely he *is* among them somewhere, and as you yourself know, these men did not die peacefully."

Maddie took a deep breath to brace herself, then faced him with steady eyes. She understood that he only wanted to protect her. He was a gentle man who obviously looked upon her as fragile. No doubt he feared that the sight of all those dead men, perhaps even her husband among them, would prove unbearable for her. But Maddie knew herself to be strong enough to endure whatever sights awaited her. Not knowing the truth would be far worse. She faced him now, intent on persuading him. "I know you mean well, and I'm grateful, really I am—but you don't seem to understand how important it is to me."

She struggled to keep her voice steady. She knew that she must convince him that she would remain calm. If she left him with any fear at all that she'd collapse into uncontrollable hysterics at first sight of her dead husband, he'd surely refuse to let her see.

"If I don't know for sure, I'll be forever haunted," she continued. "In my dreams, I'd search for him, and during my waking hours, his memory would become an obsession." She took a deep breath to fight back her tears of desperation. "I know you find it hard to believe, but honestly, sir, I have prepared myself for the worst. If I find him, and even if the sight be a horrible one, I'd mourn for him. But at least I'd know," she sighed, "and after awhile, I'd be able to bury him in my heart. I'd pick up the pieces of my life and start anew. But if I never really know for sure, I'd be forever searching."

The man sighed. "It goes against my better judgment, but I understand what you must be going through. Come down with me, then, and search. And God give you strength," he added, "if you should find him." He helped her down the steep defile to the beach below. The tidal cycle had come full-circle now. Waves which only hours earlier had crashed right up to the crumbling bluffs reached only part-way up the narrow beach. The ocean seemed exhausted, its energy depleted.

The young sheriff stood motionless, as if overwhelmed by what he saw. A wind that blew west off the ocean whipped his jacket and hair, but he seemed not to notice. Maddie, however, ignored her horror as she picked her way among the corpses. Only a few lay at her feet. The others waited, face down in tide pools or thrown against rocks. To her relief, all she saw were strangers—crew from the ship, crushed to untimely deaths by those four loathsome wreckers.

Maddie glanced from the corpses to her protector, the sheriff of Providencetown. "It's so horrible even to think about it," she whispered, instead of speaking. "So utterly horrible. Just a few hours ago, they were all alive, all healthy, and now look at them!" Their strong backs had manned a whaling ship. Their blood and bones and energy had struggled to keep their ship afloat through the storm. They had fought to hold her back from dashing upon the rocks of this lethal and isolated shore. And all for nothing; in the end, the wreckers had won. The sea had claimed its prizes.

She stepped over to a familiar-looking form lying as motionless as all the others, and found herself standing directly above the one who hauled her aboard. He had been young, merely a boy in his teens. Certainly younger than she. The sorrow and pity she felt for him, for *all* of them, almost overwhelmed her feeling of relief that Henri was not among their torn and bruised remains.

Wild hope surged up in her that he still survived, but Maddie crushed it back. These eight men were but a few of the many who had died. Even as she looked upon them now, she heard the shouts of deputies further down the beach as they still searched for others. She stared with pity and dread as they dragged the ones they found back to join their comrades.

The surf crashed against rocks. Its frothy tide swirled around boulders, booming out a tuneless dirge blended with her own sorrows and apprehensions. Thousands of tons of water that could drown or crush or sweep away the small, puny bodies of men played an unliving, undying requiem for its own victims. Yet she did not blame the water. It was itself; merely a power unharnessed, which four vile humans had used for evil. With a pang, she wondered where the surf had carried Henri — out to sea, to the bottom, or onto shore where he must surely have fallen pray to the four murderers. She dared not hope for anything better.

The sheriff leaned to her in concern. His young, serious gray eyes fixed on hers. "Are you all right?" he whispered "I could look for him myself, you know. You could describe him to me—color of hair, what he was wearing. My doing it would save you pain."

Maddie shook her head, instead of replying directly. "There are more down *that* way." She pointed south, toward the spot where she herself had first fought her way onto land. The retreating waves had pulled back from a natural outcrop of rock. As surf traveled south, the stone jetty's presence formed a sheltered cove, protecting the shoreline from the waves' worst pounding. To the left of it, sand was piled, the result of interrupted waves depositing particles of the worn-down rock. To the right, just further southward, the beach appeared sparser, but the surf more gentle. With a shudder, Maddie realized how lucky she had been. Had waves swept her a little further northward, they would have carried her into surf untamed. Its power would have bashed her like a rag doll against the outlying rocks. Had it happened so, she'd be lying dead among the poor devils who had not survived long enough to see the wreckers' rocks, or their ugly faces. "You'll find men down beyond that point who were murdered. These closer in were merely victims of the sea itself."

She turned from him and began to walk in that direction herself. From behind, she heard her rescuer's voice. "Wait," he called out to her, "I'm coming with you."

"As you wish." She stood without moving as he caught up to her. She was grateful, however, for his company. She dreaded carrying her fears and sorrow alone. They walked in silence along the thin wedge of beach that the retreating waves had uncovered. Facing toward water in the moonlight, she saw trees, sprung from seeds fallen into cracks in the glistening granite bluffs. Winds howling off the winter sea had gnarled them. Their branches resembled bones distorted by years of hardship and disease into knobby claws. Salt spray, winter cold, and the summer's heat had stripped them of all but the sparest greenery, while the sandy soil in which their roots groped for sustenance had stunted them, so trees became scarcely more than bushes. But those few trees grew high above. Below, nothing could live, except predators and carrion-eaters. As she and Sheriff Dundee walked together down the life-deserted beach, Maddie saw again the bodies of sailors beaten into early death. They sprawled upon the rock-strewn

Again they approached the bodies lying upon the ever-widening beach. Six more had been discovered, and these lay beside the others on the sand. As Maddie inched toward them, dreading yet determined to glance at their faces, she felt his living hand press again upon her shoulder. His touch lingered there as before, with almost unmanly gentleness. "How can you bear it?" he whispered. "Even I find the sight painful, Lord knows, and I am a man."

"Do you think it's easy for me?" she replied grimly. "Knowing each time that I might see the very face I dread to find?" On legs legs suddenly jellied, she dropped down. She knelt beside one whose head and face, no longer supported by the broken neck, pressed forehead-down in an unnatural position upon the sand. His clothes hung in tatters from his limbs. Rocks had torn the sturdy material into shreds. As he had fought his way toward shore, he had kicked off his shoes. His bare feet lying heels-down in the sand, gleamed whitish. He too was a stranger, like all the others freshly gathered here.

Once she had satisfied herself that none was Henri, Maddie stood and faced the men. "Are these all you found—up that way?" She pointed north.

"Aye," replied the tallest man. "I think we've got everyone there was, but we'll come back tomorrow to make sure."

Maddie fought down the urge to laugh and cry all at once. *Henri was not among the known dead!* "Thank God!" she whispered, and felt herself grow weak. Almost as if he had read her mind, the young sheriff's arm slipped around to support her. His strength alone kept her from collapsing on suddenly rubbery knees. Maddie silently blessed him for being there right then.

Even as he held her, he turned to his men. "I'll take the lady back into the hut. She can stay there until we're ready to leave. Make one more quick search along the beach, then come join us to carry back our prisoners—the scum!'' He added this last viciously. When they were alone again, he turned to her. ''I know how much you must hope for your man's safe return,'' he said, ''and for your sake, I do too. But *please*—be realistic. The odds are so slim. A falling timber from the ship could have dashed him to death, or waves could have flung him against one of the outlying boulders. Maybe he's even on the beach, but we just haven't found him in the darkness.'' He guided her back to the bluff-perched cabin. ''I have no wish to make you unhappy, madam,'' he continued, ''but I don't want you to cling to any unrealistic hopes. I'd be doing you a disservice if I allowed it.''

As they stepped back into the cabin, Maddie glanced to the prisoners. At once, she remembered what in the excitement had slipped her mind. ''My ring!'' she cried out, pointing to the eldest. ''He has my wedding ring.'' She described it to him, leaving out the means by which Henri had obtained it. ''May I have it back now please?''

As Nathan the sheriff bent over the wrecker's unmoving form, Maddie continued. ''You'll find it in his short pocket. That's where I saw him drop it after he tore it off my finger.''

With one rough thrust, the sheriff flung the man over and jammed a hand down into his pocket. Within a second, he pulled out the ring, Henri's special ring, then handed it to her. ''Curious.'' He glanced at it before passing it on. ''It looks almost Spanish.''

The thought hadn't occured to her until now, but he was right. This was not a ring meant for a sober Huguenot or his Puritan wife, but one cut and polished to glitter upon the finger of someone dark and richly dressed. Maddie frowned as she took the ring from him.

Without speaking, she slipped it back onto her own finger, then raised her eyes to her protector. "It's all I have of him now."

The sheriff and his men carried their three surviving prisoners out to the horses. The animals, who stood waiting to take all living souls from here back to Providencetown, stamped the ground impatiently. One of them neighed, while a second snorted his eagerness to be back home, perhaps yearning for a nice warm stable and a bin filled with hay.

"Ready, sir?" One of the deputies turned to his leader with questioning look. Sheriff Dundee nodded, then bent to help Maddie stand from where she had seated herself on a rock. Seeing Dundee's response, the man continued. "Good. The sooner we lock this scum in gaol, the better," he sneered at the prisoners. "Indeed, the very sight of them makes my skin crawl!"

When they had finished with the prisoners, the sheriff lifted Maddie onto his own horse. When he saw her comfortably settled, he climbed up behind her. His own arms encircled her, holding her close as his hands gripped the narrow bridle. With a lurch, they started forward.

The storm that had driven the ship up on to the reefs had died away, but humidity still hung thick in the air. Nightime heat nearly suffocated her. She sensed the storm was not yet over; lightning merely slumbered in the lull. Maddie could still feel its dormant power crackle against her skin, and she knew that it was only a matter of time until the weather, which had nearly killed her, lashed itself into fury once again.

As they rode back to Providencetown, they watched the moon play hide-and-go-seek with the clouds. Just minutes earlier, it had cast it's glow through a hole in the mists high above, but now billowing masses of storm formations skidded across the sky. As they thickened, piling upon each other, the gleam faded into shadow.

Maddie leaned back against the young sheriff as they rode, now completely relaxed, in one another's arms. She did not even try to shield her face as drizzle licked against it. She closed her eyes in contentment and listened to his heart beating against her ear. Suddenly, guilt and apprehension stabbed her, as she remembered again her husband. "What if you're wrong?" she yelled to him, over hoofbeats and the wind created by their passage. It took all her lungpower to make herself heard. "What if Henri is still alive and needs help?"

He yelled back, "If he's survived this long, he'll last until the morrow. As soon as it's light enough, I'll be sending men back up here to search one last time. We've done the best we could for tonight."

Maddie sighed. Uncertainty was worst of all. Not knowing gnawed at her innards. It paralyzed her movement, and because she could hope, as well as fear, obstructed any plans she might make. She glanced to the deputies who rode on ahead. Each accompanied one of the three surviving prisoners. The eldest, who had died, would not be buried with his victims. His clay would fill a hole in unhallowed ground, somewhere near the granite bluffs where he had ended his miserable days. "And what will become of the ones who are left?"

"Most likely they'll dangle at the end of a rope," he replied. "The whole depraved lot of them."

"A pity ending their lives can't bring back any of the others," she observed. "It hardly seems that justice is served at all." Retribution, although necessary, seemed such a futile thing in a case like this.

"Well, it's the best we can do," he replied, "...on earth."

The temperature dropped again, and the drizzle hardened into rain. Clad only in Nathan's waterlogged cloak, Maddie began to shiver.

"You're cold!" She felt his breath warm against her ear. The tone of his voice betrayed concern.

"A little," she replied, shrugging. What did it matter that she was freezing? Short of undressing, he could give her no more clothes. She had never been one to complain, and she refused to start now. In any case, Providencetown and warmth couldn't be very far away.

"This has been very bad for you." He clasped her a little more tightly. "But we're almost home.

"What will become of me then?" A quiet inn for a day or two, then out into the cold with nowhere to go? Despair siezed Maddie by the throat like a hand that wouldn't let go. She nearly choked from it. What would she do? Who could she turn to now?

"My mother lives with me now." After a silence, the man spoke in a burst, "And my ten-year-old daughter, too. My house is large—really, for just the three of us. You might as well stay with us."

"You have no wife then?" He was such a quiet and solitary-seeming man. Her impression of him had been that he lived alone.

"My wife is dead," he replied with quiet finality. "The smallpox took her about four years back."

"I'm so sorry."

"I did not tell you that to gain your pity," he retorted, "nor was I making idle conversation when I described my home. I did so to make it clear that you would be comfortable there, and in a situation where idle minds and foolish tongues could not see fit to gossip."

Maddie smiled grimly. "There will always be gossip. There always is." Bitter experience had taught her *that*, if nothing else in her short, young life. After all, it had been gossip that brought about her troubles. The fruit of malicious words had driven her from her home, fleeing in terror for her life.

The man spoke softly. "You've been hurt, I can see, and deeply scarred. Tonight was but a passing incident—unpleasant, to be sure—but the pain has been inside you from before." When Maddie did not reply, he continued, "I have no idea where you come from or what else has happened to you, but I can guess. I want you to believe now, to understand that I am your friend."

"How can you be a friend to someone who's a stranger to you? I could be a thief, a whore, or even a....a *witch*." At the last, her voice broke. She fought back tears that might reveal the truth.

"You are none of these, I *know*," he retorted. "Eyes are the mirror of the soul, and I saw in yours the kind of person you are. Their expression told me. But even if I were blind," he continued, "and your eyes a mystery to me, I would know. Something about you reaches out to me. Even though you are, as you say, a stranger, I feel as if I know you well."

At hearing his words, Maddie's eyes blinded with tears. To her chagrin, they rolled down her cheeks and spilled onto his hand. Very gently, he reached around and wiped them away. "What do you say?" he murmured. "Will you come stay with me and my mother? If you refuse, I could make other arrangements, but it would be difficult. We have no inn at Providencetown, and the hour is so late."

"Please—" Maddie stopped him. "I feel honored and grateful that you would invite me." She sighed. "In any case, what reason have *I* to feel squeamish about gossip—considering the way you found me? My concern was for you, for your family, and what you'd all have to endure when it becomes known, as it will, that I...."

"It was not your fault!" he interrupted her. "You were helpless to prevent it."

Maddie smiled bitterly. "In situations...of that sort—" She gave a mirthless, despairing chuckle. "In such circumstances, the woman is always blamed. No matter how fiercely she struggles, no matter how helpless she was to prevent it. In this one outrage, the victim is thought criminal." They rode on in silence for several long minutes. During that time, Maddie reached with her right hand and began fidgeting with Henri's ring.

"What was he like? Your husband, I mean," Nathan spoke, after a silence.

"Henri?" Maddie sighed. "He was always good and kind to me, yet I could see how hard he could be to others." She thought again of his face and of the embrace that had awakened her to womanhood. "And he was so handsome." Her eyes filled with tears. "He was tall and strong as a soldier, with noble features and auburn hair. But his eyes," she continued, "his eyes were like none I have ever seen. Even before I first looked into them, I felt their heat upon me." She choked back a sob. "Oh, I can't believe he's dead. I simply *cannot*. He was always far too alive, too vital. I hardly had the chance to know him at all."

"We're not certain what became of him," he reminded her. "And we may never know. He was a Frenchman, you said. How did you come to know him?"

Maddie started to reply. Suddenly, she remembered that anything she revealed of her background might prove dangerous. Once he learned of her father, of her home in Salem, he might trace back and learn the truth. She knew she must keep that information from him at all costs. "Things happened—" Her voice broke. After a struggle to keep from collapsing into crying, Maddie continued, "I left home with Henri never to return, and I ended up here. I'd rather not talk about how, or why."

By now, Maddie's entire body trembled from a chill especially vicious. No matter how hard she tried, she could not make it go away. "Are you all right?" He leaned to her with growing concern.

"Yes, I'm fine," she replied, but it was a lie. Her head reeled so that she could hardly keep her balance on the horse. If Nathan hadn't been mounted behind, with his arms supporting her, she would surely have fallen off.

She sensed his worried concern. "We're almost there now. You can see our meeting house steeple from here, though nothing else." Through the sparse and wind-swept branches of pines, live oak, and brush, beyond boulders impeding her view as the road curved around, Maddie could make out the outlines of the church tower. Dark-colored wood shingled its pointed roof. Whitewashed clapboard covered its outer walls. The steeple reminded her of a hand pointed upward, shaking its finger at an unresponsive God.

Recoiling from such strange fancies, Maddie wondered why her mind flowed now in such free-form associations. She felt so lightheaded, and her forehead and cheeks burned. The landscape slipped by in a blur. Weary, and still trembling both inside and out from chill and lingering horror, Maddie closed her eyes. Her mind seemed to waft away to a place and time that shed unearthly glow. "Don't worry, we'll get you there soon enough." From what seemed like miles off, she heard Nathan's voice, and felt his hand squeeze her arm.

As they drew closer, she saw gabled roofs like the ones she had known in Salem. Through the fog of her own illness, she counted about twenty households. The church still dominated her view. Its presence towered above all else. As they reached the village streets, iron forged horseshoes clattered upon the stone pavements. "I'll take you to my house first, then attend to business later. He shouted into her ear to make himself heard over the din. "My mother will see that you're comfortable."

"Is there some way to avoid disturbing her?" Remembering the hour, Maddie frowned in sudden concern. "I feel terrible that you should have to wake her on my account."

He laughed. "My mother hardly ever sleeps," he replied. "She spends hours of the night reading, improving, she says, both her mind and the state of her soul. In any case, she'd be furious with me if I neglected to tell her what happened tonight. Whenever there's excitement, she always wants to be the first to know."

Chapter Eleven

At his house, introductions between Maddie and his mother were quickly exchanged. Dame Dundee was about fifty, Maddie guessed, tall for a woman, and still slender. She wore a sleeping cap over her hair, but waving out from underneath its ruffled edges, tight gray curls framed her face. She might be called homely, but her features were nevertheless aristocratic. The facial bones were well defined, high and angular at the cheeks and square at the jaw. A strong, wide-nostriled nose, firm mouth, and surprisingly stubborn chin lent the woman an almost craggy masculinity, but her eyes softened the effect. Wide-set and gray, intelligent yet compassionate, they studied Maddie with an expression of alert curiosity mingled with sympathy. "You poor child." In a crackling contralto voice, she spoke directly to Maddie without bothering to greet her son. "You must be exhausted, weighted down like this in my son's heavy cloak. What happened to your own clothes?''

Maddie averted her eyes. The memory of how this woman's son found her still seared Maddie with soul-deep humiliation. Too embarrassed to answer, she could only shrug.

Nathan came to her rescue. "Mother—" He bent to kiss his mother on the cheek. "She's been through a shipwreck and much else tonight. I think she'd rather wait until some other time."

"Oh!" The woman seemed startled. "Of course. How thoughtless of me." She glanced to her son, with unmistakable curiosity. "So that was why you ran off so fast tonight. You'll have to tell me all about it."

"Later," Nathan replied grimly, then glanced to the door. He was anxious to be on his way and finish off the business of charging the three surviving wreckers with their crime.

"Of course." His mother seemed to know better than to press for answers he wasn't ready to give. Glancing back to Maddie, she raised her well-defined brows. "In any case, we have to get this child into some dry clothes and then to bed." She drew an arm around Maddie and guided her toward the stairs. Her contact, warm and protective, comforted Maddie. The woman's strength lent her much needed support, for by then, Maddie felt on the verge of collapsing senseless at everybody's feet. "You poor child!" she cried. "You're shivering. Are you ill, or just cold?" The warmth of her concern penetrated to the depths of Maddie's chilled soul.

"I-I'm not sure," she whispered. "I—" Her voice broke. "It's been such an evening." With a pang, she thought of the mother she had never known, and how she had grown up missing her. This woman, Dame Dundee, was everything Maddie would have wanted in her own mother.

"I'm sure it has. Now come." As she led Maddie

upstairs, the woman glanced back to her son. "How long are you going to be out, Nathan?"

"Just for a little while... I hope." He yawned. "We've taken some wreckers prisoner, and I have to charge them. It shouldn't be long."

"Wreckers?" The woman grimaced. "How awful!"

Once upstairs, she led Maddie to a cozy little room under the eaves. The bed nestled there was narrow, but it looked soft, dry, and clean. Maddie looked at it gratefully and smiled. Right then she wanted little else but dry clothes.

"So, he found you in a shipwreck." As she spoke, the woman hurried toward a highboy dresser. She pulled out a drawer and reached inside. She lifted out something soft-looking, dyed pale blue. As she handed it to Maddie, she grinned suddenly. "I must say," she said, "the quality of salvage is improving." Her eyes twinkled.

Maddie couldn't help but giggle. "Thank you," she whispered, taking the folded cloth from the woman's hands. As she opened it out, she saw a nightgown for her to change into. "What a relief!" she cried. "Dry clothes at last!"

"I'll go downstairs and make you some peppermint tea." The woman stood from where she had perched for a moment beside Maddie on the bed. "Judging from the look of you, I think you could use something warm."

"Oh, I don't want to put you to any trouble ...," Maddie protested, but not too sincerely. The mention of tea had suddenly flooded her with an intense craving for it. Seeing Maddie's protests for what they were, mere politeness, Dame Dundee went to see that it was done.

Once alone, Maddie slipped Nathan's cape from her shoulders. Because she was weak, however, she lost her grip on it. The heavy garment, water-laden, landed on the floor with a wet plop. Bending down, Maddie strained to lift it up again. Feeling suddenly dizzy, she draped it carefully over a nearby chair so that it would dry without unnecessary wrinkles.

She raised her gaze to the room's open window. Through it, she could see the rain pouring from the night sky beyond. Her naked flesh, still damp, felt chilly even to her own touch. No wonder she was shivering! She was waterlogged.

Maddie reached gratefully to the fluffy, blessedly dry gown Dame Dundee had left for her. Never in her life had she so appreciated the feel of simple linen as she did right then. Without even standing, she unfastened its top and slipped the garment over her head. She saw at once that it had been cut for a much taller woman than she, probably for Dame Dundee herself. Maddie felt as if she were wearing a tent, but its soft, caressing folds felt good. Sighing in blissful comfort, she leaned back on the bed.

A few minutes passed, and her physical uneasiness deepened. She had no idea how she could freeze and burn all at once, but somehow she was doing just that. Despite the rain, the night air sweltered, but she still shivered hot and cold all at once. She trembled in convulsions coming from deep inside herself. As she sat motionless, the room's colors took on a glowing, malignant intensity. Strange, dim sounds combined with snatches of words, flashed by her consciousness. Even her heart's beating had speeded up, fluttering as it pounded its uneven rhythm. She wondered what was happening to her. What would become of her? Was she to die here, under the roof of a stranger, never to see her Henri again until they met in Heaven? With a shudder, Maddie remembered Henri's career. She resolved then and there to meet him in Hell if necessary.

She leaned against the backboard of the bed and closed her eyes for a second. She intended only to rest them and not to sleep. Time passed that way, but she had no idea how much. When Dame Dundee returned carrying a tray of tea and a plate of biscuits, Maddie's eyes flew open in startled surprise.

"I'm sorry I took so long," the woman apologized. "But usually I let a servant light the fires and cook. I'm afraid I'm not used to it."

Maddie blinked in confusion. "I must have dozed off. It hardly seemed as if you were gone at all."

"Well, good." The woman set the tray near Maddie on a bedside table. "Then it worked well for both of us." She handed Maddie the cup and moved the biscuits within closer reach. Maddie tasted one, and found it made partly of flour, and partly of ground Indian coin. "Now drink this," the woman said, "and you'll feel better, I hope. Mint settles the stomach, and its good for a fever too, they say."

The china cup filled with tea warmed Maddie's hands. She lifted it to her lips and held it there, savoring the steam against her face. Finally, when it had cooled a little, she sipped. The woman had sweetened it with honey—a little more perhaps than Maddie would have used, but it tasted good. Butter filled the biscuits, which flaked and crumbled deliciously as she bit into first one, then a second. With a start, Maddie realized that she had every reason to be so famished. She hadn't eaten for hours and hours.

"What a pretty child you are." The woman sat down beside her on the edge of the bed and studied Maddie's face. After Maddie had finished her scones and tea, the woman leveled her eyes at her. "How did you come to be caught in a shipwreck, child," she said, speaking suddenly, "and how did you, obviously a girl of good English Puritan stock, come to end up wearing a Huguenot name like de Rohan?"

Maddie blinked in surprise. "How did you know?"

111

"That de Rohan is a Huguenot name?" The woman smiled. "My dear, I'd be surprised if it were not. I grew up in England, you see, and I knew a number of Frenchmen who had fled their homeland under the persecutions of their papist king and his army. De Rohan was a very prominent name among them. Many of their greatest leaders had come from that same family, a noble family, I might add." The woman tossed her head. "Frankly, the French were a bunch of damned fools. England gained a great many fine artisans and thinkers that way, drained from France by her own misdoing."

The woman persisted, openly curious and determined to know. "Surely you were not born with it."

"My husband...."

"Ah!" the woman nodded, light dawning. "Now I understand. You married into it. I thought you were a maiden. Forgive an old woman for snooping, but tell me about him. What's he like? How on earth did you ever meet him?"

"My husband—" Maddie sighed. "Frankly, I don't even know if I have a husband anymore. I don't know if I'm a wife or a widow." She described how wreckers had lured their storm-tossed ship to shore, and how she had saved herself, only to fall into the hands of the wreckers. She spared the woman details that she herself had no wish to relive, but described instead, how Dame Dunde's son had led her rescue.

Maddie concluded, "Henri had warned them all along. He *told* the captain not to trust the lights they saw, but he refused to listen. The captain took what he saw to be a beacon of some kind, and well—" Maddie shrugged and shuddered all at once. The memory of the ship breaking up still horrified her.

"Instead of aid, his ship grounded on the outlying rocks, then capsized. How awful!" The woman shook her head. "It seems hard to believe that men could be so bestial, so dark."

Maddie's eyes filled again with tears. She shivered now in soul-deep horror. Memory of all the murders she had witnessed congealed the words in her throat. The experience came back to her now in brutal, vivid clarity. She struggled to keep from dissolving altogether into hysterical crying. Too proud to reveal herself to someone she hardly knew, she turned her face away. The night had taken its toll. As Maddie sat there, she grew increasingly dizzy; just maintaining her balance took every ounce of strength.

The woman sensed her difficulties. She leaned closer, put one hand on Maddie's own, and squeezed it. The shape of hers was slender, with long, graceful fingers and well-shaped nails, the kind of hand Maddie had always wanted for herself. Her own seemed thick by comparison, and altogether too sturdy for her liking. "I understand," she said softly, in a voice vibrant with sympathy. "Sometimes our experiences are unbearably painful, but we always learn from them. I can guess what you must have endured, but I won't press you. In any case, I can see you're nearly dead with fatigue and ought to rest. Just remember one thing, though; I'm your friend, and my son is your friend. Both of us want to help."

"But you hardly know me," whispered Maddie. After her recent experience, so much kindness bewildered her.

"I know you better than you think," replied the woman. "Now go to sleep. Rest, and we'll talk some more tomorrow."

But tomorrow melted into the next day and the next, and still Maddie writhed, moaning and delirious, in the little bed under the eaves. For hours on end, she lay barely conscious, aware only of faces dimly recognized.

She stared at them, aware also of sweat trickling off her skin. A kindly older woman came regularly and nursed her. Sometimes the woman sat up with her, knitting in a chair beside Maddie's bed. Whenever her eyes opened, barely focused, she stared with fascination at the constant clickety-click rhythm of knitting needles. A fabric of soft, intertwined yarn grew longer and wider as time passed.

The man came too, the one who had saved her from those others. Sometimes alone, sometimes with a child, a little girl about ten, he crept in and stood beside her sweat-dampened bed and just stared.

She lived again the shipwreck. The water, swirling over her, drowned her once more with its rushing flow of strength. She thrashed against it, her frail hands and arms fighting all the weight that surged around her. She struggled to breathe as she fought her way to shore. To her surprise, cool hands reached from nowhere and held her down.

She moaned with horror as those men, the four brothers with their unshaven, leering faces, raised rocks over struggling, half-drowned seamen. She witnessed again how they struggled with their last ebbing strength against the murderers. She cried out with them as the rocks bashed the life from their skulls. She stared, the only survivor, at how those wreckers had transformed minds and consciousness into blood-gray slime. Brains no longer thinking glistened once again upon the rock-littered sand.

Unable to bear the sight any longer, Maddie cried out, and from somewhere felt a cool wet cloth upon her forehead.

They lunged at her again too, those men, and as one grabbed her, holding her tight against his body, Maddie's throat opened, pouring out her terror in a scream. They tied her down and approached, their ugly faces leering with sensual eagerness. She saw it all again, and even felt the touch of rough and calloused hands against her flesh. Horror welled up inside to overwhelm her.

"No!" she cried out. She began sobbing aloud, terrified of what they intended to do with her. She moaned, tear-blinded again as she writhed to get away. Suddenly, her eyes widened, for through the clear yet strangely distant remembering, she saw a face at the window. Hope surged up in her again as she called out for help.

Arms held her tight and warm. Her cheek fell against a shoulder and she began keening, too spent and weak now to resist the embrace. Eventually, her pain and horror subsided into a dull ache that never seemed to go away.

She found herself trapped in a tunnel of darkness searching for Henri. She called out to him, begging him to come and hold her once again. Instead, she saw only blackness. She began to cry with yearning and loneliness, and to her surprise, hands stroked her hair.

One morning close to noon, Maddie's eyes opened onto a wall that slanted outward and up into the ceiling. About seven feet beyond, sun streamed in through open casement windows. A woman, calmly knitting, sat beside her in a rocking chair. Maddie blinked away the remaining blurriness of her vision. She recognized at once her companion as Dame Dundee.

At her sudden movement, the woman glanced up from her work. Her intelligent gray eyes met Maddie's. "Well, hello!" she said, smiling. "For awhile, I thought we were going to lose you."

"What...where?" Maddie stared in confusion. "What are you talking about? What happened?"

"You've been very ill," the woman replied. "Very ill indeed. Burning with fever and shivering all at once. The seafaring life doesn't seem to suit you."

Maddie recoiled in horrified disbelief. "How long?" she whispered.

"For almost a week." Dame Dundee leaned to her and pressed the back of her hand against Maddie's forehead. Her breath smelled of anise. "At least the fever's broken. How do you feel?"

Maddie struggled to sit, but the effort took too much out of her. Exhausted, she plopped back into her pillow. "Weak," she replied honestly. "Incredibly weak."

The woman raised her brows and shrugged. "That's to be expected. We tried, but we could hardly get any food down you at all. Just a little broth, and some milk. I even tried rum, but you spit it right out."

"Oh, it was awful!" Memories were subsiding, but she still recalled enough to feel as if she had just escaped from Hell.

"Those men who attacked you...." The woman's voice trailed off. An uncomfortable silence followed.

Maddie tensed. "What about them?"

"Their trial has been delayed. You are an important witness to their other crimes, you see."

Maddie's eyes widened. "You mean I am to endure testifying at a trial?" The very thought repelled her. It would mean seeing their ugly, hateful faces again, and reliving in words what they had done to her and the others. Moreover, she would turn into a public spectacle. Everyone would know what had happened. She would become, through no fault of her own, the butt of ribald jokes and gossip.

Dame Dundee seemed to understand. "They'll make it as easy as they can for you, child," she said, speaking softly. Her gray, serious eyes studied Maddie with compassion. "The public will be barred from the proceedings, and questions will be put to you with greatest delicacy. I have already extracted that promise from my son."

Maddie turned her face away. She didn't want to describe any part of it in front of strangers. "Must I?" she whispered.

"You are an important witness," the woman replied. "Your testimony will ensure that those men get what they deserve."

Maddie closed her eyes. She leaned back against the pillow and sighed. Why was it, she wondered, that life always seemed to require such unpleasantness? "When am I to go through this?" she finally whispered.

Dame Dundee clasped her hand. "Only when you are strong enough."

Maddie's vision blurred with tears. "Oh, Dame Dundee!" she cried.

"Please, after all we've been through, call me Flora. I feel we are close enough now for that." The woman's eyes were soft as they rested upon Maddie. "Already I think of you as a daughter."

Maddie smiled through her tears. "Flora," she whispered.

"Now get some rest!" She bent and kissed Maddie upon the forehead. With a swish of her skirts, she was gone from the room.

Time passed, the silvery hours of morning melting into golden afternoon. Finally, early that evening, the young sheriff returned from his duties about the village to find Maddie still awake. She lay in bed, weak but improving. When she heard his knock on her bedroom door, she called out. He answered, then stepped inside. When she first saw him, however, she started in surprise. His face seemed haggard and unusually pale. Weariness had painted dark circles under his eyes. The expression of his face, however, was joyful. "My mother said you were better." He hurried to her side. "I had to come and see for myself."

"You are too kind, Sheriff Dundee," she smiled.

117

"And I want to thank you again for saving me. Those insufferable men...." She remembered all too clearly what she had endured.

"Could I have done anything else?" he replied, giving a modest shrug. "Could I have been such a brute as to leave you, or *any* woman, in such a pickle?"

"You're a decent man," she replied, "and I'm grateful that God sent you along."

"You had us all worried." He seemed embarrassed by the extravagance of her praise. "We thought for sure you were going to die."

Maddie smiled wryly. "I'm glad I didn't know then," she replied. "I would have worried most of all. But please, tell me—" One question obsessed her mind. "Did you search the beach again? Did you find anything—anyone?" The words caught in her throat.

He became very serious. "No, nothing. No sign of him, at least nothing we'd recognize as such." He stopped and frowned. "Strange, though. We went back to that hut, and it looked as if someone had been there after we left. Of course I don't know."

"Maybe it was Henri!" Maddie's eyes widened. Hope surged in her heart. "He could have hidden, you know, then come down after we all left...."

Nathan frowned. "Why would he have hidden? He could have seen who we were, or overheard our conversation, and guessed that we weren't more of the wreckers. Most importantly, he would have seen you with us."

Maddie stopped short, suddenly perplexed. "I don't know," she replied. "I guess—I guess he wouldn't have, once he was sure. I just don't know. Maybe he was washed up farther down the beach, and it took him time to find shelter."

Her voice trailed off. She began to realize how unlikely it all was. It was more likely that some peddler riding from town to town had found it a nice, sturdy shelter from the storm. Some stranger, not Henri, had probably spent the night there before moving on. Maddie's eyes filled with tears as she realized all too vividly that her rescuer believed, with good cause, that Henri had drowned. If she went back to search, she might even find his broken body on the rocks of some deserted cove.

"I'm sorry," he said softly. "I just don't want to raise any false hopes."

"I understand," she whispered. But she would not give up yet. She'd search until all possibilities had been exhausted. She'd wait, if necessary forever, until she knew for sure her Henri was lost for all time. She fought back the urge to break into crying.

"Those men—" the man began.

From her bed, Maddie nodded. "I know; your mother told me. I'm to testify against them."

He sighed. "The magistrates will reconvene as soon as you're able. I hope it will be soon," he added. "Even in the gaol, I find their presence loathsome." He seemed terribly oppressed somehow, and weighted down by a secret burden.

Maddie smiled at him, feeling suddenly tender. "Tell me about yourself, sir," she said, speaking again after a short, pensive pause. "I really want to know you."

He shrugged. "I'm not all that interesting."

"Tell me anyway!"

His story proved to be a simple one, and sad. He had married a local girl whom he loved. Theirs had been a happy union, blessed with one daughter who survived. Five years ago, however, smallpox had come to this village of Providencetown and had taken almost a third of its population. His wife had been among the victims. She had died, leaving him to raise their little girl alone.

His daughter was a solemn child with straight black

hair and brown eyes like his. In the narrow oval face and delicate features, however, she probably resembled her mother. When she first came with her father into Maddie's room, she stared unblinking, hardly daring, it seemed, to speak. Only at her father's urging did she return Maddie's weak, whispered greeting.

Since she had first awakened, Maddie's one constant thought had been to gain back enough strength to leave Providencetown and seek for Henri. If she could never see again with her eyes his face, she would at least search out his grave. She would kneel upon it with a spray of flowers in her arms and set them down. Even if Henri should lie instead underneath waves as salty as her own tears, she would go to him, wading barefoot, if necessary, to meet him. Life with him was everything. Without him, nothing. Rather than live on in arid loneliness, she would join him in an eternal slumber from which they would both awaken only when Gabriel blew his horn to herald all the sleeping souls to judgment.

The next few days passed quietly. She remained in her little bed, and each hour passing gathered strength back into her. Usually Flora, Dame Dundee, stayed with her, but sometimes when necessity forced her friend to attend to her domestic duties, Maddie lay alone. Her thoughts wandered always to her husband. In her mind's eye, she saw Henri's face. His features haunted her as no one else's could. Her flesh ached for him. Her newly awakened womanhood yearned, as she remembered how he had gently opened wide her bodice, the better to fondle her breasts untouched by any man before. At his memory, tears swam in Maddie's eyes. To keep from sobbing aloud and drawing even more alarm and attention to herself, she grabbed her breath and held it. Her body convulsed in silent, held-back grief.

By the third day, Maddie felt strong enough to walk.

On shaking legs, she swung herself from the bed and stood. In the summer's humid heat, the floor felt damp under her bare soles. She nearly fell, but caught herself. Bracing on a sturdy chair, she crept along, hardly daring to breathe for fear it would upset her balance. A few steps away from that chair stood a loom. When she could no longer touch the chair, she leaned to it, using this next object as a way to keep herself from falling.

A mirror hung on the wall above the dresser, and as she glanced to it, she drew back in shocked surprise. The image in its frame revealed that she had lost weight. The roundness of her face had melted away. Hollows revealed themselves under her cheekbones. In contrast to the pallor of her complexion, her eyes gleamed unnaturally bright. The face of a stranger stared back at her now, with features and expression other-worldly and almost transparent, compared to what she had been before. She wondered now if Henri would even recognize her. Would anyone, even her own father?

Flora had braided her hair and the two thick plaits of cornsilk yellow hung down now below her shoulders. The shorter strands had pulled free, wisping now around her face. It looked untidy, and Maddie, distressed by her general appearance, tore loose her hair so that it hung free, ready to be rearranged the way she usually wore it. For now, however, it hung long and free, framing her face in wild cascades of waves and curls.

A cool breeze wafted in through her room's open window. Maddie hobbled over to it now, standing just out of view beside the frame, and listened to voices in the street underneath her window. At once, she discovered to her horror that people below were talking about her.

"Horace says they found a girl amidst all the wreckage," said one whose voice carried nasally upward into her hearing.

"Aye, and a beauty too, from all reports," replied

121

another.

"I wonder what she looks like," a woman said with wondering tone, "and who she is."

"No one knows," replied the first. "No one but Nathan Dundee and his deputies, and they're not tellin'."

"Dame Dundee knows," replied the woman. "I hear the wench is staying with her."

Maddie's cheeks burned as a silence fell. Suddenly, yet another woman spoke, "This is Dame Dundee's house right here, it is."

"Maybe we can see her if we look!"

More silence, and Maddie could almost imagine them all, craning their necks as they tried to see in through Flora's windows. She thought again of the trial. With a pang, she realized that these strangers and others like them would come to the trial. Even if they were barred, they would mill about outside, hoping to catch a glimpse of Nathan Dundee's star witness against the wreckers.

Exertion and the shock of what she had overheard drained Maddie. Suddenly weak, she groped her way back to the bed, and there sank down onto its linen quilted coverlet. Later that evening, she struggled to walk again. For Henri's sake alone did Maddie fight to regain full strength. She forced herself to walk, even though recovery meant going through a trial at which she would be the main witness. To leave this house, this welcome haven, became her burning determination. The evening passed, and yet another day. Two more came and went, marking silent time to Maddie's struggles. She forced legs still rubbery to hold their weight. She walked, hesitantly at first, still reaching to furniture whenever she faltered. Finally, however, she felt strong enough and bold enough to walk directly across the room through empty space, with nothing to break her fall. For the first time, she tasted and relished again the delicious freedom of movement.

At breakfast the following morning, she found Nathan sitting with his mother at the table. Only his daughter, Patience, remained away. As Maddie joined them, almost herself again, she returned their greeting.

"You're stronger, I see." Nathan's eyes fixed on her face. Maddie sensed, with a chill, that his comment held more than mere polite concern.

She lowered her gaze. "Yes." Her voice trailed off. "Stronger."

"Here, have some griddle cakes, dear." Flora handed her a plate of thick cornmeal cakes, fried and covered with melted butter and syrup. Maddie took it from her, but set the plate down with suddenly diminished appetite.

"You and my mother already discussed...what has to be done." Nathan brought up the trial first, blurting out his words in strained and awkward tone. "You're strong enough now, and...."

"Yes, I know." She spoke with ill-concealed dread.

"I don't like it much either." His own tone was apologetic. "But the sooner that scum is hanged, the better."

Maddie sighed. "I suppose." It would not bring back Henri from the dead, or any of those others.

He leaned to her. "Maddie," he said, for they had both grown close enough in these few days to call one another by their Christian names. "I know how hard it will be for you. I won't attempt to mislead you on *that*. Going into the courtroom, people outside will stare. Once inside, though, you'll be shielded. Only the magistrates will hear your testimony."

Maddie shuddered. "But they're all strangers, Nathan, and men." How could she sit in front of them and describe what had happened, without going mad?

She understood that the brothers deserved to be hanged, but she herself wanted no more to do with them. "You saw what they did, Nathan," she said. "You and your men all saw. Why can't the magistrates be satisfied with your words and testimony?" she pleaded with him.

"Because you are the sole surviving victim. The strength of what you tell them will *ensure* a just punishment."

And so, the trial was scheduled for the next day. That night, Maddie climbed into bed plagued with misgiving and dread. She awakened already troubled to a morning gone gray with low hanging clouds and a drizzle.

She dressed modestly in a somber-looking frock once belonging to Nathan's wife, then plaited her hair. Feeling glum and sick with dread, Maddie crept from her room, downstairs to breakfast, a meal she hardly touched for fear nausea would take her.

Providencetown had no courthouse, so the magistrates were to meet in a private home belonging to one of its leading citizens. The three of them, she, Nathan, and Flora, rode in a covered cart to it, and on the way Maddie endured what she had dreaded.

People who had only heard of her existence through gossip now saw her for the first time. With eyes wide, they ogled her. Some pointed, whispering among themselves, while few even followed behind on foot, straining to get a better glimpse of her. Maddie's cheeks burned. She had no idea what stories, true or false, might have circulated among them. What wild debaucheries did they think had gone on between her and the brothers she was to testify against?

Flora reached for her hand. "Take heart, child," she whispered. "We're almost there." Maddie wondered how so short a ride could seem so endless.

Finally, the cart stopped. As she climbed out into

daylight, curious onlookers crowded around her. They pressed close, obstructing her path, as she hurried with Nathan and his mother into the house where that trial was to be held.

Once inside, however, Maddie found refuge of a sort. The indentured girl who guided them to the dining hall, the house's largest room, glanced at Maddie with furtive curiosity, but her behavior, however annoying, hardly compared to the clamor of the crowd still milling about outside. Quiet reigned here. Once, however, from behind a door down the hall, Maddie heard cursing. With a chill, she recognized the voice. It belonged to one of the brothers she was testifying against. Nearly faint, she whirled to Nathan. "I can't go through with it," she whispered. Her eyes had widened with sudden dismay. Too paralyzed to move, she just stood on suddenly shaking legs. Must she to face her attackers, as well as the magistrates?

Nathan took her by the arm. "It'll be all right, Maddie. Now come. They can't hurt you now." With gentle pressure, he half-pulled her inside the room where the judges already waited.

Furniture had been arranged to resemble in its layout an English courtroom. The long dining table served as the Bench, with magistrates, townsmen of special importance, lined up behind. Someone had placed an empty chair in front of them, presumably where they would interrogate both witness and the defendants. Other chairs lined up directly ahead, facing the bench. In these sat the deputies who had been with Nathan that night, guards, and the three surviving wreckers. At opposite end of the room were three empty chairs. As they stepped inside, Nathan pointed to these seats in silent instruction. Maddie and his mother obeyed, going to them while he followed. At their arrival, all voices fell silent. Eyes followed her movements as she sat.

At once, Nathan approached the bench. "If it please your Lordships, allow Madame de Rohan to testify first, and so be done with it. The experience is going to be painful enough for her as it is."

The head magistrate nodded in solemn agreement. "Madame de Rohan, step forward, please."

As Maddie approached, walking on shaking legs, he continued. "Speak the truth as carefully as you can, because you'll be under oath. When we've finished with you, the court gives you permission to leave."

After the swearing in, Maddie sat on the special chair facing them. In spite of herself, she glanced from time to time toward those she was to testify against. Her eyes met the youngest brother's gaze, and she immediately chilled from the hatred and venom she saw burning back at her. He had not repented of his deeds. Neither, for that matter, had the others. All three sitting there looked upon her with a viciousness that left no doubt what they'd do to her, if they could. Unable to stand such hatred, Maddie turned away, but nevertheless, she still felt it burrowing into her very flesh.

The magistrates tried to be kind. They questioned her gently, sparing her as much as they could. Finally, they finished with her. After instructing Nathan to return and testify himself, they allowed him and his mother to take her home. Drained now of all emotion, Maddie hardly noticed the stares she received leaving the house.

Suddenly, a voice called out. Someone who knew her name struggled to catch her attention as he fought his way through the crowd. "Maddie Bradshaw, as I live and breathe!"

At the man's cry, Maddie's eyes widened. She glanced to the unusual movement heading toward her and saw almost immediately a familiar face.

"Edward Leich!" As she cried out his name, her voice trembled. He was a neighbor of hers from Salem

Village, a few years older than she, and a one-time classmate in the village school. She was sorry, truly sorry, that he had seen her here. Undoubtedly he was on his way home from the business trip he had taken to Boston a month ago, and once back among his friends and neighbors, he would tell anyone who seemed interested that he had seen her here. He was that sort. "What on earth are you doing in Providencetown?" He drew close, staring at her with wide, curious eyes. "And for Heaven's sake, what's going on?" He glanced around at the crowd. Edward Leich had the wit to see that she herself was the focus of attention, and he wanted to know why.

Maddie shrugged, hoping to play it down. "Oh, it's a long story. I was a witness to an offense, and had to testify." She glanced to Nathan. With her eyes, she begged him to rescue her, but saw that his gaze had directed itself elsewhere. She turned again to Edward Leich. "When will you be going back home?" While pretending to be but casually interested, she struggled to get what information she could from him. His answer would tell her how many days of absolute safety she had before people in Salem were likely to learn where she was and come after her.

Edward Leich shrugged. "Oh, in a few days, I suppose. I'm visiting relatives, you see." His eyes widened in eager curiosity. "But tell me about the crime." He glanced around. "It must have been a bad one, to attract such interest."

Maddie struggled to keep all emotion from her voice. "Oh, just some wreckers, and I happened to see what they were doing. I'm afraid it's all been blown out of proportion though. You know how gossip spreads and grows. But tell me," she persisted, "how many days? I'd like for you to take a message back up to my father, if you would." She had to know exactly how much time she really had.

Strangers, meanwhile, pressed close. The unknown young man who stood with her now became yet another object of their curiosity. She could hardly hear him speak over the din of their voices.

In answer to her question, he shrugged. "Oh, about three days," he replied. "I'll probably leave on Monday, to avoid traveling on the Sabbath."

By then, Dame Dundee had gotten her son's attention. With one simple, significant gesture, she let him know that Maddie was uncomfortable and wanted to be spirited away. He came to her now and slipped his arm around hers. "Maddie," he said, "will you be wanting to leave now?"

With a smile of relief, she nodded. "Yes, very much." Ignoring Edward Leich's bewildered stare, his unasked questions, Maddie bade her acquaintance Godspeed and climbed back into the cart that had brought her, Nathan, and his mother here in the first place. Nearly faint now from all she had endured, Maddie leaned with eyes closed, just listening to the clatter of wheels against the street as they rattled home. Once back at the house, Nathan saw them inside. He himself did not remain, however, but hurried on horseback to where the three wreckers were still on trial for their lives. He did not return for hours.

Later that evening, Flora came up to Maddie's room. Her mood had changed, becoming uncomfortably solemn. Maddie stared at her, startled and a little apprehensive. "Flora?" she whispered.

"The magistrates have sentenced them to hang," she said, without even so much as greeting Maddie. "On the morrow. I just found out about it a few minutes ago. Nathan will be delayed several hours, attending to it."

"Was there any doubt that hanging would be the verdict?" Maddie found herself surprised by Dame

Dundee's mood.

The woman shook her head. "Oh, no, not really. It's just that taking a life...hanging a man...is such an awesome weight to bear upon one's conscience. I feel rather sorry for Nathan. It's *his* responsibility, you know."

"Poor Nathan."

His mother added, speaking pensively, "I myself don't care to watch, but I suppose we could make some arrangements, if you do. The rest of the town will be there—gathering around the gallows. The hanging's to be at sunset, and they intend making quite a picnic of it, or so I hear."

Maddie shuddered. "Thank you, but no!" If she never saw those men again, she'd be grateful indeed. In any case, she had seen a hanging once; a nursemaid had taken her when she was but a child, and the sight had horrified her.

"I'm glad to hear it," replied the woman. "Somehow, I always wonder about people who enjoy that sort of thing. I know that sometimes a hanging is necessary, but allowing it to be done publically, well...." She shrugged, then added crisply, "It seems to me it only encourages morbidity among the weakminded. Far less, I suspect, does it teach the lesson intended."

Maddie averted her gaze. She remembered, with a sudden ugly intensity, how her own townspeople had intended the same fate for her.

Flora sensed, though could not understand, her mental pain. The woman reached for her hand. Hers felt warm and reassuring against Maddie's own. As their eyes met, Dame Dundee shook her head. "You poor child," she murmured. "You've been through so much. I want to help you, and so does my son." As Maddie stared but did not answer, the woman continued, "I fear for you, child. You seem to attract trouble to yourself, and you do it so effortlessly." She sighed. "It's a talent, I suppose, like any other."

At such a wry observation, Maddie giggled. Her friend continued. "Please stay here as long as you want. Under our roof, you'll have friends and protection. Out there...." She gestured toward the window and the world beyond. "Out there, you're alone. I suppose in the end you'll follow your own destiny, whatever it is, but I pray for you."

"Thank you," whispered Maddie.

She awoke at dawn the following morning. Almost at once, a cold dread gripped her heart like icy fingers. Startled, she blinked the sleep out of her eyes. She wondered for an instant why she felt so fearful, then realized why. That day, at sunset, those four brothers, murderers all, were to meet justice at the end of a rope.

She bolted up in bed, wondering why in God's name she should feel so miserable and apprehensive as she did. She should be glad for their punishment, not dreading it. After all, the crimes they had committed were undeniably foul. She realized at once the wisdom of her friend's words. To be even partially responsible for another's death had become an unbearable weight upon her conscience.

She swung her feet out of bed and stood. She saw through the window that the sky outside was gray. Through the still-opened casement windows, a breeze blew against her face. It felt warm and laden with moisture, portending rain.

Maddie went to the window and looked out. She stared onto streets almost deserted. A few people hurried past, perhaps to watch the scaffold being readied. As she watched, apprehensive yet not really comprehending why, the dampness turned to drizzle. It misted against her face, collecting in her hair, and left her nightgown hanging soggy and limp from her body. Still, she did not move away to a drier part of the room, nor did she close the window. She remained, as if waiting for some unseen thing to happen, and reflected that the day was a dismal one indeed, to be the last image those three men would carry with them to Hell.

Hours passed. To occupy them, Maddie wandered the house and garden like a wraith waiting for release from earthbound memories. A grim expectancy hung around her. A strange unease cast its pall over her mind.

And as morning brightened into afternoon, the street outside grew busier. Toward sunset, the whole town hurried past to the scaffolds built mercifully out of view.

At sunset, Flora who had remained behind, found Maddie shivering miserably in her room. The woman saw, and came to sit beside her on the bed. "I know how you must feel," she said, putting her arms around Maddie.

"It's happening right now, isn't it?"

"Yes, I suppose so, but why are you so unhappy? You ought to be glad to see them get their just desserts."

Maddie knew the three wreckers were guilty. She could not forget, however, that the same fate would have awaited her back in Salem, and that knowledge imbued today's execution with hideous significance.

Flora thought she understood. "Being responsible for another's death is always terrifying, Maddie, at least to any soul who hasn't sunk to the level of the beasts. But look what would have happened if you had not done your duty. At very worst, the magistrates might have felt forced to release them for insufficient evidence—release them to further their mischief upon unsuspecting ships."

131

Maddie could not reply, but remained silent.

Sunset darkened by degrees into a mucky twilight barren of moon and stars. Night fell, and still Nathan did not return to his mother's house. Finally, both woman bade each other goodnight and went to their separate rooms.

Sometime in the hours of uneasy sleep, Maddie had a dream. She, who had all but given up her husband for dead, saw him again.

He seemed to be groping, struggling through an unidentified tunnel toward some mysterious destination. Upon his face, she witnessed terror, and along with it pleading, as he cried her name throughout the lonely night. Maddie, bound by slumber, tried to touch him. She stretched one hand toward his, but could not meet. An invisible yet potent dimension of space held them apart. She called to him and he answered, but she could barely hear his voice. A virulent cosmic wind swept it away. Its power distorted his words beyond all recognition.

She awakened, moaning in anguish, opening her eyes onto good Dame Dundee's ceiling. A cold gray dawn had already begun crawling across the sky, pushing fingerlike smears of light into the darkness.

Compelled by a force she hardly understood, Maddie flung back her bedsheet. She swung her feet onto the floor, and with a great, shuddering breath, stood. Without stopping, she reached for one of the dresses Flora had lent her and pulled it over her head. Not even bothering to braid and arrange her hair, Maddie grabbed her friend's cloak and hurried out.

The house lay silent and sleeping as she crept down the hall, holding shoes in her hand so as to move all the more quietly. She had no wish to alarm them, or worse, to explain why she must leave right then, must return to that deserted beach to search for her husband.

The dream had left a powerful effect on her. The sight of his face, suffering and in need, tormented her. As soon as she had awakened, as soon as her mind cleared, she had vowed to search for him, and search she would. All her earlier determination had been little more than the bravado of hopeless desperation. She knew now for sure. *Henri was alive, and she must go to him!*

A farmer aided her on her journey. As he lumbered past, driving a wooden cart pulled by two thick-limbed horses, he saw her walking just outside the outskirts of town. In a booming voice, he called out to her, offering to give her a ride. He was a rose-cheeked man and simple, not from stupidity, but from lack of the more subtle learning that comes from books and teachers. He was a man of the soil and lived content with his lot, so long as crops were decent enough that he and his family felt no hunger. He had crates full of chickens he was taking to market, and their wings fluttered softly as she rode beside him.

Finally, as she came within view of that particular stretch of coastline, she bade him Godspeed. He had been kind to her and she appreciated the ride. She slipped from his cart's hard wooden buckboard, then hurried on fear-trembling legs toward the bluff-faced beach beyond.

The ship which had brought her and Henri this far south had all but disappeared. Only raw wood, waterlogged and dark, littered the beach, and even this would go in time. Waves already sucked what remained of it back out to sea. The boards and timbers would float, perhaps for years, and as time passed, the sea would polish them all into driftwood.

Water still pounded with savage fury against the great gray boulders. Beyond, clinging to a flatter, higher spot just above the high tide water mark, she saw that wretched hut.. It looked deserted now, but she remembered with hope what Nathan had said about coming back and finding it freshly used.

As her hopes had risen, he had tried to dash them gently, and he was right to do so. The likelihood that Henri still survived, that he had come to this one isolated spot and used it as shelter before moving on, was a slim one. In the cold light of morning, it seemed almost impossible.

But Maddie had to know for sure. She could not rest while doubts and dreams still lingered in her mind. Heart pounding now both in dread and eagerness, she hurried toward the hut, pausing now and then when she saw some object washed up onto the beach.

She had almost reached it when a noise behind startled her. Though soft, the sound stopped her short. A boot had kicked at a rock, hurtling it down a slight incline. *Someone was behind her!*

Startled, she whirled. She found herself staring upward toward the figure of a man who loomed directly over her. "W-who are you?" Her voice trembled. Suddenly frightened, she could only stare at him.

"I could ask the same of you, girlie," he retorted. As he spoke, Maddie chilled. She recognized his coarse rhythm of speech. She had heard it before—one night barely a week gone by now, when she had lain bound and helpless to four wreckers' gaze and touch. This stranger—he was brother to them all, and she was in his power!

Chapter Twelve

As he inched toward her, moving steadily down the in-

134

cline, his close-set eyes fixed upon her. As Maddie stared, she saw more similarities of feature. He had their jawline, also half-shaven, and the same wide pug nose.

"Good God!" she whispered. Horrified to the very core of her soul, she whirled. She fled, stumbling over rocks, her wide eyes seeing only the path of her escape.

She caught her toe in a root, then kicked free as she fought to put more distance between him and herself. Her legs, indeed, her entire body, trembled so violently that Maddie had to fight just to keep from falling down. She knew now her coming here had been a mistake, a horrible error indeed. She hadn't expected to find a surviving brother, but then, how could she have known? She knew, beyond doubt, that she had put herself in mortal danger. He was probably the only one of his clan left. No doubt he carried with him a sense of bitterness, hatred, and injustice toward those who had caught and hanged the other members of his family.

Though she ran as hard as she could, he clattered after her. As he followed her down a steep defile, his boots thudded heavily on the rock-littered waste. His breathing, hard and heavy, punctuated the scraping of his footsteps.

Maddie moaned aloud as she fled. Pure animal terror, so deep she almost felt as if she were losing consciousness of all else, possessed her mind. Worst, she was hopelessly alone. She knew, even as she stumbled and clawed her way down to the beach below, that she was doomed to endure whatever her pursuer wished to inflict upon her by way of revenge.

"No, dear God, no!" she prayed aloud, to the one who appeared to have forsaken her. First he had taken away her home by allowing her to be falsely accused, and then her husband, the man she loved above all others. Only bitter, futile desperation let her hope that he would be more merciful now.

Suddenly, Maddie's foot caught in a hole cut into the granite by years of repeating waves. Crying out in pain, she dropped to her knees. She struggled to stand again, but the pain from her suddenly throbbing ankle paralyzed her will. She moaned in horror mingled with despair, as the last surviving brother of his clan fell upon her with a cry of triumph. His hands, hard and strong, dug into her arms and shoulders as he yanked her up from where she lay. With a snarl, he flung her onto the ground facing upward.

He stared at her with hard-eyed fury. His breath, hot and fast against her face, reeked as the others' had of rum and tobacco. "Who are ye, and what have you to do with me brothers being gone?"

Maddie's eyes widened in shocked surprise. Was it possible he had no idea his brothers had already been hanged in Providencetown?

Interpreting her silence as a stubborn refusal to talk, he shook her. Maddie cried aloud from the force of his strength. He seemed to jar her teeth loose from her jaw, and as he held her, he climbed upon her. He straddled her with both legs to hold her down. "Answer me, Goddamn it!" He gritted his words through long yellowed teeth.

Maddie stared at him, mute with horrified fear. She sensed to the very core of her being that if she told him the truth, he would kill her then and there. Somehow, he would blame her for it all.

"*Answer me!*" His open hand slammed into the side of her jaw. Under its impact, her head whipped to the opposite side. She cried out at first blow, then moaned with pain. She shuddered into her lungs a great gulp of humid salt air. She lay motionless now, with eyes screwed shut and muscles rigid. She no longer dared to look, to see what he would do to her next.

He shook her again. "I want you to tell me, damn it," he said through tightly clenched teeth. "If I have to break every bone in your body, I'll find out."

"I don't know...who your brothers are," she replied half-moaning. "I have no idea what you're talking about."

"Liar!" The hand came down again, stinging into the other side of her face. Maddie dizzied under the pain and nearly lost consciousness. But he was not through with her. He grabbed a great fistful of her hair and squeezed. He yanked at it painfully as he held her down. "Goddamn you!" he cried. "You wouldn't have come here...you wouldn't have known, if you hadn't been to our cabin before. Now I want to know the truth!"

"I came looking for my husband," she replied. Too spent now to put up any more resistance, she answered him. "We-we were in a ship that wrecked right here off this cape. Your brothers did it," she added accusingly. "They put out false lights, and the captain believed he had found safe harbor." She no longer cared if she lived or died. The pain throbbed throughout her head, nearly driving her mad. All she wanted now was to sleep, to drift away into some soft darkness until this nightmare ended.

"And what happened to me brothers?" His face loomed very close to hers now, so close that she turned her own away to be farther from his. He yanked again at her hair, so hard that she cried out with a fresh, almost overwhelming pain.

"I...they...men from Providencetown saw lights. They came to investigate and saw what your brothers were doing. They-they overpowered them and took them back as prisoners."

The man spat out an obscenity. Eyes blazing, he took her cheeks roughly between his hands. "And you, me pretty wench, where do *you* fit into it all?"

137

Maddie closed her eyes to shut out the sight of him. "I was a survivor," she whispered.

"Me brothers leave no survivors." He chewed each word between his teeth. The day was growing darker. The sky overhead warned of an impending summer storm. From somewhere far distant, Maddie heard a roll of thunder.

"I think they intended the same fate for me...eventually," she replied. "But I was lucky. Those good men—"

"Those 'good men'...!" he snarled, interrupting her. "Those high and mighty swine who live so well and sneer at honest poor men. Burn them all in bloody Hell!" Maddie could not reply. Angry words of loathing and scorn congealed in her throat. She could only lie here, thinking of Henri, remembering him and the sight of all those good and decent seamen being slaughtered by this man's brothers.

"And so they came and rescued you," he continued viciously. "And now you think of them as bloody knights in shining armor, I suppose. Well, let me tell you, girlie, by the time I'm through with the likes of you, y'll pray for God to come and take you." He drew up from her, though still pinning her down with his weight. Maddie opened her eyes to see, then stared with horror into his own cold, hating gaze. "No doubt me brothers'll hang in that stinkin' rathole of a town, but believe me, I'll see to it that they get theirs back. Ye'll pay, girlie. Ye'll pay for all their sins. It may not be fair, but I've got you here and not them, and I'm content to take what I can."

Maddie wanted to scream, to cry out that his brothers had deserved their fate, and that she was glad that justice had been so well served, but she was afraid. Things would go badly enough for her as it was, she suspected. She must not antagonize him further.

138

She cried out as his hands clenched around the neckline of her dress. As indigo-dyed linen tore, with a hoarse and rasping sound, her entire body convulsed from the suddenness of his movement.

Her breasts fell out of the ruptured bodice. They lay gleaming white and vulnerable under the overcast New England sky. Her captor crouched motionless for a second, looking down at her with eyes hard and cruel. With mounting horror, she saw how his lip curled into a smile that showed no mirth, only gloating triumph. "I think I shall enjoy this, girlie," he said, still grinning. "Thy flesh is the finest I've seen for many long summer's night."

Maddie hardly dared move. She even forgot to breathe as she watched him. She stared wide-eyed as his hands lifted from where they had rested on his own thighs. She recoiled as they clamped upon her flesh. His palms sweated as they covered her, and the callouses, developed from what little honest labor he might have done, scratched against her skin.

Maddie cried out as the stranger, like his brothers, used her so roughly. He grinned with great chuckling pleasure at her fear. Her very flesh crawled with revulsion as she stared upon the heir apparent to his kin's legacy of wrecking, plunder, and rape. "Why hurt *me*?" she whispered, too terrified to scream. "I have done nothing to you—nothing to anyone."

"So what?" he retorted. "You're here, and I like it well enough now."

She could feel his desire pulsing against her belly. A savage fury coursed through his loins as he flung himself upon her with a snort of gloating pleasure. Maddie moaned aloud, numbed now to all sensations.

Just then, her hand reached blindly out. Her finger-pads touched something hard. Her grip curled around it and felt a slender object that seemed to have an edge—not very sharp, but bladelike and with a point.

As her attacker lay grunting on top of her, Maddie lifted it to view and saw that the object was indeed, as she had hoped, a knife. Though dulled, its metal appeared sturdy. Its point would still penetrate flesh, if thrust with enough force behind it. With a wild surge of hope, she raised it up. She held it with tip aimed toward the back of his neck. She intended to sink that blade clear to the hilt, if necessary, and free herself.

Suddenly, a voice calling out her name wafted over the din of ocean waves and her assailant's panting. Maddie sensed the sudden jerk of his turning almost before he had actually moved. As he yanked himself away to kneel poised and listening, he did not see Maddie lower the knife. Still clutching its handle, she concealed it underneath her skirt, and stared in the direction of his gaze.

Boots scraping down rock grew louder with each approaching footstep, but Maddie, still pinned by her attacker's arm, could not see. The voice called out to her again. This time, Maddie recognized Nathan's tone. "Over here—*help!*" she screamed to him. In punishment, a hard fist smashed against her jaw.

Her attacker scrambled off, but before she could pull away and flee, he grabbed her upper arm and jerked her upright. "Ye'll not get away from me so easy as all that." With a rough tug, he dragged her along as he scrambled up the incline to face her rescuer. As she moved, Maddie's eyes gleamed with hope. In one sweating hand she still held the knife. When the brother had dragged her within view of her friend, Maddie cried out silently with soul-deep relief. *Nathan was carrying his musket!*

With one swift move, however, her captor yanked her to him, using her body as a shield. "Aye, go ahead and shoot!" he cried, "and yer lead will go into her, not me." Maddie stared at Nathan with pleading eyes. She wanted him to help, yet knew he dared not shoot for her sake. His coming had been a great, brilliant fire of hope to her, but now it seemed as if he had no choice but to stand by helplessly, while this final surviving wrecker carried her off to some farther secret place and ravished her.

Suddenly Maddie remembered the knife. She had clung to it all along, with hands grown numb from terror, hidden still in the folds of her skirt. Still stumbling, held close to her captor, she signaled to Nathan with her eyes. He, sensing that she had some plan, some trick to foil her captor, slowly brought his musket into firing position. With one swift movement, he primed it.

At sight of him, the wrecker laughed. "Why bother?" he called out tauntingly. "Y'll not want to kill her along with me. I know you Godly apes too bloody well for all that."

Slowly, very slowly, Maddie pulled her knife arm around behind her back. Careful not to drop the weapon, she aimed its blade outward toward his belly, as she arched her spine to give it space. Suddenly, she thrust back against him. Her body became a ram shoving the blade into his gut. He screamed a surprised and angry howl and doubled over. He clutched himself where the metal had stabbed, and Maddie, sensing success, whirled away from him with a cry. To give Nathan an unobstructed shot at him, she dropped down.

"No, don't shoot!" the man cried out, half-coughing as he sank to his knees. "I cannot go for ye now."

"I had not wanted to shoot you." Nathan hurried toward him. "I had only intended to take you into custody."

The man's hands, clutched to his stomach, were bloody. Life spurted out from between his fingers. Maddie stared at him in horror. She could not draw her eyes away, not even when his gaze met hers. "Ah, go to Hell, girlie," the man snarled at her with his final breath. "You were the one what did it to me. Thanks to you, me guts are spillin' out of me like sausages...." He laughed mirthlessly, then grimaced as he raised his eyes to Nathan. "In any case, y'll not take me into custody like y'did me brothers. Y'll not hang me like ye probably will *them*." He faced Maddie again. "We'll meet in Hell, you an' I," he said, "Now that you're a killer, like me."

"I'm not a killer," Maddie retorted in a soft and even tone of voice. "You did it to yourself. I accept no guilt for being an unwilling instrument of justice."

He did not reply. His cheek rested against the stone-clotted sand. His eyes were closed, but he still breathed, though heavily and with a rasping sound that portended death for him.

"Maddie, are you all right?" Nathan stood from the wrecker and faced her. Maddie could not reply. She stared down at the man and felt only horror.

"Is-is he...." The breathing had quieted. No longer did he gasp so loudly for air. A small trickle of blood rolled from the corner of his mouth. It dripped free, becoming a small discoloration in the sand under his head.

"Not yet." Nathan's mouth stretched into a grim line.

"I didn't mean to do it. I swear!"

"I know," he replied. "It couldn't be helped. It was either him or you, and your choice was the only one possible. In any case, his life's worth little."

"To him it was," she said, speaking thoughtfully.

"He should have thought of it sooner," Nathan shrugged. "In any case, his death may prove to be a mercy for him. If he lives, I'll have to take him back to Providencetown for trial. What he did is a hanging

142

crime. He'd only follow his brothers to the gallows."

Maddie shuddered, then turned away. She felt unclean. For the first time, she noticed his blood on her hands. Without speaking, she walked to the water's edge and washed them off in the surf. Nathan followed, then took her in his arms. "Oh, Maddie, try to forget."

"I don't think I ever can," she replied. "Loathsome as he was, I'll always know I killed him." His arms, holding her close now, felt strong and reassuring. Suddenly tired, she leaned back, letting his strength support them both. Her head rested upon his shoulder. Her cheek nestled in the crook of his shoulder. "It's an awesome thing, really, to kill, even when it's someone like him."

"Oh, Maddie, I know." Nathan's voice had grown suddenly hoarse. "The hanging...." Whatever he was about to say, died in his throat. The two of them stood on that desolate beach for endless minutes without speaking, just listening to surf pounding against shore. His breath blew against Maddie's hair. His heart pounded against her back. When he finally spoke again, after many minutes had passed, he had regained control of his voice. "Why did you come here today?"

The wind, sighing westward from off the ocean, lifted her hair. Tendrils of blond-gold played around her face. "I had to," she replied.

"Why, Maddie, *why*?" The anguish of his voice cut into her heart. "You were safe. You seemed content. Why did you have to come back here?"

"He's not dead. I know it!" Tears glistened in her eyes. She hadn't want to bring him pain, but what she must do had become the most important thing in her life. "You-you said this cottage looked as if someone had come and used it after the arrests. I had hoped, perhaps—" Her throat closed so that she could not speak. In any case, she knew she had no need to finish

143

what she was saying.

"Oh, Maddie!" Nathan clung to her shoulders. "What good did it do, especially when you knew how slim the chances were?" His voice murmured low but intense into her ear.

Maddie thought again of Henri, of his eyes green as a sunlit ocean wave, intense as the visage of an eagle. She remembered again his craggy, aristocratic features—the high cheekbones, jutting nose, and strong chin. And his mouth—such a hard, unyielding mouth it could be, yet other times so tender, as when he had kissed her.

She wondered if his hair still tangled wild and long. Did he stand as straight, move as gracefully, or had hardship bowed him? Was he dressed now in tatters, perhaps starving somewhere along a stretch of deserted beach? No matter what his condition, Maddie knew somehow, with heart-exulting certainty, that her Henri lived.

"If you should ever see your husband again, it would be a miracle." Nathan's voice brought her back to the here and now.

At Nathan's words, Maddie smiled. "Miracles sometimes happen."

He retorted gently, "They happened long ago, in a different place and in ancient times, when our Savior walked upon the earth. Not now, not here in New England." He sighed. "Now come, I found *this* lying on the beach." He handed her the shawl she had brought with her when she left the house this morning.

"You're mother's shawl." Maddie took it from him. "I'm glad you found it. She'd be furious with me if I went away and left it here."

"My mother's going to be furious with you anyway," he retorted. "And it will have nothing to do with her silly shawl. She was worried sick when I left looking for you. Here, wrap it around yourself. Some delights

144

should never see the light of day."

Something in his tone of voice caught Maddie's attention. She turned and stared into his face, but saw only his blue eyes, veiled and unreadable. Within seconds of her silent, questioning stare, he whirled from her. He left her standing alone while he strode back to the wrecker still lying in a heap on the sand.

Maddie followed after a few paces behind. "Is he—" Her voice failed. She hardly dared to ask what she feared.

Nathan nodded. "He's dead. I felt no pulse when I put my hand against his neck."

Maddie shuddered. "What now? What's to be done with him?"

"I remember seeing a clamming shovel in the cabin," he replied. "It's not much, but it'll do if I find nothing else. I'll pile sand over him and rocks to keep carrion animals from devouring his flesh." He continued, speaking through clenched teeth. "It's not exactly a Christian burial in hallowed ground, but it's better than he deserves."

Maddie glanced to the man she had killed, then shuddered. "Yes, but we must be merciful." She stared with fascination at the contorted, pain-wracked mask which until only a few minutes ago had been a man's living face.

"Of course," replied Nathan. "In any case, to do otherwise would be to sink to his level."

He ran into the cottage searching for that shovel, while Maddie remained behind alone with the corpse. A strange silence had settled over the beach. Even the surf and the cries of gulls and petrils had muted in the dense atmosphere of storm-thickening clouds. Mist gathered. Water-saturated fog absorbed all sounds.

Still clutching the shawl wrapped tightly around her shoulders, Maddie stepped away from the dead man.

She wandered a few yards closer to the battleground where sea crashed against shore. There she stood, lost in thought. Finally, after unmeasured time had passed, Maddie heard footsteps coming from the cottage again. She glanced up and saw Nathan returning with a shovel.

They said a prayer over the dead man, and like magistrates sentencing a criminal to death, they invoked the mercy of God upon his soul. When their voices fell silent, ending this makeshift funeral, Nathan began to dig. First sand, to cover every trace of him, and then rocks. When he had finished, Nathan flung the shovel down and turned to her. "When I was looking for something to bury him with, I came across a cask of beer and some rum in the cabin. What say we go in there and wait until dark?"

Nathan took her arm and led her away from the newly-formed grave. "Maddie, have you any idea how you look right now? If we went back before dark, well...." He gave a low, mirthless chuckle. "I shudder to think of the gossip we'd arouse, from the sight of you riding with me through town with your hair disheveled and your clothes torn the way they are. Not to mention the ugly bruises he made on your face." He smiled, suddenly mischievous. "Why, everyone would say I beat you!"

Startled, Maddie raised her hand. She cried out in sudden pain, as her fingertips touched the cheeks and jaws swollen from the force of their attacker's blows. "You look as bad as it feels," Nathan shrugged, glancing to her. "The whole lower half of your face is all black, swollen, and purplish."

They found the rum and drank some of it while they waited. As the sky opened into a storm, Nathan started a fire. Later, as they sat together, letting its heat and light sink into them, he raised his eyes to her. "Why can't you trust me?" His question came suddenly, after a silence.

Maddie glanced at him, then smiled. "I trust you," she replied.

"No...*stop*!" His eyes darkened. "Maddie, I care about you. I am a friend, not an enemy, and I want to help. But I have to know what you're running from."

Maddie's heart pounded. Nathan had never spoken to her like this before. She wondered how much he knew. She forced a high, nervous laugh. "Running from? What-whatever do you mean?"

Nathan sighed. He moved from where he sat beside her near the hearth. Tense with his own doubts and yearnings, he began to pace the floor. "Even now you cannot bring yourself to confide in me. You pretend not to understand what I am saying, but I can see in your eyes and voice that you are lying."

"Nathan, I—" Maddie's voice trailed off. She had been about to utter a denial, but the look on his face warned it would be futile.

"I know very little about you, Maddie," he continued. "Only that you have a loving heart and a soul filled with light, despite your circumstances. Of those I have learned very little indeed, and the few facts I have gleaned," he sighed. "You have not given them to me knowingly."

"What-what do you mean?" Maddie stared, suddenly terrified at what he might know, yet compelled by curiosity to find out.

"While you were ill, in that delirium from which we feared you would never recover, you cried out. In terror, you proclaimed your innocence of some crime. You screamed for your Henri to save you from....*them*. Who are you running from, Maddie and why?"

Maddie could not answer. The very words stuck in her throat. "Why, I—" Her voice broke. She knew Nathan was her friend, and Dame Dundee, his mother, too. She understood all that, yet could not speak. Ashamed of her own hesitation, Maddie turned her face away.

"*Maddie!*" He kneeled in front of her now and took her hand. "Oh, Maddie." His voice, steeped in despair, cut right through her heart.

But still she could not speak. She dared not bring herself to confide in the one person who would be tender, who might understand, and even help. She was afraid for her very life. Instead, she only stared at his head bowed in despair. She reached her hand to him and stroked his hair. "I'm sorry, Nathan," she whispered. "I just can't. Perhaps someday, but not now. It's all too painful."

The day had all but passed, darkening into twilight once again. After a few moments of silence, Nathan stood. He glanced out the window, then helped her rise. "Well, whatever's to be must be," he said quietly. "You know I care, and want to help. Someday...." His voice trailed off. "Now come, it's almost nighfall." He slipped his arm around her and guided her outside, to the spot where he had tied his horse to a sturdy burl of once-living pine. Without speaking, he lifted her into the saddle and climbed on behind. His arms held her securely as he goaded the creature back over sand toward the high road once again.

Maddie lay back against him in the saddle. As they rode home, she stared up at the sky. It looked more or less the same as it always did, and she reflected that, no matter what happened to mortals here on earth, the cycles of heaven waxed and waned always.

The clop-clopping of his horse's hooves cast a gentle, restful rhythm that soothed her terror-worn nerves. It felt good to be in Nathan's arms, almost as much as Henri's, right then. At the thought of her husband and lover, however, Maddie's eyes filled with tears. She knew in her heart that she could never yearn for another man as she did Henri. No matter what happened, fate had doomed her to love Henri, and no other. Destiny had linked her life forever to his, and no matter what obstacles might lie in her path, she could never rest until she was by his side again.

Chapter Thirteen

Maddie faced the scolding she had to endure from Nathan's mother who had come to treat her as a daughter. A rather ill-favored and disobedient daughter, to judge from the woman's words, and the scowl that went along with them. Maddie, knowing all to well that she deserved what she was getting, merely hung her head and listened.

Finally, Flora's temper subsided and Maddie dragged wearily to bed. The next day passed by quickly as she helped her friend around the house.

Both Flora and Nathan assumed she'd remain with them, but Maddie knew, with a tear of her heart, that she would have to leave. By now, Edward Leich would have almost certainly returned home to Salem, and when he did, word would get out that he had seen her here in Providencetown.

That night, Nathan came home late. Maddie had spent the earlier hours of evening with Flora, listening to the woman reminisce about life in the Southern English countryside where she had grown up. As she left Flora's bed-sitting room, tired and ready to retire, Maddie heard a noise in the main room below. Not recognizing its source, she padded down to investigate. She met Nathan coming up the stairs. Something about his manner stopped her short. "Nathan!" Her voice trembled on its own. The look in his eyes frightened her. She wanted to run back upstairs and hide, but doubt, combined with her fear of offending one who had been so good to her, stopped Maddie from acting on her impulse.

"Maddie, come down here!" he said in a low voice, but one taut with suppressed emotion.

"Yes, Nathan, what is it?" She moved to obey on legs grown suddenly shaky. Her eyes froze upon his, and she found herself unable to tear them away. Why did she feel now so uncomfortable in his presence? What instinct urged her to run and hide?

As she moved closer, she smelled ale on his breath. She saw red veins cutting across the whites of his eyes. He breathed heavily, as if merely inhaling took great effort. Maddie understood with a clutch of her heart that he had been drinking far more than he should. "Maddie, I want to marry you," he whispered. "I want to take care of you."

She stopped short and stared at him in dismay. "Nathan," she replied. "You know I cannot. My husband is...."

"Your husband?" His lips curled into a smile. He swayed slightly as he faced her, and gave a mirthless chuckle. "Face up to it, Maddie, your husband is dead. No one could have survived."

"I survived." And if *she*, a frail girl could, then so might he have struggled ashore and escaped the wreckers' death-dealing blows.

"A lucky accident. Anyone who might have placed a wager upon your chances—"

"I care nothing for wages!" Maddie retorted. "Do you expect me simply to forget about him and marry *you*? Would you have me commit bigamy?"

"Maddie, I love you." He breathed his words

through clenched teeth. Even in the dim light emanating through the front windows, she could see how his face had paled. "I see you every day, right here in my house, and it's torture for me."

As he reached for her, Maddie backed away. Suddenly afraid of both his intensity and his drunkenness, she whirled to run back upstairs and shut herself in her room.

But as she moved, he grabbed her by the arm. His eyes glittered now like those of a madman. He yanked her to him and held her close in both arms. Imprisoned against his body, Maddie could feel the excitement pulsing through him. His breath rasped hard and fast against her cheek. His heart pounded wildly. "I love you, Maddie," he whispered. "Damn it, I love you!"

Still holding her in his arms, he whirled, pinning her back against the wall. His hands, trembling now from the frenzy of his desire, slid from behind to clasp her upon the breasts. He leaned to her, holding her tight as he gazed upon her face. "Oh, Maddie...*Maddie*!"

His hands released her bosom now. They slid instead to her shoulders, and he held her while the fingers of his right hand slid up her neck and buried themselves in her hair.

"Nathan, *please*!" Maddie's voice had all but failed her. Fear of what might happen mingled with surprise at the man's sudden change of behavior.

His breath rasped hard and fast now. His chest heaved. Sweat glistened upon his face as his eyes scanned her features. "Your skin is so white," he whispered. "So very soft and white!" He reached with one finger to stroke her cheek.

"Nathan, I—" Maddie stared at him with fear and dismay. She had always admired and respected him. She dreaded seeing him turn into some kind of lust-filled monster.

"And your neck—so slender...so graceful. Not like that of a swan's exactly," he continued, "a swan's neck would be far too long and stem-like, but yours is the loveliest that could ever be found on a woman."

"Nathan, you're frightening me!"

He continued, "And your breasts...my God, your breasts! I've seen them twice now, and each time, I've longed to take them naked in my hands and kiss them." His hands lowered again to her bosom and took possession. His breath shuddered as he inhaled. His lips trembled as he fixed blazing eyes upon her.

Maddie tried to reason with him. "Nathan, you're drunk. You'll regret all this in the morning, you know." She could cry out and arouse his mother, but would do so only as a last resort. She had no wish to bring shame and humiliation on a man who had saved and befriended her, nor embarrassment upon his mother, either.

"No!" His voice had fallen to a hoarse whisper. "You must know how I feel. *You must!* I want you to understand."

Tears sprang into his eyes now. Maddie stared horrified as he sank to his knees. His hands slid down her thighs and remained there, clinging to the folds of her skirt. "You *must* understand. Five years have gone by since my wife died. *Five years.* And through them all I've waited, holding myself back. Until I met you, I never knew for what...for *whom.* And all the while I've starved for the love of a woman."

"Oh *Nathan!*" Pity and sympathy flooding into Maddie drove out all her fear.

Nathan continued, speaking in a broken whisper, "I saw you in that cottage, that wretched shack. You were beautiful, but I felt nothing then—only the cold desire to do my duty as a lawman."

He sighed. "Afterward, when the fighting had ended, after it all, I-I looked into your eyes. I saw your heart and lost my own." His voice trembled. "It was then I knew, right then. Oh, Maddie, please...I beg of you, don't leave me. Your husband can't possibly be alive. I just don't see how. What is the point of looking for him any further? You have your whole life ahead of you, and I could make you happy. *I know I could.*"

Maddie kneeled to face him. She gazed into his agonized eyes with compassion now, stroking the hair tousled upon his head. "I had no idea how much you've suffered, Nathan." For the first time, understanding had suddenly dawned. All this time he had held himself in, trying to suppress the natural urges of manhood, and she—she had lived under his roof for days, yet had remained blind to his feelings. She had never suspected how much he ached for her. Without understanding what she was doing, she had taken from him, again and again, and had given back nothing.

And yet, he had never asked. He had been too decent to demand what another man might. It had taken liquor to send the already-heated blood in his veins flowing unbearably hotter. Under its unaccustomed influence, the wall he had built around his emotions had crumbled. The mask had fallen from his face. And even now, he had asked only what an honorable man would—for her hand in marriage, nothing less and nothing more.

With a sudden surge of compassion, Maddie smiled tenderly into his face. Her hand stroked his hair. She knew she could never give him the undivided love he really needed. She could never be his wife, but her body could buy him temporary respite from the achings of his unsatisfied desires. By deliberately sacrificing her own chastity, she might even convince him that she was indeed unworthy to be his wife, and thus spare him heartache. In any case, she would be giving him back a small measure of what he yearned for.

Suddenly remorseful, Nathan raised anguished eyes

to her. "Oh, Maddie," he whispered. "I-I'm not usual-ly like this. Not really. Not ever!"

Maddie's own glance was tender. "It's all right. I understand." She held his head gently in her hands. Knowing now that she was doing right, no matter what the world might say, she raised his face and planted a soft kiss upon his lips. With a flooding surge of warmth and even love, she encircled him with her arms. "Dearest Nathan!" As she murmured his name, she smiled into his eyes. "Come up to my room with me. Let me make amends for all the pain I've caused you."

His eyes widened with hope, with surprise. "Do you mean—?" He hardly dared believe his own ears.

Maddie nodded. "For tonight, at least, let us be together."

"Oh, *Maddie*!" His chest heaved. His hands trem-bled as they reached hesitantly to her own. With a gesture, she bade him rise from where he still remained in abject kneeling. He obeyed. With one strong arm, he helped her rise too, then followed her up the stairs.

At the door to her room, he stood, hesitant to enter. Smiling at his timidity, she reached for his hand. "Don't stand out in the cold," she whispered. "Come inside where it's warm. Come to *me*." Her fingers closed with gentle pressure upon his own. Gently she pulled him to her.

Moonlight gleamed through her window like liquid silver. It bleached a trail across the floor, then fell with fading glow upon her bed. Its clear cool light glimmered upon his features so that she could see him clearly. She could read the complex and rapidly changing emotions parading across his face.

Once inside, he closed the door softly and bolted it so that no one could interrupt. He turned once again to her and just stood, gazing upon her face with rapture and yearning.

Her own eyes meeting his, Maddie glided toward him, feeling as if she were floating. As she moved, the long, white nightdress she was wearing billowed about her legs. He stared at her as if fascinated. "I can hardly believe—" he whispered.

"Believe!" Drawing close, she reached to him. Her fingertips slid across his cheek to bury themselves in his hair. With one hand, she guided his lips gently toward her own. As they touched, his mouth against hers, Maddie closed her eyes. Her body, as if of its own accord, pressed against his.

Though he smelled of lye soap, instead of leather and the sea as Henri did, she found his scent not unpleasing. His kiss tasted different, but firm and fair nevertheless. He held her with the same passion as Henri had, though far more timidly at first. Although he could never replace Henri, he was a good man, and in a way she loved him. Maddie took her friend Nathan willingly, and even savored his embraces.

They still stood, she barefoot and he fully shod, upon the room's clean planking floor. With a smile, Maddie pulled herself gently from his caress. She stepped back from him, untying her nightdress as she did, then let it drop down around her ankles so that she stood naked before him in the moonlight.

She sensed more than heard the sharp intake of breath. She waited, standing motionless as he came to her with eyes fixed fascinated upon her moon silvered flesh.

He reached hesitantly to her cheek, then slid his fingers into the shimmering blondness of her hair. He gazed questioningly into her eyes, losing himself in two deep pools of blue.

In silent reply, Maddie reached to him. She slid her hands down the curve of his spine and held him around the small of his back. Her own waiting, pliant body pressed into his.

"I can't believe this is happening. *My darling*! Is it all a dream?"

"All life is a dream, I sometimes think," she replied. "But we are both awake."

His breath, as he exhaled, trembled. It blew warm and eager against her ear. "Now take me to bed, Nathan," she whispered. "I want to taste your love. I want to feel your pleasure."

Without speaking, Nathan moved to obey. He guided her down, then held her close for a minute just gazing into her eyes. Gently, she helped slip the shirt from his shoulders. Her fingertips stroked his chest.

Their bodies glowed naked in the moonlit bed. Their passions mingled, and when they had finished, awakening, it seemed, from a dream, they lay together in one another's arms. Each gazed into eyes smiling and tender. After minutes of joy, Nathan finally spoke, "You know, Maddie, I love you more than ever now. More than ever I want you to be my wife."

Maddie smiled sadly as she stroked his hair. "Nathan," she said, "you are precious to me, but what you ask...." She shook her head. "You know, it cannot be, and you know why."

"But tonight!" He stared at her in sudden dismay. "You gave yourself to me willingly, and you enjoyed it. Your pleasure was genuine, and so was your joy."

"I know," Maddie sighed. "But if I could have consented to marry you, then tonight—this love we shared—it could never have happened. It was only because I *cannot* marry you, because you asked of me the impossible, that I—"

"That you took me to bed out of pity?" His angry, half-whispered exclamation interrupted her. He stared at her with hurt in his eyes. He started to draw away, but her hands, reaching to clasp his shoulders, restrained him. Her own gaze fixed earnestly on his. "Not from pity, Nathan," she whispered, "but love. Oh, don't you see? If I had loved you less, I would have kept my virtue. As it was, I sacrificed it—to a man who is not and can never be my husband. Does that mean nothing to you?" She raised a pleading look to him. "Do you know what that makes me now in the eyes of the world? For them, it turns me into a harlot—a common whore."

"Oh, damn the world and all its silly gossip!" Nathan cried out, so hotly that Maddie's hand flew to his mouth to silence him. He continued, speaking in a softer voice, "I care nothing for their opinions."

"Well, *I* do," she retorted. "Yet I did what I did anyway, in spite of it all. For *you*, Nathan, because of how I feel about you."

He clasped her hands in his own. "Maddie," he whispered, "I will wait. For as long as it takes to find out what happened to your husband, to satisfy yourself that he is dead."

Maddie shook her head. "Nathan, you need a wife now, not later. For that very reason, I am not the one you should marry. Do you think I would have you spend your days and nights burning as you have done for the past five years since your wife died? Do you think I am so selfish as to allow *that*?" She kissed the palm of his hand, then continued, "What kind of a wife would I be, if I didn't choose as I do now? Would you want a woman who could care so little about the man she married? He is my husband, after all, and I still love him. What if I should marry you and he turns up alive? What then?"

She gazed at him long and earnestly, holding his eyes with her own. "And would I have you risk the state of your immortal soul, by putting before you the temptation of wishing and hoping another man dead so that

157

you could claim his wife? No!'' she shook her head. ''No, my precious Nathan, no. It doesn't bear thinking about. Yet that is exactly what would happen if you should wait for me, instead of marrying someone else.''

''But it's you I want, Maddie,'' he protested. ''It's *you* I love. I'd rather wait than settle for lesser happiness with someone else.''

With a sigh, she raised dark, sad eyes to his. ''You could learn to care. Nathan, listen to me. You know nothing about me, nothing at all. I came to you out of the night, and you took care of me. I will always love you for that, but you must understand. I am haunted—tormented by a memory that will not fade, and driven by the belief that I shall someday find my husband. I may be wrong,'' she shrugged. ''I may die alone, but I must do what I have to. My destiny lies with him, wherever he is—not with you.''

''*Oh, Maddie*!'' Nathan's voice broke with despair. Pain glimmered in his eyes.

''I'm sorry, Nathan.'' She raised her gaze to his. ''I wouldn't have hurt you for anything, but you must understand—I don't belong here. You look at me with longing because you're lonely. You said yourself it's been five years. You need a wife, and surely some handsome, good woman from here or a nearby settlement would be only too delighted to join with you in wedlock. But not me.''

Tears glistened in Maddie's eyes as she looked upon his face. She wondered, with a fleeting stab of fear, whether she was sacrificing her only chance of happiness and peace for a will-o-the-wisp that could lead only to danger and loneliness. ''I could honor you,'' she continued, ''I do already. I could serve and obey, but never could I love you—not with the deep and undivided devotion you deserve.''

''Oh Maddie....'' His voice failed him.

"Look around you, Nathan," she said, whispering. "Look into the eyes and faces of all the girls and young widows you meet, and in one of them, you'll recognize the woman you *really* belong with."

"What happens now, Maddie. To you, I mean?"

She shrugged. "I've known since three days ago that I'd have to leave here, and soon. That man I met after the trial—he was from my village. He bears me no ill will, but he'll talk, once he gets home, and my enemies will know where to find me."

"I could help you face your enemies. Help prove your innocence of *whatever*...." He faced her questioningly. "I never did find out what crime it was they think you committed."

"And it's best you never do. Just believe, on my word of honor, that I am innocent and leave it at that. *Please!*"

"I shall miss you, Maddie." Nathan's voice went suddenly hoarse. "Dear God, how I'll miss you!"

Chapter Fourteen

At breakfast the following morning, Nathan barely spoke. To Flora's obvious chagrin, he barely touched his food. Maddie only picked at hers. Despite Flora's bright-voiced attempts at conversation, all she received in reply were short, monosyllabic answers. Finally, with a sigh, Nathan stood, announced that he was off to work, and strode from the room. When he had gone, the woman turned to Maddie. "Good God, what happened? I've not seen my son in such a mood for a long time. And you too, for that matter. What's going on?"

Maddie bowed her head. "I'm afraid I told him I was

leaving Providencetown." She wanted to spare her friend all details the woman might find painful.

Flora's brows raised. "But why? You know you're forever welcome here."

Maddie smiled sadly. For a moment, she could not reply. Flora had no idea Nathan had proposed to her. The woman would never guess that her son had held Maddie in his arms, had kissed her lips, and taken her in tender, passionate love. Maddie sighed. What was done was done and she did not reget it. After last night, however, she found it impossible to remain. Even if she had no enemies pursuing, intent upon taking her back home and holding her for execution, she would still have to leave this safe refuge. But she could not tell Flora why.

Before answering, she reached to the older woman's hand and just held it. "Flora," she said with trembling voice, "I have no choice. Not now, not anymore. It's more than just the desire I have to find my husband, much more," she said. "That man you saw with me the other day, the one I was talking to just outside where the magistrates were meeting for the wreckers' trial, is from my hometown. He wished me no harm, but as I told Nathan, he'll go back and tell them where I am, and frankly, I can't afford it. Don't ask me to explain...*please*."

Flora gazed on her with calm, compassionate eyes. "I think you're right. For the time being, it's well you put yourself out of reach." She chose her words carefully. "What you're running from will pass. In a few months from now, or maybe in a year, the villagers back there will look upon this summer as a bad horrifying dream, and they'll be ashamed of how they behaved." Though spoken gently, the woman's words jolted Maddie. She stared now with wide horrified eyes.

"How—how did you...?"

Flora smiled sadly. She looked very much in that moment like a wise old owl. "I know more about you than you think, child," she said. "I guessed almost from the first what you were running from, and where."

Maddie leaned back in her chair, suddenly weak. Her entire body trembled now. She felt dizzy, as if she were going to faint. "But how come Nathan didn't...?"

"Was it any of his business? Or for that matter, was it any of mine?" Flora shook her head. "Oh, child, so many times I wanted to say something to you, give you words of comfort. But I knew how afraid you were, so I held my tongue. I often wondered if I was doing the right thing."

"Oh, Flora!" Maddie suddenly felt exhausted and relieved.

"Just what do you intend doing now? I really care, you know."

Maddie shrugged. "I'm not sure. Henri mentioned once that his ship was docked in Boston's harbor. He said it was his own."

"A trader, eh, or perhaps," the woman added jokingly, "a pirate."

Maddie struggled to keep from revealing the truth. She reflected that people often unknowingly spoke the truth in jest. The woman continued. "Do you know its name? What he christened it?"

Maddie nodded. "Yes, it's called the *Genvieve*—but I have no idea if it's still there. It's been quite a few weeks, you know. By now, it could have set sail...with or without its master." Tears filled her eyes at the possibility of Henri's ship going on without him.

"But perhaps it remains, waiting for its captain to return," said Flora, interjecting a word of hope. "Or perhaps it waits for the captain's bride."

Maddie shrugged. "I have no idea, but it's my only hope. I want to go and find out, as soon as I can figure

161

out a way to get all the way to Boston," she sighed. It seemed so hopeless, now that she thought about it. How could she make her way from this isolated spit of cape all the way to Boston?

Flora smiled. "That, child, is the least of your problems. I can help you there, and with ease."

Maddie's eyes widened. Her heart pounded now in wild hope. "Would you? Could you?" She leaned across the table to her friend.

"I think so," the woman continued. "I have friends in Boston, the Atwoods. A good family they are too, and all quite fond of me, or so I flatter myself to think," she added with wry humor. "I could make an excuse by visiting them. In any case, I've wanted to go there for a good long time."

"How would we get there? Boston is such a long way off." It seemed an eternity of distance to her right then.

"We'll sail, child," replied the woman. "How else?"

Maddie's eyes widened. "You'd really come with me?" It seemed too good to be true. She'd be glad for her friend's companionship, yet surprised at the same time that a woman so old would willingly undertake the rigors and tedium of a journey of so many miles.

"Of course I'll go with you. It's not proper for a young lady to travel so far by herself, and you'll be welcomed at the Atwoods with me along."

"Oh, thank you!" Maddie replied with breathless gratitude.

Flora's eyes narrowed. "In any case, you with *your* knack for getting into trouble, you'll need someone sensible to watch over you."

Maddie reached to squeeze the old woman's hand. "It will be a fine time for both of us," she cried, and her heart beat faster as she thought of how the journey would bring her one step closer to Henri, and one further away from Andrew Mathias and the Salem Village witch-hunters.

"We'll go by gondola," the woman continued. "My late husband's friend Henry Potter has a fine one. It's small, but sturdy enough surely to carry us over the waters ot Boston. Sailing is far more pleasant and comfortable than going overland, and in most ways safer."

Maddie closed her eyes and sighed with pleasure. "You know, this has worked out very well indeed. In any case, it's better, I think, that I should leave." She had hurt poor Nathan enough already. To remain would only keep the wound open.

"I know," Flora replied quietly. "Life must go on as best it can."

Three days later, they were to set sail out of Providencetown, heading north once again. Morning had dawned that day fair and clear with blue skies, crystal air, and clouds of pure white turned to gold in the sun behind them. Their gondda was, as Flora described, a sturdy craft about ten feet long from stem to stern, with its wooden exterior painted gray. A lateen sail reached like a single wing from a mast that reached at an angle from its base. Henry Potter was too old himself to accompany them, but had given the responsibility to his son Jack. An able and capable man himself, Jack Potter would ferry them up the coast and into Boston Harbor.

Jack was a congenial man, about twenty-eight, who talked constantly about his new baby daughter. Maddie, who remembered with horror her previous shipboard experience, found herself staring out into the gentle blue-green sea with wondering delight.

Her trip this time seemed blessed. A gentle wind wafting once northward pushed them where they wanted to go, while the sea itself, once angry and boiling with storm-tossed energy, lapped at the sides of their craft with docile tongues of water.

Indeed, hardly any time at all had seemed to pass

before, in a distance, they saw the farmlands surrounding Boston, and finally the city itself. Jack steered their boat into the harbor and straight to a pier where he tied up securely. After assisting both women to land, he bade them Godspeed and promised to return in two weeks, weather permitting, to bring them back home.

Boston was a busy town, self-important as the capitol of the great commonwealth, and it was worldly, compared to Salem. Carriages clattered over the stone-paved streets. In them, Maddie saw women dressed in shocking fanciness. Cufflets and collars of lace, that would have been banned in Salem, decorated their dresses. Fastening them, she saw string ties dangling little crocheted bells. Most shocking of all, small feathers had crept into hatbands, which by Puritan standards should have been left unadorned. Maddie found herself studying this finery with interest, visualizing how such lace and frills might look on herself. Suddenly she felt Flora's eyes upon her. Startled, she glanced up and saw the woman smiling in amusement. "Such frills and furbelows," she said, "they're hard to resist, aren't they?"

Maddie's face flushed in embarrassment as she lowered her eyes.

As they rode along in the public coach, Flora told Maddie about the family they were to visit. "Josiah Atwood and I became friends when we were children," she said. "We both grew up not far from where he now lives." Flora sighed. "But childhood friends grow apart. When we were both seven, his father bound him to a trader for his apprenticeship. I remained at home, of course, and learned what I needed from my mother."

"Did you see him much after that?" Childhood friends had a way of slipping from each other into lives of their own.

"Oh, yes," Flora smiled nostalgically. "Later on, we

became sweethearts after a fashion. He courted me, but I suspect he felt as little passion for me as I did for him. Finally, just afer I met Joseph, my husband, he wed another friend of mine. Her name was Sarah Hartman, and she had been widowed young and left with three children of her own. Within two years after their marriage, he fathered two more." She smiled, then added wryly, "I never asked, but I suspect Josiah approves of large families."

She sighed. "Time passes so quickly though. They are all grown now, just like my Nathan. Still, through it all we have remained fast friends, the three of us, and I must say he's done remarkably well. At age twenty-two, he bought his first ship, and the following year, he acquired three more. Twenty years later, Josiah Atwood owned an entire fleet. His traders traveled to Europe, the Indies, and even to Africa, where he exchanged New England rum for slaves, chocolate, coffee, and spices."

As they rode along, Maddie glanced around in fascination. She had never before seen Boston, the Commonwealth's greatest city.

The buildings on the harbor's edge were obviously warehouses, to store the goods and spices brought to New England from far across the sea. The bustle of workmen loading and unloading ships provided a fascinating specticle. The smell of spices, sweet and pungent, dried fish, and the sweating bodies of those who handled them, had sent her senses spinning.

Now that she was here, she hardly knew where to begin. She had seen how tired Flora looked and knew right away that they couldn't begin any inquiries that day. In any case, she herself had become a little weary. The early rising, then sitting out in the sun all day in that gondola had drained her. Overwhelmed from the first by the bustle around her, Maddie knew she could get nowhere until she collected her thoughts and made some plan of action.

The streets of Boston were crooked, and most of the houses built of wood, with a few of brick or stone. Near the harbor were inns and taverns that faced directly onto the street. Farther out in more genteel neighborhoods, houses large and graceful nestled on plots of well-tended land planted with grass, trees, and blooming flowers. Soon they arrived at the Atwood's home. Maddie saw at once how proudly it displayed the family's wealth.

The building itself was an imposing structure of brick imported from England. It stood three stories tall with window and door frames set in ivory-hued oil paint. Curtains of heavy Belgium lace covered the windows. Roses rambled up its outer walls. The house itself stood back from the street, on grounds that stretched for over an acre. Green grass covered its soil like a carpet and sheep grazed there, watched and tended by a negro child. Zinnias splashed color in borders along its drives, while willow and oak trees, ash and crabapple, provided a haven of shade for those who might wish to sit underneath them.

The day Flora had decided to come, she sent a message warning the Atwoods to be expecting them. As the two of them climbed down, aided by their hired coachman, they saw the front door flung wide. Obviously the note had reached their hosts in time. With cries of joy, their hostess ran outside and embraced her friend.

After a hasty introduction, all three swept back inside. Maddie trailed behind, slightly bored and ill at ease. She listened to endless questions, exclamations of delight, and gossip about people she had never met.

In addition to Josiah and Sarah, the Atwood household consisted now of an unmarried daughter, and Josiah Atwood's ward, his nephew Peter. Peter was about sixteen years old. He was a quiet young man, pale from his studies but strong-looking, with a body that would turn to fat if not exercised. From the start, Maddie wondered about him.

He moved with barely controlled restlessness. His hazel eyes, which radiated intelligence, also snapped dissatisfaction. His young features suggested strength of character, though Maddie suspected that he would be thwarted from ever really using it.

When introduced, he greeted her politely, but with little interest. When he learned that she had survived a shipwreck, however, his apathy transformed at once to fascination. For the rest of that first evening, he followed her around, asking question after question, until his uncle ordered him to stop pestering her.

But he had aroused Maddie's curiosity. She felt compassion for him, too. Within the few hours since her arrival, Maddie had observed enough of him to understand how much he hated the protected genteel life he led here with the Atwoods.

In conversation, he admitted no interest in his studies. He openly hated the idea of the career his strong-willed uncle had planned for him in the family business. He was as eager a boy as any, and he yearned for adventure. He believed manliness went with danger, and that the quiet life was a sign of something else. His uncle, though well-meaning, was trying to suffocate him, or so he believed.

"Working in the family business would be all right, if only my uncle would let me train to be one of the captains aboard ship, or the one who makes contact with foreign traders, but no," he sighed, "Uncle Josiah wants me to study *accounting*!" He spoke the word as if it were an obscenity, and looked so miserable that Maddie wanted to reach out and pat his hand.

"You'll be old enough soon," she said, consolingly.

"You can strike out then and do anything you want."

"By then, it will be too late. I'll be in a rut, perhaps even *married*." He continued bitterly, "Besides no one can argue with my uncle. No one! He thinks he knows all the answers."

Maddie shrugged. "Sometimes you have to take things into your own hands." To a certain extent, she herself had done it. For the sake of her hosts, however, she dared not pursue the subject any further.

At dinner that night, Flora herself brought up the purpose of Maddie's journey here to Boston. "She's looking for her husband, Josiah," she said, turning to her friend.

From the start, Maddie had been impressed by her host. Josiah Atwood cut a fine figure. He stood almost six feet tall, trim for a man his age, with iron gray hair and well-chiseled features. As they sat at the dinner table, eating off translucent blue-and-white plates imported from China by way of Europe, he turned to her. His lips twitched with a wry, amused smile. "Ach, what a careless knave he must have been to lose such a lovely lady as yourself. Or were you the careless one, Madame de Rohan?"

"Neither." Maddie shrugged. She explained how the ship they had been sailing in had run aground. She told him everything she dared, leaving out only the more horrifying, embarrassing details. When she had finished, she raised wide, pleading eyes to him. "Oh, sir," she whispered. "You have interests down at the harbor. Perhaps you know. Perhaps you've even heard of it. His ship was christened the *Genvieve*. Do you remember seeing it there? Perhaps it's still docked at one of the piers."

The man shook his head. "I know of no such ship, Madame," he replied. "But that in itself means nothing. I rarely get down to the harbor any more, and when I do, I pretty much attend to my own business and ignore anything going on around me. The sea as such has never interested me. In any case, the harbor's a fine one, and many ships dock and set sail from it. The *Genvieve* could have set sail without me or any of my workers knowing about it.''

Maddie's heart sank. Finding what happened to the *Genvieve* promised to be a bigger job than she had anticipated. "Well, I have no choice but to try. I'll be going down there tomorrow to inquire.''

Josiah Atwood drew back. "Not alone, you won't! The waterfront is no place for a woman—at least, not for a *lady*. I won't hear of it.''

"But I have to,'' retorted Maddie. "It's my only hope.''

"Someone will go with you then.''

That was fine with Maddie. From the start, she had dreaded going alone. She had noticed how rough men had stared at her and Flora as they walked to the streets. The wait for a public coach had seemed to take forever. All the while, she had burned under the gaze of strangers' hungry eyes, and she suspected that only the older woman's presence had held them at bay. Flora spoke up. "I already told her I'd go.''

The man's brows beetled together, "No, two women is the same as one alone.'' He turned to Maddie. "You must take a man with you.''

Maddie started in dismay. "But-but *who*?''

"I'll go with her, Uncle Josiah,'' Peter spoke up suddenly.

The man started in surprise. "You, Peter? Why, you're only a boy!''

"I'm sixteen,'' he retorted, "and as strong as any older man.''

"I had more in mind a servant, Peter,'' replied his uncle. "I'd rather you stay home and attend to your

169

studies."

Peter's aunt Sarah came to his rescue. Indeed, she spoke up so quickly that Maddie wondered if perhaps the woman sympathized with her nephew's distaste for his accounting studies. "Now, really, Josiah!" she scolded him gently. "And where are we supposed to find such a servant? The only one I can spare right now is old Tim Boot, and he's a little feeble to be hoofing all over God's creation. In any case, I suspect Madame de Rohan would want someone a little more...well, able-bodied...while she searches the harbor. I just don't think old Tim'd prove much of a protector, should she need one."

The man seemed clearly displeased. "All right, but only during the afternoons. In the mornings, Peter, you study. I cannot allow you to neglect your education. You'll be taking over this whole business some day, you know."

Maddie glanced to the boy and smiled. She could tell by his air of suppressed exultation that he was overjoyed to be released even half-days from his tedium. She turned to Peter's uncle, genuinely grateful. "Thank you, sir," she whispered. "I feel confident that I'll be safe with Peter."

The next afternoon she started out with high hopes. Those hours spent searching ended, however, in the pits of despair. With Peter by her side, she spent six whole fruitless hours asking everyone if they knew of a ship called *Genvieve*, and to her dismay, no one claimed even to have heard of it. Early that evening, she left the harbor in despair. As the sun set turning the sky blue-gray, Peter led her by the arm back to where he had parked their carriage.

They started to ride back in silence to the Atwood mansion. Suddenly, he spoke. "Maybe you got the name wrong," he suggested.

"No, I heard it quite clearly," she replied. "At least three of those people were lying when they said they hadn't heard of his ship. Three people!" She shook her head. "Why would they do it?" Maddie refused to give up. She vowed to go out the next day and search again. There must be *someone* out there willing and able to tell the truth. Peter, of course, was only too happy to go along.

"I can't tell you how much I've enjoyed this," he cried. "The sounds and the smells...." He turned to her, suddenly guilty. "Oh, I know it's been rough for you, and I'm sorry, but frankly, I'm glad to be going out again. I really hate being stuck in that room with all those bloody books."

Maddie smiled sadly. "I know." She felt glad that at least one of them was happy.

That night as moonlight streamed in through her sleeping chamber's lace-curtained window, she lay in bed wide awake and just stared at it. Her heart beat too hard for peaceful slumber. Thoughts of Henri rushed through her mind. Stirred, unsatisfied desires had left her restless. The day had proven such a horrible disappointment, yet things that happened had tantalized her too. She saw now how big the place was, how many people there were to ask. All she needed was one person to give her the information she sought. Perhaps that someone had been sleeping in a waterfront inn, or working at a pier far away from where she made her inquiries.

A strange excitement consumed her now. Today on the waterfront, Henri had seemed closer to her than ever. Indeed, his presence was more real, more alive now, than since the dark, unforgettable night when ocean waves had torn him from her reach. Surely such a feeling meant something.

As she lay there in bed, she hungered for him. She

longed to see his face again, and her flesh ached for his touch. Her heart pounded with eager anticipation. A strange warmth had spread through her being. Its glow rendered her soft and yearning for his manly love and tenderness. She remembered again the brooding pain in his eyes, the lips that could melt all her maidenly fears with one kiss.

At his memory, a pang of grief pierced her heart. Tears welled up in her eyes. Unable to stand it any longer, Maddie moaned aloud. She screwed her eyes tightly shut to wring out the tears that flooded them. She clung to her pillow with both arms and pretended to be holding the man she so desperately yearned for.

The next day she searched, and then again the next, until finally, a week passed. As her escort, Peter couldn't have been more delighted, but she sensed that Josiah Atwood, though civil, was growing restive. The man sensed some threat in his nephew's yearning for the sea, and therefore felt uncomfortable that Peter should spend so much time down at the harbor, where the sea and its wild men might influence him. As time passed, Maddie began to sense subtle pressure to give up.

He found her early one evening in the parlor. "Madame de Rohan," he said suddenly. "I'd be the last one to destroy your hopes, but you saw how it was. Surely if a ship called the *Genvieve* had docked here in Boston, someone would have seen it."

"Someone did," retorted Maddie. "I know it. I'm sure at least three of the people I talked to were lying—for some reason."

"But why? Why bother to lie?" He obviously believed that Maddie, in her desperation, had concocted a hopeless fantasy.

"I don't know," she replied. "But I saw it in their eyes."

Maddie could not recall her dreams that night, but

she awakened with the urgency that she should go out again and search for him, and immediately. The day had dawned sunny and hot. Even the light, fine-woven linen of her nightdress chafed unbearably against her skin.

For her searching, she chose as usual a dress more soberly proper than cool. Made of twill, long-sleeved, and tinted gray, not even a collar decorated its plain appearance. When she had finished fastening it, Maddie reached for her comb. She plaited her hair into braids and wound them into a tight bun. As she left her sleeping chamber, she glanced to the mirror hanging on its wall. When she saw her appearance, she smiled. She looked modest and plain, and even a little drab. Exactly the way she wanted to look for the kind of places she planned to go.

Downstairs Maddie found Peter in the study, sighing unhappily over his books. "Peter!" she whispered to him. "Come!" When he looked up at her, she smiled. "Today's going to be the day. I can feel it in my bones."

His eyes widened. He leaped up from his studies with a delighted yelp. "We're in luck," he cried. "Uncle Josiah is in Amhurst today on business, so he'll never have to know that I left early." He glanced to his books with a grimace. "Have you ever thought about how dull numbers are? How really deadly dull?" When Maddie shrugged, he went on, "Columns, and ever more endless columns of figuring, and in it all, no food for the soul. It's like turning one's mind into a desert." He sighed. "And my uncle wants to sentence me to spending my whole life doing it, just because when I was four years old, I could add and subtract better than all my little friends." He made a disgusted noise, then led her by the arm through the kitchen. He guided her out the back door. "We'll have to ride in the delivery cart today," he

173

said, speaking suddenly. "My aunt and your friend took the carriage to go visiting. The other is about all we have."

It was more than most people had, even here in the affluent section of Boston. "The delivery cart is fine," Maddie smiled.

The vehicle in which they finally set out for the harbor district was a rude, unpainted cart with heavy wheels that clattered horribly. The Atwoods kept it to haul flax, corn, and vegetables from their landholdings just outside town, while they themselves usually rode in the carriage. Compared to all the elegant two-wheeled chaises she saw skimming past, or to the five or six private coaches, this cart was rustic indeed. In it, she felt like quite a spectacle. However, Maddie was grateful for it. For the distance from Atwood Manor to the harbor, it was better than walking.

This time they clattered to another part of the waterfront. Within an hour, Maddie found a little man with glistening, red-rimmed eyes. He studied Maddie for a moment, then spoke with a shrug. "There be a merchant over on Water Street," he said. "A ship's outfitter named Seumas Hawkes. He uses some fanciful sort of name for his business, but that's his own handle. He's the one what outfitted Rohan's ship. That much I know," he added defensively, "and that's all I know."

But he had told her a lot. First of all, he gave her hope of tracing her man. Secondly, and perhaps without intending to, he revealed that he knew who the *Genvieve* belonged to. She hadn't mentioned Henri's name, only the ship's, and from that one slip, she suspected that the little man knew more than he was admitting.

But she sensed he would not reveal anything else. She thanked him, genuinely grateful for that little scrap of information he had thrown her way, and hurried back to where Peter stood waiting, a few feet behind. "Water

Street, Peter," she cried, "and let's hurry. It's the first real break I've had all week."

Water Street lay far away, both in spirit and in distance, from the Atwood home. Indeed, it faced the harbor, looking outward on one side to all the ships that wafted landward from open sea. When Maddie saw it, she sighed inwardly with relief that Peter was along. She was glad of his protection, for it was a tough district indeed. Shuttered warehouses intermingled with taverns where thirsty sailors just ashore could find a drink, a meal, and perhaps a wench, even in Puritan Boston. Rough-looking men loitered on its intersections, some even whistling as she rode past. They stood in groups, talking, and even those who remained silent studied her with sensual interest. Their eyes skimmed her body as if mentally undressing her. Maddie's cheeks flushed with embarrassment. She tried not to look at them. Every once in awhile, however, she'd glance beyond the wagon to some interesting sight and meet someone's eye. Whenever it happened, her contact leered, or called out some obscene invitation. Maddie didn't like the area at all.

"You sure Water Street's the place?" Peter stared at her doubtfully. He too seemed uneasy down here.

"I was told where to come," she replied, "and this is definitely it." She glanced up in time to see a sign, then sighed in relief. "Ah, there it is—Seumas Hawkes. This is it." The cart pulled over to the side, to the edge of the street where it would not be in the way, and stopped. As Maddie slipped from the seat, she raised her eyes to her friend. "Please wait for me here, Peter," she said. "I shouldn't be long."

Without waiting for a reply, Maddie smoothed her skirts, then hurried toward the front door of this establishment owned by Seumas Hawkes, who was apparently the only man in Boston who might know what happened to her husband.

"Oh, Henri," she whispered, turning the knob, "I'm coming. Just be patient, darling, and don't forget me." As she pushed open the door, a bell tied directly above jingled.

Inside, she saw a long desk, completely blocking access to the storage area beyond. It was an ordinary warehouse, not sinister at all, but plain and homely. At her approach, a clerk glanced up from some invoices he was working on, then moved to see what she wanted. "We don't serve individual customers," the clerk said curtly. "We trade only wholesale."

"I'm not a customer," she replied. "I came to see Seumas Hawkes."

Maddie looked around now in curiosity, rather than dread. The place had a pleasant odor, one of cinnamon and spices, of tea and cocoa, sandalwood and rose attar, mingled with underlying muskiness and the all-pervasive smell of fish from the sea outside. Boxes labeled with strange markings lined the shelves. These extended into the shadows behind, and their supports groaned from the weight of this treasure brought from all over the world. All the Hindu cloth, all the golden thread, coffee, perfumes, spices, china, and silver would wait here, until Seumas Hawkes saw fit to sell them at a good price.

At her reply, the man drew back in obvious surprise. "May I have your name, please, and the nature of your business with Mister Hawkes?"

"I'm Madame de Rohan," she replied. "My husband is supposed to have traded with Mr. Hawkes, and I'd like to discuss something of a confidential nature with him. Would you please go and see if he'll receive me?"

No longer Maddie Bradshaw, but Madame de Rohan. The transformation of her name still startled her. The flavor of its syllables tasted unnatural in her mouth.

She reminded herself of their marriage vows, taken in secret upon that windswept moor above the ocean. She saw again the love radiating from his eyes. How could she ever doubt, or draw back from that fact that she was no longer a maiden, but a wife? What did it really matter that he was a pirate, who traded stolen treasure for his necessities? She still loved him more than life itself.

The clerk returned. "My master will see you right away." He led her through the wooden gate separating clerk's stall from the entrance, then pointed up one dusty aisle. "Go straight back," he said, "then turn right. You can't miss his office."

Her heart pounded both in eager anticipation and in dread, as Maddie hurried to meet Seumas Hawkes. She passed wicker woven crates and cases of little wooden boxes and came into an unlit area steeped in deepest shadow. Here Maddie glanced around, fearfully wondering what to expect. Finally, she passed beyond the far end of the aisle to a space behind. To her right, ten or so feet away, she saw a light beaming through an opened door. Eager now to confront Hawkes and find out what he knew, she almost ran to his office.

Seumas Hawkes was a thin man, in spirit as well as body. His head was almost bald, save for a wisping half-moon of fuzz between his ears. Skin dry like parchment stretched taut over angular cheekbones and jaw, sinking into the hollow cheeks between. A beak nose jutted out from between two slightly bulging gray eyes. These stared at her suspiciously as she approached, while below his nostrils, the lips pursed together in seeming disapproval of her intrusion in his domain.

"You claim to be Rohan's wife." No graceful ameneties for him. Here was a man who came right to the point. He studied her coldly, with subtle, yet obvious contempt. "What are you really doing here? What do you want?"

Taken aback by his cold hostility, Maddie recoiled. "I—someone at the harbor told me you were the one I should see. He told me you were the one who outfitted Henri's ship."

"I sold Rohan some commodities," replied the man. "That's far different from outfitting his ship. Food...clothes...rum and some tools. He paid me in cash, so I consider the transaction closed." His thin lips pressed together as if to cut off any more words. Maddie stared at him in dismay. He was the only one who could help her. If he refused, all would be lost. Only the distant and unappealing hope of Okracoke remained, and she had no idea how she'd get there, so even though she sensed it would prove useless, she threw herself on the man's mercy.

"Please...I'm trying to find him." She clasped her hands together and squeezed nervously. The interview was going badly, very badly indeed. "We were on a ship together which wrecked off the great rocks near Providencetown on Cape Cod. We became separated. The storm did it to us," she added, "and those waves." Remembering them, Maddie shuddered.

She continued, "I have no idea whether he's alive or dead, none whatsoever. All I know is that he had a ship called the *Genvieve* docked here at Boston Harbor. He told me that himself." She sighed. "I came here as soon as I could, but when I asked around at the harbor, nobody seemed to know. Finally, one man was able to tell me what I wanted. He said the *Genvieve* had set sail already—a few weeks ago. Unfortunately he had no idea where it was headed, or anything else about it. He knew nothing, except that you had traded with my Henri." Maddie raised pleading eyes to him. "Oh, you are my only hope, sir. My only chance to find him. Please, it cannot hurt you to give me a little information, and I won't take much of your time."

178

He moved closer. His eyes remained fixed on her face. "Prove it, madam," he said suddenly. "If you are truly his wife, then you must be able to prove it. Rohan would see to it that you could."

"I have no documents with me, if that's what you mean." She felt suddenly breathless. "Only the ring he gave me when we exchanged our vows."

"Show it to me," he demanded. "I'll be able to see from the ring whether you speak the truth."

Maddie raised her hand. The ring, restored from the wrecker's pocket, glistened in black, gold, and ruby splendor upon her left middle finger. The man took her hand and studied it. After endless moments, he released her. Maddie drew her hand away and let it fall into the folds of her skirt.

"You are indeed Rohan's wife," he said, "and God help you." He spoke more to himself now than to Maddie. "I would not have believed it, but this ring you wear proves it. He tore it from the dead finger of a Spanish Grandee, you know."

Maddie drew back surprised. "He told me it was from an Arabian Mogul."

Hawkes smiled. "Aye, but I had to be sure. Somehow that ring could have been stolen, but only someone close to Rohan would know its true history. In any case, he's worn it proudly ever since I've known him, and it's been his pride and joy. Indeed, until this trip, I have never seen him without it." He had seemed to soften toward her.

Maddie's eyes widened. Her heart pounded exultantly in her chest. "This trip? He was on board the *Genvieve* then, when it set sail?"

Hawkes raised his almost-invisible brows. "Would ship set out without its captain?"

Maddie's heart nearly exploded with joy. "Then he's still alive!" She clasped her hands together and nearly fainted with relief. "Oh, I'm so glad!"

"Alive as ever," he replied, "but dark and brooding, as I've never seen before. I asked about his ring and he told me he had lost it. I was surprised to hear that he'd allow that to happen, but now I understand. He must have thought you dead."

"Where did he go? Where was he headed?"

The man's pale eyes studied her now, almost with pity. "Why do you want to know. Why are you asking?"

"Why?" Maddie stared at him incredulously. "Because he's my husband. I'm his wife. A husband and wife belong together."

"I was afraid of that," he said, then continued, "You seem like a nice enough maid. Gently bred and virtuous. Go home to your parents. Rohan isn't a man for one such as you."

Maddie drew back. "How dare you!" Her eyes widened. "Our vows were taken before God. I am bound to him for life!"

The man shook his head. "Then God pity you, madam," he replied. "I have no wish to insult you, but I know him—probably better than you do. He is an honest man in his own way, or I would never have traded with him, but he is also hard—like iron, and cruel as a man can be. He is famous in all the Indies for that cruelty. The transplanted Moors, Saracens, and Africans call him by the names of their own heathen devils, and the Spaniards do too, in their own tongue. Even his own people," he continued, "call him *Le Diable*." He fixed sad eyes upon her. "Do you think that you could possibly be happy with such a man?"

Her Henri, called a devil? Impossible! She refused to believe any such thing about the man she loved; the one who had always been kindness itself to her. "No!" she cried. "You lie. Henri is kind, and as gentle as can be.

180

He is no devil."

"It is as I feared; you do not know him," he retorted.

"I do too, and obviously better than you do. Now I tell you once again that I belong with him. Now tell me please—where is he headed?"

He sighed. "Do you know where the King's colony of Bermuda is? Have you any idea how far away it is, and how dangerous? Can you even imagine how hard it will be to find him, once you get there?"

Maddie drew back in dismay. Bermuda might as well be on the far side of the world near China, instead of in the West Indies. How could she get there with no money of her own? Once there, how would she live? Tears sprang suddenly to her eyes. She realized God had put many miles and days between them.

"Go home and wait patiently." The man took her arm now and led her to the door. "Word will get back to him that you still live. In any case, you have no choice. You cannot go to him, not alone. Those colonies further south—they're wild. The only white women who live there are prostitutes, not gentle ladies such as you, while the men—" He shook his head. "They're wild men and rough. You would not stand a chance. They would tear your virtue to shreds before Rohan ever saw you again."

But Maddie had no home to go to, no refuge but the arms of her husband. "You may be right," she retorted, "but I'm going anyway."

"God help you then," he replied somberly.

Numb with horror at how far her beloved was from her, Maddie left Seumas Hawkes' office. She hurried down the corridor past the desk clerk. With trembling hand, she yanked open the bell-jangling door and slipped outside.

Almost immediately, someone tugged at her sleeve. A voice rasped in her ear, "If ye want to see yer husband

181

again, follow me."

Chapter Fifteen

A shabbily dressed man emerged from the shadows surrounding Hawkes' front entrance.

Maddie stopped startled. Her eyes widened with newfound hope. "My husband?" she whispered. She glanced out onto the street where Peter in his cart waited.

"Ye *are* Madame de Rohan, are ye not?" Black eyes peered with fanatic intensity into hers. The face was gaunt, and almost too swarthy for a white man, yet his sharp-edged features pointed to northern Europe, not Africa, as his ancestral home.

"Y-yes, but—How did you know?"

"Word gets around. Ye been askin' folks questions, and they put two and two together and it sometimes comes out four. I found out this mornin' where ye was headed, and I followed." He grinned. "Ye'r a pretty easy one to follow. They's not many who look like ye, down here by the harbor. I knew where to come; I came and I saw."

She glanced at Peter still waiting in the cart. "Just one moment please," she said. "I have to tell—"

His hand fell on her arm. "I cannot wait. There isn't time." The man's voice rasped low and urgent. "He waits impatiently, knowing ye are here now, yet unable to come."

"Why not?" Maddie wanted to know why Henri had seen fit to send this stranger. She stared now with bewildered suspicion. "Surely if, as you say, he knows where I'm staying, he could have sent a message."

"He lies injured, and sometimes delirious," the man replied. "Perhaps even dying."

Maddie recoiled. "Dying?" Her eyes widened in horror. Henri was too alive, too vital. A man such as he could not come to such an end. Her heart refused to believe it. Fear, however, made it flutter. "But how?"

"Some men pulled him ashore close to here...from a shipwreck which left him broken. They brought him to me, ye see, because they knew I was with him in the old days further south." The man continued, "Most times he just lays a-moanin', but sometimes he wakes, and then he asks for ye. Word came yesterday that ye were here in town. Someone on the dock, a friend of mine, talked to ye and told me that ye was looking for him. I found out today where ye got sent. Rohan was awake then, and went beside himself with joy. He insisted that I come down here and wait until ye arrived."

"B-but Hawkes said Henri sailed with the *Genvieve*." Suddenly suspicious, Maddie held back.

The man shrugged in reply. "Maybe Hawkes had some reason for tellin' ye what he did, but it ain't true. Believe anyone ye please, but if ye'r comin' with me, then hurry up. This may be yer last chance to see Rohan alive." Without waiting for her reply, he started moving. Maddie wasn't sure now who to believe. Feeling the prize worth the risk, however, she followed. After giving one last backward glance to Peter, whose eyes met hers in startled surprise, she ducked behind the stranger into a nearby alley. Thinking quickly, she had decided just to take her chances.

The alley they traveled was narrow, and it led through what seemed to be the underbelly of Boston. The butt-ends of shabby buildings clapped up in the early days of the town's infancy, now tumbling down piece by piece, board by board, faced one another across a passage too narrow for any but foot traffic. People lived in these buildings. They called to one another from open second-story windows. The stench of rotting garbage and excretia and the remains of fish mouldering in the summer's heat nearly suffocated Maddie, as she hurried behind this stranger who had come to her out of nowhere. Litter tossed about the hot, water-laden breeze that blew off the sea skidded past her feet. Loiterers, bleary-eyed and smelling of rum and ale, stared openly as she passed, and crooned rude suggestions.

But Maddie was willing to endure all of it for the sake of being reunited with her Henri, who waited in some no doubt wretched garret for her arrival. As they hurried along, Maddie's thoughts strayed from her husband long enough to think of Peter. At once she felt a pang. When their eyes had met that last time on the street, he had looked so startled and dismayed. She hoped he'd not get into trouble on account of her.

The man tossed his head to the left. "This way, madam," he said, and then to make sure she understood, he motioned with a sweeping hand gesture. A second alley butted their own. Without speaking, she followed, as he led down this one.

Buildings loomed tall and steep and rickety above them like bluffs. The wood, exposed to winter snow, spring rains, and summer sun, had grayed, and its fibres had softened and decayed. A curious pall hung over the atmosphere here. A silence completely devoid of human voices oppressed her. Maddie glanced around and shivered as her eyes met those of some derelict, the only person besides the two of them in this back alley way. The expression in those eyes was indifferent, yet strangely wary, those of a wild animal surviving in its natural habitat. She hated this part of town. She dreaded being here, yet would do anything to see her husband again.

"How much further?" She glanced around. Her leader, however, did not reply. Instead, he motioned her to follow down yet another alleyway. Too intimidated now to argue, and knowing that she'd be lost finding her own way back, Maddie could only follow.

Suddenly, ahead, loomed a building. It was the oldest she had seen so far, perhaps indeed one of the first built here.

"He's in *there*." The man pointed to it, then sprinted on ahead of her to the front door. After glancing back to make sure she still followed, he opened it and nodded for her to step inside.

Sudden apprehension jellied Maddie's knees. "Henri's in here?" she whispered. She stared with sudden plummeting doubt at the building. What a dismal place to find him! She could not imagine someone as fastidious as Henri enduring such a wretched spot.

As if reading her mind, the stranger spoke to her. "I know it ain't fancy, or even clean, but it's the best I could do. I'm a poor man, and he's in no position to argue. I'd do better if I could, but I can't. This is where I live. Now hurry up!"

As she moved forward, Maddie's heart swelled with anticipation even as it fluttered in dread. If he was not a friend of Henri's, then why would he have bothered waiting for her? Why would he lie? In spite of her fears, her reasoning forced her to believe him.

She stepped into the foul-smelling hall, and looked around. As so often the case in old buildings, the interior was in better condition than the outside walls. Her heart fluttered again. What would she find—the man she loved and had married, or a broken wreck? Would he even remember her, or had the injuries shattered his mind and soul for all time? "I'm afraid," she whispered.

"Why should you be? He's yer husband, ain't he?"

The man's cool practicality was like a bucket of cold water splashed upon her. "Now come along. He's upstairs."

He led her up four flights into a garret passage, dingy from too few windows and stifling hot in Boston's humid summer. "He be in there, Madame Rohan," he said, motioning to a closed door. "You'll find yer husband in the bed there, sweatin' like a hog, and—"

"Hogs don't sweat!" Maddie found herself strangely angered by the comparison. "And my husband in no way resembles a hog."

"Be that as it may, y'll find yer husband in bed, sweatin'."

The door swung open. As it did, Maddie saw not a bed but a short wall forming a crude entranceway into the larger room beyond. As she stepped inside, nearly tasting the heart's blood that seemed to be pounding in her mouth, he closed the door behind. As it latched, she heard a soft click.

"Henri?" Maddie's voice nearly failed her. Even as she rounded the entrance, she called out to him, hoping to hear a cry of joy, or at least a word of recognition. But as she stepped into the room itself, Maddie's eyes widened in horror. Her throat closed, and strangled the scream that would surely have pierced the silence. There was no bed, no Henri lying there. She recoiled, her entire insides melting into horror, as she stared, numbed with shock, into the gloating face of Andrew Mathias.

Chapter Sixteen

"What have you done to Henri?" She gazed uncomprehendingly at the man who had tried to have her arrested and hanged back in Salem. She froze where she stood, her mind reeling in shocked confusion. Hadn't it been enough for him to falsely accuse her of witchcraft, and see her torn from her home? What had compelled him to follow her all the way to Boston? "How did you get here?" she whispered, "and how did you know where I was?"

"I've been waiting." He smirked at her, obviously savoring his triumph. She saw a mad gleam in his eye.

"Where is Henri?" She stared at him with loathing and horror.

Mathias shrugged. "How should I know?" he replied. "Perhaps he realized the strumpet you are, and abandoned you."

Maddie drew back. "Strumpet...I?"

Mathias's eyes narrowed. As she stood, so stunned she couldn't even move, he inched toward her. His gaze riveted upon her. "Still the face of an angel, I see." He clamped his hand around her jaw. She saw with horror how his eyes burned hot and intense. "And you fooled everybody," he continued, "everybody but me. But I know." His breathing had become deeper and faster as he talked. "Setting yourself up in front of men...in front of *everybody*, as an object of desire."

So that was it! He blamed her for the feelings of lust that had swelled unbidden from his own breast. Maddie's eyes widened as she stared at him. Tears sprang to them from pain. The pressure of his fingers against her flesh hurt horribly. She had no idea what he was talking about. "What have I ever done to you or anyone else?" Was this whole grim charade of pursuit a way of punishing her for the forbidden desires she had unknowingly aroused in him? She realized now that the man was undoubtedly insane.

His hand still around her jaw, he gave her head a shake. "Liar!" he snarled. "I've seen it in the way you

187

hold your breasts so high as you move. The way you flourish your skirts. Oh, but you pretend!" His chest heaved now. "Your little chin raises so high at the merest suggestion of anything indecent, and yet all the time your body....it invites. It teases. It pleads to be taken." By now he had become quite breathless. His hand slid from her jaw, down her neck to her chest, where it lingered for a moment against her pounding heart. "You must be afraid," he whispered. He smiled. His eyes gleamed maniacally now.

But Maddie was too proud to admit fear to this man, whom she had already grown to despise. "How did you find me?" She leveled her gaze to his. She forced her voice to remain calm. She buried the fear in her eyes beneath a veiled hardness.

"I thought you had slipped through my fingers," he continued, "Indeed, I had despaired of ever finding you again. Especially," he added, "since those weak-willed fools I rode with placed their own comfort above the capture of Satan's tool."

So that was how it was. The others had sensibly turned back, going home where they belonged. Only Andrew Mathias, gripped by obsessive hatred, had continued on. Still, what he said had not answered her question, so she put it to him again. "I want to know how you found me, how you came to know I'd be in Boston."

His lips curled into a smile. "I see no reason to deny you that knowledge," he said. "It was Edward Leich who enlightened me."

Edward Leich, of course! Up from a business trip, and visiting relatives in Providencetown. Seeing her was as much of a surprise to him as it was to her.

Mathias continued, "He mentioned it to me quite by accident. Imagine his surprise when he found out you were a fugitive witch!"

"An *accused* witch," she retorted. "It's hardly the same thing—especially with you and that hag Goodwife Jameson doing the accusing." Her voice hardened. "Tell me the truth! Is it that you're still angry because I refused your hand in marriage, or is it because I resisted you that Sabbath in the cemetary?"

She had hardly finished. She had just begun to draw in a breath to start again when she saw what the punishment would be for her boldness. The whites of his eyes reddened. Their pupils enlarged until the central disk hid the drab gray-brown of the irises. His face contorted now in fury.

Andrew Mathias flung his hand back to gain momentum, then whipped it forward. His blow stung against her cheeks. "Devil's strumpet!" he cried. Suddenly his hands curled like claws around the neckline of her bodice. With a snarl, he yanked it open.

Tiny mother-of-pearl buttons flew in all directions. They clattered onto the bare wood floor, as he ripped the top of her dress from her body. Maddie cried out. She tried to cover herself with hands now trembling, but he tore them away.

The chemise she wore underneath, woven of flimsy cloth, yielded easily to his rage. His movement bared now what she wished to hide, and he took them as his prize. Lifting them roughly from underneath, his cadaverous fingers stroked them. From the look of triumphant satisfaction she read on his face, Maddie knew that this was what he wanted all along. From his mouth, however, poured words of hypocrisy and denial. "Thy paps are a temptation to all but the strongest of men, girl," he said. "The Devil has equipped you well."

"God gave me these," she retorted, her eyes blazing.

"Blasphemer!" He let loose of her breasts to grab her by the hair. One hand on each side of her head curled around the locks which had been so demurely braided.

189

With one angry movement, he tore them free. As his fingers squeezed around them, nearly tearing the hair out by its roots, he shook her. Maddie cried out with pain and fear. She refused, however, to give in to him willingly. "I speak the truth and you know it, Andrew Mathias. That's why you're so afraid to hear my words," Maddie shrieked at him, as she thrust suddenly against her enemy with all the strength she could muster. She kicked him hard and whipped away from him. Sobbing aloud now from pain as well as terror, she dashed past him for the door leading out into the hall and freedom.

She flung her hand onto its pull and yanked, nearly tearing her arm from its socket when the door refused to yield. With a despairing cry, she tried again, but with no luck. She heard it rattle against the frame. From beyond, the metal bolt scraped against itself but remained firmly locked. Her betrayers had bolted her securely inside. "No!" she sobbed, now in despair. "Please, no!" Too weak to fight anymore, she sank to her knees.

"You have no choice, Witch." From beyond, Andrew Mathias' voice reached her. Its tone was hard and cold, foreign to all mercy. "You will come back with me to Salem to face your just fate." He was upon her now, speaking through clenched teeth that doubtlessly ached to sink themselves into her flesh. He reached to grab her by the arm, to yank her up, and force her to endure more beatings, more humiliations, but his movement galvanized her. Maddie leaped up, forcing the trembling legs underneath to support her weight. Fighting free, she dashed past him.

The room's only window opened out onto the alley below and she ran to it now, intending to fling herself out to whatever fate she might meet, rather than to endure what Mathias intended. But when she got to it, and peered down into the cavern formed by her own prison and the building across the way, she lost her nerve. The room stood three stories up, an unmeasurable and terrifying distance from the ground. As she stood, paralyzed by fear, he dashed up to her. This time he caught her. He yanked her away and flung her down. Maddie screamed as her knees cracked against the floor.

He straddled her now, pressing into her with his weight. "Witch!" he whispered, then yanked her roughly around. Maddie's eyes widened when she saw what he pulled from inside his coat jacket—a small whip with leather thongs.

"No!" she cried, and tried to shield herself with raised hands.

But to no avail. Its sharpened edge stung into her flesh. It sliced into ribbons what remained of her bodice. Maddie sobbed aloud as pain seared through her. She tried to writhe away from it, but with no luck. He brought it down again and then again, until he had torn every shred of clothing from her back. When she lay moaning, weak from spent emotion, and almost unconscious now of pain he seemed to relish inflicting upon her, he took her, his hands roaming free with a possessive roughness that under other circumstances would have sent her clawing to escape. Right then, however, Maddie lay half-dead, unknowing, and uncaring of anything he might do to her. Finally, even he saw that she was beyond suffering. Unwilling to let her enjoy the mercy of unconsciousness, he pulled away.

"You tried to escape your fate, Witch, but you cannot," he moaned through gritted teeth. He kneeled over her now, straddling her as he yanked her limp and unresisting arms behind. She hardly fought as he bound them with rope. "You will remain here, in this room, until it is convenient for me to return you to justice. There, in Salem, you will be held with all the other witches in the gaol, then tried before the magistrates who alone in their wisdom will decide your fate." And then he bound her ankles. As he tightened the knot around them, his hand lingered upon her legs. She shuddered to feel his fingers on her.

Maddie slumped there, bound by rough hempen coils that scratched against her skin. Dizzy with pain and nauseous from the smell of her own blood and sweat, she hardly comprehended anymore who she was, or why he saw fit to punish her. She stared dully, as he set up a small cross carved of wood in front of her. "Contemplate your mortal enemy, Witch, and show the grace to throw yourself upon His mercy. Your body, a tool of evil, will writhe as it deserves from a hangman's rope, but pray, if you still can, for the life of your soul."

"Pray for your own, Andrew Mathias!" she cried out defiantly. She remembered all too well what he had just done to her, and she understood that someone so consumed by hatred and lust could never be blessed—not even by his own stern Puritan God.

However, he paid her no heed. He merely walked to the door, then called out to his accomplice. Maddie heard the bolt click open, and shut again, then footsteps down the hall fading into silence.

An eternity passed, and as consciousness more or less returned, it brought with itself an awareness of pain. The ropes proved too strong for her efforts to pull free. She nearly went mad from sheer discomfort. Her bones and muscles seemed alive with fire.

Returning consciousness brought with it despair, too. She knew what would happen to her once Mathias returned her to Salem. In the goal, the warders would stip her, shave all the hair off her body, then examine her for 'witchmarks', secret nipples used to suck demons. After all that, they would torture her for the names of her accomplices—others who practiced the

192

heinous crime with her, and in her pain and terror she might cry out, accusing other innocents, just so that they would stop.

Afterward, she would be tried, found guilty, and hanged, dying the slow death of strangulation. Tears of pain and fear and indignation bleared her eyes. What had she ever done to deserve all this? Who in her life had she ever hurt? A chilling thought prickled her scalp, and a feeling like ice trickled down her neck and spine. Perhaps God had abandoned her, no longer caring that she had lived all her life in virtue, studying His word, and praying every Sunday in a meeting house dedicated to Him. In his place, Mathias had come, her enemy and tormenter. Bound by ropes tightly knotted and locked in a room high above the ground, Maddie saw no hope that she might do other than end her life by a noose back in Salem. Most galling of all was the thought of Mathias' smirking face gloating at sight of her final agonies, for undoubtedly he would take pleasure in watching.

Chapter Seventeen

Maddie had no idea how long she had been imprisoned there, but it seemed like several eternities. Even in daylight, the shadows cast by the building veiled the room in dimness, and the air remained stiflingly hot. Maddie's eyelids drooped. Grogginess, discomfort, and heat lowered her into a state of semi-consciousness.

Suddenly, outside, she heard a noise, a scuffle of some kind. Dreading the worst, her heart pounded wildly. Had Mathias finally returned? Was it now her time to be taken, bound in ropes, back to the sight of her father, friends, and enemies in Salem? What was the fight going on outside about? In spite of the heat, goose pimples raised on her flesh.

Suddenly, the door unlatched. A foot kicked it open. Her heart pounded harder now. She wondered what new ordeal she was to face. Feet stepped over the threshold. Steps grew louder, as someone walked toward where she remained knotted and imprisoned in one corner.

Familiar footsteps they were too, but she wasn't sure whose. Not Andrew Mathias's; she knew that for a fact. They stepped lighter than his, and springier, yet right where wall ended and the little corridor turned into the room itself, they stopped altogether, as if the intruder, sensibly cautious, wanted to take his bearings and expose himself slowly to whatever lay beyond.

Finally the footsteps started up again. The unknown person moved forward and Maddie waited, her eyes fixed upon the spot where he would appear. As he stepped into view, she saw him. She cried out with joy, as she recognized Peter, not Mathias or the other unknown scoundrel. "Peter, my God! How did you ever find me?" Her heart pounded in exultation at the sight of him.

His own eyes widened in horror at her plight. "Madame Rohan!" His voice failed. "What-what happened to you?"

"I was lured here by the promise of seeing my husband, but instead all I found was an old enemy," she said firmly. "Now please—untie me!" She had no wish to wait like this for him to free her at his leisure. In any case, untied she could run and fight, if Mathias returned. Bound, she was helpless.

"Oh, yes, sure." Young Peter seemed almost reluctant to approach her, as if embarrassed beyond all control. He edged up to her, his eyes averted from her torn dress, bared breasts, and whip-striped flesh. Moving awkwardly, he reached for the rope knotted behind. She felt, rather than saw, his fingers fumbling with it.

"How did you get into the room?" She remembered the scuffle she had heard right before he entered.

"Your jailer posted a guard," Peter answered grimly. "Luckily for us both, he was a dirty old dog, reeking of whiskey and hardly able to stand. All I had to do was overcome him. He's still there—out cold."

Maddie shuddered. "He was probably the one who lured me here."

"He was," replied Peter. "At least, he was the one I saw you with, right before you ran off. You should have called to me to come along. As it was, I had to tie the horse, and then it was hard catching up." As Peter fumbled to untie her, Maddie grew impatient.

"Have you no knife?" she cried. She was tired of her bonds and ached to be free.

"Knife?" Her suggestion startled him. "Yes, of course. I should have thought of it myself." He was a young lad, and inexperienced. Out of the corner of her eye, Maddie saw him blushing furiously. Obviously the sight of her bare flesh had clouded his mental process.

As for a knife, she knew he carried one. Though he had no real need for such a weapon, he lived out youthful fantasies in which he dreamed of using it. Like any overprotected boy, he saw only the glories of a free and dangerous life, but none of its hardships and dangers. Right then, Maddie was grateful for it.

Finally his knife had come in handy. He slipped the blade between the ropes and her skin, sawing outward until finally he broke through, freeing her wrists and hands first.

Maddie's flesh, bound for what seemed like many hours, had numbed, yet burned at the same time. As he flung the rope aside and began working on her ankles,

Maddie struggled to move her arms, but could not. She realized then she'd have to leave them hang from her sides until sensation returned. The same with her legs. Once freed, she collapsed into Peter's arms and waited for circulation to prickle itself into her extremeties again.

"Are you all right?" He seemed genuinely concerned for her.

Maddie nodded. "I will be, as soon as I can feel my legs and arms again." She glanced to him in grateful relief. "But how did you know where I was?"

"I left the cart and followed you," he replied. "I hope it's still there, or we'll be walking home. You sure moved fast. I nearly lost you twice."

"Thank God you didn't!" Maddie replied with heart-felt joy.

"Anyway, I saw where they took you, and after a bit, followed you in. Luckily, the place is deserted, so when I heard voices up above me . . . ."

Maddie smiled. She closed her eyes and sighed. "Thank you," she whispered. "Thank you so much." If he hadn't come, the result would have been unbearable. "Help me to stand," she said.

With his strong arm around her, she clambered up on feet still half-numb and painfully sensitive to the pressure of her own weight. She knew, however, that they had to leave as soon as possible. This garret prison, in the heart of Boston's warehouse district was too dangerous. While she got used to standing again, Peter unbuttoned his shirt, then handed it to her. She slipped her arms into its sleeves.

Just as she had finished fastening it up, a voice from beyond startled them both. "So, Witch, you found another ally!" Horrified, Maddie glanced up to see again the glowing, malevolent eyes of Andrew Mathias.

"You!" she whispered. She drew back. Her flesh

196

crawled at the very sight of him.

Peter took a step forward. "Is he the one who did this to you?" His voice rumbled low and menacing in his throat.

"He's a madman." Maddie dared not take her eyes off Mathias. "He takes pleasure in cruelty, and he hates me. Yes, he's the one." As she stood there, for the first time unsupported by Peter's strength, she blessed fortune that almost full sensation had returned to her legs and feet. She could even run now, if necessary and with Peter along, she stood a chance of breaking free.

Mathias reached inside his coat. Maddie's eyes widened as he whipped out from its hiding place a pistol, which he aimed at the two of them. "You'll not get away from me so easily, Witch. Not even this brawny dupe of yours can help you now." As he spoke, his upper lip curled into a snarl. He stepped toward them one pace closer. "In any case, you have blinded him. You . . . the Whore of Babylon," he spat out. "You, Lilith . . . you, Delilah . . . you, Jezebel, and Salome, and all the other harlot servants of the Devil who ever tempted a Godly man. With your body and beauty, you have stolen his reason. God pity his soul."

Maddie's own gaze fixed upon her pursuer and hardened. "I have done nothing," she replied, coldly. "I am but a mirror, reflecting back what you yourself are, what you yourself think. Look to your own mind, Andrew Mathias, for the evil you see in me." She felt strangely calm now, and in full possession of her senses. No longer would she cringe in fear. Mathias was a fool, acting right then on emotion. She would use reason instead, and somehow make her escape to safety.

Peter, to her relief, appeared just as calm as she herself. From the corner of her eye, she saw him glancing around, looking for something with which to defend himself against their common enemy's pistol.

197

Just then, Maddie noticed a bottle lying on its side near her foot. Blown of thick green glass, it had probably once held rum. It was empty now, and its bubbled walls caught glints of light from what little sun still shone through that window. Dust lay thick upon it, but the container itself looked sturdy as ever, and intact.

Maddie's mind raced. The room was empty, save for that bottle and the cross, now out of reach, which Mathias had set up in front of her. She knew, somehow, that she must lay hands on that bottle and use it to distract her enemy long enough for Peter to act. She prayed that her young friend should prove quick of wit and movement. Acting together was their only chance, for even now Mathias advanced, pistol in hand, a sadistic gleam in his eyes.

"I-I feel faint!" Speaking with a sigh, Maddie caught Peter's eye for an instant, then flung the back of one hand to her forehead. She staggered until she stood directly above the bottle, then crumpled, falling on top of it.

"Madame de Rohan!" As she sank, she heard Peter cry out, but she dared not acknowledge him. Her seeming weakness concealed her intentions. As she fell, Maddie's right hand grappled for the neck of the bottle. With a sharp movement and a cry, she flung the glass container at Mathias's head.

Her unpracticed arm missed, as she had feared, but the movement and the bottle hurtling close past his temples distracted him. He glanced away for an instant, and in that one flash of time, Peter lunged. He flung is weight against Mathias. His hand grabbed hold of the gun wrist, forcing the weapon upward. In reaction to Peter's assault, one thin, pale finger drew back. It squeezed the trigger, igniting an explosion from its barrel. Lead and fire tore into the ceiling directly above Maddie's head. Bits and pieces of plaster fell down into her hair.

With a cry of relief, Maddie stumbled to her feet. She saw at once that Peter still struggled. Mathias, in almost animal frenzy, fought fiercely. His hands curled around Peter's throat. Unable to bear the thought of Mathias winning, Maddie flung herself at him. She grabbed one ear in her hand and twisted. The other curled around a great fistful of his hair. Using both hands and knees, she kicked and tore at him, until Peter broke free and forced Mathias to the ground.

"Get that rope he tied you with," he cried. "It'll be a pleasure to use it on him."

Maddie hurried to obey, bringing the cut but still substantial lengths back to Peter, who bound them around the ankles, hands, and wrists of their attacker. "What a swine he is!" Peter murmured aloud as he knotted the last piece of rope. "We'll leave him here. He'd make his escape in time, no doubt, but not before we report him to the authorities."

"What about the other?" Maddie glanced toward the door. If Peter had overcome Mathias's partner, then he must still be outside, perhaps waiting. Peter reached for the pistol Mathias had dropped. As he stood up, he answered, "He's still out cold. Drunk to begin with, then hit over the head. The man won't be bothering us." Peter turned to her. "Well, what now? Shall I take you home?" Maddie turned from him. Her heart felt as if unseen hands had wrung it as suddenly and violently as a wet rag. "I . . . If I give up now, I'll have come here to Boston for nothing." Her voice trembled as he spoke. "I followed that man because he led me to believe Seumas Hawkes was lying. I see now that I was wrong. I could tell Hawkes was sincere. I should have believed him when he told me Henri had set sail for the West Indies."

"The West Indies?" At mere mention of it, the boy's

eyes widened. He stared at her with eager interest. "What will you do then—write him a letter? If you do, and need someone to deliver it, look no farther than myself, for—"

"No!" Maddie shook her head. "I will follow him." Henri was the other half of her soul, her life, her destiny. She could not bear the thought of being separated from him. These past few weeks had lain upon her like pure torture. In any case, where else could she go? She had no home, now that all Salem Village had branded her as a witch, while Providencetown, where she had known kindness, held only the awkwardness of a love she could never hope to return. Fate had burned all her bridges behind her. Her only direction was forward now, to the man she had joined in a whispered vow before God.

Maddie took her rescuer now by the hand. She focused blazing eyes upon him. "There shall be no letter, Peter," she said. "When I spoke of following him, I meant it . . . as soon as I can find a way to get there."

The youth stared at her in dismay. "But the dangers, Madame de Rohan! The difficulties!"

"I shall have to live with them," she replied. "Nothing remains for me here . . . no home, no love, no future. Oh, Peter, I belong with him. He is my husband." Suddenly, an idea came to her, one that might serve both of them. In her eagerness, Maddie clutched one of his arms. "Your uncle . . . he's in shipping. Do any of his ships go to the West Indies?"

Peter frowned. "Some of them do," he replied. "Why?"

"Are any of them in port right now? I mean, that plan to leave Boston and head south?"

Peter shrugged. "Just one," he replied, "the *Anadeen*." He stared at her, bewildered. Maddie reflected that, though Peter was extremely bright in many ways, in others he was almost a dolt. Anyone of quicker wit would have seen why she was asking what she did. Nevertheless, joy filled her breast at his answer. "When does the *Anadeen* set sail?"

"Tomorrow," he replied.

"Then I'll be on it."

Peter drew back, genuinely horrified. "You haven't a hope in hell that he'd let you sail on it. The rigors of the journey would be too much for a woman, or so he'd say. In any case, the crew is made up of common men. They're rough, and superstitious, too. They believe a woman on board is bad luck." Peter sighed. "Even I know that, and I'll never have the chance to go to sea."

His words of discouragement only steeled Maddie's resolve. "I have been through far worse than mere discomfort, Peter," she replied. "I've faced danger too, and I learned that you either die or you survive. I'm no longer afraid of either."

"But they still won't let a woman on board. I know my uncle, Maddie, and I can tell you—under no circumstances would he consent."

"No one need ever know," she replied. "It shall be our secret." A plan conceived and born of desperation had formed in her mind.

Peter stared at her now in genuine alarm. "But, how? What do you mean?"

Maddie shrugged. "I am slim, am I not, Peter? Dressed in a loose shirt and vest, in trousers and heavy shoes, would I not resemble a boy? Especially once I cut off all my hair. A boy will board that ship, and I shall turn up missing."

He shook his head and drew back. "Never!" He stared at her body, at the half-open shirt and the skirt still hiding her legs. "Never in a hundred thousand lifetimes could I ever believe you were anything but a woman!"

He spoke with such intensity that Maddie laughed. "You're wrong, Peter, and you shall be my accomplice. You shall lend me the clothes I need, or else I'll take them from one of the servants. Tonight, when everybody else is sleeping, I shall steal out of the house to the harbor, and stow away in your uncle's ship. By the time they find me, the ship'll be out to sea, and it'll be too late to send me back. By then they'll be on their way to the West Indies, where I intend to go, come Hell or high water." Her eyes met his and held him. As she spoke, she saw his mounting excitement, and his wistfulness. He yearned to live the life he envied her for pursuing, and by the time she finished describing her plan, his face had flushed. His own eyes danced with eager anticipation. "If you go tonight, and put yourself at such risk," he said, speaking suddenly, "then I'm going with you."

Chapter Eighteen

He pleaded with her. "It's better that I'm along. Oh, don't you see? You'll have a protector. We can both put out to sea, and if they catch us, the worst they can do is make us work. It's what I've always wanted anyway, but my uncle still insists that I stay home and learn the business . . . study accounting and all that."

Maddie's eyes met his. "I know," she said, speaking softly. The move, she knew, would be good for both of them. His thwarted wanderlust was driving him half mad. She saw too that while he showed great physical bravery, he lacked moral courage. Though nearly full-grown, he feared the force of his uncle's personality. Unless he took a brave step now, he would spend his life

202

doing what he hated, just because his guardian willed it. She could be his goad. He needed to find his own path, and she wanted a traveling companion, someone to stay with her in the dangerous new lands to which she would travel. The Atwoods might curse her, but in the end, if they loved Peter, they would come to understand.

By then they had hurried out of the room and down into daylight. As they passed, they glanced to the man who lay motionless in their path out through the hall. She recognized him at once as the one who had led her here. She wondered in passing how much Mathias had paid him for the service. "I want to thank you, Peter." Suddenly breathless, she glanced to him with genuine gratitude. "I hate to think what would have happened to me, if . . ."

"Well, you're doing a pretty good job of saving me," he retorted, smiling at her. "I was trying to think of some way out, but I would never have latched onto the idea of simply stowing away."

The cart drew up to the house, into the drive, and clattered around back to the stables. Peter helped her down and led her gallantly toward the kitchen door. "I'll see you get the clothes you need. They'll be in your room by this evening."

"When shall we meet?" She raised her eyes to him.

"How about midnight?" he replied. "Down here by the stable gate."

With no further words, they parted, spending the rest of the evening pretending business as usual. This proved difficult at times. At dinner, Flora asked Maddie what she had learned about her husband that day, but Maddie only shrugged, feigning discouragement. It broke her heart to have to lie to her friend, or even to mislead her subtly, but she knew she had no choice. If any of them even suspected that she might try to join her husband out in the West Indies, they would have the wit to figure out at once how she intended accomplishing it without any money. Maddie resolved then and there to leave a note behind. No doubt one of the servant girls would find it the following morning. In the letter, Maddie would beg her friend's forgiveness. She would explain as best she could why she had gone off without even so much as a good-by. She could only hope Flora would understand. She would miss Flora, and think of her often. She hoped someday she'd be able to see her again.

The evening dragged by. Each hour seemed to go slower than the one before. By nine, Maddie could stand to remain downstairs no longer. Making small talk under such circumstances drained too much energy. It took all her self-discipline to act as if nothing had happened, when in truth she was bursting with excitement and nearly beside herself. She had to get away. Claiming a headache, Maddie begged to be excused. She threw Peter a glance, then bade the rest of them all goodnight. With a sigh of relief, she hurried upstairs.

She found the clothes Peter had smuggled into her room folded neatly on a chair. On top of the pile they formed rested a pair of scissors. With these, she would cut off her long feminine locks.

She set the scissors aside to examine the garments she was to wear. A coarsely woven shirt, tattered kneebreeches, and darned stockings—perfect for her masquerade as a poor but honest boy stowing away on board ship. Anything better would arouse suspicion if they were caught.

Maddie felt a rush of admiration for Peter's intelligence. She knew he had probably found an identical outfit for himself, probably from an indentured servant in trade for something better. Maddie smiled. No doubt he had been dreaming and planning about making such an escape for years.

Silently blessing him, Maddie slipped out of her dress. Heart pounding eagerly now, she stepped into the pants, then pulled on the shirt, stockings, and shoes. When she had finished, she stood before the mirror examining the profile of her body. In these clothes, she did indeed cut the figure of a boy. The blouson style of her shirt and the tattered waistcoat hid the swelling of her breasts. Her hips, blessedly slim, lost themselves in those baggy trousers. All she needed now was to cut her hair. To prepare herself for that, she wrapped a towel around her neck. With trembling hands, she lifted the scissors to her hair.

As she stared into the mirror, she sighed. Her hair, when combed and unbraided, hung lush and beautiful below her shoulders. She hated the thought of losing it. The promise of Henri, however, sustained her. Only for him was the sacrifice worth it. She closed her eyes, took a great shuddering breath, and opened them again. Very bravely, she pressed the blades around a thick hank of hair. She winced as it fell with a plop onto the floor.

Half an hour later, Maddie examined her new appearance in the mirror. Dressed in those clothes, and shorn of all but the innermost few inches of hair, she looked more than ever like a handsome boy. With a pang, she wondered if Henri would even recognize her when she saw him again.

From downstairs, she heard the great clock in the hall shifting its gears in readiness to boom out the hour. A clang, and then its basso profundo voice chimed eleven times.

Maddie knew she must be on her guard now. The time was almost here. She had promised to meet Peter out back at midnight, and she knew she dared not be late, for fear he'd lose his nerve. She spent the remaining three-quarters of an hour writing a long note to her friend Flora. When she had finished, she gathered the few things she was taking with her and slipped from the room. Barely able to contain her excitement, she padded toward the back door. Taking care to unlatch it quietly, she slipped outside into the night.

Peter too had been eager. Already he waited for her, pacing about like a caged animal and wringing his hands, fearful, perhaps, that she might change her mind, anxious that she shouldn't. He was likewise dressed in ragged clothes. "Oh, I'm so glad you're here!" he greeted her, with obvious relief.

"Shhhhh!" Maddie raised a finger to her mouth to quiet him. After glancing around to make sure his voice had aroused no one, she asked the question that had been worrying her. "How will we get there?" she whispered. She noticed the bulging bundle he carried tied up in a rope, and assumed it to be a change of clothes.

"We'll have to walk, I'm afraid." He took her arm and led her down the front walk toward the street beyond. "I was afraid to arouse anyone's suspicions by hitching up the cart," he said aloud in a normal tone of voice, though cautiously softer than usual.

"It's all right," she replied with a shrug. "We're not all that far away." In any case, the soft night air would clear her head.

They moved downward from the luxurious outskirts of town where the Atwoods made their home, toward the district where the common folk lived. As they drew closer to the older, shabbier part of town, and the harbor district, the wide tree-planted streets narrowed. Buildings instead of trees lined them on both sides. The paths were dark. Only the sound of a lone baby crying broke the silence covering them like a shroud. Walking around, they saw no one but themselves up at this hour—not even a town crier seemed to be out at that time of night. For the sake of caution, however, she and

Peter stayed to the back streets and alleys.

"We're almost there," he reassured her.

Maddie nodded. She needed no such comfort, but suspected that he did. "I know," she replied. "You seem to forget I've been down here before."

"Oh, so you have."

By then, they could hear water slurping up between the pilings and jetties of the harbor. Faint from beyond the town's sheltered cove rumbled the distant rhythm of surf. "Do you know which dock it's at?"

"Yes," Peter nodded. "My uncle doesn't realize it, but I make a point of knowing exactly at what pier each of his ships is harbored, when it comes in, and when it sets sail. I know, because I've always dreamed of doing exactly this." He gave a short, self-disgusted chuckle. "But how could I have guessed," he added, "that I'd be doing it with the company and encouragement of a girl?"

Maddie smiled. "You'll have to forget that now, Peter," she said. "In fact, don't even say the word 'girl' around me, except the way you would to any other randy young lad. Remember too, my name's no longer Maddie, but 'Mather' instead. That's close enough to cause confusion, I think, should you accidentally slip." She could have told him she was no ordinary girl, but instead the bride of a pirate, but she held her tongue. The fewer who knew what Henri was, the better, so far as she was concerned.

Peter nodded, then grabbed her arm to pull her into another direction. "This way!" he whispered. "And be very quiet. With luck, their watchman will be asleep. Just in case he's alert, though, we ought to be extra careful."

As they stepped from behind the buildings down by the water, Maddie got her first unobstructed view of the ship that would take them both south—Peter to adventure, and her to Henri.

It bobbed wide and huge in the water beside its wooden dock. Both anchor and lines secured it. Its hulk of painted wood loomed a dark, almost pitch-black silhouette against the night's purple glowing dimness. Only its sail, half drawn and hanging flaccidly from a crossbeam, caught and reflected back a pale glow from the stars.

They stole closer, moving as softly as possible across the pier's wood surface. Maddie stared at the great beast now in awe. Though she had seen ships before, she had never encountered one so big. A ship like this was a small city in itself, a floating colony to venture into open sea. Maddie stared, awed at the way its size dwarfed a little gondola floating nearby. It even made the ship that saved her and Henri from the storm that distant night look tiny by comparison.

It was still firmly anchored and tied, and a plank sloped downward from its deck. Men had left the *Anadeen* to go into town to drink and spend time with friends and wenches there, and for their sake, the walkway remained easy access for those who wanted to return at a later hour. They climbed up the plank and on board ship.

Almost immediately, they saw the watchman standing with back to them, silhouetted against the night. He stood facing outward toward land, staring, it seemed, to where the harbor curved away into sea. In his hand he held a pipe. A flare of fire went up from his hand as he relit it. Puffing contentedly as he drank in the reassuring sight of land, he never noticed the intruders who had slipped on board.

At sight of him, they both crouched down. Their part of the deck lay in deep shadows which helped, since neither felt like taking any unnecessary chances. They crept past, hiding themselves as they moved behind some boxes piled on deck. These would either be set ashore, or carried, perhaps tomorrow, down into the hold. For the time being, however, they made a wonderful hiding place.

"What do we do now?" whispered Maddie. She glanced at Peter with wide, questioning eyes. He loved ships and the sea. Surely he'd know better what to expect on them than she. Her hunch proved correct. Perhaps from all the months and years he had fantasized such a thing happening to him, he had worked it all out.

"We'll make it over to where they hold the lifeboats," he said, still whispering. Maddie nodded. It seemed a good enough plan to her. With him leading the way, they padded past the sentry to the boats.

Maddie saw at once what fine hiding places they'd be. Each was large enough to hold ten men. The crew had stored them upside down. The empty space underneath those bulging sides and curved bottoms formed wooden tents for Maddie and Peter to crawl into.

Once safely in hiding inside, he smiled at her. All she saw of it, however, was the dim flash of his teeth. "This is better than I expected," he whispered. "And with luck, we may ride all the way to Jamaica without anyone on board being the wiser."

A sudden uncomfortable thought raised Maddie's apprehension. "What'll we do for food?" She stared at him, suddenly angry at herself for not thinking. "And water?"

"Don't worry," he replied. "I have skin flasks of water, about three pounds of cheese, and some bread." Maddie sighed gratefully. So that was what he carried in his bundle. *Good for him!*

"But what if we run out?" she whispered, suddenly anxious again.

Peter reached from darkness to pat her hand. "Don't

worry so much," he replied. "If necessary, we can probably get more from the galley. If it's like other ships, that's down below, and I think I know exactly where." He smiled. "We won't go any hungrier than the crew, and all we'll want for is rum."

Night passed into morning. Light crept in under the edges of their lifeboat, so that by noon they could see much more than just each others' dim and shadowed forms. Maddie glanced to her friend. "When will they be setting sail?"

"Today," he replied, "as soon as they finish loading—at least, according to Uncle Josiah's schedule. Until then, I hope, they'll all assume back home that we're out looking down by the harbor, as usual."

Almost at once, a shout resounded from below. A cry went up for all hands to come back aboard. Footsteps pounded on the decks, and even where they crouched, they could feel the vibrations. Voices, rising in excitement, shouted to one another on the pier.

The general bustle mounted for awhile, and then, the ship finally gave a lurch. It rocked in the suddenly disturbed waves, then began to move. Maddie felt a sensation of looseness underneath her belly as she half-lay, half-crouched in her hiding place.

"Well, it's done!" What she could see of Peter's face looked triumphant. "Once we're out to sea, there'll be no dragging us back."

As the ship glided toward open sea, the sounds of shore faded into the cries of birds. The ship's fittings creaked, and the water gurgled below. In the harbor, at the water-facing edge of Boston, the air had smelled of cooking. The atmosphere had stunk of unwashed mens' bodies, and of discarded fish parts left to decompose in the summer's heat. The harbor shore had smelled of spices, too—all manner of them, both rare and common. The fragrance of coffee mingled with them, and chocolate. The harbor was a magic place to her—one where all the peoples of the world met and mingled by way of their merchandise. As the ship glided into open sea, however, all those odors faded. They drifted into the fresh tang scent of salt. The stink of rotting fish faded into the gentler odors of things still living in the water below.

As day passed into evening, Maddie blessed luck that neither she nor Peter was inclined to seasickness, for nausea and its result would have created an unbearable mess. Finally, night fell. Maddie slipped out of hiding. With relief, she stood among the overturned hulks of lifeboats and savored merely being out in the open again. The fresh air smelled good to her. The night, though dark, seemed beautiful.

The water below was black underneath the heavens, but a moon, glowing in a thin, silvered crescent, highlighted the ripples with pinpoints of diamond brightness. The two stowaways grew to love the darkness. By day, they concealed themselves, not daring to move. By night, however, they stole a few, luscious moments of freedom.

They ate sparingly of their food and drank as little water as possible. Even so, by the end of a week, they had used up all the food Peter had brought along. They fasted for two days and would have gone longer, but their water had fallen dangerously low as well.

As soon as night came, he turned to her. "I'll slip down into the galley and try to steal some more supplies for us," he whispered. Without further comment, he crept from under the boat into the night surrounding them.

An hour passed, and then another hour, or maybe it only seemed so. No matter what, Peter did not return, and by daybreak, Maddie climbed back under the lifeboat all alone.

Another day passed, and she ran out of water. By then, hunger had subsided to a dull ache, but her thirst intensified. Her throat burned. At dusk of the second night, she heard Peter's voice outside calling to her softly.

"Where have you been?" she cried, then started to crawl out to meet him.

"No, stay there." From where he crouched, he handed her a cup. To her relief, he had filled it with water. "I'm sorry I couldn't lay hands on any food. This is the best I could do."

"What happened?" She stared at him, disappointed and bewildered that he could have failed so.

"I got caught." He glanced uneasily over his shoulder. "And they've put me to work. I wanted to come back to you yesterday, but they were watching. Tonight was my first chance."

"Oh, Peter, what are we going to do?"

"Jump ship when we get to Port Royal, and find out from there where your husband is in Bermuda." Peter shrugged. "There's little else we can do. With luck, I'll be able to slip you enough food and water to keep you going until then."

Maddie smiled grimly. "With luck . . ." she chuckled. "Our luck hasn't run all too well."

"So here is where I find you !" Suddenly, a deep and booming voice startled them both. Maddie drew back at once into her shelter, while Peter leaped to his feet. Heavy boots set up a clatter as their intruder strode over to where Peter stood, too paralyzed to move.

Chapter Ninteen

"You plan to steal a lifeboat and sail home, boy?" the voice rumbled, ominous and mean. "Or maybe it's someone you've come to meet up here. I saw how you slipped away with that water cup in your hand."

Hamlike fists grabbed hold of the boat under which Maddie cowered. She stifled the scream that threatened to tear out as those same hands flung the boat up and away from her. She crouched exposed and terrified. Her eyes raised from boot level to the uniform of a ship's officer.

The man spat in disgust. "God's Death, another stowaway . . . Pah! Just what we don't need! Well, you'll have to work your way over with this other young scoundrel here, then make your own way back. And when I say work, I mean *work!* Now, what's your name, boy?"

Maddie answered him in as deep a voice as she could. "Mather, sir," she said respectfully, in order to placate him.

"Well, Mather, you'll be up at dawn, swabbing the decks, and after that, you'll bring breakfast on a tray to Captain Tillotson, and when you've finished, I'll find some other work for you to do. Both of you damned young fools are going to slave your arses off all the way to Hell and gone."

Maddie did not reply. She felt grateful enough just to know she'd be getting regular rations of food again. As for hard work, it had never terrified her. All she dreaded now was the possibility that her new shipmates would somehow discover that she was no boy, but a woman.

During the following days, she learned that disguising her sex was far more difficult than she had imagined. She and Peter were to share a hammock below deck, each taking turns sleeping in four-hour shifts. Their bunkmates were a rowdy crew. All of them were older, with hard stringy bodies and beard-stubbled faces. One, more repulsive than most, with missing teeth and a single eye, seemed to take a special liking to Maddie. "Ye both be damned fools to stow away like you did," he said. As he talked, he stuffed a particularly rank-smelling tobacco into his pipe. He rocked back and forth on his hammock as he continued, "Damned fools both of ye, but then, I guess we all are. Get a little money, get drunk and spend it all, and have to come back to this." He gestured scornfully. "Back to this for all our stinkin' days." He reached for Maddie's arm. "But a pretty fellow like you can make money in other ways." He gave a throaty chuckle, then continued, "Some men really miss the wimmen once they get out here, but luckily not me. I always did have a taste fer boys—especially pretty ones like thee," he crooned familiarly, oblivious to the way Maddie pulled away. "Me, I'm a homely bastard, an' I knows it. I'll never get no where but with me money, but thee—" He grinned, exposing tooth-scattered gums. "Yer a fine lookin' lad. Almost as pretty as a wench, and there be plenty'd pay for a night in thy company."

Horrified at the thought, at its implications, Maddie recoiled. "I'll make my money honestly," she cried.

"Then ye be even more of a damned fool than I thought," he snorted almost gleefully. "But you'll change. You'll either stay pretty and get rich, or end up ugly and poor . . . like me." He began laughing.

Repelled by his very presence, Maddie hurried up to the main deck. Shortly later, she found Peter. "Peter, what are we going to do?" She glanced around. "Sleep-

214

ing down there with those men—it's impossible. One of them actually leches after me as a boy. How long can it be until they figure out what I am?" The tides and functions of a woman's body were different from any man's. The monthly changes alone could betray her.

Peter shrugged. "Pray we get a good strong wind to take us there fast," he replied. "I don't know, Maddie. I had hoped the problem wouldn't come up."

The day had started out bad and got much worse. The ship ran into a squall and no one slept for hours. Finally, when it was over, Maddie collapsed exhausted into her hammock and fell totally unconscious for hours. When she awakened, she realized almost at once that something was wrong. With mounting horror, she realized her blouse lay open and her breasts exposed. That repulsive old salt who had leched after her as a boy now leaned over the hammock where she lay. As his eyes met hers, he broke into a grin. "Now I knows the truth about ye, maidie," he said, "but I'll make ye a deal. Service me and I'll keep quiet." He reached, sliding his hand inside her blouse. With an angry cry, Maddie flung him away. She yanked herself up and fumbled as fast as she could to close the buttons of her shirt. She glanced around and saw that the only other man snored soundly in his hammock hanging over in a far corner. Unable to bear even being in her discoverer's presence, Maddie leaped to her feet. His hand, swift as lightening, closed around her wrist. "You're not going anywhere yet, maidie," he said. As he tried to force her down she slammed the heel of her fist into his jaw and shoved free.

His grip tightened, clamping viselike around her bones. In pain, Maddie cried out. In her struggles, she kicked a lamp which fell with a clatter onto the floor. Others, hearing the racket, peered down just as her discoverer stamped out the small blaze that had started from it.

"Hey, what's going on down there?" Their voices boomed out to echo in the enclosed space where she and the one-eyed man fought.

He grinned triumphantly at her. "What's it to be, maidie?" he whispered.

At sight of him, nausea welled up inside of her. She knew beyond all doubt that she could never bring herself to buy his silence that way. As he reached again for her breasts, she shoved his hand away. "Get away from me, pig!" she cried. Even imprisonment would be better than making love to him.

"What's going on?" cried yet another. Even as he called out, he descended the ladder from above to see, for himself.

"We got us a woman on board, Jake," her attacker cried out in falsely righteous dismay. "This one here ain't no lad, but a lass."

The second man stopped short and stared at Maddie with horror widened eyes. "A woman . . . ? It's a miracle we haven't gone up on the rocks somewhere."

Almost instantly the word spread, until it seemed that the entire ship droned with it. Maddie stared with horror as they gathered around, each crewman eyeing her with varying degrees of hostility, interest, and dismay. But fear ruled all other emotions.

Not that any of them wouldn't have taken her to bed, had they been ashore. None would have spared a rowdy remark if she had merely passed them by on the street, but on board ship, superstition had taken grip of their reason. A woman meant bad luck. Her presence meant to them a storm in open sea, with waves like moving walls of water to wash them overboard and splinter their mainmasts. A woman brought rocks, and treacherous outlying shoals. To them all, a woman on board invited death, and they had just found out they had been living with Death since the ship had first set sail from Boston harbor.

"You . . . damn you!" one of them, suddenly an enemy, cursed her.

"We'll take her to the captain," a cooler head said. "Let him decide what to do with her."

"What about the other one?" cried yet a third. "He may be a wench, too."

"We'll strip him and see for ourselves."

Strong arms lifted her up the ladder onto deck. There they carried her along in a living wave to the captain's quarters. They cursed her, while bemoaning their own bad luck.

The emergency was too serious for amenities. Without bothering to knock, they kicked his door open and flung her inside. Their strength catapulted her so hard that she fell sprawling at his feet. "We got a woman on board, Captain!" cried one, and the general hubbub of voices mingling did not drown out their words, or their fear.

The captian glanced from them to her, and back to them again. "You are dismissed," he said.

"But what about her?" cried one.

He remained cool, and it was Maddie's greatest hope that he'd react sensibly, without the insane superstition of his crew. "I wish to interrogate the prisoner alone. Now please leave, but never fear, I shall take action."

"Throw her overboard!" cried one. Another shouted out for her to be clapped in irons.

"That will be my decision," he replied, and his voice hardened. "Now leave." Its tone invited no argument, so his men obeyed, grumbling among themselves as they filed from his quarters.

Once they were alone, Maddie raised her eyes to his face. She had met the man only when taking breakfast trays to him, and he had always scared her. He stood almost six feet tall, graying-blond of hair, with a strong, hard body. He fixed cold, blue eyes on her now. His face, red from sun and wind, had set in an expression angry, yet chilly calm. He studied her for several endless minutes. When he finally spoke, he did so with a hardness of tone that chilled her. "By what right do you intrude upon us, girl?" he asked. "You had a lot of nerve. I suppose you can offer some explanation?"

Forcing herself to be brave, Maddie fixed her eyes upon him. "I have indeed, sir," she replied, "though perhaps not one satisfactory to you."

"Well," he said, "I should like to hear of it." He fixed his icy eyes on her face.

"I am searching for my husband," she replied, "and I learned he is heading toward the West Indies. Someone who knows told me, you see. He said my Henri's ship set sail out of Boston only two days before I arrived."

The captain's eyes softened a little. "Perhaps he wanted to leave," he said. "You're a pretty lass, even disguised as you are in breeches, with your hair cut like a boy's. But some live to regret a marriage made in haste. Perhaps your husband did likewise. The last thing he may want is a wife following after him."

"Oh, no!" she cried. "It's not like that at all. We had only just married, you see. We were on a ship heading south, toward Boston, but off the Cape a storm blew up. To add to our troubles, wreckers lured us ashore by flashing lights." She shuddered. "Oh, it was an awful sight, sir, to see a fine ship like that split apart on the rocks to become little more than scrap. A sickening thought indeed."

"Is that when you lost your husband?" He seemed more interested now. Her story had captured his imagination. Perhaps he too had encountered wreckers.

Maddie nodded. "He was helping the crew when it all

happened. I never saw him again."

"Well, how do you know he's still alive? Wreckers have a way of leaving no survivors, you know."

Maddie shrugged. "It was only a feeling I had at first, so I made inquiries. Then I met someone in Boston who knew Henri. This man saw him after I last did, and he said that Henri had set sail on his own ship out of Boston harbor heading southward to the West Indies. In any case, I would have known. When someone loves the way he and I love each other, one just . . . *knows.*"

"Your husband is a ship's captain then?" Interest heightened in the man's frosty blue eyes. "Perhaps I even know the fellow. Who is he?"

Suddenly she realized that Henri and Captain Tillotson had sailed the same waters down there. She felt a sudden clutch of fear. If what Seumas Hawkes said was true about Henri's reputation, then this good captian would surely have heard of him. She stared now, dismayed and unable to speak.

"I asked you a question, madam." His voice grew cold again. "What is you husband's name?"

"R-Rohan," she whispered. "Henri de Rohan." She added irrelevantly, "He is a Huguenot."

"Rohan!" The man practically spat out Henri's name, following it with a string of obscenities. "A Huguenot perhaps, but a pirate most certainly! Why, the scoundrel robs everyone. Even I myself, while captain of a fleet less well-gunned, have lost a ship to him and his lackies. It was only luck what saved me from being sold or killed!"

To Maddie's horror, Captain Tillotson advanced on her now with suddenly hate-burning eyes. He reached with both hands and grabbed her by the shoulders. Maddie cried out as his fingers dug into her flesh.

He shook her roughly. Maddie stared now terrified, into anger-reddened eyes. "You almost fooled me, woman," he said. "I almost felt sorry for you . . . you, Rohan's wife!" He flung her back against the wall and pinned her unmoving with his strength. "What are you really?" He faced her with deadly quietness now. "A spy?"

"No!" She stared into his face. "If I were a spy, would I admit who I am? I'd lie and say another name. And would he, who loves me, put his wife into the danger of spying upon his enemy?" She glared at him defiantly now. "Indeed, I didn't even know what Henri was until after I married him, but I love him anyway."

His eyes narrowed as he studied her face. Maddie liked not at all what she read in his. She could not tear her gaze away. She stared in horrified fascination. "What are you going to do to me?" she whispered.

Without speaking, he raised his hand to her face. Two fingertips touched her lips. "Woman," his words, when he finally uttered them, came through clenched teeth. "Thy mouth has been forever poisoned for kissing his, thy soul forever tainted. Your really ought to die."

Maddie stared, too terrified by his fury to speak. He continued, "You want to know what I shall do with you? Well, I'll tell you. I'll take you over to Hispaniola and sell you into indentured servitude to the Spaniards. I'm sure there are many among them who would be pleased indeed to own the bride of the one they call *El Diablo*."

Maddie's eyes widened in horror. "No . . . please. I know nothing . . . nothing at all about it. I married a man, not a devil. I've never even seen the West Indies; neither Jamaica, Bermuda, nor Hispaniola either. I am innocent of everything but loving my husband. I am no pirate. *Please!*"

Without answering, he reached to a cord hanging from the ceiling and yanked it. Within seconds, the first mate, the black-bearded officer who had discovered her presence aboard ship, appeared. He stepped inside the captain's quarters now and waited for instructions.

Maddie's heart plummeted when she saw Peter in chains behind him. The man's great hand had clenched around her friend's upper arm. With a growl, he pulled the boy inside. As Peter moved, the metal links clanked together creating a din with each step he took.

At sight of him, the captain spoke in hardened voice. "I want you to put this—this *baggage* in chains straightaway. When you've finished, take hold of that boy. Tie him to the mainmast and give him forty lashes. He knew all along what she was, yet brought her aboard anyway. For all I know, he's even another one of Rohan's lackeys."

Maddie's eyes widened and her heart plunged. She had not intended for Peter to suffer. Indeed, she had no idea that this might happen. "Why him?" she cried. "He has done nothing."

"He brought you aboard."

"He came with me. That's his only crime. He met me on the dock and assumed me to be a boy like himself," Maddie pleaded for her friend. She was willing, if necessary, to take the greater punishment in order to spare him. "It was at my urging that we sneaked on board. He only thought to stow away and have a little adventure. He had no idea that I was a woman, nor the wife of your enemy."

"No, Maddie . . . ." Peter tried to stop her. He moved forward, but the first mate, his hand still clamped on Peter's arm, yanked him roughly back.

Maddie ignored him. She whirled instead to the Captain to fix wide, pleading eyes on him. "He did not know till afterwards that I was a girl, and even then not that I was married to any but an ordinary seaman. Oh, sir, if you must punish someone so harshly, let it be me."

The captain's heart remained hardened. "You will both be punished, but each in your own way. If it was your idea all along as you tell, then he'll be whipped for his stupidity."

Maddie's eyes met Peter's. She saw reflected in them the same terror and dismay she felt herself. Panic threatened to overwhelm her, and she knew she must not allow herself to lose her head. She determined to save Peter from such misfortune, even if she herself suffered all the worse. After all, he'd still be at home, in the protected security of his loving family if it were not for her.

The first mate grabbed hold of her arm and gave it a tug. As he started to drag her out and below to her imprisonment, Maddie called out to the captain. "You work for Josiah Atwood, do you not?"

"What of it?" He half snarled at her now.

"No matter what Peter might have told you, his real name is Peter Atwood. He's Josiah Atwood's nephew, and his legal ward and heir."

To her dismay, the captain was not moved. "Aboard this ship, *I* am master. At sea, my word is law, not Josiah Atwood's, and as for the boy—he's damned lucky I'm merely ordering him whipped, instead of thrown overboard to drown." His eyes flashed cold fire as he glared at his mate. "Now take her. Take them both, and obey my orders."

"With pleasure, sir!" the man replied.

Maddie stared back at him in dismay as her captor dragged her toward the door. She glanced to Peter as she passed. Her eyes met his one last time, and in them she read soul-deep terror for what was to come.

Chapter Twenty

The first mate flung her into a small airless room far below the ship's main deck. Cut into the cell's heavy iron-reinforced door was a small barred window. Through it she could see, if she wanted to, the passage beyond.

The man faced her one last time before leaving. His great red hand still grasped tight around her arm as he spoke to her. "If it was up to me," he growled, "I'd fling ye both to the sharks. You've been nothin' but trouble to me, ever since the *Anadeen* set sail." He shoved her, pushing against the small of her back. Maddie cried out. As she crashed to her hands and knees, she heard him slam the door behind, leaving her completely alone. There she remained, doubled over on the floor. Lying motionless, she listened to footsteps clattering away into silence.

After the initial shock wore off, Maddie gathered her strength together and stood. To be sold into indentured servitude was a fate that horrified her.

Her own family's laborers had enjoyed good treatment. Her father was fair to them and kind by nature, since he believed all humans to be God's children. Only when they proved lazy or dishonest did he ever resort to punishment. She knew, however, that too many indentured ones suffered a crueler fate. Indeed, most fared worse than slaves.

Slaves, bought outright for life, were considered valuable property. Their owners, if they had any sense, would treat them well, so that they'd live a long time and thus pay back their purchase price with profit. An indentured servant, however, was only bound for a span of years, and many of their temporary masters flogged as much work out of them as they could. Her own fate would be much worse than theirs, since Tillotson intended bonding her over to her husband's enemies.

Quivering now with desperation, Maddie's first thought was to escape. If she could but free herself from this cell, hide until the ship moved within sight of land, then fling herself overboard, she'd have a chance to remain free. Even drowning in ocean waves would be better than what the captain intended for her. With any luck at all, she'd float and splash her way to shore. Even if she found herself in wild Indian territory, she suspected that even the most savage of redskins would prove less coldly merciless than the captain and crew of this now-hated ship.

As her heart pounded, Maddie glanced around. Hope died, however, at what she saw. Heavy wooden beams supported a wall of rough-hewn planking. Only through the window cut in the door could she look out, and as for the cell itself, she could see that other prisoners had languished here before her. One of these, perhaps unbearably bored, had scratched his initials into one beam with his thumbnail, or perhaps with a nail worked loose.

At the thought of finding a weakened part of the wall, Maddie's heart fluttered with eager young hope. She peered around, but in the cell's twilight dimness, could see little. To help her search along, she ran her hand over each board, groping for something, anything, that might help her escape. After perhaps an hour of fruitless search, however, she gave up. With a sigh, she slid off her feet and hunched disconsolately on the floor.

Suddenly, from above, she heard a sound which congealed her blood—a cry, unmistakably from a man. Her heart almost stopped. She listened more carefully now, scarcely daring to breathe. A whine ending in a moisty splat against something soft, followed by another scream, chilled her flesh. The voice shrilled out pain and suffering, and as it repeated alternately with the lash, Maddie's stomach churned. She recognized the cry. Though anguished and distorted almost beyond recognition, the voice was certainly Peter's. Nephew of the fleet's owner or no, the captain of this ship had chosen to discipline him as he had threatened.

The sound, repeated over and over, became unbearable. Maddie cringed from it. She could almost feel the lash upon her own back. She gave an anguished moan of sympathy and tried to block out his cries by holding the palms of her hands against her ears. Why couldn't she have slipped on board this ship alone? Why had she brought poor Peter along?

Even through her muffling hands, she heard the lash whining its hateful chant, as it sliced through the air to land on his flesh. Eventually, however, she heard only the lash, and no longer Peter crying out. His silence was worst of all. She pictured him unconscious, his back a mass of clotted blood and welts. Her imagination running wild—she could even see him dead, callously thrown overboard to become food for whatever flesh-eating creatures might lurk below.

She would have ached with pity for anyone going through what Peter was, but knowing it to be her friend, and worse, believing herself responsible, Maddie especially suffered. Regret tormented her. If he had never met her, he'd still be safe in Boston. He might be bored, but what did that really matter? At least he'd be fed and warm. Certainly he'd never have known the sting of a whip upon his back.

Tears filled Maddie's eyes. She had encouraged Peter,

and all for the wanting of a traveling companion. What would become of him now? Would he end up down here, imprisoned for the duration of their journey, or worse, would Peter Atwood, heir to the largest shipping company in all New England, be sold like her as an indentured servant to some plantation in the wilds of the West Indies?

Finally, mercifully, the noise ended. The cries of pain and the lash faded into silence. It came as a relief at first, but turned, as it continued, even more forboding.

Worry haunted her now. Where was he? What had become of him? Was he all right, or had those angry sailors killed him? Endless hours passed that way. Finally, exhaustion set in. Even though guilt and dread tormented her, Maddie fell into a fitful, uneasy sleep. She had no idea for how long.

Later, she awakened to the sound of movement outside in the corridor. She bolted upward with a start. Her eyes widened and her heart pounded in sudden fear.

She scrambled to her feet. On trembling legs, she crept across the narrow confines of her cell to peer outward into the darkness beyond. But strain as she did to see through it, the ink-black space revealed no answers to her. She could not see who, or what, approached. All she could do was make out the dimmest shadows of a man moving toward her. He carried in his hand a hooded candle. Maddie waited. Her heart pounded horribly, but she was too terrified to do anything but stand motionless where she was and watch.

Suddenly, a sound cut through her very being. Its suddenness nearly made her cry out. "Ssssst— *Maddie!*" A whisper whose very unexpectedness nearly sent her collapsing to the floor. Eyes wide with hope, she clung with her fists to the bars. "Who is it?" she whispered back.

"It's me . . . *Peter*."

Maddie nearly fainted with relief. "Oh, Peter. I was so afraid for you. Are you all right?"

"I'm alive," he replied. "That's about all I can say." He turned the candle around so that its light faced toward him.

Maddie gasped at the sight of him. He was no longer the boy she knew but a man turned bitter. He had aged, it seemed, at least ten years. His features were drawn and haggard now. His hair hung in limp and weary-looking strings, while in his eyes she saw a hardness that hadn't been there before. Maddie sensed at once that the punishment had not broken his spirit. The cruelty he survived had transmuted it into a cold, bitter anger.

He bent down when he got to her door, so that she could see only his hunched-over back. While she waited, she heard metal scrape against metal as a key turned. He stood back up, then opened the door slowly. As he moved, she could see how blood had stained his shirt. The door's unoiled hinges creaked. Maddie's muscles tensed at the sound, and she made a grimace of fear. She dreaded someone might hear, for in the night's silence it seemed a terrible din.

"Peter," she whispered, "dear Peter." She slipped out of the cell into the hall to join him. "How did you . . . ?"

"I killed the guard they posted and took his keys." He glanced back the way he had come. In his eyes, she caught a furtive glitter.

"What they did to you . . . I could hear it all. The lash, your cries of pain . . ." Her voice trembled.

Peter's jaw set. His face had taken on an angry cast. "Don't cry for me, Maddie," he said. "You did what you could to prevent it. In any case, they're going to live to regret it. I swore to that—forty times . . . once for each lash that dug into my back." He grabbed her by the wrist with his free hand and pulled her along. "Now hurry, but for God's sake, be quiet!''

Without bothering to explain, he led her, half running, up to the main deck above. She followed, not even daring to ask what he had planned.

As they rounded a corner, Maddie saw the watchman standing alone. Startled, she stopped short, but Peter tugged her along. The man stood facing outward toward the sea. They moved as quietly as they could to avoid rousing his attention. Suddenly, a board creaked as they passed. The guard whirled. His eyes glittered with recognition as he saw them. Before he had the chance to cry out, however Peter lunged. With a snarl, her friend hurtled at the guard with both hands out, ready to grab. His momentum knocked the man off balance, and he landed on top. Arms and legs sprawling as he fell with the enemy, Peter pummeled him with both clenched fists. The man groaned under the force of his blows. Maddie's eyes widened in horror, as she saw the way he seemed to relish reducing the man's face to a jellied mass of blood and bruised, swollen skin.

"Peter, that's enough!" She stared shocked at the boy's newfound viciousness. He had hurt the guard far more than was necessary for their escape. Indeed, he seemed more like a savage right then, than a young gentlemen raised in civilization.

Feeling faint, Maddie clung to a rope to keep from toppling over. She had never seen this vicious streak in him before, and it frightened her. She had been afraid at first that the guard would somehow rise up and overpower her friend. For once, however, luck was with them. Surprise had stripped the man of all his strength. Under Peter's weight, he writhed once or twice upon the ground, then lay still. Maddie crept toward him on legs suddenly shaking. "You didn't *kill* him, did you?" she whispered.

With a start, Maddie raised her eyes to him. She saw

again for a second the face of a stranger—hard-featured, with tightly set jaw and angry eyes. Almost at once, however, his expression softened. "Oh, Maddie," he whispered, and took her hand. He led her to the lifeboats. When they reached them, he turned. "Help me lower this thing down," he said. He had cut free a coil of rope that used to be tied to the mainmast. He wrapped it around one boat's oar sockets. Maddie helped by holding part of the extra rope while Peter lowered their escape craft to the water. "I hope you can climb down this," he said. He glanced to her, and in the moonlight, she saw the suddenly doubtful expression of his face.

Maddie shrugged in reply. "I don't have much choice, do I? At least I know from watching how it's done." Luckily she had not changed out of the breeches she had been wearing when they had discovered her true sex.

"I'll help you down to it." He tied the rope's other end to a length of the railing. Maddie climbed over, and as she straddled it, he held her steady. "Just cling tight to it with your feet as you descend," he whispered. "If you don't, you'll get rope burns."

Maddie gritted her teeth and nodded. With slow, painful movement, she began to descend.

Peter was right about the difficulty. Hanging on was a struggle. If she loosed the grip with her feet, her weight would drag her down too fast. If she loosed it with her hands, she'd hurtle into the night black sea below.

Maddie fought her way slowly downward. Sometimes she slipped, and each time burned her hands horribly. Tears of pain welled up in her eyes, but she squeezed them out and clenched her teeth to keep from crying out loud. The last thing she needed right then was to let some silly tears blind her so that she could no longer see the lifeboat. Below, the tiny wooden dinghy in which they would make their escape grew larger, ever larger. She was almost right upon it now. Suddenly above, she heard a shot. Someone had discovered their attempted escape!

Chapter Twenty-one

"Hurry, Maddie!" Peter's voice screamed out at her from above. As she dangled, she let her eyes skim down and saw that only a few feet of rope remained between her and their boat. Her glance darted up again, just in time to see her friend climb over the ship's rails, then slide down until he hung just above her. He teetered midair while crewmen, armed with guns and sticks, gathered above. The hempen coil gave a yank as one clambered over to follow them down. "Maddie, hurry—*please*!"

She knew she had to get out of his way quickly. As she slid those remaining few feet, she hardly noticed how the rope burned into her palms. Suddenly Maddie heard a cry above. Her eyes widened at what she saw. Crouched in the boat now, clinging to its sides, she stared with horror at Peter hurtling through space.

He landed with a splash in the water. It seemed forever until he finally surfaced again several feet away, and even as he sputtered, blowing water from his mouth, his arms raised and he began to splash over to her. Crying out encouragement, Maddie leaned to him, while above, two more men had gathered on deck. Even down here, she heard their voices thundering through the nighttime's silence.

"Peter, hurry!" Maddie screamed at him. The rope

bound their boat to the ship like an umbilical cord, and she had no knife. The knot nearest her was slippery, she saw, and tightly pulled. Her hands trembled too much to untie it. If anything happened to Peter, she'd be trapped.

Peter splashed madly to catch up with her. Finally he drew close enough for her to grab at him. Both her hands clung to one of his arms. He struggled to hoist himself up over the rim of their dinghy. With a great heave, he flung himself inside. He cursed breathlessly as he swung his legs up and over and the boat nearly capsized. He steadied it quickly, however, and even while it still rocked back and forth from his momentum, he reached for the knife hanging in its sheath from his belt.

"Peter, hurry!" Maddie glanced up to see a musket aimed at them.

"Those bloody bastards!" Peter slashed through the rope holding them prisoner to the mother ship, then jammed his knife back into its sheath. In one swift movement, he grabbed both oars. Using them as poles, he shoved them frantically away. "Bless the darkness, Maddie," he whispered. "In daylight, we wouldn't stand a chance."

Suddenly a shot exploded. Maddie screamed as a molten ball of fire whined toward them. Blessedly, it missed. It hurtled instead into the sea nearby. Waves splashed up from its impact, knocking them about, but doing no harm, and steam sizzled into the air.

Another fiery thunder exploded from a musket's barrel, and then a third. Both shots landed frighteningly close. Maddie clenched the rim of their boat with both hands and hardly noticed how white her knuckles had grown.

For a while, the shots missed, but then their luck changed. One ball of fire found its mark. Maddie screamed as it tore like a shooting star right toward

231

them. As it passed, part of its outer halo of light and heat burst like a fiery explosion into Peter's shoulder. The boy's mouth fell open in surprise as its momentum thrust him backwards. He crashed on his shoulder blades against the boat's wooden rim. At once, his hands flung out to the sides. His fingers uncurled, letting loose the oars.

Instinct propelled Maddie forward. She lunged for the oars, grabbed them as they dropped, then scrambled frantically to begin rowing. She had no idea what gave her such unnatural strength, but she blessed it. All she knew was that the two of them must escape, or else be dragged back into the ship, whipped, and killed or sold into slavery.

As she struggled to escape, she prayed. Her Puritan soul clung to the hope that a Greater One might help. Aloud, breathless as she struggled, she beseeched the merciless God who had cast her out to take pity now in this most dire moment of need.

Either by God or by chance, a cloud blessedly moved across the sky. Darkness obscured the moon once again and blotted out the light it had cast upon the ocean below. "Dear God, please, for a little while longer, keep it dark, and please,"—she added futilely—"let my friend's wound turn out to be a small one." Tears streamed down her face as she pleaded to the vast silence around her. "I couldn't bear to think of him dead—not when I was the one who lured him out here. *Please!*"

Maddie stared at Peter in horrified fear. He lay on his back now, moaning aloud with his eyes closed, blood spreading in a thick, dark stain across his chest. His lips had parted. Sweat glistened on his skin. Maddie wanted to help, to comfort him, and do something to dress his wound, but she could still hear the muskets still firing at them, so since she had no other choice, Maddie rowed.

Fighting fatigue, she struggled to get them safely away. She gasped air into her burning lungs and cringed with pain. Finally, when they had drifted beyond range of the ship's weapons, Maddie relaxed. Still catching her breath, she bent forward to gaze at her friend.

"Peter," she whispered, "are you in much pain?"

Without speaking, he nodded.

"Can-can you talk?" Now that they had more or less escaped form the *Anadeen*, Maddie realized she had no idea what Peter's plan might be for getting them to safety.

At her question, he nodded, "Yes." He could barely gasp the word aloud.

"Now that we're off the ship, where do we go?" Or had he merely trusted to luck?

"Look around you, Maddie." He could barely speak, but he struggled to make himself heard. "You'll find some spots on the horizon, patches down near the water, darker than anywhere else. It's land. Some kind of land, and that's where we've got to go." He tried to smile at her, but could only grimace. His body convulsed, and then he coughed. Looking up, Maddie saw what he meant. At sight of it, her heart pounded with relief. A tiny rim stretched along the top of the ocean's far horizon. If they could only get to it, they'd be safe.

"Do you have any idea what it is? Where we're going?"

Peter only grunted. He had begun shivering now as well. Wet clothes clung to his trembling body. Salt water mingled with his spilled blood. She stared at him suddenly frightened. "Hang on, Peter!" she cried. "I'll get us there somehow . . . I hope," she added in a whisper, as she glanced back at the *Anadeen*. It floated in water some distance away from them now. Though the moon had come out from behind its cloud, a fog hazed their view of it. It settled in upon the mother ship as a mist, and thickened around their own dinghy.

Maddie glanced up with dismay to the land so far beyond. Darkness had been their friend, but it could turn into an enemy. Soon fog would block even the sight of that horizon. Not able to see, she might row the wrong way, or too far, and they'd be lost. Though exhausted, Maddie began to move again. Time was too precious to waste. A new determination gripped her. She'd get them there somehow. "Hang on, Peter!" she cried. All her will, all her strength poured into pushing those two oars.

Too rapidly, her surroundings faded. Air around them thickened into a blackish gray. In her desperate haste, she had drawn close enough to land to know that, if she could but keep going in the same direction, she'd probably hit the shoreline soon.

She endured, almost too exhausted to move, yet knowing she must. Wounded and wearing wet clothes, Peter would not last out the night, unless she got him dry and warm somewhere. Finally, blessedly, her oar struck a rock beneath the water's surface. Maddie had almost fallen asleep when it happened. She had been laboring in automatic motion, but when she felt the impact, her eyes sprang open again. Her heart pounded now, suddenly revived. She stood up from her spot in the boat. Balancing on spread legs, she poked one oar into the water below. When its paddle stuck solid surface, she moaned with relief. She had gotten them somehow into the shallows lying just off shore.

With a sigh, Maddie settled back down. She rowed a little further until the bottom scraped against land. From there, she'd have to drag them ashore. To keep her clothes dry, so that Peter might wear them later, she slipped out of her shirt and breeches and left them neatly folded inside the boat. Naked, she climbed over its edge into the water, then with a groan pulled the little craft toward the beach.

The ocean felt cold against her naked skin. It washed around her, waist-deep. These were not the vicious waves that pounded the bluff-lined shores of New England, but instead a gentle current. It coaxed her toward shore, instead of lifting her high and hurtling her down.

Blessedly, the beach was smooth, not rock-strewn like those of Massachussets. Only a few large boulders here and there, but mostly sand to walk on, so it wasn't difficult to wedge the boat onto dry land. In the dark she could not see the terrain. She only knew it was solid and dry. It waited as a haven for them, and she blessed it.

Exhausted but not yet resting, she crouched down beside her friend. Peter still lay inside the boat. She saw with relief that he still breathed, but he seemed barely conscious. Though the wound on his shoulder had stopped bleeding, the bullet had torn a great patch of his flesh away and it looked bad. "Peter," she whispered. "Can you move?"

"I think so," he replied. "You'll have to help me though." His voice trembled as he spoke, and his teeth chattered. "Lift me up, will you, but be careful."

Timidly, Maddie moved to obey; she cringed to see him grimace in raw pain. The very sight of his suffering almost killed her nerve. She stared now at him with uncertainty. "Are you sure you want this?" She forgot even her own nakedness.

"Have I a choice?" His question reminded her of what she already knew. "No, Peter, I guess you don't." Leaning on her shoulder he stumbled up the beach until he could walk no longer. With a groan, he collapsed to the sand in a heap. Blessedly, the spot where he fell was high above the tide mark. The sand underneath felt warm to her bare feet, and dry. Maddie knew he'd be safe and comfortable here for the time being.

So much still had to be done. She left him where he lay and returned to the boat. Her trembling hands reached for the towrope, and she flung it over her shoulder. Groaning in exhaustion, she heaved forward. On trembling legs, she dragged it up from surf's edge. She slogged inch by inch across the soft, resisting sand to where her friend still lay.

By now she had a plan. She would use that boat as a shelter, just as they had done when first stowing away. When she had pulled it near enough, she let go of the rope. The dinghy dropped to the sand, a dead hulking weight, and lay where it fell.

When she had steadied herself once again, Maddie turned to Peter. Slowly, painfully, she peeled the wet, blood-soaked clothes from his body, replacing them with her own dry things, still folded in the boat. Her naked flesh glistened wetly under the night's dim glow. Her breasts had hardened from the chill. Tiny bumps had raised all over her. Suddenly, with a rush of heat spreading quickly, she sensed that Peter had come awake and was watching her. Startled, she whirled to him. Her lips parted in shocked surprise when she found his eyes open, and his gaze fixed upon her breasts and belly. His eyes seemed almost to burn into her flesh. While she stood, too shocked by her realization even to move away, they skimmed lower, down her firm, pale stomach to the rounded womanly swell of her hips.

Standing naked in front of him, Maddie blushed, painfully self-conscious now. Was it her imagination, or were his eyes lingering upon the blondish curling hairs underneath her belly and between her legs? Was he even trying to imagine what it might be like to press into the warm, moist haven hidden between her thighs? She saw now a swelling of his flesh that hadn't been there before, and it embarrassed her.

Suddenly ashamed, Maddie whirled from him. With

one swooping motion, she dropped to her knees and crouched, so that only her back remained to him. "Go to sleep, Peter," she whispered. She knew that, if she tried to speak aloud, her voice would tremble. Until this moment, she had never thought of him as anything but a boy—certainly not as a man. She wondered now if he had regarded her all along as a woman to be desired, or if he too had changed in this unexpected instant. Perhaps it came as much of a shock to him as well.

"Maddie, I . . . ."

"Go to sleep, Peter," Her voice came louder now, and firmer. Despite her struggle, or because of it, she had regained her self-control. "You've been hurt and you need to rest. I'll join you presently, and we both can . . . *sleep*." Her voice trembled upon that last word. In spite of all her suffering and exhaustion, she missed Henri more than ever. She ached to feel his arms around her. She had never forgotten the feel of his breath upon her skin, like a soft and secret caress. Nathan's love had done nothing to quench that fire. Neither would Peter's yearning. Gently, she lowered the boat over him as a shelter from night time's chill.

With heart pounding strangely fast, Maddie waited outside, shivering a little in the fog, as she listened for his breathing to soften into the even, regular rhythms that told her he had fallen asleep. Only then did she join him underneath. Exhausted, she fell into a troubled slumber.

She awakened at the first dim rays of dawn filtering underneath their shelter. Her first thought was for Peter. She glanced to him and saw with relief that he had survived the night. Something, however, either instinct or premonition, made her uneasy. Unable to bear lying where she was any longer, she slipped out, then stood looking around her. The sky above glowed pink and blue in the morning's light, and in it, she caught first glimpse of her surroundings. She saw a desolate driftwood-strewn beach. Behind it tangled the green of undergrowth and trees. Though richer in both color and abundance than the wild places of New England, the wilderness here seemed somehow threatening. Maddie guessed it to be because of its very unfamiliarity, rather than anything having to do with these woods themselves.

Taking a deep breath, she turned toward the sea. At once a cry of dismay escaped from her lips. Her heart fluttered with horror. She saw that the *Anadeen* loomed larger on the horizon than she remembered. "Oh, no!" she whispered. "They're coming for us!" Terrified for them both, Maddie flung the boat back and away from Peter to expose him now to the light. "Peter!" she cried. "Wake up!"

But Peter only groaned. He did not seem to know what was going on. Maddie saw to her horror that he lay barely conscious. His face flushed now with fever. When he opened his eyes, they fixed on her a glassy stare. "Oh, dear God!" she whispered.

With trembling hands, she pulled back his shirt to expose the bullet wound, now festering red and swollen. Panicked, Maddie glanced up again. The *Anadeen* had drawn still closer, blown by shore-seeking winds. While they had probably not yet spotted her and Peter, Maddie saw them all too well. She guessed with sinking heart that its crew intended to disembark at this unknown place to look for them.

Escape became her first priority. Maddie glanced back at the tangle of green beyond the beach and blessed luck. The wilderness that had been so threatening just moments ago now seemed a haven. Hiding would be easy in all that rambling undergrowth.

With a strength born of terror, Maddie grabbed Peter under the arms. Huffing and puffing, she dragged him moaning and painwracked, to where sand thickened into topsoil. Listening to his cries, screams of pain, and half-conscious moans, she knew she might be doing him serious damage. Only the realization that the *Anadeen's* crew would hurt worse gave her the strength to inflict such tortures upon him.

"I'm sorry, Peter, but they're coming for us, and we've got to hide!" She knew that his mind lay beyond understanding, but she tried to explain anyway, probably for her own sake more than his.

Once she had dropped him into the bushes and marked the spot, she scrambled back to their boat. She had been naked until now, but could stay that way no longer. She jammed her own legs into Peter's still-damp breeches. She tied the sleeves of his shirt around her waist. Come what may, she could not afford to lose those few precious scraps of cloth, nor the treasures of flint and steel he kept in his pockets.

The *Anadeen* was still far enough away. The little boat, half-hidden among the few boulders that littered this unfamiliar beach, probably remained hidden from view. *They must not find our dinghy!* The thought burned through Maddie's mind. *They must not!* Bent double, Maddie dragged it now as far as her strength could carry it from the spot where they had first landed. Huffing and puffing, she coaxed it off the beach to the forest's edge, then covered it with fallen branches, vines, and brush. She prayed their pursuers would not discover it there. If they did, she hoped they'd be content to take it with them, and not search for those who had stolen it.

Once finished, Maddie ran back to where she had abandoned Peter. She found him conscious now, though barely so. Still wracked from pain and fever, he stared at her with wild, uncomprehending eyes. "You have to do as I say, Peter!" Maddie glanced out toward the ocean, still visible from their hiding place. "Wake up—it's our only chance." She struggled to keep fear out of her voice, but failed. Her words trembled in spite of everything. "Now come!" She grabbed his good arm and yanked on it.

With a groan, Peter obeyed. He stumbled to his feet with difficulty, swayed, and almost collapsed as he struggled with her deeper into the forest. A few yards seemed to stretch for miles and take forever. Both of them struggled together against his pain. Both suffered together his fever. Finally, Maddie glanced back. Only when she could no longer see the ocean did she let him rest. The best chance, as she saw it, was for them to get as far from any animal or Indian trails as they could. Sheltered by forest, they could hide until the *Anadeen* and all its crew sailed away.

Finally, she noticed the way his knees buckled. She realized at once that Peter could go no further. With a sigh, she eased him down. She covered him with brush, and then went back and did her best to cover their trail of broken branches and weight-crushed undergrowth. Her greatest hope was that the crew of the *Anadeen*, being men of the sea, would overlook signs that a land-bound Indian, or even a fairly experienced white settler, would notice right away.

Within an hour, their pursuers had landed. Even from where they hid, Maddie could hear their voices. Men shouted to one another down the shoreline. Sometimes they cursed. Within a few minutes, Maddie realized that she had made one big mistake. She and Peter had left footprints in the sand leading directly to where they had stumbled from sandy beach into the woods. In covering their trail, she had forgotten to smooth these away. With sinking heart, Maddie realized that someone had noticed. She heard her enemies crashing from that spot through brush to search for them. Maddie prayed that they'd be harder to follow here than on the beach.

Peter had gotten worse by then. He had lapsed deeper into delirium. He had begun moaning and even sometimes mumbling aloud. As men's boots crashed closer, Maddie moved in desperation to clamp a hand over Peter's mouth to silence him. She feared she would suffocate him this way, but saw little choice.

Her heart pounded. It seemed nearly to explode in her mouth. As she listened, not even daring to breathe, the searchers crashed by, only a few feet away from where she cowered with her friend. But for once her luck held. Unused to ways of land, the men could not see past the mess of undergrowth to where the fugitives trembled so dangerously close by. Finally they went away. Long after they were gone, however, the westbound winds wafted their curses back to Maddie's ears. She heard their muttered complaints of ill-luck. She cringed at their shouted oaths so blasphemous. Maddie waited until their voices had faded into silence. Only then did she remove her hand from Peter's mouth.

They were safe for now. Maddie stood up, grimacing with pain as she straightened her back. On legs still trembling, she crept outward again toward the sea. Standing at wood's edge, she squinted at the great water beyond, and watched the *Anadeen* sail off without them. Confident now that their pursuers would not return, she checked where she had hidden the boat. When she found their little dinghy still untouched, she hurried back to Peter. She knew she had to do something to help him.

Nearby she saw a bare spot where only grasses and a few brambles flourished. Stones piled into pyramids suggested that this might have been an old Indian burial site. Whatever purpose it once served no longer mattered. It would do well enough now for their own needs.

Exhausted almost beyond endurance, she went back to drag him there, feeling as she moved a second wind.

As she lowered him down in the clearing, she wondered what on earth she'd do if he died. He was so far gone. Her mind raced. Night would soon fall, and with it would come a chill she knew he couldn't possibly endure. Her first thought was to start a fire. Luckily, he always carried a flint. She found it now. After gathering kindling into a small pile near where he lay, she struck the flint. A spark caught a dried leaf and its tiny flame grew and spread, eating its way to the deadwood log she had found.

Maddie sighed with relief. Fire was such a blessing. It would keep them warm, and scare away any night-feeding wild animals. If there were Indians about, she'd just have to take her chances that they were friendly. She knew, however, that her work wasn't over yet.

After a short rest, she gathered some long branches. When she had collected a pile of them, she arranged the softest and springiest as a bed for him, to protect him from the cold damp ground. With the rest, she built a crude lean-to over where he lay. When she had finished, she bent to examine his wound.

She stared with dismay. It definitely festered now, and she saw just by looking that his only chance lay in having all the shot and damaged skin removed as soon as possible. Heart pounding in dread, Maddie reached for his knife. She thrust its blade into the fire, then started to cut at the filth that had gathered around the hole in his torn shoulder.

At first touch of the blade, Peter cried out in pain. His agony was so intense, and his scream so loud, that she nearly dropped the knife. Maddie stared horrified at the way he writhed violently away from her. It had to be done, however, so she steeled herself to try again. She cut around a particularly loathsome chunk of debris and infection, then nearly fainted as he screamed. In the voice of a stranger, he spat out a curse. Maddie drew back, chilled to the very core of her being. She was not too good at this, and she knew it. She had never dressed a wound before. Doing it now made her queasy. She feared, too, that she'd cut into something important, perhaps injuring him all the worse. She stared at him with wide apologetic eyes. "I'm sorry, Peter," she whispered, "I . . . you . . . you've got to have it done. If I had any whiskey, I'd give it to you, but I don't, so try to be brave—*please!*" In any case, he'd surely die if she didn't try.

Despite his cries of pain, she cleaned the wound, flinching inwardly at what she was doing, yet knowing that she must. Finally, she finished, and dressed the wound with the only thing available to her—the white, fluffy seedpods of summer flowers. With trembling hands, she squeezed these together like bolls of cotton and pressed them against the hole in his flesh. Next, she laid a sleeve torn from his shirt over them all, then stepped away. Emotionally spent, she collapsed against a tree.

But soon hunger pangs tormented her. She knew that Peter too must be in dire need of energy from food. She found a stand of bushes bright with berries. She tasted one. Watery but sweet, it would serve well enough. She gathered as many of these as she could carry, eating some herself on the way, then pressed them one by one into Peter's mouth. She knew their juice would sustain his need for water. The pulp would nourish him. She ate a few more handfuls herself, then settled back exhausted.

Gradually Peter grew stronger. His fever broke and his shoulder seemed to be healing. Despite her crude surgery, the flesh had formed a decent scar. During the passing days, they lived on shellfish washed onto the beach, washed them down with berries. One day, a trapper passed by, a rough-looking man dressed in skins, with a gray grizzled beard and bright blue eyes. Taking the chance that he'd be friendly, Maddie called out to him, asking where they were. He seemed astonished, not only by their presence, but that they'd even have to ask. "Ye be on one of the outer islands. Mainland be within view on the other side.

"What mainland?" Maddie could hardly contain her excitement. The man was not Indian, but white, and he had spoken English. "Might we be near one of the King's colonies?"

"Aye," he replied. "Ye be in the Carolinas. One of her outer islands, but didn't ye ken?"

"The Carolinas?" Maddie's eyes widened. Things were better than she dared hope. "Ocracoke?" She remembered the last words Henri had spoken to her while standing on the deck of that doomed ship. If she could only get to his friend Pierre Dumont on Ocracoke, then at least he'd know she was still alive. Perhaps she could even wait there, under Pierre Dumont's protection.

"Nay. This island don't even have no name, at least not one in English, but Ocracoke be nearby though. You can get there by boat, if ye've one." He glanced to both of them questioningly. "Ye've got something, I presume, else how'd ye get here in the first place?"

Maddie shrugged. "A tiny one, not really fit to go far, though we'll take our chances if we have to." Her heart pounded wildly now. What a relief to know they were so close to one of Henri's contacts! She glanced uneasily to Peter. "My friend though—he's not much for rowing."

The day was warm, so Peter had left off his shirt. The

man glanced to the scar still red and swollen on his shoulder and nodded. "Aye, hardly fit at all, I should guess, but ye can come with me. I be heading back there in a day or two in me own boat. If ye wants, I'll take yer own in payment for the ferryin'."

"That will be just fine," Maddie agreed. "We'll not be needing it once we're there. I know of someone in the settlement," she explained. "A friend of my husband."

As his eyes flitted from Maddie to Peter, he squinted, as if in surprise. "Ye knows someone *there*?" He shook his head. "Must be mistaken, girl. The two of ye looks like good sorts. Maybe yer friend be in the backwoods. There be some Christian folk in the woods, but I'd advise ye to stay away from that settlement. Especially *thee*." His eyes fixed again on Maddie. "Them what lives near the water be a rough crowd, and nasty."

The trapper, named Hiram Simms, made camp with them another week. He dressed his skins, stretching them across tree branches until they were stiff. All three ate gamey-tasting meat from the animals he had slaughtered, some of it fresh, the rest dried over the fire he kept constantly going for the purpose. Finally, old Hiram was ready to move. On that day, all three of them set out in his own boat for Ocracoke.

Once there, the old man bade them good-by. "Just keep a-movin' in that direction," he said, pointing. "The town's right on the water, and ye'll be able to smell it even before ye sees it." And then he was gone, carrying with him their thanks and blessings, as he disappeared with his skins and traps into the woods.

Maddie saw at once that anyone who chose to live here could exist comfortably, if he but knew how to cull the land's riches. Terrapins, green and solemn, crawled from the marshes. They waddled over mud to bask in the sun. Fish gleamed as they wriggled back and forth near the surface of a freshwater pond they passed.

Waves from the outlying sea washed tiny crabs and clams onto shore for them to gather and eat. Birds flew here too, some large as chickens, but with strange feather markings, and ducks cried out, flashing by in the branches above.

She and Peter walked in silence, just looking around. Spindly pines reached skyward just beyond the cordgrass growing at edge of a salt water marsh. They passed live oak and hickory intermingled. Fan-shaped fronds of some exotic bush she had never seen before fluttered as they reached from their single trunk growing in the mucky soil. They gleamed in the sun. The fringes of their green-tufted tops seemed to whisper to one another as they rustled in the wind. Finally, late the third afternoon, they walked within view of the waterfront settlement.

Remembering the old trapper's warning, she and Peter decided to spend the night on the beach and approach cautiously by daybreak. A little uneasy now, they didn't even light a fire, but instead covered themselves with sun-warmed sand for heat. Toward daybreak, Peter shook her awake. "Maddie!" His voice pierced her sleep clogged mind. She blinked dully and struggled up to consciousness. "W-what? What do you want?"

"I've been thinking. If this place is as rough as all that, then you shouldn't go into it at all. You stay here and let me find your husband's friend for you. Once I do, I'll come back and get you."

Maddie reached to him. "No, Peter, really, I—"

Peter shook his head. "I've made up my mind. Listen, I don't want anything to happen to you. If you hadn't taken care of me the way you did . . . ." He looked very brave right then, and so touchingly young. Maddie laughed bitterly. "Taken care of you? Oh come now, Peter! If it hadn't been for me, you'd still be back in Boston, safe and warm. No, I owe it to you. I'm coming with you." Maddie sat up, still groggy, and rubbed sleep from her eyes.

"No, you're not!" Peter squeezed her shoulders, then pushed her back down. "Now just wait here, and that's an order!" With those words, he ran up over a bluff and disappeared from view.

With a sigh, Maddie waited where she was. She did not relish going into town alone, but hours passed. Still Peter did not return. Night fell, and cold hours melted into ever-deepening anxiety. What had happened to Peter? Where had he gone? She dreaded that he had run into trouble he couldn't handle.

Chapter Twenty-two

The settlement, when she finally followed after him, frightened her from the start. Rough men loitered in its single dirt-paved street. They sat in the opened doorways of shacks, or under tall gnarled trees, wasting time. They swatted mosquitoes while drinking from green glass bottles of rum. Looking at them, Maddie blessed luck that her hair was still short and that she wore boy's clothes.

Even so, bloodshot eyes glanced at her from all sides as she passed, then glanced again, seemingly startled. Animal-like moans of lust escaped from their throats. Obscene words of proposition shocked Maddie into walking faster. One even laid his hand on her arm, intending to grasp and perhaps drag her down right there in the street, but she resisted. "Let me go!" she cried, then yanked free. Suddenly afraid, Maddie glanced over her shoulder. Whether they believed her a young boy or a woman didn't matter. Too many of these rough men considered her fair game. With a clutch of fear, she thought of Peter. Had something like this happened to him? What had become of him? Was he all right? Maddie felt horribly alone right then, and afraid for her friend.

Flies and mosquitoes buzzed everywhere. Even as she hurried along, she slapped at them. Humidity nearly suffocated her. Though she dreaded winter for its cold and ice, she hated the climate down here in this lawless settlement.

Sitting outside his shack, an old man smoked a pipe. He seemed less filthy than most of his neighbors and glanced to her with indifference, instead of lust. Heartened by such a reaction, Maddie approached. "Pray, sir," she began. "Could you tell me where I might find Pierre Dumont? I know he owns a tavern, but I know not where."

"Aye," the man nodded. "But a young fellow like you'd find only trouble in his place."

"I have no choice. I must leave a message for someone, and he told me to leave it with Pierre Dumont."

The man scowled. "And who'd the likes of you be leavin' a message for?"

"For Henri Rohan."

His eyes widened. "Rohan?" he cried her husband's name, almost in a gasp. At once, his look grew crafty, disbelieving. "But what would a young stripling like you be wantin' with Rohan?"

Maddie decide to lie. "I have a message from his woman," she replied, and tried to sound the way a young, rascally boy might talk. "A fine wench," she added, speaking in a braggardly tone. She had seen enough such boys by now to know how they'd talk.

"Ah, what a pity." The old salt chewed thoughtfully

on the stem of his pipe. "If you'd but come ten days ago, you could've talked to Rohan himself."

Maddie's eyes widened. "Ten days ago?" She had just missed him then. If only the southward wind had blown a little harder!

"Aye, ten days or so, give or take a few," he nodded. His mouth stretched into a grin that revealed missing teeth. Tobacco had stained the few that remained. "Come to trade good Spanish gold for Virginia tobacco and ham," he added. "We takes a lot more kindly to his sort here, than in Virginia."

Remembering how much the *Anadeen's* captain had loathed Henri, Maddie could only stare dumbly at the old man. She still found it a shock to think of him as an outlaw. Angrily, she found herself defending him in her own mind. He had always proven himself good to her, and gentle, and she believed it to be his true inner nature. Religious bigotry alone had driven him to this hated, evil life, and now the whole self-righteous world condemned him for it. She realized with a sudden rush of insight that just months ago she too had been smug, confident of her own virtuousness. In her well-protected ignorance she would have believed herself superior to Henri and all his kind. Now that she had joined the ranks of criminals, however, her outlook had changed.

She stared. "Tell me, where was he off to? A man in Boston knew that he intended sailing to the West Indies, but he might have already been there and gone again. I cannot just sail from island to island."

"Aye, it isn't a good idea," he agreed, then added with a shrug, "but I be not sure where Rohan has went. Even late as a year ago, I'd a guessed Tortuga, but now I ain't so sure. The Frenchies have gotten as ill down on all his kith and kind as the Spaniards. Most likely I'd guess St. George in Bermuda—if he's not gone and left for Madagascar, that is. The Gov'nor of Bermuda be still friendly to the likes of yer man, so long as he gets his cut of gold and riches they brings back. Not like Jamaica," he added, "where the bleeders have started hangin' Rohan's kind."

Maddie nearly fainted. The mere mention of Madagascar, a place so unthinkably far away, horrified her, as did the thought of someone capturing and hanging Henri. She thanked the man, however, then went where he directed to the Mermaid Tavern, Pierre Dumont's place. Somehow, she would find her way east and south to Bermuda first, then learn if she could where Henri had gone. Unless, of course, Pierre Dumont knew something the old man didn't.

The Mermaid Tavern was a dark and murky hole. The damp air reeked of ale gone bad, of rum and unwashed bodies. About seven men sprawled around a rough-hewn table. Each swilled from a bottle of his pleasure, one man to a bottle. They talked to one another in low rumbling voices. As she stepped inside, however, all conversation stopped.

"Well," crooned one. "What a fine boy. Almost as pretty as a wench, that boy be."

Maddie blushed, but met their eyes. "Which one of you is Pierre Dumont?" she demanded.

A pause followed. All eyes glanced to one another. Finally one set of eyes, black and glittering, fixed on her. A swarthy face now turned in her direction and its owner stood. "I be Pierre Dumont," he said.

Maddie nodded. "Good. I have to speak to you alone."

He glanced to his companions, then motioned her over to a table in the far corner. "What be you wanting?"

"I have a message from Henri Rohan," she said, facing him. "He told me to come to you if he and I became separated, and to leave word. He even said you'd take care of me until he returned, although I do not want to ask you to do it."

The stranger's black eyes peered suspiciously but with interest. "Who be you that Rohan would care?"

Maddie shrugged. "I guess it's all right for me to admit it to you," she said. She glanced doubtfully to the others. "I am Rohan's wife, and I want him to know I'm alive and looking for him."

Dumont glanced to his cronies. A strange silence had settled over all of them, and it worried her. The atmosphere felt strained in a way Maddie didn't like. "Come into the back room, Madame Rohan." He nodded to her now with exaggerated respect. "There be somethin' I got to show you. Somethin' left here by your husband. Now come, it'll be all right." He sensed her apprehension and made effort to dispell it. "He left it for you, and it's waiting. Something in the way of money," he added, whispering into her ear. "You see now why I don't want to flash it out *here*, in front of all this riffraff."

Maddie nodded, then exhaled a deep, relieved breath. No wonder he wanted her to go into the back room. It would indeed have been madness to hand over money in front of these others. However, something about the man left her uneasy. The glint in his eyes was of cruelty, not merriment. His face was hard, and seemed a stranger to compassion.

"Well, are ye comin', or aren't ye?" His voice had taken on an impatient edge. "I want to get back to me card game."

"Yes, of course I'm coming." Maddie followed him toward a leather-covered exit in the back. "Perhaps you might even help me further with very little trouble to yourself."

"Aye?" His reply was guarded.

"I want to join him down in the Indies," she said.

"Perhaps you could advise me how to board some ship heading there. Surely Henri has friends among the other captains who stop here. Perhaps one of them could help."

He smiled a strange grin. Maddie didn't like the way his eyes glittered. "I think that can be arranged," he said.

The others had fallen silent, still listening as the two of them walked toward the back room. Maddie blamed idle curiosity. When they both reached this inner chamber, he pushed back the leather, and motioned for her to pass in ahead of him.

Once inside, Maddie drew back in horror. She cried out, then turned to flee, but it was too late. His bulk blocked her from escaping. His strong arms reached to grab hold of her own. She writhed to free herself but found escape impossible. She could not even hope to run past him now, through the front room to the dubious safety she'd find outdoors.

She glanced back, staring in horror at what she had seen. A dead man lay in that room on his back against the dirt floor. Blood stained his clothes. It caked to his limbs. The face stared upward through wide, unseeing eyes no one had bothered to close. The man had been, when alive, about forty, with flowing gray-brown hair and fine chiseled features. All the blood had drained from the once-tanned face. The wide, thin-lipped mouth had drawn back in a silent scream that sickened her.

Maddie could only whimper, "W-who . . .? Who is he? What has he to do with me?" She pulled her head back in an attempt to look into her captor's eyes, instead of at the corpse. "What do you want of me?" Was she to join this poor creature in death, or endure, as once before, the hated caresses of men who proved to be her enemies?

His chuckle came from deep within his throat. It

vibrated throughout his whole body into hers. "It seems I win this round," he said, still chuckling. "Me against yer precious Rohan, and I gets the pretty little wifie."

Maddie went suddenly breathless. "I-I thought you were his friend."

"Hah! I ain't his friend. That be Dumont right *there*," he said, pointing to the corpse. "I-I, Jed Hawkins—I'll live to see that buggerer and all is kith run through with my sword, or marooned."

Maddie grew suddenly faint. So he had lied to her about his identity. She had been too trusting! She glanced again to the dead man and berated herself for her own stupidity. She should have known. A man named Pierre Dumont was not likely to speak with the accents of a London slum Englishman!

Still holding firmly, he whirled Maddie around. "Bolt the outer door, boys" he shouted to his mates. "We're gonna be havin' some fun, we will, and at Rohan's expense. This fair baggage be our game now."

"No!" Maddie screamed. She tried to struggle free, but his grip was like iron. She clawed helplessly at his arm, but her struggles only tightened his hold. Terrified, she felt the breath pressed out of her. She gasped in air to keep from suffocating.

"I've done nothing to you!" she cried. "To anyone. I am only a wife looking for her man. You have no right." She screamed again as he hoisted her up onto his shoulders. She kicked and pounded with clenched fists against his spine and shoulderblades, as he carried her out into the tavern's main room. Tears of fear and humiliation streamed from her eyes. "No!" she cried again. "Damn you!"

"Shut up!" he snarled.

"No!" Maddie screamed.

He flung her down onto the table, onto their scattered cards. She writhed to get free, but strong arms held her.

Hands clamped to her thighs, their pressure digging into the soft, white flesh of her inner legs. Fingers ripped away her shirt. She cried out, then sobbed aloud. Tears of pain blinded her as the sturdy linen of the tearing shirt cut into her skin.

Hands toyed with her breasts. They squeezed and molded her nipples, hardened in spite of her terror. Her pants slid from her kicking legs. Someone's red and hairy hand swooped between her legs. Its caress pressed deep and hard into her. Blood rushed suddenly to her head, as fingers explored where no decent stranger's should have dared. Maddie choked aloud her humiliated disgust.

"Why the Hell are we shootin' hot air?" cried one of them. "While you boys decide what to do, I'm a gonna take my turn."

Tears streamed from Maddie's eyes. She moaned aloud as he mounted her, then rammed the hard, pulsing tool of his passion inside her. "Damn you!" she gasped. She clawed, wanting only to hurt him. Laughing, he grabbed both wrists and held them painfully tight until he had finished with her.

One followed after the other in an agonizing blur of pain and humiliation. Finally they finished, leaving her to lay in a drained and moaning heap. A soul-deep despair settled in upon her.

She stared, eyes dry and hardly even caring if they killed her. She felt so dirty. Not even a thousand baths could wash away the filth. They had polluted her inside and out. Her arms, thighs, and belly felt sticky with the residues of their passion, congealing now upon her. How could Henri want her after this? She had become a loathsome creature, most of all to herself.

"I pretended that I was Rohan—the great *Diable*." Hawkins began to strut around, in vile imitation of Henri's proud stride.

Another turned to Maddie and grinned at her. "What'll we do with her now?"

Maddie's eyes widened in sudden fear. Surely they'd kill her. She forgot for the instant that she no longer wanted to live, that death would come as a blessing.

"If *you* don't want 'er, I'll take 'er." One of the others grinned at her in a gloating, possessive manner, then reached with one dirty finger to stroke below the earlobe. "She'd make a fine wench to have around, she would. Them fancy ladies from New England, they know how to do a whole lot. She could cook and sew for me, as well as bed me down and blow me."

Jed Hawkins grinned. "You want to die young or somethin', Archer? No, Rohan'd only come back and kill you. I've got a better plan. One that'll make bloody sure our Rohan never beds his sweet little pussy again."

The first man stared in horror. "You don't mean to *kill* her, do you? Surely that'd be a terrible waste."

"Not kill her." Hawkins chuckled again. "Not *kill* her, but sell her." He turned to his mate. "Are we not sailin' this very morrow for Araby?"

"Aye, but—" The man to whom he spoke looked clearly bewildered. "But you'll have no need of a wench on board ship. We can get all we want whenever we raid a town."

"Not Rohan's wench, you fool. Look at her." He motioned to her. "She's young, and Lord knows she's pretty. What heathen sultan wouldn't pay a pretty penny for a fair morsel like her? Especially if he be knowin' she's the wife of *Diable*, who's been sometimes raiding their trading ships? Why, you'd be makin' an easy fortune for a days work at the slave market in Madagascar."

Understanding dawned on the other man's face. Triumph and greed mingled with sadistic glee. "Aye," he replied. "She's a fine piece, sure enough, and they likes 'em blond."

Jed Hawkins chortled. "And think of how it'll be when Rohan finds out that his pretty wife be all clapped up inside some harem, sold to a sultan. He'll burn for her, he will, and find no way of getting at her."

Maddie stared at them with helpless horror. Choking back the urge to scream, she forced herself to stay calm. "He'll kill you, you know, when he finds out. What pleasure can this all be, if you end up dead men because of it? Mark my words, Rohan will have his revenge."

Her argument startled two of those five men. Because her words rang true, they stared to one another, suddenly silent. All their mirth vanished, as they fixed bleary eyes upon one another in sudden fear.

Her first attacker thrust his own doubts into their hesitation. "Bull—that's what I say. You can all defend yourselves well enough. He is no devil, but a man just like the lot of you. Anyway, they's five of us and only one of him. Now I ask ye—how can he kill us if we stand together?"

"He has followers," said one of them who seemed more frightened than the others. "I used to sail with him, and I seen how he likes to fight and kill. He didn't get his name *Le Diable* for nothing."

"Maybe so," retorted Hawkins, "but we've got followers, too, and friends who hate him to his very bones."

Maddie stared hard at the men who seemed so consumed with hatred for her husband. Jed Hawkins had a rum-hoarsened voice, grown harsher now from lust-thickened anger. His black eyes flashed from time to time with the cold fire of a fanatic, and these reminded her, somehow, of Andrew Mathias. She knew she could never reason with him. Her words would never frighten him. Her only chance lay in convincing the others. Exploit their fears, and hope they gang up on Hawkins and let her go.

Her eyes fixed on his companions, especially upon the one most terrified. "This man isn't your friend, you know," she said in a steady voice . . . "True friends would have your interests at heart, as well as their own, but—" She nodded toward Hawkins. "He wants only to bring my husband down. Why do you suppose my husband got the name *Diable*? Because he fights like the very devil himself, that's why!"

The others fell into uncertain silence. Maddie realized, with a surge of triumph, that her words were having their effect. "Maybe he'd never find out," one of them murmured uncertainly.

"He'd know." Maddie fixed steady eyes on him. "Even if none of you admit what you've done, he'd know. I've been seen coming here. It's known that I seek Henri Rohan. People know, and they'll talk. They'll figure out soon enough who was behind it all, and who his accomplices are."

"Yer a cool one, you are." Hawkins eyed her with a hard and suddenly interested gaze. "But it'll do you no good. You'll be comin' with us when I set sail for the eastern Indies. I'll have my fill of ye on the passage over, and when we get to Madagascar, I'll put ye in the market up for sale."

With those words, he whirled to the others. In a voice deep and hard, he thundered out his intent. "That's what I mean to do, and do it I will. Now if any one of you has any ideas of stoppin' me, I'd advise you to think again." Hawkins was lean, but had a sinewy strength that reminded Maddie of a ravening, half-starved animal. As he faced his compadres with blazing gaze, they recoiled. "And if I hear that anyone of you's been spreadin' it around . . . ." His black eyes narrowed. "I'll kill you deader'n old Dumont back there, and I'll do it piece by piece."

Maddie stared at him, then shuddered. He was danger, death, and hatred in the form of a living man, and the very look on his face terrified her. "Now help me get her all bound up!" He barked out orders. Too cowed to argue, his cronies obeyed, tying Maddie's wrists and ankles with stout rope. After they had wrapped a handkerchief around her mouth, they left her alone for just a few minutes.

From the back room, Maddie heard scuffling and the drone of their muted voices. Finally they returned to where she lay. When she saw the large sack woven of tow in Jed Hawkins' hand, her eyes widened. Tow was cast-off fibre from the spinning and processing of flax into linen—stuff too course for bedsheets and clothing. In Massachussets, farmers and householders wove it into sacks, or gave it to the very poor. In the South, she knew, owners ordered it sewn into clothes for their field slaves.

Without bothering to speak, he stuffed her inside as if she had been but a pile of old clothes, and she, bound with rope and still naked, found the woven cage unbearably itchy. After they had tied her in, they hoisted her onto their shoulders. She hung there, dangling toward earth. As they talked, she realized that they had forgotten for the most part how they had forced themselves into her. Or perhaps it simply wasn't important to them—merely a passing pleasure. She had now become merely freight to be loaded upon Jed Hawkins' ship—an especially valuable piece of cargo, to be sure, but essentially merchandise bound for the slave markets of far-off Arabia.

Finally, the stale, bad-smelling air, the horror, and the pain of her ordeal all combined to overwhelm Maddie. As they carried her down the street toward the inlet where Hawkins' privateer frigate floated in dock, she slipped from consciousness, but even then she could not escape. The horror pursued her in the form of a nightmare, in which she was awake but held captive in some Turkish brothel, surrounded by eunuchs. No matter what she had endured before, she had always clung to the hope that somehow, somewhere she would find Henri once again, but now she despaired.

Chapter Twenty-three

Maddie awakened to find herself already inside the ship, alone in a cabin, her wrists and ankles bound to the cot on which she lay, still naked. Angrily, she fought against the ropes, but found them too sturdy to resist. "Damn!" she cried. In despair, she fell back against the mattress. Tears streamed out of her eyes, trickling over her cheekbones, down along her hairline, then dripping off her jaw.

She glanced around, searching desparately for some way to end her life then and there, but found nothing. With soul-deep despair, Maddie knew she had no choice but to endure. Through unshuttered windows, she watched day pass into night. Remaining alone, she marked the hours by the way the light shifted and darkened in the sky.

Suddenly, the door to that cabin clattered open. Her eyes, which had closed in an uncomfortable slumber, flew wide at the noise. Her lips parted in a soundless cry of dismay to see Jed Hawkins standing there. He towered over her for a moment then strode to the cot. She drew a sharp intake of breath as he swooped down. He kissed her roughly, biting her bottom lip then forcing her mouth open onto his. Maddie tried to writhe away, but the ropes were too strong. In her struggles, they cut into her wrists and ankles.

Her flesh crawled with loathing as he touched her, but she could do nothing to defend herself. His hands slid without tenderness over her breasts. They explored everywhere, and all she could do throughout the whole, humiliating experience was to bite her lip, screw shut her eyes, and endure.

Tears welled up again as he mounted her. Her body convulsed in a soul-deep shudder as his flesh pierced into her. Lying helpless under the wild churning of his loins, Maddie prayed to God for a quick and easy death to over-take her immediately. When he had finished, she opened her eyes to glare at him. "May the Devil take you!" she gasped.

He only laughed. "Is that any way to talk? And where'll *you* be, lass? In Heaven, with all God's sweet angels? Nay, I'll see thee down in Hell with me, when *our* time comes to meet again."

As a cry of despairing rage burst from her mouth, he suffocated it with a kiss. Finally, mercifully he finished with her. He left her lying there still tied, as his own private hostage until the journey's end, when he would sell her for jewels or for gold; he left her alone while he himself went back outside to enjoy the sun on deck.

Time passed. Maddie had no idea how long. She lay naked in her misery and knew that each passing hour swept her farther away from all hope of rescue, of freedom, and closer to the fate she dreaded more than death itself.

That night, after Jed Hawkins had come and left her a second time, Maddie suddenly heard a noise. While she watched, dreading, the door to the cabin opened just a crack. She stared with wide, horrified eyes as the intruder waited, perhaps to see who lay inside.

Finally, the door opened wide enough to let a man slip in from outside. He was a squat little fellow with pock-marked face and loose, gaudily colored clothes. Suddenly afraid, Maddie recoiled, dreading yet another attack on this nightmare voyage.

"I knew you'd be here now," he whispered. "Please be quiet." He closed the door behind, then stood just staring at her nakedness. "I didn't know he left you in this state, though, or I would have brung you some clothes."

"What do you want?" Maddie stared at him. In his hand, she saw, he gripped a knife. "What are you going to do to me?"

"Get thee back to thy husband." His voice fell soft. As he glanced around, unexpectedly furtive and purposeful, Maddie's soul flooded with newly surging hope.

"My husband?" she whispered. "Have you word of Henri?"

"Aye, sort of."

Maddie frowned. 'Sort of' didn't sound too promising.

He explained. "Thy husband has long since sailed, but they's other captains from his fleet, and one was docked just off Ocracoke when you was there. He heard just too late from some stranger that you was taken by Jed Hawkins while lookin' for Rohan." Hope beat faster in her heart.

"Where is he now, this captain?"

"He be on a ship just beyond this one, and waitin' to take you on board once I free you." He used his knife to hack into the ropes binding her wrists. He had just cut through, freeing both when suddenly outside and coming toward them, they heard footsteps. "Here!" He handed her the knife. "Hide this away until you get a chance to use it!" Leaving her alone, he ducked behind some clothes hanging over in one corner.

Maddie's eyes widened. Unable to think of any other

261

place to hide it, she slipped it underneath her. She waited, heart pounding in her mouth as the door to her prison cabin crashed open. Would Hawkins notice her hands untied, cut free? Her eyes rolled from side to side, searching for she knew not what.

She need not have worried, however, for the very stong smell of rum that wafted in with him told her he had been drinking. He seemed barely able to stand up now, moving unsteadily across the floor right toward her. "Ah, there you are, me bonny lass—still soft and sweet and willing?" He stumbled. He fell upon her with a painful crash, then almost immediately went limp. A gentle snore issued from his lips.

Maddie waited, heart in mouth, until she was sure he had truly fallen asleep. With trembling hand, she reached under to where she had hidden the dagger.

His mouth hung open. Below, his throat lay exposed. It gleamed reddish with a prominent Adam's apple that bulged. Glancing one last time to her unknown ally, Maddie rested the blade of the dagger against one side of Jed Hawkin's throat, then pushed inward. She used all her strength to slice through flesh and cartilage. Gritting her teeth, she held the knife, now slippery with Hawkin's blood, and kept right on digging in.

Hawkins gave a gurgling moan. His eyes shot open. He stared with uncomprehending pain. For the rest of her life, Maddie knew she would never forget the way he looked at her. He tried to struggle free. He writhed, but the little man, who had dashed out now to help her, held him down while Maddie finished the job. Finally, he fell silent.

Maddie let the knife drop. It landed on his chest, then clattered to the floor underneath. She drew back, nauseous and gagging in disgust. His blood covered her now, warm and wet against her bare skin. Retching, she pushed free and stumbled to a basin that stood in one corner, filled with the wash water Hawkins had used earlier that day and not bothered to empty. She soaked a cloth in it and wiped herself clean as possible.

Her helper glanced uneasily toward the door. "Get dressed, and hurry!" His fear penetrated the silence surrounding them now. "There may not be much time."

Maddie nodded, grabbed a pair of Hawkins's own knee-breeches and a shirt, and pulled them on. She followed the little man into the corridor beyond. Under her bare feet, the wood planking felt clammy and wet. A patch of slime grew in her path. She nearly slipped and fell, but caught herself just in time. "Be careful!" He led the way out onto the main deck. It was the dark of the moon. Although the sky was clear, free of clouds, a velvety blackness lay over them like a diamond-spotted cloak. The salt air hit her with a tang that made her nostrils tingle, and she sensed in the silence a poised mood of waiting.

By then her rescuer had extinguished his light. The two of them crept, feeling their way along. Maddie followed him, hand on his shoulder, as he groped across the deck to the railing beyond. Maddie glanced around, then smiled with approval. All in all, it was a perfect night for making an escape.

Suddenly the little man grabbed her arm and yanked her to a place further to stern on the railing. She glanced down where he pointed and saw a rowboat manned by three sailors. "You'll go with them," he whispered. "I'd come too, but I have to stay aboard Hawkins's ship and keep me eyes opened."

Maddie stared at him in wonderment. Whatever the favor Henri or the other fleet captain had done him must have been great indeed, for this fearstricken little man to have helped her as he had. "Thank you," she whispered, and wished there was time to find out.

"Well, begone now, and good luck." He held her

arm as she climbed over the railing to the outer rim of the ship's top deck. Uneasy in the presence of a rope ladder, Maddie clung to the railing with sweaty palms, while her bare foot groped gingerly for that yielding top cross-tie. She lowered to it, and found that it did indeed support her weight.

Clinging for dear life, she crawled like a spider down the side of the ship. Its size seemed to have expanded, in the few moments between glancing downward from deck, and actually descending. Afraid that she would drop into the ocean, Maddie clutched ever more tightly to keep from slipping away.

"How much longer?" she whispered to herself. "My God, how much more of this can I take?" She glanced up and saw that the little man who had set her free, Rohan's spy, had already disappeared.

"Just a little further now. Just a little more." From below, Maddie heard soft voices calling out encouragement. A few more rungs, and strong hands gripped her around the waist and hips. They held her tight and firm. As they lowered her into the boat, Maddie let go of the ropes. Her hands, numbed and falling asleep, began to prickle.

She clung to one man's neck as he set her down, then collapsed exhausted on a hard planking seat. She watched, exultant but weary, as they rowed from the great, broad ribs of her captor's ship. She closed her eyes as they moved off into blackness, their presence as yet undetected. "Where is your ship?" she whispered. She was too tired to speak aloud.

"Not far, but just out of sight," one man answered her. "We'll take you to our captain."

"What I don't understand is how you got word to that fellow to set me free."

One of the sailors chuckled. "That's easiest of all. We already knew you were on board, but in port Hawkins had posted armed guards outside his cabin. Guess he was afraid someone would find out, and try to rescue you, so Captain Abraham planned to get you out of it in open sea. When that fellow saw it was clear to cut you free, he signaled us with a lighted candle.''

"I see, and what happens to me once you get me on board your own ship?''

The man shrugged. "Our captain doesn't confide in us," he replied. "You'll have to ask him yourself." At seeing her twinge of fear, he spoke to reassure her. "Our captain is a friend of your husband's, madam. He will not hurt you."

Only half believing him, Maddie gave him a weary smile. Finally, after what seemed like hours of rowing, she saw their destination. The black silhouette of a ship very similar to Hawkins's own loomed ahead. Its name, *The Maidenhead*, had been carved across its sides, then painted white. A row of lanterns lit its top deck now, a beacon so that the men sent to fetch her could find their way home. When she saw, Maddie sighed, relieved that she'd finally be on board some other ship. What was he like, this Captain Abraham, she wondered. Would he be someone crude, terrifying, and cruel, or gentle like Henri?

The ship's belly nestled in the water. As they drew up to it, Maddie's heart pounded. Yet another rope ladder lowered, but this time, large strong hands reached down and pulled her to safety.

Finally she saw him, the captain who had masterminded her rescue. They had led her to his cabin. The door swung open onto a scene of almost Oriental opulence, and her eyes widened with disbelieving wonder.

"Welcome, Madame de Rohan. Please come inside." A voice, low and melodious, greeted her. "I am Abraham Castaneda, ship's master, and I see now that

265

you are every bit as beautiful as my friend described. I had not believed him, but now I do.''

Maddie stared around, awed by these richly decorated surroundings. Tile painted with intricate scrollwork covered his lower walls. Dark wood carved in an openwork of intertwining vines and leaves trimmed his door. A carpet woven of scarlet and black, indigo and ochre, rested upon the floor. Instead of proper chairs or cots, pillows furnished the cabin. Sewn in all manner of fabric, of brocade and carpeting, of silk and linen, some were small and some huge. All lay in a pile upon his rug. Lamps of polished brass carved in filigree hung from the walls. Their light flickered out with light-dark shadows that added their own rich pattern and rhythm to the walls.

The captain of this ship was like no one Maddie had ever known—either in looks or manner. His blue-black hair curled out from his head in wild, almost Blackamoor ringlets that trailed halfway down his neck. His dark tan face was smooth shaven. His eyes, like two bottomless pools of night-black water lit by stars, studied her from under heavy, straight brows. His lips curved with almost African fullness. When he smiled, however, his face lit up in a boyish grin that made him seem younger, less brooding than he had at first. Most startling were his clothes. He wore not trousers, but a robe of whitest linen embroidered at the yoke in white silk. From a chain around his neck hung a talisman of gold, cast and worked in a pattern of barbaric complexity. Rings glittered upon each of his brown fingers. Pierced into one earlobe gleamed a gold earring.

"You-you are with my husband in his fleet?" Maddie stared in disbelief. What connection could this exotic stranger have with Henri? How would they ever have met?

"Madame de Rohan—" He spoke English well, but

with the musical intonations of a language Maddie did not recognize. "I know you have many questions and I will delight in answering them, but I can guess how these past days must have wearied you." With a sweeping gesture, he pointed to a door further inside. "Just beyond that portal you will find a basin of water. I have no dresses to give you such as the ones women wear in your own country, but I have set out a robe which I trust will serve a similar purpose." He grinned, suddenly mischievous. "You will find it comfortable enough, but undoubtedly not to your own taste. After you have changed out of this—this clothings,"—he grimaced slightly in distaste at the baggy, dirty looking breeches and shirt she wore—"you will dine with me. I will join you, and we shall talk." He nodded to her, then stepped away. He turned, walked to the door, and opened it. With a swish of his white linen robe, he slipped outside, closing the door behind him.

Maddie was grateful for the water and change of clothes, yet suspected, with a twinge of dismay, that his offer might have been inspired by motives other than mere graciousness. After all, she had spent two weeks masquerading as a boy aboard ship heading south, then another uncounted number of days in the wilderness. In all that time, she had found no chance to bathe, nor in Jed Hawkins's ship, either. Her lips twitched with a rueful grin, as she wondered if his kind offer had been merely a polite way of telling her that she stank. Certainly he himself seemed clean enough.

Eager to wash away all traces of Jed Hawkins and his friends, Maddie turned to the basin. Rose scented-water filled it. Towels and a robe of linen hung where she could reach. Sighing in contentment and delight, Maddie scrubbed herself clean in the perfumed water, savoring each moment of her bath, then wiped herself dry.

She reached now for the garment Castaneda had laid

out. Obviously one of his, it hung too big on her, but its linen was of the finest quality, and embroidery crusted it thick and rich. With a needle and thread, she could make it fit.

When she had smoothed it into place, she glanced to herself in his silvered glass mirror, then started in surprise. Weeks of working aboard ship had tanned her skin. Though she had cropped her hair, it had begun growing out now, and curved in waves around her face. She had changed, to be sure, but not so much that Henri wouldn't recognize her if he really wanted to. She wondered again with a pang whether he'd be glad to see her, or sorry.

Feeling refreshed for the moment, Maddie slipped from that little chamber into the main room once again. When she saw what waited there, her eyes widened in surprise. Upon a low, long table newly set up rested a carafe filled with wine. A dish covered with a bowl of woven reed held chicken lying amidst a steaming, aromatic sauce. Suddenly desperately hungry, she plopped down onto the pillows resting behind, then wolfed it all down.

Somehow, in waiting for Abraham Castaneda to return, Maddie fell asleep. When she opened her eyes, hours later, she saw daylight streaming in through the portholes lining the outer wall. The long table had disappeared, and she lay where she had leaned, on one huge satin covered bolster. She stared disoriented at first, wondering how she had gotten where she was. Suddenly it all came back to her. Maddie smiled at her good fortune. At last, she was among friends again.

Just then, someone knocked upon the door. "Come in," she called out for whoever it was to enter, and in stepped her host.

Gone was his robe. Leather trousers, boots, and a flowing linen shirt replaced it now. Open at the throat, his shirt revealed the black hairs curling upon his chest. His talisman glinted gold in the morning's light, and very beautiful. "I thought I'd let you sleep last night," he began.

"Thank you," she replied. "I must have needed it."

"Yes, I think so." He glanced to the door. "Pedro, my cabin boy, will be bringing us coffee," he said. "May I join you?"

"Of course," Maddie smiled at him. He had a pleasing face, really, and his dark eyes, though brooding and alien-looking to her sensibilities, were gentle.

"One of my men said you had questions." He did not bother with the conventional pleasantries. Nor did he seem inclined to volunteer information. Maddie realized that anything she wanted to know, she'd have to ask.

"I have so many," she replied. "Who are you? I mean, how did you come to know my husband, or for that matter, how did you find out who I was, and what had become of me?"

"One at a time!" The man laughed.

Bursting with curiosity, Maddie stared at him. "All right then, how did you and Henri ever get together? You're not someone I'd have guessed would be his friend."

Castaneda's eyes darkened, becoming sorrowful. "I met him on my way back to Spain, a prisoner from Hispaniola, to stand trial and probably forfeit my life. We will not discuss how or why I was taken, but when your husband captured that ship, he freed me. I joined him then and there, first as a crew member, then with my own galleon, as a captain in his fleet."

"So you're a Spaniard then?" Maddie's eyes widened. Somehow, she would have guessed him a Moor, or even an East Indian.

"No," he replied with a clipped, abrupt tone. "I am not a Spaniard."

After the boy brought coffee and pastries, Maddie nibbled and sipped, as she listened to the man describe how he had learned of her plight. "A few of my men were ashore—luckily, my more reliable ones. A stranger approached one of them, someone claiming to be a friend of Rohan's. He described how Hawkins had captured a beautiful woman claiming to be Rohan's wife and had taken her aboard his ship. He said he was there when Hawkins had captured her."

Maddie's eyes widened. It had to have been the man who took her warning to heart that afternoon in the tavern. Apparently fear of Rohan proved greater than his loyalty to Jed Hawkins.

Castaneda went on, speaking gently. "All we knew was what the man told us. That they had you on board, and that the ship was bound for Madagascar where they intended selling you. At first, we thought it might be a trap, but my man had the presence of mind to demand that the stranger describe you. What he said matched Rohan's description of you." Castaneda shrugged. "Well, you know the rest, because my man found you, and now you're here."

Maddie met his eyes. As she smiled at him, his own face seemed to light up. "Thank God you found me," she whispered. "And bless you for going to all the trouble you did to save me."

His dark eyes grew very serious. He studied her intently for several seconds before speaking. "A loyal wife is a treasure beyond all reach. Men have died for lack of one, or suffered." He continued, "I saw how my friend grieved when he believed you dead. He was beside himself." Maddie sighed, suddenly relieved. His words had lifted a great load of doubt from her mind. Now that she knew Henri still loved her and hadn't forgotten her, all her toil and sufferings had meaning now. She would go to him, and they would both spend

270

the rest of their lives in perfect love and happiness.

Suddenly, from below, a cry pierced the air. At once, its noise galvanized the man into action. He paled, then almost at once, his swarthy cheeks flushed with excitement. He leaped to his feet. Without speaking, he whirled, turning his back to her, and ran to the door. He flung it open with a clatter. Like a cannonball, he hurtled to the main deck.

Curious, bewildered, and alarmed all at once, Maddie ran behind. Outside she could almost taste the fear and excitement that filled the air. Its presence throbbed so thick and heavy that even she, a stranger, felt gripped by it.

The sun was shining bright and hot. The sea sparkled azure blue. Elevated over the main deck just outside his cabin, she watched the long, steel blades of swords whining as they slashed through air. Metal clanked against metal, to mingle with men's cries and yells. They ran to and fro, manning cannon, drawing swords, or scrambling over muskets piled high on deck, as their ship floated closer, ever closer to another. Movement from above caught her eye. She glanced up and saw tied to the main mast a Jolly Roger, a flag of black with its heart a skull and crossed bones. At sight of it, Maddie shuddered, yet stared fascinated at the way its tattered edges fluttered in the breeze.

Castaneda's ship, *The Maidenhead*, drew ever closer to its prey. Heavy cannons burst great exploding tongues of fire and thunder into the shattering wood of the Spanish ship's main deck. Her sailors fought back as bravely as they could, but their weapons were inferior and their ship too unwieldy to outmaneuver their attackers. Armed with only two light cannon and some muskets, against the *Maidenhead's* arsenal, they didn't stand a chance.

While Maddie stood and watched, her eyes glazed

with horror at the sight, the *Maidenhead* drew close enough for its crew to leap aboard the ship they intended capturing by force. The fighting began, hand to hand.

Black smoke billowed everywhere and its oily stench mingled with the acrid smell of power burnt with exploding force. On both ships, men lay wounded upon the decks, moaning with pain from arms blasted off, or deep holes bored into chests and bellies. Bodies, dressed in dirty, bloodstained rags writhed with the life still within ebbing out. Others, less wounded, stumbled to flee. Those remaining crouched with intent to kill, to fight, to attack or to defend, and even from where Maddie stood, high above the battle, she could smell the sickening sweet stench of running blood.

Suddenly it was over. The surviving Spaniards surrendered and were taken prisoner, and their ship and all its contents became the property of Castaneda and his crew. Maddie stared around her in horror. So much pain and death and bloodshed! What had it accomplished? A little material wealth changed hands, to be divided then squandered in the nearest port. Suddenly she realized that Abraham Castaneda, her husband's friend, was watching her. She met his eyes with her own, then turned quickly away; she felt sickened and disgusted by what she had seen. She wanted only to be left alone.

He met her later standing on deck overlooking the sea. He moved beside her and just stood watching the waves ebb and flow. "You are a strange one—especially for Rohan's wife." His voice had softened; so too had his eyes. "You try to be so kind, even to your own enemies. Does it not occur to you that if you spare them, they will only turn around at first chance and stab you in the back?"

Maddie turned to him. She spoke to him in a hard,

unrelenting voice as she stared into his eyes. "And were those strangers your enemies? Did they attack you?"

He glanced out at the sea, staring in silence for a moment, then turned back to her. "They are Spaniards, Madame," he said. His voice had chilled. "All Spaniards are my enemies. I do to them what they would do to me."

Maddie turned to him. "Why are you so sure of that? Why are you so desolate? Perhaps if you'd but give them a chance, they'd befriend you, instead of—"

"What a sweet child you are," he interrupted her. "Even after what you've been through, you still believe the world is good, and all men in it basically kind."

Maddie tossed her head. "And what about you, sir?" Her eyes burned into his. "Are you not as naive, believing all the world to be so evil?"

"I am a realist!" His voice took on an hard and angry edge. "I see the world as it *is*—with all its cruelty and stupidity."

"And so you hunt and kill and add to its pain!"

"I am a part of this world, and therefore share in its evil." His mouth set in a grim, bitter line.

"And yet you saved my life and freedom." Maddie leaned against the railing and studied him. A gentle wind lifted and turned locks of his blue-black hair. She gazed into his eyes, but saw only impenetrable depths. At first, she believed him entirely gentle and good. This morning, however, she had seen he could be savage, too. What a paradox he was, and how unlike Henri.

"I did it for the sake of a friend," he replied in a curt voice.

"But there are men who would betray a friend," she retorted, "yet you did not. Instead, you changed your plans to help him, even when he himself did not realize he needed your aid. I think you are a hypocrite, sir," she added. "You pretend to be so hard and cold and brutal, but you are not."

As he drew back in startled surprise, she smiled. "How did you come to be what you are?" she asked. "Why a sea brigand, instead of a farmer or a priest? In many ways, you remind me of my husband, even though you are so different. He carries a bitterness just as proudly."

Castaneda smiled now. "A curious way of putting it, but true, I suppose. Your husband and I share a great bond. Perhaps it is why we became such close friends."

Maddie glanced to him in bewilderment, wondering what on earth he and Henri might have so in common. As if sensing her thoughts, he answered her. "Your husband and I are both outcasts, Madame," he said in a low, intent voice. "Outcasts in our own land and ruined because of it. Rohan is a Huguenot, while I, God help me, was born a Jew in Spain, where since the days of those Most Catholic Emperors, Ferdinand and Isabella, my kind has had to hide the truth and pretend to be Christian instead, or die in exile."

He continued, "When I was very young, someone betrayed my family. Every one of them died at the hands of the Inquisition but me. I escaped with the aid of my old nurse. I was only five years old at the time, but I have never forgotten seeing my father and sisters marched off by soldiers."

Chapter Twenty-four

The next few days flew by breath-takingly fast. They saw a great many islands now, tiny ones with white sand shores. In the center of others loomed steaming peaks, their bottoms ringed with lush green growth.

She had reached a new understanding with the captain of the ship, and they had spent many long, full hours talking. He told her all about his days with Henri, and of the rich, deep fullness of their friendship. He told her too, about the place where they were going; how Bermuda was a group of coral islands of stunning beauty. He told her about the pigs that roamed its interior, the descendants of animals stranded from shipwrecks. The Spaniards who first discovered these islands had not bothered with them, considering them valueless, so they lay unclaimed until 1609, when a British ship had wrecked upon its shores. Its crew, not knowing of their earlier discovery by Juan Bermudéz, had named them Somers Islands, after their admiral, Sir George. Though claimed in the charter of the Virginia Company, for almost ten years the territory had been administered jointly by that company and the crown. "It's a friendly place, Maddie," Castaneda told her. "One of the few islands left where our ships can go and feel welcome." He sighed. "I'm sure in time that too will change. Governor Bennett is our friend, so long as we share our spoils with him, but he'll not last forever. When he goes, the Crown will probably send out someone like governor Lynch, and then Bermuda will go the way of Jamaica." The latter, Maddie knew, had sworn emnity to all pirates.

"What will you do then?" she whispered.

Castaneda shrugged. "Then it's off to Madagascar, I suppose, or God forbid, find an honest trade."

Bermuda loomed up from the distant mist as a vague mirage at first. With each approaching mile, however, its islands grew wider and more beautiful, until at last Maddie could see waves frothing upon chalky white shores. Behind them swayed tall skinny palms. Below, green and flowering bushes tangled around the base of their trunks. In the center of one large stretch of land, she saw a volcanic cone.

Their destination was St. George, on St. George Island, capital city and friendly port. They sailed around her first, then slipped past one outjutting point into her main harbor. The day sweltered as they put into port. Hot and humid, the air nearly suffocated Maddie. The sun beat down like a ball of fire in the stunningly blue sky.

When his men had finally secured the Spanish ship and their own at the docks of St. George, Castaneda led her off. He trusted his lower officers to oversee without him the unloading of their captured wealth. "I know a good inn right nearby. I'll get you a room there. Once you're settled, I'll start looking for Rohan. There are only a few placed he likes to frequent here, so it shouldn't take more than a couple of hours. When I find him, I'll bring him back to you."

"But I want to go with you!" Maddie objected to being shut away in some dark room, just waiting and not knowing. She had endured too much of that already.

Castaneda glanced at her, then looked quickly away. "No, I think not," he said, with a determined tone of voice. "These places where I'll be going . . . they're not for your eyes."

Rebellious but knowing better than to argue, Maddie walked by his side. She had worn for the journey ashore a pair of trousers and a silk shirt. Sandals of leather tied around her bare feet, while her hair, still short, hung curly and free. To the casual onlooker, she looked like a mere boy, and she wanted it that way. She felt somehow safer in such a disguise, and knew that, if necessary, she could walk the streets like this, and search for Henri herself.

Her friend and protector Abraham Castaneda had shed the comfortable robes he wore in leisure. He dressed instead in boots, gray linen breeches, and a loose-cut shirt that billowed from his shoulders. He tied it at the waist with a sash, then buckled around it his knife belt. With his blue-black hair, snapping eyes, and swarthy skin, he looked more than ever like some scourge of Allah come to conquer. Maddie's eyes sparkled as she walked beside him proudly.

Most of the women she saw on the streets were negresses, tall and well-formed, with black skins glistening under the sun. They dressed in bright but usually tattered ruffles and carried themselves proudly, with backs straight and heads held high. The few white women Maddie saw did no credit to their race. Obviously prostitutes, none seemed terribly young or pretty. Their clothes, jarringly bright, only served to accent their aging pallor. Cheap jewelry glistened from throats grown puffy or scrawny. Ashamed for these sad creatures, Maddie turned her gaze quickly away. She tried not to look at them again.

The buildings at water's edge were shacks. Somehow they reminded her of the white prostitutes she had seen. Their walls, built of driftwood and scrap, had bleached almost white under the sun. Sea grass, dry above but soured in its bottom layers, thatched their roofs. An occasional warehouse stood tall and massive beside these other hovels. Built of brick imported from England, of Bermuda cedar, or of volcanic stone, they looked solid and closed in. A few private coaches rattled down the streets, and a few horse-drawn carts, wagons, and men on horseback, but nothing else. The two of them had no choice but to walk.

"The inn I'm taking you to is a villa, actually, and pleasant. You'll stay there while I go to look for your man. You'll *stay*," he added warningly. "You will not leave. I forbid it." He knew by then the kind of woman she was. He had sensed how impatient of danger she could be when intent upon finding Henri.

"You *will* hurry, won't you?" she whispered. "You must know how I long for him." She knew that, if necessary, she'd disobey him. For the moment, however, Maddie wanted him to believe she'd do as he told her.

"I do," he replied, "and I also remember how deeply he mourned for you, when he believed you dead."

The inn stood at the edge of town. Maddie's spirits soared when she saw her room. Waiting here would be easy. Fresh breezes wafted in through its netted mesh windows. The view of street below and ocean beyond nearly took her breath away. A dim and faded yet adequate mirror hung on one wall. It showed how much she had changed. Its silvered reflection reminded her of something that broke her heart. She had come far, far away from the sober Puritan world of Salem Village, Massachussets. With a pang, she realized that even if someday she went back, her return would be but a visit. By the very look of herself, she knew she could never go home to stay. An exotic stranger peered back at her now. Neither father nor former friends would see anything else. For all intents and purposes, Maddie Bradshaw, Puritan maid, had died in that shipwreck off New England's rocky shores near Providencetown. Madame de Rohan, a pirate's woman, had replaced her.

For the first time in weeks, she thought of her father. She pictured in her mind's eye how he looked sitting in his favorite chair, smoking a pipe. Suddenly angry at herself, Maddie tore her thoughts away from it all. Her childhood, her life in Salem Village lay in ashes now. 'Do you think it does any good to pine for what is long gone?' she scolded herself furiously. 'You can never go back. Never! You're an accused witch who fled. You have nothing anymore, but yourself and the home you make with your husband.'

At thought of Henri, the man who had spirited her

away from certain death, Maddie smiled with tender eagerness. The thought of seeing him again thrilled her. Impulsively, she moved toward the window. Restless now and eager to embrace him, she leaned on its sill and peered out. Standing on the street below, three brown-skinned musicians sang in some strange tongue. Homemade musical instruments accompanied the lilt of their melody with a counter tune and drum beat. Their melody stirred her with its rhythm. Their song transformed into a memory that stung tears to Maddie's eyes. Its sensual beat reminded her of how she and Henri had lain together naked, their loins moving in time to one another's passion. Suddenly a stab sound of anguish seared through her. Crying out, Maddie flung hands over her ears and whirled from the window, unable to bear any longer her yearning.

Turning back, she stared past the gaily dressed street singers, and strained instead to see any sign of Henri or Abraham. She saw, however, only strangers—mostly black-skinned or brown, but sometimes rough-looking whites. These lower orders walked on foot. Anyone of substance or dignity, whether white or of color, rode in carriages.

It maddened her to know that Henri was so near, yet so far away. Her entire life depended on Abraham Castaneda now, and more importantly on his ability to search out Henri and bring him news of her arrival. Though she trusted him, doubts assailed her. Did the young captain know every tavern or private house where Henri might go? What if he had friends Abraham knew nothing about? Finally, Maddie could stand it no longer. She had to leave, to search for him herself. For protection, she had dressed as a boy, but even so Abraham had seen fit to add to her safety. Perhaps sensing that she might disobey, he had left her a knife—a nasty little stiletto with leather-bound handle and its own sheath.

She had no idea how to use the thing, but its very presence gave her comfort and a gay sort of courage. Dressed this way and armed, she would overcome all dangers. After all, had not Providence brought her thus far? Would God not lead her now the rest of the way? The thought heartened her, so much that she very carefully avoided remembering all the dangerous and unpleasant experiences He had also seen fit to throw her way. It did no good to think of them now.

Having finally made the decision to take matters into her own hands, Maddie felt as if a great weight had lifted from her soul. She hummed a merry tune as she moved to the door of her room.

Chapter Twenty-five

Even so close to midnight, the streets below still hummed with noise and activity. She sensed that the taverns in this wild, open town would remain serving all night, and Maddie spent the next several hours searching for him. As time passed, activity in the streets quieted. Women disappeared completely, and even most men took shelter.

At the far edge of the city, at the very end of a long, dirt-paved street stood yet another tavern. Coming upon it, Maddie groaned. Hope had ebbed to weariness by then. She felt that she had been in hundreds the past few hours. The very sights and smells of this one, though no worse than any others, now sickened her. Tired of her search, Maddie decided that, since she was already here, she'd make this one her last stop. If she did not find him inside, she would go back to the inn and try again tomorrow.

As she drew close to its front door, she heard the low rumble of voices erupting now and then into brief arguments that subsided almost as quickly as they began. Somewhere above, from an upstairs window, she heard a snatch of a song crooned in a rich, honey-soft voice.

The quiet down here below in this deserted street swallowed it, however, just as it blotted out all other sounds. Maddie's heart pounded as she approached the door. Each time she entered one of these places, she felt a fresh surge of fear. Would there be in this one a man not intimidated by Henri Rohan's name?

A thickset mulatto sat upon a stool just inside. At her approach he fixed cold, beady eyes on her, but said nothing. "I'm looking for someone," she said. She stared at him, suddenly uncertain how to proceed.

"An' who be that?" His tone was insolent, with more than a twinge of scorn.

"Henri Rohan," she replied. "Some people know him, I hear, as *Le Diable*."

At mention of Henri's name, his thick lips curved into a smile. "Aye, he be here, but almost ready to go into the back. He might not want to see the likes of *you*, boy." His brown eyes squinted at her.

Maddie's heart pounded wildly. *Henri was here!* No matter what he was doing, she knew he'd be glad to see her. As Maddie moved among the tables toward where the man pointed, however, she glanced around suddenly uneasy. This place was darkest of all the taverns she had seen, and the men who frequented it, the roughest. Her heart felt as if it had swollen to twice its size. It fluttered eagerly, yet fearfully. She strained her eyes to see where her husband might be sitting. A deck of sorts ringed the outer edge of this entire room. Tables filled with people took up space here. The heart of the room lay about two

281

steps lower. A sunken area about fifty feet square, it held more tables. These, covered with tankards and surrounded by men sitting on benches, filled all available space. Maddie's heart sank. So many men and tables! In this dim light, she'd have to move closer to see their faces.

A few brightly painted women mingled among the men. Some had already found a companion and sat upon his knee sharing brew or rum. These doxies fondled their men in ways that shocked Maddie's Puritan soul. She remember the Hell preached back at the meeting house in Salem. She began to wonder now if Hell might really be a noisy, ugly tavern like this.

As Maddie descended the steps, she caught movement out of the corner of her eye. She glanced up in time to see a man stand. He was a stranger, and not alone. A raven-haired woman, a mulatto to judge by her features, moved with him. Both staggered arm in arm toward a set of shuttered doors just beyond.

Suddenly, in the very heart center of the room, she saw Henri. Her heart pounded now in wild exultation. Almost at once, however, Maddie's mood plummeted. A woman was sitting on his lap. She was a dark, exotic creature with mixed blood lineage. She was lush, as the tropics are lush. Her hair was black as midnight and thick with curls. It cascaded down her strong, brown shoulders in wavy tendrils.

A dark red dress imprisoned her body. From it swelled breasts round and full and almost bursting free. These, lighter than the skin usually exposed to the sun, reminded Maddie of two ripe tropical fruits.

Large brown eyes glittered triumphantly as their gaze caressed Henri. Her full lips, painted red, parted in a sensuous laugh that revealed strong white teeth. The woman's firm, brown arms hung around Henri's neck. Her hands, well-formed, moved gracefully as she stroked his cheek.

Standing there watching it all, tears flooded Maddie's eyes. It hurt especially much that he seemed to be enjoying himself. An impulse to run grief-stricken from the place almost overwhelmed her. Only the memory of all she had endured to come this far held Maddie back.

Instead of fleeing, she moved closer. She blinked back the blur filling her eyes so to see more clearly what she was about to face, then reminded herself that Henri believed her dead. Suddenly, she could wait no longer. With a deep breath, she hurried to him. "Henri!" Her voice trembled, barely audible, as she called to him. Her knees felt as if jelly had replaced bone, and to steady herself, she leaned against a chair.

Her call, though soft, must have been loud enough to reach ears yearning to hear her voice again. With a cry, Henri turned as he glanced up. Surprised, amazed, he drew in a sharp breath. His eyes widened with unmistakable joy. "God in Heaven, it's you!" It was a thrillingly familiar voice, one she sometimes thought she'd never hear again. At sound of it, Maddie struggled toward him through the crowd, bearing a radiant smile. Her heart pounded now in exultation. Tears streamed unashamedly down her cheeks as joy mingled with relief. Thank God he hadn't forgotten her. He still loved and wanted her. Maddie thrilled at how he cried out her name in such tender disbelief.

At sight of her, he shoved away from the table, then twisted upward as he struggled to his feet. "Oh, my darling!" His voice failed him. It hoarsened to the point where he could barely whisper. So utterly had Maddie's presence startled him, that he had forgotten all else in his effort to go to her. Heedless of the woman still on his lap, he had leaped up. With a startled squeal, she slid from his legs. Flung outward by his movement, she fought to keep from falling to the floor. Catching her balance, she stared with surprise from Henri to the newcomer he seemed so glad to see, and perceived almost at once the truth that this was no boy, but a woman beloved to Henri.

Her brown eyes widened, then narrowed, as anger became a cold, calculating intent for revenge. Her thick lashes fluttered as her glance darted back and forth from Henri to Maddie, to Henri again. An angry flush spread across her dark tanned cheeks, as she glared at the way Henri flung himself into Maddie's arms.

Her chest heaved. Her eyes flashed fire as she stood unwilling witness to their reunion. Her full lips peeled back from teeth parted, as if poised to tear the flesh from Maddie's bones. She pulled back her arms in fighting stance, clenching her fists. Her legs had spread to a posture ready to attack. Maddie glanced to her and felt a pang of apprehension. She saw purest hatred snapping in those wild dark eyes. In Maddie's joy at finding Henry, however, the woman's presence faded into unimportance. She became but a bad dream—one that had passed quickly through her mind, and out again with the waking dawn.

Maddie trembled in his arms. She clung to him as if afraid that the tides would come between them once again. More than ever, she yearned for him to take her as he had done once before. He had awakened her sleeping womanhood. She ached now for him to satisfy her again. "Oh, Henri!" she whispered. "It's been so long. How I've wanted you. How I've searched and prayed I might find you alive!" To her surprise, she spoke in a strangely breathless voice, as if she had been running a long, long time.

"Oh, Maddie, I had believed you dead." He stroked her hair, then bent to plant a kiss on her. All strength drained away from her. In its place surged a warm and yielding desire. She pressed herself against him, weak

284

from longing, yet elated beyond her wildest dreams. "Oh, take me, Henri!" Her voice trembled. "I am yours. Do whatever you will with me. That's all I want. It's all I ever wanted."

He peered into her face, then slid the fingertips of one hand down her cheeks. At his touch, a thrill rippled across her flesh. "You look exhausted, darling, yet beautiful. Sit down and tell me how you've come to be here. This miracle . . . ." His voice trailed off. It seemed he only wanted to look at her. He clung to her tightly until his warmth became hers.

"You've no idea what I've gone through to get here." Now that it was over, Maddie felt as if she had awakened from a terrible nightmare. "No idea at all. If I had loved you any less . . . ."

Henri held her close. "Thank God you love me as you do then," he whispered. "For by the Lord, I had thought the best part of my life was over."

The dark-skinned woman had disappeared, but as Maddie saw a flash of red near the door, she glanced back to Henri suddenly troubled. That woman had looked her way one last time, and the hatred Maddie saw in those eyes had sent chills of fear down her back. "Who is she, Henri?" she whispered. "That woman you were with, I mean?" She wasn't jealous anymore, but merely curious. She had already seen from his re-action how little that woman really meant to him.

"She is no one, and nothing—nothing at all to me," he said intensely. "Try to understand how it was Mad-die. I thought you were dead. I didn't see how you could possibly have survived. I barely did myself, and I am a man used to the sea. I had assumed that you, a fragile girl—" He shuddered.

"I understand all that, darling," she whispered, "but who is she, anyway?" She glanced after the woman ap-prehensively. "She frightens me somehow."

He shrugged "Oh, just a local girl. Someone who passed the time well enough for me. A warm body to cling to in the night."

"That warm body is very angry with you," she replied, then clung tighter to her man.

"Forget her!" He tossed his head. "It doesn't matter. She's nobody. Just another woman for sale, bought with a few shillings."

"Well, I don't like her, Henri," Maddie shivered suddenly. "She frightens me."

"Never mind!" Henri pressed his lips to hers. A thrill shivered through Maddie. Her flesh heated under his embrace. She wanted to leave now, to move far away to some isolated spot where they could be alone, away from the gaze of all these rough men who sat leering at them. "Oh, Henri, le.'s not stay here! Let's leave. I don't like it here at all."

Held in his arms, she could look beyond his shoulder to the door through which a few men with women disappeared. As she clung to him, held tight in her husband's arms again, she saw that door open. A man stepped out, returning alone to the central hall. His figure lay obscured in the shadows. At first, she saw only his silhouette, but as he drew closer Maddie's eyes widened in horror. Suddenly frightened, she stiffened in Henri's arms. She knew that face, and would have done anything to forget it. The hard and melancholy visage of Andrew Mathias drew closer. Suddenly their eyes met. In his, she read the message of her own doom.

Chapter Twenty-six

"Maddie, darling, what is it? What's wrong?" Henri

had sensed her sudden terror. He drew back and studied her face in alarm. "Dear God!" His eyes widened in shocked dismay. "You're white as death!"

"I saw him!" She trembled, unable to stop. "Right here just now. Oh, Henri, I saw *him*." Was it really possible that he had followed her, even here to this distant outpost of English civilization? How would he have known where to look?

Suddenly, with a shock of horror, Maddie remembered how she and Peter had discussed their plans late that afternoon when Peter had freed her from the Boston garret where Mathias had held her prisoner. The man had lain bound on the floor, seemingly unconscious, but he must have overheard. Aflame with thoughts of revenge for the hated woman who had bested him not once, but three times by then, and with nothing to lose because her father had ruined him in business, he had followed her south. It had to have happened just that way, with him using his low, vicious cunning to pick up bits and pieces of her trail. Maddie could think of no other explanation.

But why? No matter how much he hated her, any revenge he achieved would bring only limited satisfaction at best, yet his pursuit must have cost him endless trouble and expense. She couldn't understand such a mind as his. She realized with a chill that only a madman obsessed would have followed her that way.

In her frenzy, Maddie wiped the back of one hand across her eyes. She wanted to blot out vision of his dreaded, seemingly inescapable presence, and she succeeded. When she looked again, Mathias had disappeared, but his leaving provided no relief. Maddie glanced around in an uneasy fear. Had he been only a mirage, a trick her tired mind had played on her? She shuddered. As she felt in her very bones the overwhelming presence of evil, however, she knew that An-

287

drew Mathias did indeed lurk nearby. "Hold me close, Henri!" she whispered. "I'm afraid."

"Who did you see, Maddie? Maddie?" Alarmed because of her terror, Henri obeyed. He gathered her ever more snugly into his arms.

"Andrew Mathias. I saw Andrew Mathias. He followed me down here. I know he did."

"Who?" Henri blinked. He had obviously forgotten the name. Perhaps he had never known it from the start. Maddie knew, however, that if he saw, he'd recognize that fanatic who had thundered after them on horseback that dark night so long ago.

"You remember him, even if not by name," she said. "He was the one who followed us when we ran away. He was the one who planted that false evidence against me."

"Ah, *him!*" Remembrance dawned. For him too the memory was unpleasant. "What on earth is he down here for?"

"He never gave up. He followed me to Boston. He intended dragging me back to Salem, but with the help of a friend, I escaped him. He nearly killed me though, and now he's here, probably to try again." He was like a devil—uncannily able to sense her direction, and to follow her anywhere. She wondered with despair if she would ever be free of him.

Henri stared at her. Doubt mingled with concern on his handsome, brooding face. He would see that Mathias never came near them. In Salem, Mathias had enjoyed influence; he owned property, a business, a position of some importance. Here he was just another traveler passing through on his way somewhere else. Maddie began to feel a little easier now.

A small, nagging fear, however, clung like a burr to the back of her mind. Try as she might, she could not be rid of it. She glanced uneasily over her shoulder, as she remembered how Mathias had stalked her so many miles out of hatred, just as she pursued Henri out of love. Surely he would stop at nothing to destroy her. He would wait and watch until he found a way past the shield of her husband and protector.

"And you saw him here? Are you quite sure?" Henri didn't really believe her. Indeed, she wouldn't have believed herself, if she had been someone else. It all seemed so preposterous, somehow, and yet she knew. Henri continued, speaking soothingly, "Let's go then. We'll leave Bermuda soon as we can. Tomorrow, if you like."

"Yes, please!" Maddie clung to him. "Take me away. Get me out of here. This place suffocates me now." Foreboding surrounded her, choking her and clouding her mind. As they stood to leave, Maddie clung to him for support. Exhausted from searching, and now trembling with horror, she could hardly move.

Outside in the balmy night air, Maddie's fear evaporated. A wind whispered from off the sea just beyond. The dry, feathery fronds of palms rustled in its flow. The breeze stroked them both with moist, salt-scented caress. Gradually Maddie calmed. The sight of him had been fleeting. Perhaps she had, as Henri suspected, merely seen someone who looked like her old enemy. Maybe her tired mind had been playing tricks on her, materializing half-forgotten terrors out of thin air. As they walked side by side down the night-deserted streets, Maddie could almost smile at her fear. Even if Mathias had indeed followed her here, what harm could he do? She had her husband now, and he would protect her. They hurried down a hillside street closer to the harbor. From here Maddie saw water glittering under the stars and moon above. She smelled the clean salt tang wafting in from the sea, then sighed in satisfaction.

"Oh, my darling, you have no idea! I'm so happy to

see you," he cried out his joy yet again. "But tell me, how did this miracle come to pass? I want to reward those who helped you, and punish anyone who tried to hurt you."

"Henri, please!" She shuddered as she clung to his arm. "Leave off this talk of revenge. Evil ones make their own hells." She felt so lighthearted now, so overwhelmed with joy. "Do what you will to reward my friends, of course—especially Abraham Castaneda." She shuddered. "I hate to think of what would have happened, had he not heard of my plight and arranged to rescue me."

"Abraham—I should have known," he added, "from that flamboyant shirt you're wearing, if nothing else!"

Maddie chuckled, then continued in a serious tone, "He is a good friend, Henri. He arranged for me to be spirited off Hawkins's ship and rowed to his own. On board, he showed me every hospitality. By the way, he may still be looking for you."

Henri frowned. "Strange, he should have known right away."

After a silence, she turned to him. "Where are we going?"

"Back to my ship," he replied. "Then tomorrow we'll leave St. George."

Their feet clattered noisily on the wooden pier at water's edge. Laughing aloud, they leaped onto the gangplank of Henri's ship, *Genvieve*. Hand in hand they ran, feeling the wood spring and give underneath their pounding feet and weight. As they passed, Henri nodded to his watchman. "Disturb me only for emergencies."

He guided Maddie to a narrow stair leading upward to a door closed above, the Captain's cabin. Would his be opulent like Abraham's or spare and austere like the one aboard the *Anadeen*? Though curious, she didn't really care. Her only desire was to lie naked in his arms. "I love you, Maddie!" he whispered as he swept her inside. "You have no idea the agony I went through when I believed you dead."

Transported with joy, Maddie breathed his name like a prayer. "Oh, Henri!"

The inside of his cabin lay in shadows. Suddenly one darker than the others moved, coming toward them. "Henri!" Maddie whirled to him. With trembling hand, she tugged at his sleeve. He too had seen. His body tensed. His muscles hardened for attack, and his hand swooped to the knife hanging in his belt.

The shadow moved closer. It took form, becoming the shape of a woman. When he saw, Henri relaxed. His arm dropped away from where it had reached poised for his weapon's handle. Almost at once, however, he tensed again.

He recognized even sooner than Maddie who it was who lurked waiting for him. The lush, red-clad form of a woman he wanted so much to forget moved toward them now.

"So my man has found another, has he?' A honeyed voice purred with quiet, yet evil intensity. Black eyes glittered with malevolent hatred. The full lips had pulled back from white teeth in an almost animal-like snarl. The curling black hair tangled more wildly now, framing a sweat-glistening face. Even in darkness, Maddie could see that the woman's body poised for attack. Her fists had clenched into weapons she obviously ached to use against someone.

"Why did you come?" Henri's voice had fallen, becoming little more than a hoarsened whisper. "You should have known you wouldn't be welcome here any longer."

"I do not care if I be not welcome!" The woman

291

glared at him. "You be *my* man now, not hers anymore. I am an island woman. You should have known you cannot throw me away so easy."

She glanced to Maddie with withering scorn. "Her kind, Rohan—she be pretty now, but not for long. Too many men and strong island sun be too much for her. In the end, she wilt like some dead flower." Maddie chilled. The woman's words seemed more a threat or a curse than mere prediction.

"I want you to leave!" Henri's voice hardened. His jaw set and his chin raised high, giving his face a defiant air. "I don't know how you got on board, but—"

"You crazy, mon?" Her voice shrilled with scorn. "You watchman let me on, like he always do. He know me. He thought I meant to wait for you again, and I let him think it." She glanced to Maddie with hatred. "I come on board often, sweetie," she smiled, but with a strange glitter in her eyes. "*I* be his woman now."

"Well, you won't be coming anymore." Maddie surprised herself by the very boldness of her reply. "You might as well know, I am his wife. Henri will be spending his nights with *me* from now on."

The woman's eyes widened. They glowed an unearthly white around the pupils. They glared at Maddie, then whipped away to burn themselves into Henri. "You promise me, Rohan!" She spat her words in rage-hoarsened voice. "You promise me that *I* be your wife, not *her*."

Henri leaned to her. "I did not know my wife was still alive, Chloe. When I promised you, I really believed her dead."

"You lie!" The woman's lips peeled back from her teeth. Suddenly she turned to Maddie. "But maybe he *not* lie. I say we should put truth to his words." Suddenly, with a snarl, she lunged. Her hands clawed toward Maddie's throat. Maddie cried out. The hurtling weight knocked her off balance, sending them both crashing to the ground. Maddie fought to keep the woman's nails from her face; she could tell from that distorted expression that her rival would gladly gouge out her eyes.

Maddie struggled to defend herself, but the woman's strength overwhelmed her. Even Henri, who had flung himself down trying to pull the woman off Maddie, could only struggle against her at first. Anger-maddened, she had gained amazing strength.

She growled like an animal from the back of her throat. Her teeth clenched, flashing white, and spittle ran down her chin. Both her hands clutched around and yanked great hanks of Maddie's hair. Maddie screamed in pain. She sobbed aloud as she struggled against this woman gone suddenly insane, while Henri loomed above them.

Finally he managed to overpower her. He dragged his former mistress to her feet, pulling her from Maddie, who lay gasping for breath on the floor. With an angry curse, he twisted both arms behind her back. Furious at what the woman had done to his wife, he shook her fiercely. "Damn you!" he snarled. "I ought to kill you for this!"

"Go ahead!" the woman yelled back at him. "And you shall see what it be like, to have my ghost haunting you for all eternity."

Angrily, Henri yanked harder on the arm twisted behind her back. In pain but still defiant, the woman screamed, then spat a curse at him. Holding tight to his writhing prisoner, Henri half-dragged her to the door, then kicked it open. Standing in its frame, he bellowed a command for someone to come help him. Feet thundered below on the main deck. Men's voices shouting wafted up to Maddie's ears.

"Two of you—up here!" Henri de Rohan, captain

and master of this ship, called out to them. Two men hurried to obey. Henri shoved the woman at them with the same distaste he might show for a wild animal. With a cry, she landed in their arms. Maddie shrank back. She stared in pitying horror as she saw tears streaming now out of those brown eyes. With a pang, she realized that in her own way this woman had loved Henri too.

She started to murmur a word of sympathy, a plea for mercy to her husband, when suddenly the woman pulled free. She whirled from the men to fix blazing eyes on Maddie. "You will be sorry you ever come into his life, woman!" She spoke with low, purring intensity that sent chills down the back of Maddie's neck. "And you—" She turned now to face Henri. "You will be sorry you threw me away. You may laugh, but we in the islands—we have ways to make our enemies pay for what they do to us. In time, you might even pray for death."

Henri turned to his men. "I said, take her away!" He no longer looked at her, but stared into space, jaw clenched and features hard. Maddie saw that the woman could expect no mercy from him now.

All the way down and off the ship, they heard her screaming. Curses spewed from her mouth, and Maddie, still lying exhausted on the floor, shivered from the impact of such raw, naked hatred. Once he had overseen the woman's removal, Henri returned to Maddie. He kneeled beside her and gathered her into his arms. "Oh, my darling, are you all right?" His breath blew warm and soft against her cheek.

Unable to speak at first, Maddie drew in great shuddering breaths. "Oh, she's awful, Henri. Utterly awful, and so strong! If you hadn't been here, she would have killed me for sure. At the very least, she would have blinded me."

"My God, you're trembling!" He held her close for a

moment, then lifted her up. Her legs felt as if they would collapse. Henri's strength, however, supported her all the way over to his bunk.

"Sit here." He lowered her down. "I'll get you something to drink. Lord knows you probably need it."

To give them light, he fired an oil lamp bolted to one wall. Shadows from it flickered and danced over everything, as Maddie looked around. The furnishings, she saw, were simple. A slim mattress covered his bunk, and upon it spread a woolen blanket. "You and your friend . . . live very differently aboard ship." To be honest, she preferred the elegance of Castaneda's cabin to this spare and spartan simplicity, perhaps because Henri's cabin reminded her of what she had seen aboard the *Anadeen*.

Henri shrugged, then tossed a smile at her. He seemed to know what she was thinking and found her amusing. "It's comfortable enough," he said. "Too much luxury is fine on land, but while sailing, it makes me fat and lazy." He returned, carrying a bottle filled with dark liquid. In his other hand nestled two glasses. He set them on his built-in desk, then filled each. "Here, drink this." He handed one to her. Maddie raised it to her lips and sipped. It was rum, thick and black as the molasses from which it had been distilled. "I love you so much, Maddie," he whispered watching her.

"And I love you, too!"

She let him wrap his arms around her. She moved her own to hold him close, to press her breasts against his chest. Through them, she felt his heart beating. She realized at once that both their bloodstreams pulsed with desire and yearning for each other's touch.

He had untied her silken blouse by then, and gently folded it back. His right hand cupped the firm, high globe of her left breast, warming it under his palm. She raised her face to him. Her lips hungered to taste his

295

own yet again. He pressed his mouth to her, parting hers with his own, then slid his tongue deep inside.

A spasm of desire convulsed her. She clung to him tighter now, as if she dared not let him go. "I would rather die than lose you again," she whispered. As she spoke, she released him from her embrace. Her hand now slid across his thigh, then timidly reached to touch the fire of his manhood. Under her fingers she felt his desire and knew, with glowing rush of satisfaction, that he wanted her as desperately as she yearned for him.

"You must not say such things, Maddie," he whispered. "Or even think them. To do so is to invite disaster."

"But how can I want to live if you're not here to share my life?" His hand had slid between her legs. As he touched where she had so longed to feel him, a yearning burst of fire thrilled across her flesh. The pulse in her throat had begun wildly to flutter. At her question, however, he pulled back. Though holding her still where she ached the most, he gazed upon her with serious expression. "My life is turbulent, Maddie. You already know, I should imagine, the worst of it."

Maddie faced him with loving, troubled eyes. "I've heard what I've heard—that the Spaniards and French whom you rob call you *Le Diable*. That you're the most dangerous pirate in all the Caribbean, or so they tell me."

She burned for him to finish what he had started. She wanted him to take her, to possess her with the fierce and burning power of his manhood. Only in wild, blinding desire fulfilled could she forget everything that now haunted her, but maddeningly he still held her without moving. He studied her a moment sadly. "And would it make a difference if they all spoke the truth? If I am indeed a brutal, bloodthirsty outlaw?"

Maddie fixed her eyes on him. She could not have

known how luminous they glowed in that dimly lit cabin, nor how beautiful she looked, all bronze and gold. She could not have guessed how the firm, young softness of her body melting under his touch had aroused him. He had never really admitted to her how much more she meant to him than life itself, nor how hard he prayed that fate would not tear her from him, as it had all the others he had ever loved.

"Henri!" Maddie reached for him now. "I can no longer stand back and look down upon those who walk paths the world condemns. Those same 'good' people who robbed you of your birthright—the conventional, the devout and law-abiding—they have robbed me, too." She smiled bitterly. "You forget that I am considered a witch. Is it not fitting that I should couple with *Le Diable* himself?"

He laughed. "Oh, Maddie!" he cried her name in a softer tone, then kneeled over her. His hands roamed, warming her flesh wherever they fondled, lingering especially upon her breasts, then again between her thighs. His breath blew like a soft caress against her neck, and his tenderness thrilled her.

She ached. She yearned for him to take her to himself, and yet, with sweet, tender cruelty, he held back. A languorous warmth had heated her flesh. It mingled in a strange union with the growing pulsing urgency that nearly drove her mad from wanting him. "Henri!" she sobbed his name aloud, as she writhed in his arms.

How could he do this? How could he tease? She moaned, imprisoning him with her arms and legs. Her very body begged him to take her. Finally, when she could stand it no longer, he thrust forward with one powerful swoop. His weight and heat and strength smashed against her. A convulsion of pain-yet-pleasure screamed through Maddie's flesh. Her lips parted in a moan of sweet, agonized delight, then faded into a sigh. Clinging to him, she smiled as her body moved with his own in perfect harmony.

Chapter Twenty-seven

As they lay in one another's arms, reality filtered back, bathed in a glorious glow. Colors had heightened for her now, and sound clarified. The moment of their love lingered on, floating into all eternity. "I never want to leave your arms, Henri," she whispered.

"Nor I yours."

Maddie felt a pang. "What will become of us now?" How could such joy possibly last? Surely life, as it always did, would come between them somehow to destroy their happiness.

"I don't know." Henri grew suddenly sober. "Anything can happen to me, and in case I should die, I want you provided for."

Maddie recoiled. "Henri, do not speak of death! I forbid it." The very thought chilled her.

Henri raised himself up onto one elbow to gaze at her. "Maddie, darling, we have to be realistic. I fight, and I'm sorry to say, I kill. Someday, someone stronger or luckier may come and kill me, too."

"Henri, I don't want to hear it!" His words turned her joy into fear and desolation.

"But you may have to face it someday. I want you to be prepared."

Maddie clung to him. "No, please! I don't want to. Why do you have to live the way you do? Can't you leave the Spaniards alone, and run honest trading ships? Or find something on land?"

"This is the only life I know anymore, Maddie. In any case, it's got beyond me now. People know me. The name they have given me, *Le Diable*, it strikes fear and terror into their very hearts. Why, even if I denounced this life, they would still come after me. Think of how important the man will be who kills me." Henri smiled upon her tenderly. "No, my darling, I'll be safer going on as I have. In any case, I'll be leaving these islands soon, on my next trip."

Maddie stared. "Where will you go?"

Henri shrugged. "Spain is played out. There's little left, and in any case, the climate here is changing. Of all the places I once used as a safe harbor, only St. George remains, and even that will change in time."

He glanced around and sighed. "I had been making arrangements with you father to cope with it."

"Arrangements?" Maddie started. "Have you heard from Papa?"

He shook his head. "Not since we left, no. I had been looking to New England," he continued. "Despite its miserable weather, it's a friendlier climate now, to my kind." He smiled ironically. "The tradesmen and government types in those northern states care not how you gain your wealth, so long as you spend it there, and behave in an orderly fashion while you're doing it. I had planned to establish safe harbor in Salem, and perhaps I will, despite the way they treated my wife." He smiled down at her with roguish grin. "It's got good deep water, you see, and its merchants carry all the things I need. Boston is too populous, and New York, too. Things have a way of getting out of control in places like that."

They spent the night in one another's arms, then sailed from harbor the next day's dawning. The sea, an azure blue, reflected the glowing sky. Feather clouds gleamed there, and while Henri attended to his duties,

Maddie spent the time alone, staring fascinated at the movements of water and air.

They sailed southward for three days. On the afternoon of the fourth, Maddie found herself leaning against the railing of his ship. Facing outward toward the green and jagged islands passing, she lifted her gaze to Henri, who had stopped for a few minutes to talk with her. "Where is this place you're taking us to?"

"It's an island called Dominica. I have a villa there, overlooking the sea."

"How soon will we come to it?" She could go on like this forever.

"We're almost to it now. You'll see it in a few moments, but my villa is around the other side from our approach."

True to his promise, she saw it soon after. They sailed further, until the *Genvieve* rounded a point into the island's superb natural harbor. A few other ships floated there, and since Henri seemed neither surprised nor dismayed, Maddie guessed these were either friendly, or else belonged to his fleet.

Up a hill directly above loomed a fortress-like edifice of stone, and it looked for all the world like a small walled city. Henri pointed to it now. "That's where we're going, darling. It's my own Spanish fortress—at least for a while longer. Few know of it, and fewer still would dare to storm it."

Maddie squinted to focus a better look. "Your villa is up there? Somewhere in that fortress?"

"The whole place is my villa," he replied. "A haven for me and my men. As I said before, it used to be an old Spanish outpost, built in their days of arrogance, when they and their neighbors in Portugal actually believed each could own half of all the New World, merely on the word of their bloody Borgia pope."

He chuckled, then laughed out loud. "How ironic,

300

really, is life! The place is mine now, trod upon and owned by me, a devil-bedamned Huguenot!''

Horses waited at land's edge to take them up the narrow, steep path to the settlement above. Maddie's own, a white mare, waited patiently as Henri helped his wife to mount. She rode behind him side-saddle, and as they traveled uphill in single file upon their sweating, puffing beasts, they talked. Finally the path widened, and they rode side by side. When they could finally speak to one another without shouting, Henri turned to her. "A man of God lives among us here," he said. "A former priest who left the Church to follow a light of his own. He'll marry us this very evening, if you consent."

Maddie smiled. "As far as I'm concerned, we're already married." For better or for worse she had bound herself to him for all time.

Henri reached and squeezed her hand with his own. "My darling wife, what an unusual woman you are. Any other would have cared most of all about the public display. Only by having it witnessed by a hundred casual onlookers would they have considered themselves truly married." He went on, speaking tenderly, "But you—all it takes to satisfy you is a vow whispered in secrecy, and you've deemed it adequate."

He smiled. "But I want it public. I want my own men to know you as my wife, and to treat you with all the respect I demand for you. It's for your own protection, too," he added. "If you should ever return home, perhaps with a child in your arms, you'll need proof of your wedlock to keep the respect of your neighbors."

Henri's men greeted him with joyful shouts. She and her husband walked with them the rest of the way up the steep hill through the gate to his own quarters—a castlelike structure in the center, with smaller buildings clustered around. Once inside, Maddie stared around her in awe. A massive table of some dark wood carved intricately filled the central hall, and around it lined chairs fitted with velvet-covered seats. Rugs from far-off Araby covered a cool, flagstone floor, while tapestries, depicting scenes of medieval pageantry, hid its stone walls. He carried her at once to the bedroom. This great vaulted chamber furnished in the same grandiose Spanish style lacked coziness, but Maddie knew that with Henri, it would be comfortable enough. "They left all their bedding and their art when they fled," he said as he carried her over to the bed, then lowered her down. A window curved at its topmost edge into an arch let daylight into the dim, stone-walled room. Through it, Maddie saw blue sky and clouds skidding by, not at all like the gray skies of home.

"Oh, Henri, you've brought me so far away from where I was born, and I've changed so much that, when I look in a mirror, I hardly recognize myself."

"Do you regret what's become of you?" He faced her now with suddenly serious eyes.

Maddie smiled. "No, of course not, but sometimes when I think back, I marvel at how ordinary that Sunday I met you started out to be, yet by its end, I not only made a blood enemy, but fell in love, too." She thought again of Andrew Mathias, and wondered with a shudder what he might be plotting against her now.

Henri stroked her hair. "Dear Maddie, I'll leave you now. Prepare yourself for tonight while I attend to matters of my own. I'll see to it you have everything you need." He kissed her once upon the lips, then went away.

Maddie had been standing at that window, looking out on to the ocean so blue that glittered seemingly directly underneath, when two servants came, carrying cloth of white silk. They fitted her then went away. A few hours later, they returned, carrying with them a wedding gown trimmed in lace. Because lace was forbidden to adorn the clothing of Puritan women, who were supposed to look sober and devout at all times, never frivolous, Maddie had never owned anything so richly decorated. When she saw, her eyes widened in delight.

"And this pretty thing be for you, too," continued the old negress. "Master wants you to wear it tonight." The woman handed Maddie a small, mahogany casket. Maddie opened it, then gasped with happy surprise. A necklace of perfectly matched, pink-tinted pearls lay inside. With hands trembling, she lifted the string up and fastened it around her throat. Its color, like the first glowing of dawn, matched the blush that raised now to her own cheeks. "It's beautiful!" she whispered. Henri was so good to her. She had loved him before. More than ever she adored him now.

"I tell Master you like. He be happy to hear it."

Later, Maddie met her husband in the great central hall downstairs. When he saw her, his eyes lit up, and he smiled. "You look so lovely, Maddie," he whispered. "You were meant to wear fine clothes like this and be admired. The Puritans, I fear, waste their pretty women."

Maddie lowered her eyes. At his words, a hot blush burned across her cheeks. "Thank you, sir," she whispered, then flashed him a quick, suddenly shy smile.

Some of his men played musical instruments. To the accompaniment of guitar, fife, and horn, the two of them walked, side by side toward a short, sunburned fellow standing apart form all the others, holding a bible. In front of the assembled company, Henri and Maddie repeated their vows. Afterward, amidst cheers, they embraced in a fine, lingering kiss.

The feast that followed their wedding was one Maddie would always remember. A calf roasted whole glistened on a hand-turned spit. Suckling pigs decorated with tropical fruits graced the long, wooden tables, along with carafes of strong wine and sweet whiskey, but she and Henri did not remain. They wandered instead to the garden. There, among fragrant jasmine blooms, amidst wild ginger and roses, pungent geraniums and night-glowing hibiscus, Henri lowered her down.

Her lips parted to inhale a delighted shuddering breath as his weight pressed upon her. A thrill of pleasure rippled through her flesh, as he tasted upon her mouth a honeyed kiss. She reached to him, quivering with anticipation as he gently untied her gown. She trembled at the mere sensation of his touch upon her breasts and belly. Tonight was a special moment. For the first time, she was his wife in the eyes of society, as well as God. While others feasted at their wedding banquet, she and Henri savored the moments alone.

Each time seemed fuller, more exciting than the last. His caress transported her into ever higher heavens. His body, lean, hard, and tanned, pressed down against her softness. His arms encircled her. As before, she surrendered; united with his passion, she yearned to lose herself, to become one flesh with him for all time. Thrills of pleasure rippled up her spine, across the back of her neck, then through all parts of her, like white, pulsing bursts of fire.

"On, my darling, my darling!" Maddie clung to him with both arms, pulling him closer, as if by sheer effort she could melt into him forever.

"I love you," he murmured. "More than life itself do I love you, and it terrifies me."

"Don't be afraid. I'll always be here, always yours so long as you want me." Maddie smiled up into his eyes, and tried to hide the sickening heart-flutter of premonition that warned he'd be the first to go, cut down by the weapons of his enemies. Tonight was their wedding night, and Maddie would let nothing, least of all her own fears, dim its pleasure.

In a distance they heard the ocean roaring, a rhythmic drone, of breakers crashing against rock, eating land into steep, eroded cliffs. Strains of music wafted out to them from inside. Suddenly, however, Maddie felt the shock of something cold and wet biting into her passion-heated skin. A drop, and then another coming faster, warned of a storm beginning. Henri too had noticed it. Leaning on one elbow, he smiled down at her. "Come, darling, I think it's best we go inside. In any case, I'm hungry."

At mere mention of food, Maddie realized that she too felt ravenous, now that the other appetite had been satisfied.

Once inside, he set her down on a divan at the head of the table, then joined her. "Some wine!" he cried, clapping his hands, "and make mine red." At once, a Blackamoor, one of his men, poured and carried two carafes to them—one red and strong for the man, the other sweet, fermented of ripe tropical fruits, for this wife. Later, Henri carried Maddie upstairs to bed.

The following week passed by in a tumult of stormy weather. Rainstorm intensified into hurricane. Winds screaming up and out of the ocean churned the breakers to frightening heights. They crashed into shore, battering rocks and trees, then ripped oceanward again. The power of the wind flung bits of stone off the parapet just outside their room. Rain poured down in blinding sheets. Stinging wind-driven pellets of water splattered against the roofs and shuttered windows, but neither she nor Henri cared about the weather. They spent their nights and days together in that great vaulted bedroom. With the storm for music, they lay and laughed and loved in one another's arms.

Finally the storm cleared. One day Maddie woke up

to the sound of silence, instead of rain. Curious and hopeful, she pushed open one wood-shuttered window to gaze outside at a sky still blackened with clouds. Through one small hole, however, gleamed a faint, dim patch of blue.

Suddenly Maddie spotted a ship below, a very small one, slipping past the straits into the harbor where all the other ships still lay blessedly undamaged, waiting for future conquest. For some reason not even understood, she felt a chill dread to see it there. Within the hour, the captain of the ship had arrived in their fortress with a message for Henri. Maddie followed him downstairs, breathless and strangely afraid.

As the stranger waited in the great hall, Henri approached. Maddie walked by his side, though a step or two behind. "Welcome," Henri greeted the man. "But please—tell me who you are, and how you know of my fortress."

"My name is Dante Thibold. I am merely a trader of sorts, running supplies between these islands, but I came to you for another reason than to sell." As they waited, curious, he continued, "You have a comrade, Abraham Castaneda by name."

Henri tensed. "What about him?" Maddie's heart began to flutter. It seemed to rise to her throat and choke her.

Henri's eyes narrowed. "What about him, sir? You must know I am anxious for word of him."

"He is in some difficulty, I'm afraid." The stranger handed Henri a note. "He managed to smuggle this out to me from where they're keeping him—in the dungeon of Port Royal."

Maddie drew in a sharp intake of breath. Her heart fluttered in fear and horror. Abraham Castaneda, her friend and Henri's *imprisoned?*

"They plan to put him up for trial, and no doubt,

hang him. Bennett in Bermuda is our only friend left, I'm afraid. You yourself know how Lynch is, Rohan, and that's why the Crown made him governor. Now that they don't need you any longer, now that the Royal Navy is strong enough to protect these island dominions, they're trying to wipe us all out. As for Lynch, he'd as soon order Castaneda hanged as look at him.''

Maddie chilled. It was too awful. She pressed close to Henri and leaned over his shoulder to read Cataneda's note. The handwriting she saw was strange to her, barely readable. Though ornate in its basic letter formation, she could tell the message had been scrawled with urgent haste. ''Henri, it might be a trap.'' Suddenly apprehensive, she whispered into his ear, ''Are you sure this letter is really from *him*?''

Henri's mouth straightened into a grim line. ''It's from him all right. I'd recognize his handwriting anywhere.'' He turned to her. ''Maddie, wait for me upstairs. I want to discuss matters further with this messanger, and I can do it better alone.''

With heavy heart, Maddie obeyed. In her bed chamber, she waited, hours it seemed, for him to return. Unable to stand it any longer, she hurried back downstairs. To her surprise, she found the place almost deserted. Her eyes widened and her heart sank when she learned the truth. Henri had gone in haste to deliver his friend from certain death by hanging, and he had done so without saying good-by, in order to avoid her tears. Angry, hurt, and fearful, Maddie turned away from the servant who broke the news to her.

The days passed somehow, into weeks. Was it boredom, or something else, that made her notice strange changes in her body? Standing on the parapet overlooking the harbor one bleak and windswept afternoon, Maddie pressed a hand to her breasts as she remembered the days and nights of love she had shared with Henri, and she knew, as only a woman can, that she was carrying his child.

As she stood there that afternoon, thinking and planning for the unborn child's future, Maddie saw a ship waft silently toward the harbor from open sea. As it drew closer, she cried out with delight. By its flying colors, she recognized the *Maidenhead*.

Castaneda had escaped! He had returned to safe harbor. Surely her husband, if he was not on the *Maidenhead* with his friend, would be not far behind in his own ship, the *Genvieve*.

Castaneda rode uphill on a mule, while she ran down to him on foot. He met her more than half way. His eyes widened in surprise when he saw her. "Maddie!" he cried out her name, then climbed down. "How good to see you again, but you shouldn't be walking on such rough ground in kidskin slippers. They're too thin. You'll hurt your feet."

"Oh, Abraham, I'm so glad you're free. When we heard you were arrested in Port Royal, waiting to be hanged, well—" She tossed her head. "We were beside ourselves, as you can imagine. Tell me, is Henri close behind? Did he have much trouble freeing you?" Her voice trembled with excitement. Words gushed from her in a torrent.

Castaneda drew back in horrified surprise. "Port Royal? What are you talking about?"

Maddie stared at him dumbfounded. "Your letter, of course. Don't you remember? A man named Dante Thibold delivered it to us a few weeks ago. He said you smuggled it out to him from the dungeons at Port Royal."

"I never heard of any Dante Thibold, and I wrote no such letter." He clutched her by the shoulders. "Nor was I ever in Port Royal, Maddie, nor in its gaol. I had some trouble in St. George where I left you, and it took me almost a week to get away.''

He stared apologetically at her. "How glad I am you found him, or you would have been left stranded. When I finally broke free, you had gone. I was on my way back here, to leave a message for Rohan, when that terrible storm came up and forced me to put in at the nearest port."

"But your handwriting! Henri recognized your handwriting." Maddie stared at him in mounting horror.

Castaneda's mouth tightened into a grim line. "Well, it must have been forged."

Chapter Twenty-eight

Icy fear gripped Maddie's soul. She stared at him now, too paralyzed to move. "Henri," she whispered. "He's gone off to free you. He believed that letter!"

"Dear God! That means he's in Port Royal now," he said bleakly. Judging from his tone, and from what she already knew of Governor Lynch, Jamaica's new overseer, Maddie understood that Port Royal was the most dangerous place of all for Henri to be. "What will we do?"

"I'll disguise myself and go after him," he replied. "It's the least I can do for him."

"I'm coming with you."

He started. "Maddie, you can't. It would be too dangerous."

"Do you think I can stand to remain here, knowing the both of you are in danger? I'd go mad! In any case, sometimes a comely wench can prove useful. She can get into places and situations where a man would never be trusted."

"If anything ever happened to you—"

"I'm going into it with my eyes open," she retorted, "and I think I know the risks as well as you do. You seem to forget, Abraham, that I love my husband, and I'll do anything it takes to free him. *Anything!*"

He glanced to the fortress above, then to her. "How many men are in there still?"

"Just a handful."

"Then maybe it's safer to come with me, after all," he said with a thoughtful frown. "The forgery and false information are obviously part of a conspiracy, and that means our enemies now know the location of Henri's fortress."

Maddie chilled at a sudden, horrible thought. "You mean they lured Henri to Port Royal just to capture him?"

Castaneda spoke quietly. "Why else? I would think it has to be the case. Whether that messenger was an agent of the governor or the minion of one of Rohan's other enemies, does not matter. He's in deep trouble. We can learn the truth when we get there. As for now, we can only hope for the best and prepare for the worst."

Port Royal, until recently one of the richest and most corrupt cities in all the Caribbean, was now a town on the rise. Built outward from the shacks still blighting the waterfront, she saw signs of the town's change and transformation. Edifices of stone or brick—government offices and mansions of the newly wealthy—had risen up in a separate, newer district. They overlooked sunlight-speckled lawns. Fine tall palms and flowering bushes shaded the carefully laid-out walkways. Already, the marble carved portrait of some former governor graced Port Royal's main square, and all this construction proved to Maddie what others had already hinted. The winds of time had brought change to Port Royal, blowing out the old days. The bucaneers, the pirates, maroons, and privateers who used to gather here were gone now, swept away forever and replaced, slowly and clumsily, but with increasing force, by a new sea breeze of prosperity supported by sugar-growing, rum, and slave trading. Henri no longer belonged to this place, nor did the man who walked by her side. The middle classes, newly wealthy and smugly energetic, had replaced them all.

Suddenly, a chaise rattled past. Maddie glanced at the passenger riding behind its driver, then startled, whirled to take a better look. To her dismay, she recognized someone she had hoped never to see again. Well dressed in rich clothes, a woman of color sat alone on a seat wide enough for two. She sailed along in a cloud of silk chiffon fluff. Peach colored, its ruffles and lace contrasted and set off her creamed-coffee-colored skin. Her hair swirled upward in elegant cascade, and proud of her own superiority, she gazed outward to the street below. Her dark almond-shaped eyes glittered with haughty contempt. As her gaze riveted around to meet Maddie's, however, she too started in surprise. Her black eyes narrowed, then lingered upon Maddie and her companion. Shocked, Maddie grabbed Abraham's arm. When he looked up and saw, he too gasped. "Chloe!" he barely whispered aloud the woman's name. "How in Hell . . . ?" His words trailed into silence.

Chloe's eyes studied them both as if to memorize what she saw, then with a stick of silver-trimmed ebony, she tapped her driver's shoulder. He, a black-skinned man, perhaps a slave, slowed down. He leaned back while she whispered something in his ear. He nodded and whipped his horse again. At once, the rig lurched forward, thundering almost at a gallop around the nearest corner. Maddie stared after, chilled. "My God!" she whispered. "What does it mean?" That her bitterest rival should be here in Port Royal right now of all times unnerved her.

"Oh, it's probably nothing," Abraham's reply came in a voice too shaky to be convincing. He gave her hand a reassuring squeeze. "It's probably just a coincidence.

Suddenly, he squeezed her arm and pointed. "This tavern—I used to come here with Rohan in the old days. Let's go in. Perhaps we'll find someone who remembers us, perhaps even knows . . . ." His voice trailed off. A spark of hope, a glimmer that some crony still willing to be friendly might have heard what happened to Rohan once he reentered this unfriendly port, heartened him. "You'll have to come in with me, unfortunately." He frowned, obviously considering the place unsuitable for her. "But you should be all right . . . with me."

The air inside hung damp around them, and smelled of beer and salted fish. He left her sitting at a table, while he went off. Uneasily, she glanced to him and saw him deep in conversation with the barkeep. Finally he returned. She sighed with relief as he sat back down. Other men in that tavern hall had been eyeing her.

He looked around, then leaned to her. "I learned something already," he said, barely above a whisper. "The proprietor of this place is an old friend of mine—Jack Trimble by name. He's out just now, but his steward thinks he'll be back soon. He might know something. When he returns, I'll try to talk to him."

"Oh, I think I'll go mad!" Maddie's heart fluttered.

"In the meantime," he continued, "talk is loose in a place like this, so it's possible we'll hear something on our own." However, just then Jack Trimble returned. He was a squat man with wispy brown hair and gray eyes, wearing rumpled clothes. The minute his gaze fixed on Abraham, he cried out, then motioned for them to follow into a back room he used as his office.

"Jack, this is Madame de Rohan," her friend gestured to Maddie as she followed them in. "She's just as anxious to learn what happened as I am."

"No doubt." He studied both of them for several seconds without speaking, then shrugged. "Well, I'm sorry to say it, but things are looking very bad for him. Very bad indeed." Fear clutched Maddie's throat. "He sailed into Port Royal some time last week—a stupid thing to do!" He spat. "Anyway, *they* were all expecting him—the King's troops and everyone. That's really all I know."

"What do you mean, *they*?" Abraham leaned forward with face tense. His widened eyes had fixed on the proprietor's. Maddie didn't even have to ask if Henri had been arrested.

The man glanced to Castaneda and shrugged. "He's a very big catch, you know." He frowned to both of them. "Why on earth did he come, anyway? He knew what it's like here now. Everybody does. Why, in God's name, why?"

Her friend's mouth hardened into a grim line. He explained to Jack Trimble how their enemies had set Henri up with the forged letter. When Abraham had finished, Jack Trimble let out a sigh. "So that was it. Who do you suppose—"

"I don't know," Castaneda interrupted him, "but when I find out, I will take pleasure in killing him . . . *inch by inch!*"

"That won't bring Henri back!" Maddie broke into their conversation. "Run him through, if you will, when you find him, but first things first. Now we must figure out some way to save Henri."

"It will not be easy, Madame." Trimble sighed. "My brother-in-law is a warden in the gaol, and he's the one

313

what told me where they're holding Rohan. They'll keep him down in the seventh dungeon, he says, until they get around to hanging him.''

Maddie chilled. Death by hanging was considered no doubt a fitting end for an accused pirate. Castaneda leaned forward. His face had taken on a steely, intent look she had never seen in it before. ''Why have they waited so long?''

The man shrugged. ''Information. They want to pry information out of him, about his men and the number of ships in his fleet, things like that.''

''He'll never betray his men!'' cried Maddie.

Trimble turned to her pityingly. ''M'lady, they have ways of making it damned uncomfortable to hold back on them.'' He glanced to Castaneda. ''You know what they have hidden down in those dungeons. As I told you, Rohan is already condemned. Only Lord Carstarfin, the Chief Magistrate, or else the Governor himself, could commute Rohan's sentence now, and they're not likely to. They hate Rohan, most of all because he ain't English.''

Castaneda nodded. Maddie chilled at the sight of his grim horror. ''Can your brother-in-law tell us the location of Rohan's cell?'' Castaneda stared hard into the other man's face.

Trimble shrugged. ''I already know, but it'll do ye little good, I'm afraid. Here—'' He handed her friend a rolled-up parchment. ''Here's a map of the dungeons. I pinched it from me brother-in-law only yesterday. You can see by looking just how hard it would be to storm it. Prob'ly impossible.''

''Perhaps we can find another way, then,'' Maddie said suddenly, breaking into their worried silence. ''What if I were to go to the Governor himself, and plead? After all, Henri would not even have come near Jamaica, if someone had not lured him.'' She stared long and hard at them both. "Nor has he committed any crimes here."

"The man's very presence in this town is considered a crime, as is our own," Abraham retorted grimly. "I'm sorry to say it, Maddie, child, but if they took the trouble to lure him here, they'll not let him loose upon the pleading of a woman." He fixed his eyes deep and sad upon her own. "Not even a woman as beautiful as you."

Maddie sensed the sorrowing, brutal reality of his words. At the same time, however, she knew her own desperation. "What have we to lose by trying?" She whirled from her friend to Jack Trimble. "I, for one, am willing enough to chance it." With a despairing sigh, she tossed her head. "What else can I do? Sit and wait for news of his execution? No, I cannot!" Her last words were a cry of anguish.

"I would trade all I have," whispered her friend, "to gain love such as yours. Nevertheless, I forbid it, just as Rohan himself would, if he but knew." He took hold of her shoulders, squeezing them hard. "Do you think he'd forgive me, Maddie, if I allowed you to do what you just suggested? Dear God, he'd run me through with his own blade."

Sorrowing and angry, Maddie turned her eyes away from him. Was she the only one with the courage to act, she wondered in bitter, despairing rage.

In the end, fate took the mater from their hands, in the form of a summons from Chief Magistrate of Port Royal, Joseph Carstarfin. Luckily, Abraham had gone out with his friend at the time, leaving her, they believed, safely alone in her rented room. She heard a knocking at the door. Expecting her friend's immediate return, she flung it open. Instead of Abraham

Castaneda, however, stood a stranger, a liveried servant of mixed white-African lineage, who handed her a silver-edged envelope. Maddie's heart pounded as she tore it away and unfolded the paper inside.

Madame de Rohan,

Your presence here in Port Royal has come to my attention, leaving me no choice but to contact you. With fatherly concern, I would urge you to leave this town immediately. If, as I fear, you choose to ignore my good counseling, then come immediately, accompanied by my servant Hugo, and I will grant you an audience, although I cannot promise what you might desire.
Sincerely,
Joseph Carstarfin.

Maddie's heart pounded, as she scribbled a message to her friend who would return she knew not when, then followed alongside Hugo the messenger, to meet with Joseph Carstarfin. When she met him, the chief magistrate proved to be a hard-eyed man about fifty-five who cut a dashing figure. Despite the summer's heat and humidity, he wore a wig powdered white as was fashionable in his native England. His breeches, sewn of nubby linen dyed soft brown, reached just below his knees. Ivory piping trimmed their bottom cuffs, while fine silk hosiery covered his calfs and disappeared into shoes of black kid leather, decorated with a large, tooled silver buckle on each. He wore a jacket of that same fabric, cut lower in back, like the petals of a tulip, and nipped tight at the waist. A cravat of finest chiffon, white and blue of woven stripes, covered his throat. Maddie saw at once that he was no mere dandy, however, but an able, ruthless administrator of his duties for the Crown. In his thin yet sharp-planed face, intent eyes of almost navy-blue peered out from underneath thick, black brows that seemed always to scowl. His hooked nose reminded Maddie of the beak of a predatory bird, while his mouth, thin-lipped and set in a taut line, hinted at a nature that could turn on its enemies with cold and merciless fury. His jaw was square, his chin strong and cleft. It was a handsome, well-formed face in its own way, yet Maddie looked into those intelligent cold eyes and shivered, suddenly afraid. She began to wonder what she had gotten herself into. Only the knowledge that this stranger might be her only chance to help Henri kept her from turning with a cry and running away. Facing him now, Maddie curtsied. "Y-your Lordship?" Terrified, her voice trembled. "I am only a wife coming to plead for mercy . . . for my husband."

A strange heat prickled up her neck and across her cheeks. It tinged her skin a delicate pink, the color of some rare flower. She stood before him now in the prettiest dress she had carried with her from Dominica, a cotton frock painted at the bottom with flowers. Its bodice scooped low, cut square, but the lace trim ruffled at its edge concealed more than it revealed of the soft, white swells of her breasts. Her chest now heaved in the intensity of her emotion. Her pulse fluttered in the hollow of her slender throat. Although she had carefully combed and arranged her hair only a few hours ago, the wind of her ride over had disheveled it. The hated but useful boyish cut of earlier weeks had grown out, but her returning curls were still short enough to be unruly. Their tendrils fluffed and curved around her cheeks, flushed rosy now. They surrounded her face like a golden halo.

The words poured from her, pleading words calculated to melt his heart. As she spoke, she remembered her last conversation with Abraham Castaneda. It had taken place earlier that afternoon, right before he had left with Jack Trimble. "I have no idea how to help, Abraham," she had whispered, "but you must understand that I'll do anyting, no matter how odious, to get Henri out of there. *Anything!*"

She remembered her own words with special clarity, now that she saw the way Carstarfin's eyes lingered upon her breasts. She tingled as his gaze slid up her neck and face, then dropped lower, to the place where tight-laced bodice met the ten yards or so of cotton gathered into her skirt. She knew beyond a doubt that he was thinking about what lay underneath, visualizing white thighs and the warm, secret place between. Watching him watch her, Maddie vowed a silent secret oath that she'd gladly trade anything he wanted of her, if it meant Henri's freedom and life.

Suddenly, the door behind opened. As a dark clad figure stepped into the room, Maddie's eyes widened. She recoiled in shocked surprise. Terror welled again within her as she found herself face to face with her old enemy. "No, not you!" she could hardly whisper. Her burning eyes now darted from Mathias to Carstarfin, back to Mathias. "So it was you all along! You're behind all this. I should have known." How he must hate her. How that hatred must haunt his life.

For one brief instant, Maddie even felt a surge of pity for the dark, obsessed man who had followed her so far, but then it ebbed away, driven out by anger. What had she ever done to deserve such vengeance? If anything, he had wronged her. That attempted rape in the cemetary had been a horror. His planted evidence, silently and falsely accusing her of witchcraft, could have gotten her killed. She shuddered even now to remember that Boston garret where she had lain for hours, bound, at his mercy. She turned her mind quickly away. Would he never be satisfied, she wondered. No doubt it had been his idea to lure Henri here, and no one else's. Maddie frowned. But how had Mathias known of

318

Henri's friendship with Abraham Castaneda, and how deeply it ran? How had he possibly acquired a sample of Castaneda's handwriting in order to forge it?

"I want to know," Mathias broke into her thoughts, "how did you get here? How many accomplices did you bring? We know of at least one."

So that was it! She had been offered this audience only so they could interrogate her. "I brought no one with me," she replied, lying defiantly. "I was already in Port Royal by accident when I learned."

"You lie!" Mathias swung his arm around, then slapped her hard on the face. Maddie glared at him with blazing eyes and vowed she would not give him the satisfaction of crying out.

After slapping her, his fingers lingered against the burning, reddened skin of her cheeks. They slid down her neck, then across her throat. With a clutch of horror, Maddie sensed, as clearly as if his mind had been an open book, the erotic thrill he took at estimating how much hempen rope he'd need to knot around her smooth, white throat a noose. At once, her heart pounded desperately hard. To steady herself, she took a deep, slow breath.

"Mathias, leave her be!" Carstarfin whirled on him. "I won't have you bruising her." The man's eyes lingered on those swells barely visible above the neckline of her dress. "She is a woman, after all."

Mathias continued interrogating her, but his hands hung now by his sides. His voice, hard and cold as steel, however, cut through her like a knife. "We know you were with him on Dominica when our letter was delivered. You came after him, and were seen on the streets with one of his men. Answer, Madame de Rohan, or it will be very bad for you."

Maddie lifted her eyes to glare at him. "I do not know what you're talking about."

"You were seen in the company of Abraham Castaneda, his best friend. Where is he now?" Mathias was relentless.

Maddie chilled. They knew the room where she was staying. Otherwise, how could they have delivered the message to her? It was only a matter of time until Castaneda returned. Would they have someone waiting there to ambush him? Suddenly a surge of hope washed over her. Perhaps they did not entirely trust their source of information. Maybe they weren't sure. By then, Maddie realized who their betrayer was. In her mind's eye, she pictured that raven-haired quadroon dressed in a peach-colored chiffon riding so erect, so proudly in her open carriage down the streets of Port Royal. She began to understand that somehow, in the days following her reunion with Henri, Mathias had found and allied himself with Chloe. She alone had seen them here, and she must have reported it. "I've never heard of this . . . this fellow you're talking about." Maddie met his eyes. Determined to brazen it out, she swore she'd die, rather than betray her friend.

"Liar!"

She choked down a cry as Mathias lunged for her. Careful not to bruise her where it showed, he grabbed her by the shoulders. His long, bony fingers dug painfully hard into her flesh.

"Mathias, leave her be!" Again Carstarfin spoke. Maddie turned to him gratefully now, relieved to find at least some decency in him. With new hope surging inside her, she leaned to him, hands clasped in pleading supplication. "Sir, my husband committed no crime in this territory. Why have you imprisoned him? What has he done to hurt you, or this island domain?"

The man's expression hardened once again. "I am an officer of the Crown, Madame," he replied. "What hurts England and her allies hurts me. We are in an uneasy but necessary truce with Spain and Portugal, and anyone who captures and plunders ships of these sovereign nations, while remaining in or near English waters, hurts England."

Maddie raised tear-filled eyes to him. "Oh, sir, is there nothing I can say to convince you?"

His gaze fixed upon her for several endless seconds. "Convince me? No, Madame, but perhaps you may yet sway me by other means." His eyes lingered upon her. "I am most amenable to gentler methods of persuasion."

Maddie drew back. "What do you mean?" She knew what he wanted, but wanted to hear it from his own lips. He gestured at Mathias to leave. To her relief, her old enemy obeyed. When she and Carstarfin were alone, he continued.

"I think you *do* know." He moved toward her. "I am a man far from England, and the women I encounter here—" He spat scornfully. "They are either street drabs, or black. Of the two, I far prefer the negresses, because at least they're healthy, but I've yearned for a young and pretty white woman to lift my spirits, and I find you as toothsome a wench as any I've seen since leaving Mother England."

Maddie stood unable to move, just watching as he drew closer. She had expected this. Now that it was actually happening, however, she quivered with horror. A tremor of revulsion rippled through her flesh as his finger stroked the side of her neck. Nevertheless, she held to her purpose. She would not be swayed to refuse anything that might help her Henri.

She forced her voice to remain calm. "Are you telling me then, that I might buy my husband's freedom?"

"Rather crudely put, my dear," he replied, smiling. "I don't particularly fancy your way with words. Let us just say that I asked, and you, honored to be of service,

321

agreed. In gratitude for the delight of your favors and to please you, I release one relatively unimportant wretch from the gaol, commuting his death sentence to exile.''

"Put it any way you like, sir," she replied, "so long as I can see my husband freed, I will do what you tell me.''

"You are so agreeable." He led her beyond the outer office to his private quarters on a higher floor. Rich carpeting covered his floors here, and whitewashed walls glittered with paintings held in gilt frames. Its furnishings were some of England's finest, transported to the islands by ship. "Please make yourself comfortable, my dear," he gestured for her to sit, then turned to a cabinet where bottles of rum and strangely colored liquors stood. He pulled one of these down, then poured its contents into two flower-etched goblets. One of these he handed to Maddie. "Drink up, Madame de Rohan," he said, then sipped from the brim of his own. Maddie obeyed, but hardly tasted the cloying sweet wine inside.

She sat where he directed upon a divan. She wondered how many other wretched wives might have tried to buy their husband's freedom in exactly the same way. Knowing such thoughts did no good, Maddie drove them from her mind. Carstarfin was her only hope, and she would play it out to the bitter end.

"What a beautiful creature you are!" He lowered himself down beside her and reached for her hand. "Here, come closer, child." His fingers stroked her hair. "Spun gold," he whispered. "It's like silk, and such a delicate perfume. You deserve so much better than you've received."

Maddie did not answer, but instead averted her eyes. With trembling hands, she raised her glass to take yet another sip of the wine. Soon she began to feel its effects. She courted intoxication knowingly now as a way to endure her coming ordeal. When she had finished, she asked for another glass.

Smiling, he stood. "Perhaps it's better this way, this first time, for in spite of everything, I can see you're a very timid lass." He sat back down and handed her the newly refilled goblet. "And more than a little afraid of me, but you need not be. It is true that I am ruthless where criminals are concerned, but with women, I am always gentle." He watched her drink.

Maddie raised her eyes to him, then quickly glanced away. Her gaze darted to the closed door through which Mathias had gone. "But what about him?" She nodded scornfully in his departed direction. "Andrew Mathias must not come near me. I hate him. He frightens me!"

Carstarfin nodded. "As you wish. In any case, I myself want no intrusion when we are alone."

Under the wine's warming glow, her nervousness faded. She still found him repulsive, but the drug alcohol had blunted the edge of her despair. Joy at seeing Henri once again would some day sweep away all thoughts of its price.

"Your breasts—" He pressed his hands to them. "Even under that prim little frock, I can see them. Such tender little buds they are, too." He ran his fingers over the buttons binding her bodice. Maddie did not resist. She leaned back motionless as he unfastened each one. When her dress hung open, he slid his hand inside, warming her flesh with his own heat. Maddie closed her eyes as he freed her body . . . . She lay almost insensate, as he fondled each nipple, and when he took possession of her, mastering her with his manhood, she had already found a way to bear his unwanted passion. She let her thoughts roam far away. His hands became Henri's hands. To her mind's closed eyes, this stranger's lips, his weight, and the heat of his passion, became her husband's. By pretending him to be Henri, she'd live through all this somehow.

When he had finished, Joseph Carstarfin held her in his arms. She lay with eyes still closed, so that she wouldn't have to open them onto the moment's ugly reality. "Oh, my beauty," he whispered, then pressed another kiss onto her unresisting mouth. He nuzzled her neck. "What a prize you are for any man to take and never share. You are a golden creature sent to me by God to ease the loneliness of my days. You will stay with me always, as my consort."

Maddie's eyes flew open. Horrified, she pulled away from him. "What are you saying, sir?" She gasped aloud. "I am a married woman, like it or not! My husband is alive and I intend to join him. You did indeed give me your word, you know."

"I was afraid you'd react that way, Madame," he replied coldly. "You are too fine a lady for such scum as Rohan. You'll stay with me instead." His eyes had hardened.

Maddie stared with horror. "Stay with you?" She felt herself sinking into a swoon. "No, sir, my place is with my husband, with Henri, the man I love."

"If you insist upon being stubborn, then you give me no choice. You will go with me in chains to watch him hang. Then you will be Rohan's widow, and free to marry me."

"No!" Maddie broke into a sob. She would go mad if she saw her husband die. Her whole life would end right then and there. She turned to him with soul-deep despair. "You promised. How could you?"

"I promised before I understood what delight I could find in your arms. All is fair in the capture of a woman, Madame. In any case, you have little say, since I hold all the power." He spoke the truth, and she knew it. He could have Henri killed in a moment. Maddie turned to him is despair.

"And if I agree to stay with you—what then? Does

Henri go free? If you say so, how do I know you'll keep your word?"

"You will know your husband is free," he replied, "because you will see him loosed with your own eyes. Indeed, if you stay with me, I will even give him a small boat for his escape—though it be far more than he deserves."

A sudden hope warmed her. Maddie turned to him now with defiant eyes. "And if you force me to stay, what then? Do you believe he'd not come here to rescue me?"

"He will not, Madame."

"Why not? He's not all *that* afraid of you."

"He won't, because I'm imposing one other small condition upon you—a minor one, compared to the first, but necessary, and I'm afraid I must insist."

Maddie's heart plummeted. "And what be that?" she whispered.

"You will tell him face to face, and with your own words, that you will stay with me. You will tell him it is by your own choice and wish, and that you no longer want anything whatsoever to do with him. If you refuse, or if you fail to convince him, then I take back my offer to free him. Instead, as before, you will see him hang, and you yourself indentured to me for life."

Maddie turned her face from him. Her eyes glistened with tears. "What choice do I have, sir?" she whispered. Her husband's life, at the price of her own freedom and future happiness, or his death. In any case, the outcome would leave her desolate. With a sigh, she turned once again to her captor. "Very well, I accept your conditions. Both of them. I will renounce my husband."

Chapter Twenty-nine

Lord Carstarfin rang a bell on his desk. Immediately, a soldier, accompanied by Mathias, appeared at the door. "Bring Rohan up here." With a wave of his hand, Carstarfin dismissed the young man in uniform who was to summon and escort Henri to these chambers from his dungeon cell. As the soldier turned away, Carstarfin called after him, "And see to it that he is well guarded!"

"That 'knave', as you call him, is more of a man, sir, than *you* are," Maddie retorted in hot defiance.

Carstarfin's eyes narrowed. His face hardened. "Be not too quick with you insults," he said, speaking coldly. "Remember, it is only by my grace that your husband will live. For that matter," he continued, "be reminded of your own home back in Salem, and how the righteous drove you out."

"By *his* false accusation!" she screamed, as she whirled on Mathias with one arm held out and finger pointed.

"Not by mine, Madame, but by the devil-sent anguish of Goodwife Jameson," he retorted.

"You put her up to it, no doubt!"

"Enough!" Lord Carstarfin silenced them both. "I care not a whit for these bickerings. Your suggestion, Mathias, was a good one, and you, my dear," he said, turning to Maddie, "you brought me one good hour of pleasure, and I anticipate many more."

Maddie averted her face so that he could not see the tears in her eyes, but failed to hide them. "Instead of weeping, you should rejoice. Have not circumstances lifted you? For the life of a worthless rogue, you gain so much. You were but a doxie when you came to me—a common knave's woman, and now your are to become a lady."

Maddie did not reply, although harsh words burned to fly out at him. Until Henri was safe, she dared not resist anything Carstarfin demanded.

"Be warned, lady," he continued. "If you mean to betray your agreement, you will be punished."

Maddie felt herself grow faint. Formless sound roared past her ears. "I will not betray my word," she whispered, "so long as you do not break your own promise to me."

After an eternity passed, she finally heard footsteps in the hall. A knock rattled Carstarfin's outer door. At once, everything took on a horrible intensity for Maddie. The whitewashed plaster walls blinded her now with their brightness. The paintings hanging there overwhelmed her with the gaudiness of their reds and pinks and shades of blue. She saw every wart upon the faces of her captors, every mole, and all the misdirected hairs that sprouted between Mathias' eye brows. A curious grin of triumph flickered across Mathias's face, and upon Carstarfin's played a combination of anticipation and impatience.

Carstarfin called out in answer to the knock. At once, the door clattered open. Soldiers of the King thrust one heavily chained prisoner inside. They shoved against the small of his back, nearly knocking him off balance, but he, proud and unbending, struggled to regain the step he missed.

Maddie's heart lurched when she saw him. She nearly cried out with shocked dismay to see the horrible change in him. He had lost so much weight. Lines of pain and weariness had etched themselves upon his features, while his complexion, once brown from rays of the sun, had paled to a waxen sallow gray. He glanced first to the men with defiance still burning in his eyes. Maddie's heart throbbed with pride when she saw the way those others in the room cringed when he focused on them. Suddenly, he turned to her. He drew back; his lips parted in shocked surprise. "Maddie!"

"Aye," Mathias stood between them. "Thy doxie sits with us now, and here she'll stay, by way of her own choice, as mistress of Lord Carstarfin, the man who sentenced you."

Henri whirled to her. He stared in horrified disbelief. "Maddie!" he whispered. "Is this true?"

Maddie could hardly face him. She could not bring herself to meet his eyes, so lowered hers instead. "It is true, Henri," she replied. "I am staying here with Carstarfin."

She ached to tell him why. Her soul screamed out with anguish at the thought that he would go away believing her faithless, but she had no choice. If she failed to convince him, then she would see him hang.

"Tell him, dearest Maddie," said Carstarfin. "Tell him how you promised to stay with me. How sweetly you offered." Her captor turned to Henri once again. "See that divan?" He pointed to the couch where he had taken his fill of her body. "Well, regard it with respect, my dear sir, for right there, I took thy woman down. And a fulsome wench she was, too," he added. He smacked his lips. "Her kisses were sweet, and her embraces as warm as any I have known."

Maddie's heart plummeted. She stared with horror at the look of shocked anguish on Henri's face. He stared at her, then said in a voice that almost failed him, "Maddie, this can't possibly be true. Surely he forced you."

Maddie exhaled with a shudder. She fought back her

tears. "Yes, Henri, it's true." She was afraid to speak out loud, for fear she'd burst into crying. "I felt ashamed at first, but he gave me such pleasure I could not think of leaving him."

"One more thing, Rohan," Carstarfin continued, "thy marriage to this woman is invalid. Your chaplain was no man of God at all, but a rogue. Nor was the union recorded on any official rolls. This woman knows, and wishes to sign a statement to that effect, thus freeing her from any further entanglements with you." He held the paper up to Henri's face. "You *can* read, can you not?" He spoke purringly, but with a cutting undertone of sarcasm.

"Probably better than you!" Henri replied in a surly voice. As his eyes glanced down the paper, however, he visibly paled. Maddie's heart ached to see his face. When his own eyes met hers, she tore hers away. It was too painful.

"The lady has not yet had the opportunity to sign it," said Carstarfin. "Perhaps she will do it now." He turned to Maddie. "Come, my dear, I have a pen already waiting." He laid the paper down on a polished ebony table. Maddie stood. Without speaking, she moved on trembling legs, trying not to notice how Henri's eyes burned into her. To force herself calm, she gulped a deep breath. Suddenly, she realized that the whole point of her betrayal had not been mentioned. No word had Carstarfin spoken about freeing Henri, and she would not go on until she saw it done. "But sir,"—she turned now to the chief magistrate—"had we not agreed that his miserable presence upon your territory is odious? Had we not spoken of driving him out?"

"Driving me out?" Henri's voice hardened. His lips curled in disgust. "I thought you planned to hang me, Carstarfin."

Lord Carstarfin shrugged. "Believe it or not, Rohan,

I am a sentimental man. Your woman gave me such pleasure, and so sweetly, that I felt rather sorry for you who would be losing her, and felt moved to pity."

"Oh, that's very good of you, I'm sure!" Henri did not bother to conceal his scorn. "Like a rat from a sinking ship, she leaves me, now that I am down. What a fine couple you two make!" Maddie felt herself grow faint. With all her will, however, she struggled to hide her feelings.

"I will forgive you for that impertinence," Carstarfin said coldly. "I know the King's examiners have done their best to interrogate you. No doubt you're tired, and not clear of head for thinking."

"Interrogate—hah!" Henri spat it out. "You mean torture!"

Carstarfin turned to his soldiers, ignoring Henri. "We are all going to the harbor together, and you with him. The three of us will follow in a coach." He turned once again to Henri. "You are far luckier than you deserve, Rohan. By my sufferance and mercy, you will be set free, with a boat to sail you away. We will follow simply to watch. We want to be sure that you are off our land for good, and I warn you—if you should ever return, I will see to it that you hang!"

"Return?" cried Henri. "To what?" He glared with hard, loathing eyes at Maddie. "To my oft-mounted hobbyhorse, who deserts me at first sign of trouble? No, thank you!" His gaze burned now into her own. "I thought you were different," he whispered. "I believed you were good, like no woman I had met in many a long year, but I was wrong. You pious gray-clad wenches from New England may indeed be the worst."

"Henri, I—" Maddie stopped short. Carstarfin stood beside her now. The pressure of his hand upon her arm reminded her to stay silent.

Maddie consoled herself with the thought that her

330

own misery had bought Henri his life. No matter how much she grieved or suffered from his hatred, she knew she had made the right choice. Perhaps someday he would come to understand and forgive her.

The three of them followed in an open rig as Henri was led to the harbor. At Carstarfin's orders, soldiers unlocked the chains binding him and set him free. Maddie watched as he climbed aboard the sloop that was to carry him away. He turned one last time to gaze upon her, then quickly whirled, as if sight of his wife had proven too painful. Tears blurred her last view as he disappeared to the deck beyond and started the small craft moving.

It lurched into the open sea beyond, taking with it the only man she had ever loved. As she, Carstarfin, and Mathias, still in their rig, lurched forward to leave, Maddie turned back in her seat for one last look. As she did, her eyes widened. A cry escaped from her lips, parted to catch a sudden, searing breath—*Carstarfin had lied to her!* As Henri reached harbor's edge for open sea, three armed frigates flew toward him. Flying the Union Jack, they blocked his way past. They surrounded him now to prevent his escape.

Maddie broke out with a keening moan, as cannon lowered and aimed themselves at Henri's boat. She realized then that she had denounced her love for nothing. Carstarfin had never intended setting Henri free. Instead of hanging, he had become sport for sailors.

She whirled on him now. "You!" She screamed. With her hands curved into claws aching to gouge out his eyes, she lunged, but Andrew Mathias grabbed her wrists from behind.

"Where is Satan to help you now?" he cried, laughing. "Why can you not help your man?" With one hand, he held both her own by the wrists. His other arm, pressed tight around her, mocking her struggles, while his palm possessively squeezed the high, firm globe of one breast.

"God damn you to Hell!" she cried. Tears seared her eyes. They rolled out in a stream. Their hot salt wetness burned her cheeks. Somehow, she struggled free. She crashed over Carstarfin's knees falling to the ground below. She sobbed aloud in pain and fury as she stumbled to her feet. Knowing that both of them had leapt from the rig to follow, she ran back toward water's edge to watch with horror the scene unfolding in the water beyond. Almost immediately, they caught up and grabbed her.

As she writhed in Andrew Mathias's arms, she saw from the corner of her eye yet another carriage. It clattered over stones and stopped next to them. Chloe, Henri's woman scorned, sat proudly with head held high, dressed in a gay gown of silk dyed red. Red, for celebration? Scarlet, to match Henri's blood that would surely flow? The creature glanced to Maddie in cold triumph.

Suddenly a noise out beyond distracted them all. Her eyes froze open with horror, as the ships swept all at once down upon Henri's little boat. From one, a gigantic tube of iron on the top deck aimed, then suddenly burst a flash of fire. A booming report followed a few seconds later, shaking the ground underneath their feet. Its force hurtled into Henri's boat. Its impact burst the little craft into flame. Maddie screamed one dying strangled cry, then fainted dead away.

Chapter Thirty

At once, she struggled back to consciousness. As another shot rang out, her body tensed. "No!" She let out a choking sob. In a frenzy, she whirled on Carstarfin. "How could you? How dare you? You bloody, filthy liar!" She had bought Henri's freedom with her body, only to have this man cheat her.

He turned to her now. "Do you think I would release a dangerous criminal like Rohan just for you?" he shrugged. "In any case, he has a sporting chance."

Maddie writhed to get away from the soldiers holding her now. Her breasts heaved with the exertion of her struggles. Her hair tangled wild and golden around her face. If she could but break free, she'd surely lunge at him and do what she could to make him regret his betrayal. From far out on the water, she heard explosions of cannon, of guns aimed, and fireballs screaming.

Suddenly her eyes widened. Her heart swelled with sudden joy. Though the sloop was little more than a smoking hulk, it still sailed free. The great unwieldy frigates still pursued, instead of returning to port in triumph. They hadn't caught him yet, nor knowingly killed him. Henri might still go free! Maddie raised her face toward the sky now. "Dear God!" she whispered, "let him get away. Oh please, God, free him and punish his enemies."

Mathias broke into her prayer with cold voice "More likely he'll be on *our* side than Rohan's, Madame. After all, why should God abet a common criminal?"

Furious, Maddie whirled on him. "Because Henri Rohan is a better man than you, Andrew Mathias!" She spat it out at him. "He is no sanctimonious hypocrite—" The palm of his hand silenced her, but only for the moment. As before, she clenched her teeth to keep from crying out. "You are a swine!" she whispered, "and a blackguard, all the worse for pretending to be Godly."

Suddenly, the noise over the water caught their attention. All the others, including her captors, whirled in its direction. The three frigates sailed into open sea in hot pursuit. "Go, Henri!" Maddie screamed to him. She urged him on with all her heart and soul, even though she knew he couldn't hear. Her voice shrilled into another wordless scream, as all three ships disappeared beyond the spit of land.

No longer able to see, Maddie went limp. She closed her eyes and prayed a whispered entreaty for Henri to escape. She wanted nothing more. Revenge on Carstarfin and Mathias would be nice, but she'd gladly do without, if she could have but that one wish granted. Even if she never saw Henri again, she wanted her beloved alive.

Carstarfin turned to the soldiers. "Take her back to my rooms."

"You must be joking!" Maddie's eyes popped wide. "Do you expect me to yield myself to you now? By God's death, I'd rather spend the rest of my days in a prison cell than in your arms!"

"You speak hastily, Madame. In any case, it would be a terrible waste and I'd never allow it."

Maddie whirled to Chloe now, suddenly enraged. "It was *you* who told them I was in Port Royal, wasn't it?"

The woman glanced to her in cold scorn. "So what? In any case, they would have found and arrested you soon enough." She glanced to Mathias and smiled.

"My husband is a very clever man."

At her words, Mathias stepped away, as if detaching himself from both women. Maddie's eyes narrowed. Suddenly, she knew for sure. Carstarfin was crude. He would have acted with the sword, beheading Henri with his own hand. Only Mathias possessed the kind of cold, relentless cunning that would have come up with such a cruel torture. Maddie smiled, but bitterly. Perhaps Mathias had outsmarted himself. In their days together at Dominica, Henri had told her many things. Most fondly did she remember now his accounts of narrow escapes. She prayed this would prove to be his latest of many. A little bewildered about one thing, however, Maddie turned to Chloe. "But how did you and Mathias come together? You were worlds apart."

Chloe's full lips curved into a mocking grin. "My husband,"—she nodded toward Mathias—"he noticed me at the tavern that night. He saw from where he stood how Rohan treated me. He called me to him afterward, and he say we should go and talk. I tell him everything I could, and a few of Rohan's other enemies tell him the rest. I stay with him that night, then later we marry."

"I hope you enjoy him then, your fine, new husband." Maddie spoke with ill-concealed sarcasm.

They locked her in one of Carstarfin's own private rooms, an elaborately decorated cell about ten feet square with a small, high window overlooking the street four floors below. She sat in silence here, upon a fussy little velvet upholstered chair. Tears of despair glistened in her eyes. She knew her life had ended for sure now. Even if Henri should still have survived, he hated her now. He had cast her from his life forever, and she couldn't really blame him.

Without even thinking, her hand pressed against her

belly, where the baby lay growing inside, Henri's baby, only a few weeks old. She vowed that she'd do her very best to care for it well. After all, the child would be all she had left of her beloved. For the infant's sake, if not for her own, she must endure.

To take her mind off her pain and sorrow, Maddie walked over to a shelf of books propped against one wall and reached for one. When she opened it to read, however, she recoiled. She had never seen such a book as this. It pages described indecent acts in elaborate, painstaking detail, following the movements of lascivious gentlemen and willing women, like none Maddie had ever met. When she turned the page and saw an obscene woodcut illustration, Maddie slammed the book shut. With burning cheeks, she shoved it back where she had found it among the others.

Carstarfin returned a few hours later. He threw down a package he was carrying, then settled in a chair facing her. "You!" she whispered. "What do you want?"

"Life goes on, my dear. You must learn to live with what fate doles out to you, and for the moment, I am its best offer."

"Then I'd rather do without, thank you!"

His eyes narrowed. "I'm afraid you have no choice. You are mine now, booty confiscated from my fallen enemy, and I claim you for my own." His voice dropped, iron-hard.

With a cry, Maddie turned from him, but he grabbed her wrist. "Let me go!" She fought against him. "You touch me, and I swear I'll claw your eyes out, you . . . you liar! You filth!"

"Flattery will get you nowhere!" Holding her wrist, Carstarfin stepped around the chair held between them. With a yank, he drew her close. Maddie struggled to writhe free, but he imprisoned her by both wrists. With a cry, she fell off balance. He clamped her against himself for a moment, then backed her over to a wall. Once he had pinned her there, Carstarfin freed her arms.

She tried to force herself free by clawing at him, but her strength was no match for his. With one swift movement, he tore her bodice open. Its tearing thundered in her ears, seeming to echo off the close-built walls. The friction of cloth tearing burned into her. Sobbing aloud, Maddie cried out in pain.

Almost before she knew what had happened, he grabbed her by the hair. As she struggled, tears of anger and frustration rolled out of her eyes. He finished off her skirt, ripping it from her thighs as if it had been but paper. He ducked her flailing arms, then flung her down on the bed. By his power, he took his pleasure of her, while, she, writhing in futile desperation underneath, could only curse at him.

He had perfumed his body in oil, less manly than sickeningly sweet. His breath, hot and fast upon her face, smelled of chocolate, and she saw to her horror that his red-rimmed eyes had turned glassy. When he had finished, he laid upon her, still panting. He gazed into her face. "You know, it wouldn't be so crude for either of us, if you'd but relent, and give yourself to me willingly. It wouldn't kill you."

Maddie choked back the urge to retch. "Never!" she gasped, "I'd rather die!"

"And what good would *that* do? Either for you, or for that wretch?" he retorted. "By the way, you'll be pleased to know he might have escaped . . . but don't expect him to come back looking for you, even if he survives."

"No," she replied bitterly, "*you* saw to that well enough."

Carstarfin stood. While she watched, too despondent to move, he pulled back on his breeches and strode from the room, leaving her alone.

The days passed by slowly, but mercifully, each of them ended, sooner or later. He came up once a day and forced himself upon her. Each time he finished, he pleaded with her as before to give herself willingly, but Maddie always refused. Her only consolation was that she never saw Mathias anymore. Her gaoler at least had the decency to honor that one request.

In those nightmare days, she thought often of Henri, and of those idyllic hours she spent with him in Dominica. Tears swam in her eyes as she wondered if she'd ever see him again.

Time hung heavily on her hands. She saw with the passing months that the rhythm of her body changed. The old familiar cycle that came and went each month had dried up right from the first in her new condition. Her flesh became instead fragile, like an egg. Her swollen breasts hurt to touch. Her belly began to spread. The rich gowns Carstarfin had ordered for her no longer fit.

Three months passed, and then a fourth. Her weight became cumbersome, her movement awkward. By then, Carstarfin had left her out into the rest of his apartments. Convinced by her guile that the child was his, he trusted maternal instinct, and the unfamiliar burdens of her condition, to keep her docile. Maddie, for the sake of her unborn baby's safety and later good treament, let him believe what he wanted. She even pretended to have accepted her lot in life. For the sake of that unborn child, she even gave her hand in marriage to him. Though her gorge rose at the final vows, she spoke them aloud in a private but legal ceremony. In the end, she nurtured one grim satisfaction. Carstarfin had no idea that she'd still try to escape.

Chapter Thirty-one

Finally, during a moment of confusion, Maddie made her break. During the changing of the guards downstairs, a man tried to shove his way past, claiming that Carstarfin had sentenced his brother falsely. Maddie heard the din. Alone at the time, she had slipped from Carstarfin's private quarters into the more public rooms downstairs. As she padded in soft sandals down his carpeted steps, her heart had pounded, seemingly in her mouth.

The guards, their attention occupied by that man, hadn't noticed Maddie cowering behind. Knowing that her chance might be now or never, she lunged past them outside into the sunlight of freedom.

Desparate to find a contact—someone who could take at least a message to Henri—she ran along streets only half-remembered toward Jack Trimble's tavern. He was the only one she knew here in Port Royal. He would have to do.

How long until Carstarfin discovered her gone? What would he do? Negresses and old pirates populated the district where she found herself. The only women here of her own race were prostitutes, while she, pale skinned, blonde, and obviously pregnant would surely stand out. If Carstarfin sent soldiers, as he surely would, he'd find out soon enough that a woman of her description had passed through here.

Somehow she found her way. Finally she arrived at his tavern. With a sigh, she pushed her way inside. Picking her way carefully between the heavy tables, she hurried up to the bar. When the barkeep saw her, he stopped what he was doing and hurried toward her. "You!" he whispered. "Why did you come back here?"

Maddie didn't bother to explain. "Your master—is he here?"

"No, but why . . . why would you want anything to do with him?" He seemed strangely defensive.

Maddie's eyes widened. "Please!" she gasped, "please let me wait in his office!"

He frowned. "Well, I don't know. Something's up, isn't it? He won't like it, if I do something that gets him in trouble."

"*Please!* No one will know." She glanced wildly around her. If she had anything to offer in the way of a bribe, she'd give it to him gladly, but she had nothing—only her body, which in her current swollen state wasn't enough.

Mercy seemed to overpower his uneasiness. "Well, all right." He nodded toward the door. "Hurry in then, but keep quiet." For more than an hour, Maddie waited in there for Jack Trimble to return.

Finally, he stepped inside. He stood in the doorway, stiff and hostile at the sight of her. His eyes narrowed. "Madame de Rohan . . . or is it Dame Carstarfin now?" he said, with an icy sarcasm that brought a blush to Maddie's cheeks. "I heard you were no longer using your husband's name. Are you officially divorced?"

Maddie slid a hand over her forehead. This was going to be far worse than she had anticipated. "Please! Appearances sometimes lie."

"Indeed?" he said coolly, with eyebrows raised.

"You-you are a friend of my husband's, are you not?"

"Which husband?" He was going to make it difficult for her.

"Rohan, my only true husband. Are you still his friend?" She stared at him with desperate urgency.

"I served your husband when first he came to these islands. Of course, I've changed since then," he added guardedly, "I have become as law-abiding a citizen as thy man Carstarfin." Again, that cutting sarcasm.

"Please!" Maddie shuddered. "Carstarfin isn't my man—at least, not by choice. Do you see him often—Rohan, I mean?"

"What's it to you?" A definite surliness had crept into his tone.

"A great deal." Her voice dropped to a whisper. "I'm not an enemy. No matter what it may seem, I'm not." She clasped her hands together as she pleaded, then moved closer. "You're the only one who might be able to get a message to him, or to Abraham Castaneda. You're my only hope. I don't ask you to admit anything. I know how it is here, but please—I beg you to pass on word of me, if you have the chance."

"And why, Madame, should I bother?" His eyes chilled her now. His voice had hardened into scorn. He stood in front of her with arms folded across his chest. "As I have it, from too many good sources, you turned from him and gave yourself to Carstarfin. You betrayed him, Madame, threw him to the dogs when it suited your fancy. You let him die."

"No—it's not like that at all!" Maddie flung herself at him, but he threw her off. Pushed off balance, she crumbled to a heap on the floor. She remained on her knees in a gesture of supplication. "Please listen! At least hear me out. I did not give myself to Carstarfin willingly. I sold myself, in return for Henri's life. Carstarfin led me to believe I'd only have to give him an afternoon's pleasure, and since it seemed a small enough price to pay for my man's freedom, I consented."

"I heard otherwise," Trimble interrupted her. "It's said you denounced you husband in front of Carstarfin and other witnesses. It's even said you signed a paper denying your marriage."

Maddie turned away in despair. "True," she whispered, "all true, but for that very same reason." Her voice trembled as she explained, "Carstarfin wanted to be sure, you see, that Henri would not come back and try to rescue me. To insure it, I was to face my husband and tell him I wanted to remain with Carstarfin by my choice. If I refused, or if I failed to convince my husband of this lie, I'd be forced to witness his hanging. If I succeeded, then Henri would go free."

Maddie moved toward him. In her agitation, she clutched his shoulders. "What would you have done, sir?" She let go, then whirled from him. With a sob, she crumbled into a chair. "In either case, I was damned. Damned to Hell on earth, and for eternity, too. I either sacrificed my virtue and, as its reward, witnessed his execution." She sighed. "Right or wrong, I did what I believed was right, and I insisted, as a precaution, that I witness his safe departure from Jamaica. I did not know Carstarfin would trick me the way he did. I suppose I should have suspected, but foolishly I trusted him."

She turned to him now with wide eyes, pleading for him to believe and understand. "They never found his corpse. D-do you happen to know, . . . is he still alive? I feel in my heart that he *is*, but then I couldn't dare think otherwise."

He seemed to soften just a little. "I have heard nothing, and that is the truth, although I do not know if I'd admit otherwise to you." He shook his head. "I've heard neither bad news nor good, but then it means little enough. He could have found his way into the belly of a shark."

Maddie fell into a dreading silence. With a twinge of

fearful uncertainty, she touched her belly where Henri's child lay. This was a possibility she had thought about all too often. Jack Trimble studied her intently. "Even if I believe you, Madame, one thing puzzles me. Why did you take so long to come?" He leaned to her. On his face, she saw a bewildered frown.

"I've been kept prisoner," she replied, "guarded day and night. I've not been allowed to go out—not even under escort." She described the weeks shut away in Carstarfin's rooms. "Today was my first chance. A man tried to push past the guards, and in the confusion, I ran out." She raised a pleading look to him. "Oh, sir, I understand why you refuse to admit you know Henri, but if you should hear that my husband is alive, could you get word to him somehow? I can't pay you anything, but . . . ."

Suddenly fists pounded on this inner door, then it opened, flung back by Trimble's barkeep. She saw at once that the younger man had paled in fear. "Soldiers out front, sir, and they be asking about this here woman."

Maddie's flesh chilled. With a cry, she leaped to her feet. "They mustn't find me here. Is there another way out?" She glanced quickly to the shuttered window.

"Aye." He helped her scramble onto the sill. "Hurry now! Up the end of the alley, you'll find a way leading back onto another street—if they don't catch you first. Now hurry."

He shoved her out. Caught off balance, Maddie fell to the dirt below. Pain stabbed through her knees where she landed, but she gritted her teeth and stood. As she limped to what she hoped was safety, she tried to ignore how her skin, raw and exposed after scraping the top layer away, tingled in searing pain. She stumbled up that alley fleeing in breathless terror. She flung a look over her shoulders whenever she heard a noise, but saw nothing. Suddenly, where it joined the street, she hurtled smack into the arms of a soldier.

His grasp closed tight around her. Like a vise, he held her to him. Maddie struggled, writhing to break free. "Let me go!" she cried. "You have no right!"

"By orders of Lord Carstarfin, we have every right," he answered her in a stern voice, then called out to his comrades. Boot soles clattered over the stone-paved street beyond, as those others approached. "I've got her, and a lively one she is, too," he cried. "But Lord, how pretty—even pregnant. No wonder our man Carstarfin wants her back so badly."

One of them clamped manacles to her wrists. When she kicked, they tied her ankles. Screaming as they lifted her onto a horse, she sobbed aloud in angry fear. With one of them riding behind to hold her tight, they galloped back to Carstarfin's mansion.

At the orders of Andrew Mathias, who stood waiting for them, the soldiers dragged Maddie down steep stone steps and flung her into a cell below street-level. She struggled against them, but could not resist as they clamped her chain-bound arms and legs securely to the wall. As the metal door clanked behind them, locking her in, Maddie sobbed in despair. Shivering both from chill and terror, she waited alone, seemingly forever. Finally, a shadow from the hall beyond moved closer to the door of her cell. Maddie's heart pounded in hope and dread as the door creaked open. When she saw who entered however, and caught the look of triumph upon his gaunt, self-righteous face, her hopes shattered.

Andrew Mathias stepped inside, one pale hand clutching a cat-o-nine-tails, a tiny but nasty-looking whip. Very lightly, he tapped that whip once, then again and again, against his palm, while his eyes, dark and cold, fixed upon her. While she waited, staring and unable to speak, he reached out. Maddie screamed with terror as those long, damp fingers curled around her dress. He ripped the cloth right off her shoulders.

Chapter Thirty-two

She awakened later, her swollen eyes opening onto the ceiling, not of that dungeon cell, but on Carstarfin's inner chamber. She ached all over, and when she moved to touch where it hurt the most, across her breasts, she discovered with horror that ropes bound her wrists. She lay belly up and helpless under the gaze of Andrew Mathias, who stood looking down at her with contempt.

"So, Madame, you thought you'd defy the wishes of your betters and try to get away." He drew closer. His eyes, cold as ice, revealed a cruel glint. "Perhaps that criminal still has friends on this island. If so, we'd like to know about them."

"I know of no one." Maddie would not betray Henri's friend.

"Then where did you go, Madame, after you slipped free? We want to know."

Maddie did not reply. She lay silent and tried not to look at him. A cry of pain escaped from her throat, as with his flattened hand, he stung a blow across her jaw. "Answer me, damn you, or I'll use *this!*" He still had the whip with him. He cracked it now in the air, just above the baby lying inside her belly.

Maddie bit her lip. She'd try to convince him with a lie. "I had hoped to find a ship that would take me far, far away from here," she said. "I learned soon enough that it wasn't as easy as I had hoped."

"And you went nowhere else."

"No."

"Liar!" He slapped her again, this time harder. His blow caused the opposite effect from what he probably intended. Instead of yielding, and telling him what he wanted to know, she forced herself silent. He continued speaking now in deliberate, measured tones, "Our men found you in a back alley quite far away from the harbor."

"I got lost." She glared defiantly into his eyes.

"Lost?" He gave a short, harsh laugh. "We have reason to believe that you hoped to find an ally of Rohan's in one of the taverns."

"Well, you believe wrong," she retorted. "If my husband has any friends here, I do not know of them. I merely went from tavern to tavern, begging for a ship that would take me on as passenger . . . to *anywhere!*"

"How did you hope to pay for your passage?" His voice dropped to an insidious purr.

"In any way I could, sir," she replied. "If necessary, the same way I had hoped to pay for Henri's life . . . and probably with better luck, since sailors are not cheats like you and your master."

"You are a whore!" he spat at her through taut lips.

Maddie glared at him. Though she was afraid, desperately so, she despised him to the very core of his soul. "I used to be a virgin, sir and a dutiful daughter, too," she reminded him, "but you yourself changed all that. You and your lies drove me from home at threat of my life, and I had to survive as best I could. Is it any wonder that I've hardened somewhat along the way?"

While she spoke, she saw Carstarfin step into the room. He stood behind Mathias and just watched them without speaking.

"Be done with your impertinence, Witch!" Mathias cried.

Carstarfin's eyes too were cold, though not with the hatred radiating from Mathias's. He glanced now to his subordinate. "It is not necessary, I think, to keep her so firmly bound." He turned again to Maddie. "We both knew she might try to slip away. It was our fault, really, for allowing ourselves that one small lapse of carelessness." He moved toward her, still studying her with thoughtful gaze. "From now on, we'll be more careful. In any case," he added, "the problem will soon take care of itself." He seemed very pleased about something.

Maddie stared at him fearfully. "What do you mean?" she whispered her question through cracked lips. What did he intend doing with her?

"I'm resigning my post as chief magistrate, and going back to England. You'll be coming with me. Over there, you have no friends, no associates. Under those circumstances, I think you'll be more docile." His words were like a death sentence. Maddie's eyes widened in horror. "England?" she whispered.

Carstarfin smiled. "That's right, England. And until we leave next week, I put my friend Mathias in charge of keeping you safe."

Those five days dragged by in a slow, unending Hell. Mathias spent those entire days with her, watching, just watching, until she thought she'd go mad. One afternoon when she could stand it no longer, she confronted him. "Why don't you just kill me now, while you have the chance? It's what you always wanted, isn't it?"

"My wants don't enter into it, Madame. True, I'd as soon see you dead, but Carstarfin holds the power here, not me, and you've bewitched him. That child you're carrying," he nodded toward her belly with a sneer, "it's probably Rohan's bastard, but Carstarfin, poor fool, believes it's his own."

Maddie chilled. He had come too close to the truth. "Carstarfin sired this whelp I carry, not Rohan, and you are an idiot."

Mathias leaped to his feet. His face had paled at her insult. His lips, now white, drew back against his teeth, Maddie recoiled as he lunged at her. In one fist, he grabbed a handful of her hair. "On this island, I have but little power as yet, only what comes from my family and my sugar-processing interests, but if I ever find you again, and if you've left Carstarfin's protection, I swear to God I'll kill you with my own hands." Maddie did not cringe. She glared unblinking into his face, and maintained a scronful silence.

With a strangled cry, Mathias shoved her away. This pushed knocked Maddie off balance. As she fell, crashing to her knees, her hands reached out to protect the unborn child still sleeping inside her. Kneeling on the floor, she glared after as Mathias strode from the room, slamming the door behind him. Blessedly, she did not see him again for the rest of the day.

Finally the time of their departure dawned. By then, Maddie was almost relieved to be going. At least she would never lay eyes upon Mathias again, because he, and Chloe, were remaining behind.

While Maddie stood at the rail of their ship, she watched as it lurched free from its moorings at harbor. Port Royal, that wealthy, corrupt city, grew smaller and smaller to her eyes as they glided out to open sea.

Carstarfin, standing next to her, reached for her arm. Maddie, in revulsion, yanked away. After a silence, he spoke. "I hope you'll soon come to your senses for the sake of your baby, if not for your own. You'll make it so much easier on yourself if you learn to accept what you cannot change. I could treat you well, very well indeed, if you'd but allow me."

Maddie raised her chin. "You betrayed me. You raped me, kept me prisoner, and when I escaped, you added to my misery by sending soldiers to drag me back, and had me whipped by Andrew Mathias. Oh yes, in deed," she tossed her head scornfully, "you're so good, it makes me ashamed of my ingratitude!"

He sighed again. "Mathias carried things too far. Listen, I had no idea he intended chaining you down in that cell. I never ordered that."

Maddie set her mouth in a grim line. Because of Carstarfin, she'd never see Henri again. She prayed that her beloved would learn the truth, at least, of that hated denunciation. Perhaps, God willing, he'd come to understand someday that she had done it only for his sake.

Carstarfin touched her again but Maddie stiffened. The months of pregnancy had been a blessed relief from his attentions. Ever since her body had begun to swell, he had left her alone. As she walked away from him now, she knew he would not follow or send anyone to accompany her. He trusted to maternal instinct that she'd not try to end her life, and he was right. The child within was all that remained of a precious love now torn from her. Standing alone, Maddie stared down at the water and sighed. England was so far away, and even though her parents had both come from there, she considered the country a foreign land.

Daylight dimmed in late afternoon, becoming in time night's darkness. In its hours, Maddie endured the sounds of Carstarfin's snoring. She hated him. Lord God, how she hated him! Mathias had egged him on, but he alone had used his power to ruin her life. Finally, morning dawned. While Carstarfin still snored, Maddie stood up and dressed, putting on a frock of linen dyed gray in a pattern of watery-looking ripples, and then slipped from the cabin. Once on deck, she saw that thick whitish fog shrouded everything. Vapors swirled in a moist caress against her face, and as she stood at the railing on deck shivering, she pretended that she was in another time and space, where all the past few months of her life had never happened. In the mists of this strange, unearthly morning, Carstarfin and Mathias no longer existed. Salem and the witch hangings became an ugly fiction, a mere bad dream gone forever, and she herself had never been born, but simply had always existed, forever a part of this fog.

Such a feeling could not last, however. The fog thinned. Looking out over the curve of far horizon, to the place sailors of long ago believed marked the earth's end and eternity's beginning, Maddie saw the first visible rays of sun—hazy at first, but gradually clearer in form, as its heat and light burned off the vapor of cloud descended.

The sun glared higher in the sky, now a deep, brilliant blue, and the day wore on, growing impossibly warm. In mid-afternoon, Maddie's eyes caught sight of another ship. At first but a speck on the horizon, it moved toward them, growing distinctly larger. Gradually others noticed, too. No one seemed alarmed at first, because the strange ship flew the colors of France, a friendly nation. The crew, although curious and even a little cautious, conducted business as usual. As the French frigate drew closer, however, the collective mood of indifference heightened into worried fear.

"Wonder what they want of us?" She heard a sailor asking himself, as he hurried past.

"He's still drawing up to us," muttered another. Someone else shouted for the captain. There were few passengers on the *Dundee*, but all of them sensed the tension now hanging thick in the air. They clustered on deck, straining to watch. The crew tried to signal the approaching vessel with flags. When the strangers aboard did not reply, tension turned to active fear. "Do you suppose it's a pirate?" whispered one.

"Oh, Lord, no!" a woman muttered in horror. "Surely a pirate'd not be flying the *fleur de lis*!"

"Well, you never know," Maddie broke into the conversation now. "Sometimes they fly false colors, then at close approach, raise their own flag. You see instead the Jolly Roger, and then you know, but by then, it's too late." Maddie liked none of her fellow passengers very well, so she took grim satisfaction in frightening them. She turned to Carstarfin standing beside her now, and flashed a cold smile. "Perhaps it's even *Le Diable* himself, free now, with a new ship and crew. He'll remember you for sure, and what fine sport he'll make of you."

"Rohan is dead." Carstarfin retorted, with more hope than conviction. "He could never have survived those infested waters."

Suddenly, as the ship drew close, too close, the *fleur de lis* plunged down from where it flew up on the mainmast. With breathtaking speed, a black flag crossed with skull and bones flew in its place. Maddie could almost smell and taste the fearful horror surrounding her now.

"All passenger below!" a voice shouted, in command for them to clear the deck. Most were only too glad to obey. They stampeded like frightened cattle, cramming themselves down hatches meant only for single file. Women sobbed aloud. They screamed in fear, while men muttered curses under their breaths. Carstarfin, as terrified as any of them, was among the first to hide.

At the hatch leading below, Maddie stopped. Instead of following the others down, she leaned back against a mast. She did not want to cower in the darkness below as if she were part of the cargo. She would watch. The crew, engrossed in its own desperate struggles to save the ship from capture by pirates, did even notice her standing there.

Running footsteps clattered across the deck. Men grabbed great coils of rope and flung them to others, or lifted them up under their arms and fled somewhere else with them. All the while, the hot sun beat down. She smelled and saw the sweat of terrified men as they ran past her. It soaked their shirts or glistened upon their naked backs, as they bent and strained to load cannon and muskets, or to set the mainmast and rudder in position to flee if possible, their attacker's terrible advance.

Suddenly, a cannon thundered out. Its boom blasted a hollow-sounding report from its muzzle. Almost at once, Maddie smelled the acrid reek of burnt powder. Another shot, and a great ball of fire ate into one of their secondary lateens.

A third explosion, and then her own crew answered back. Blasts from afar mingled with those on board, one exploding after another, in urgent, hot-smelling rhythm. Temperatures on deck were almost unbearable, as sun's heat mingled with cannonfire. Another shot, another, then another, and from far-off, a man screamed. Still the pirate ship drew closer, until Maddie could see clearly its crew running back and forth on deck.

While some manned cannon, others clutched muskets aimed to blast out the hearts of those who would invade their ship. As Maddie stared paralyzed with fascinated horror, first one and then another of the *Dundee's* crew dropped down, shot and killed by their enemy.

Those who fell did not die without a fight, however. Men on board the pirate vessel had perished, too. They lay with arms blown off, or skulls shattered. Their blood oozed as thick and red as that of her own ship's fallen crew.

The stench of blood nearly overpowered her. It mingled with the smell of gunpowder. Suddenly nauseous, Maddie turned away. She clamped a hand over her mouth and stumbled to the hatch. She would have joined the others below, had not the *Dundee* given a lurch. Its force sent her sprawling to her knees. From where she lay on deck, she saw the pirates now boarding their captured prize.

They were an ill-assorted lot, all sunburned and ragged. Knives and guns armed them. Some even carried stilettos clamped between their teeth. With cries and curses and shouts, they swung their swords into the flesh and bones of vanquished crewmen. Their war-whoops shrilled the air. They fired their pistols skyward, or aimed at random to send someone sprawling in death to the ground. Eyes red with passion of battle, they fired into the backs of those who fled. A few of the *Dundee's* crew escaped with their lives into the sea, only to be torn apart by sharks waiting there below. Maddie stared sickened and overwhelmed with horror.

The pirates swarmed everywhere. Most were of European lineage and armed with weapons familiar to Maddie, but other races sailed with this pirate band, too. Dark-skinned North Africans, with flashing teeth and eyeballs, wielded great-bladed machetes. Scimitars flashed in the hands of Turks. As they lunged, they cried out a savage appeal to Allah. They mowed the hapless crewmen down, slashing their flesh to ribbons. As heads fell or arms flew off, they shrieked with a cry that curdled Maddie's blood. She stared, suddenly paralyzed with horror. She had never seen anything like it. Unlike Castaneda's crew, who went about it in an almost businesslike manner, killing only when necessary, these pirates seemed actually to enjoy setting blood flowing, and turning living men to corpses. Suddenly, one of them turned his attention to her. Maddie drew back, terrified to the very core of her being. Their looks of savage desire threatened violence.

With a cry, one man lunged for her. His black eyes glittered. His swarthy face flushed as he hurtled himself toward her, jabbering something in a tongue Maddie did not recognize or understand. She did not need, however, to discern his words to know what he was thinking. She read it all too clearly in his eyes. Before she could scramble to her feet and run away, he grabbed her by the arm and yanked her to him. Holding her tight against him, he dragged her out into the center of deck.

"No!" Maddie writhed, wide-eyed with horror, as strange men moved toward her. She nearly fainted dead away as they advanced like a living tide. In their reddened eyes and bulging trousers, she saw her fate. What did they care for the baby growing next to her heart? She was a woman, young, helpless and golden-haired. She was theirs to overpower and take.

Chapter Thirty-three

Suddenly, a voice thundered out. "That woman is for me!" It bloomed, from somewhere out of sight. Its tone was hard and strong, calm, yet taut with fury barely suppressed.

She saw his shadow first, then raised wide, horrified eyes to his face. He stood tall and strong, with tangled hair and a beard so thick and curly that it hid his jaw and chin. What little skin showed was dark. Though his eyes were European, of a glacial shade of gray, the sun had burned his complexion almost black. His hard-eyed gaze flitted tense and alert from his men to the blood-washed deck, and then to her. His eyes reminded her of an eagle's, constantly on search for the living flesh of weaker creatures on which to feed. "You will not touch that woman!" he shouted, "not any of you—upon pain of death." His voice, calm and deep and vibrant with scorn, had a strange effect. His men stepped away from her. They stood without moving, rooted to the spot where he had encountered them. No one argued, no one dared. He, leader of them all, turned to the man who had first grabbed her. "Akbar, you and the boy will guard her. See that she does not escape." He whirled now upon the others. "The rest of you," he cried, "bring up the other passengers and tie up the surviving crew." He snarled out his orders. Maddie frowned; something about him seemed familiar.

A young man joined his crewmates on deck. When she got a better look at him, she stared in shocked disbelief. "Peter!" What was he doing *here*, among such savages? She was too surprised even to be horrified by his transformation into one of them.

The leader moved past her, and spoke to someone in a normal tone of voice. At once, Maddie glanced to him, then stared in shocked disbelief. Suddenly she felt as if someone had kicked her in the stomach. Shock mingled with wild joy, as she recognized in his words a beloved voice.

He had changed so much since that last time in Carstarfin's apartments. The beard and tangled hair hid the clean-lined face of her husband. Her heart sank. Without even so much as acknowledging who she was, Henri had claimed her as his booty—his prize of war in the capture of the *Dundee*. She glanced at him with dismay. What did he intend doing with her, now that she was, in his eyes, a captive enemy?

Time and circumstances had tranformed him into a stranger. The sun had burned him a deep, reddish brown. He dressed now like a Moor. His clothes were dirty. A wild printed scarf tied around his head hid the tangles of his hair. He had armed himself with a scimitar, an evil-looking curved sword. Fresh blood stained him. Glancing from Henri's retreating back to Peter again, she confronted him. "Is it really you,

Peter?'' she whispered. She had a thousand questions to ask him, yet hardly knew how to begin.

"Maddie, I have to obey." He seemed clearly uncomfortable. "You heard what he said—for all of us to leave you alone, and for us to guard you, and he means it. Not one of his men would do otherwise. You are his now, and he seems to hate you. But why? How? I thought you were his wife."

"It's a long story, Peter. As for the other, I understand. I can see how terrible he must be when his orders are disobeyed. You must do as he says, no matter what, but tell me—how did you come to join him? Where did you go when you left me on Ocracoke?"

Peter shook his head. "It was terrible, really. Some ship needed extra hands, and so two men from its crew kidnapped me. In St. George, I escaped, and it was there I met Rohan and signed onto his crew."

All survivors were on deck now. The other four women and eight men from the passengers, including Carstarfin, stood huddled together apart from Maddie. The women were all crying. One old crone prayed aloud through her tears for God to spare them, but God seemed to be elsewhere. Maddie alone stood calm. She knew she would have to pay for the suffering she had caused Henri, and she resigned herself to it. Whether death or torture, she was prepared.

He was a stranger to her now. He strode back into sight and faced them all. He stood with legs spread and arms folded across his chest. For endless silent moments, he studied them. As he glanced her way, Maddie's blood chilled. She saw only hatred in his eyes; no trace of tenderness now remained. With the exception of Peter, his new crew seemed half-savage, and they frightened her. His eyes darted from one to the other of his men. Finally, he spoke. "I claim no interest in this ship's cargo. What's here will be divided equally among the rest of you." He whirled. As his eyes fixed on Maddie, however, she knew the worst was coming. "I claim as my prize only this wench, and promise death to anyone else who touches her!" As he moved toward her, Maddie trembled. At a signal from his eyes, three of his men grabbed hold of her arms. They imprisoned her unmoving, as Henri drew close.

Every eye on deck fixed upon her and the pirate captain. "So, we meet again!" He stared with contempt upon her. Maddie's reply froze in her throat. She could only stare at him. Without waiting for her answer, he whirled. He faced the others assembled there. "Look well upon this woman!" he shouted at them all, "and know that she is everything a woman should be! She is a seeker after gold. She lies, whispering false promises of love with her lips, and she betrays the trust of those who would protect her."

Maddie's cheeks seared with the heat of her humiliation. She stared in mounting horror. "No, Henri!" she whispered. "You do not understand."

Henri ingnored her. "She is even, some say, a witch, a hound of Satan in the form of a beautiful woman."

A collective gasp tore from the passengers. Maddie's eyes fixed with loathing and hatred upon Carstarfin, who stood among the others. She could not blame Henri for his bitterness. What else, after all, could he think? It was Carstarfin's fault alone that Henri now stood publicly denouncing her. He could have refused Mathias's bright plan. He could have ordered Andrew Mathias away, yet he did not. Carstarfin was the cause of Henri's misery, too, but the others did not know, did not understand. They stared at her now in horror.

"I never betrayed anyone by choice." She pointed to Carstarfin. "That man coerced me into denouncing you. For the sake of your life, or so I believed, I gave myself to him and signed that false document. My only

357

crime was stupidity, not faithlessness."

Henri ignored her protest. His lips curled into a smile. "How fitting it is, then," he continued, as if she hadn't spoken. "how fitting that she should come to me, the one known throughout the Caribbean as *Le Diable*. How fitting that I, called a devil by one and all, should cleave unto myself a bride of Satan!"

As he whirled back upon her now, ominous hatred glittered in his eyes. His gaze fixed upon her now, and chilled her. "And you will all see for yourselves, what it is Satan offers to his obedient wicked. Let your eyes behold the sweet, ripe fruits of his temptation!"

Within a sudden movement, he grabbed her finespun blouse. His steel hard fist clenched the delicate fabric between five fingers and a thumb. With a savage cry, he yanked down.

Maddie screamed as his strength jolted her. The fabric tore, revealing the luminous flesh of her breasts, now swelled with milk for his child. Tears of pain and humiliation streamed down her cheeks now, as she stood naked in full view of crew and passengers. Men still held her so that she could not fight free and cover with hands and arms her flesh. She could only turn her face away, so as not to see all those who now stared at her with horrified fascination. Her cheeks burned hot with shame.

"See then," he proclaimed, "see what a mistress of the Devil uses to lure men's hearts! Are they not beautiful, these fine, white breasts? Would not any strong-blooded man ache to fondle these? Soft and lovely are the tools of Satan, but deadly."

Suddenly fingers dug into her jaw. He held her by the chin and forced her head around, to gaze again into his eyes. "No one betrays me, Madame," he whispered. *"No one!"* He turned to his crew. "Take her to my cabin, mates, and lock her in. As for the others," he whirled back to his remaining captives. His eyes narrowed as he studied them a moment, and then he said, "I want *that* man hanged." He pointed at Carstarfin. "Hang him, just as he would have hanged me in Port Royal. Do it right now, so that I can be sure it's done." He whirled to Carstarfin who stood cowering. "Be thankful...be thankful that I do not torture you first, the way you tortured me. I, at least, am merciful. I give my enemies a quick death. I do not let them linger in pain and misery the way you do." He turned again to his men.

"Leave the rest of them here to watch, and the wench, too," he added, gesturing to Maddie. "Leave them here until I decide what to do with them."

Even as they dragged Maddie up the steps to Henri's cabin, she saw from the corner of her eye that someone had already flung a rope over one beam of the mast. As they half-carried, half-dragged her inside Henri's private space, she heard Carstarfin screaming like a frightened pig, knowing he was being led to slaughter.

Chapter Thirty-four

They locked her in Henri's cabin, but not until after the men held her in full view of Carstarfin's death. Maddie shuddered just remembering it. He had squealed in fright. His eyes had rolled until she could see only their whites, and she pitied him as much for his cowardice, as for his fate. As they led him to the noose, he had tried to break free from their grasp. He had struggled to get away, but with no luck. He should have known better. Where could he have run, but overboard? Sharks still churned in the bloody waters below. In any case, they would have torn him to bits. At the sound of his cries, Maddie had flinched. His death had been horrible to watch.

It wasn't that she cared about him. Indeed, she had good reason to rejoice at what he suffered. Hearing him scream for mercy, however, Maddie had stared with loathing pity. She could not help but shrink away from the terrible finality of his punishment.

After a seeming eternity, silence returned. The pirates who held Maddie thrust her into Rohan's cabin and locked her in. Here, only the faint and distant voices of men calling to one another or speaking among themselves reached her ears now. She collapsed onto the bunk where Henri had last taken her with great tenderness. She knew she'd enjoy little love from him now. It was to be her prison cot, a cold, hard bed where she'd sleep alone. At thought of the love she had lost, Maddie sobbed aloud. She dreaded what he might now intend for her. The bitterness of his hatred chilled her to her bones. She thought again of Carstarfin's death and shuddered. Was Henri planning the same for her? Maddie trembled. He was such a stranger to her now, angry and unpredictable.

Hours passed, and Maddie drifted into a light, uneasy slumber. She had been dreaming, having a nightmare actually, when suddenly the door to her prison clattered open. Framed in it, Henri stood glowering at her.

With a cry, Maddie drew back. Protectively, her hand flew over her belly, to hide from his violence her unborn baby. She saw at once how his brooding face had hardened. His eyes burned like two coal pits from Hell as he towered over her. He stood without speaking for what seemed like endless eternities. Instead, he just studied her. His contempt radiated out of him like fire. She could see that his teeth had clenched. His nostrils had flared as if he were breathing flames. "Henri, I—"

Maddie's voice trembled as she gazed upon him, in longing mingled with fear.

"Shut up!" Her words had broken the terrible spell of silence that had held them both unmoving. His heels clattered as he strode over to her. He drew close, and with one swift thrust, grabbed her under one arm. She cried out as he yanked her to him. A jab of pain seared her as his fingers dug into her flesh. His body became like a wall, and she, imprisoned by its strength, pressed to him. Helpless and frightened for her very life, she trembled in his arms. He held her with one hand. His other grabbed a great wad of her hair. This he squeezed so tightly in his fist that he seemed to be tearing it out from the roots. Tears sprang to her eyes as he used those curls to yank her head backward. It seemed that he wanted to look more closely and with greater loathing upon her face. "Motherhood becomes you, my darling." His words were a snarl, barely audible, yet all the same he spoke with the frightful intensity of an enraged animal. "It plumps you out and flushes your cheeks." His heart pounding wildly against her told her that her presence still aroused him, perhaps against his will. Her own fluttered now in shrinking fear.

His presence surrounded her. His heat burned her. In that close, airless chamber, she felt as if she were suffocating. She closed her eyes so that she would no longer have to look upon his.

"Look at me, damn you!" His hand released her hair only to swing down to grab her jaw. Maddie cried out. She crumbled sobbing into his arms.

But he would not let her fall. His hands curled like talons around her arms. "Your tears do nothing for me, madam," he spoke in a cold, hard voice. "You're wasting them on me. Save them for your other lovers—those who do not know you so well."

"I have no lovers." Maddie could barely speak. Her

body shook in uncontrollable spasms. "You are the only one."

"If that be the case, then I pity you," he smiled bitterly, "for I am no longer your lover, nor your husband, either."

"Henri, I—" Maddie reached to him, but he flung her away. He grabbed her again by the arms, then yanked her to his bunk. Maddie gasped aloud, blinded with tears as he flung her down. The bitter intensity she saw in his eyes terrified her. His hands came at her curled into claws, ready to tear. His fingers reached for her bare breasts. His weight pressed down upon her. He crushed her now, and didn't seem to care. Maddie felt as if she could hardly breathe.

His passion, once gently tender, now took her with cruel roughness as he claimed her as his own. His lips pressed hard upon hers with unyielding intensity. His hands were uncaring, like those of some hateful stranger's. One reached down between her legs. His fingers in harsh caress sent blood searing to her head. "No, Henri!" she cried, sobbing and gasping all at once, "not like this!"

"How then—like some long-lost lover?" His reply, brutally sarcastic, cut through her. Instead of love, he took her now in anger and with hatred. Maddie's eyes swam with tears. She could tell by the very feel of him that she meant less now than the most debased slut he might find on the streets of Tortuga or St. George. His swollen, throbbing manhood thrust into her now with such force and rage that Maddie cried out. Her body convulsed in a spasm from his power. Finally, he finished, collapsing away from her like an exhausted animal. Choking in horror, Maddie writhed to be free of him.

With tears searing in her eyes, she stumbled from his cot. "Damn you, Henri!" she whispered. "You feel so injured because you think I've betrayed you. Well, go ahead. I no longer care. You've finally convinced me that your love has been false all along."

He jolted upward. "Just what the Hell do you mean, woman?" he cried. "Nothing I ever gave you was false, yet all I got for it in return was a stab in the back."

"I followed you halfway around the world, Henri," she cried, "I suffered to find you. Lord knows I've suffered!" She remembered bitterly the faces of all her enemies and attackers. "Do you really believe, after all I went through, that I'd turn my back on you at first chance?"

She whirled from him. In agitation, she began to pace the floor. "You saw me with Carstarfin. You listened to words I was forced to say, and you believed the worst. Had you but loved me enough, you would at least have asked yourself if there might not have been another reason. You might at least have reserved some small doubt for my sake, but no—you showed me no mercy in your heart."

"What the Hell do you mean, 'words you were forced to say?" Henri's voice remained hard, yet his tone betrayed startled bewilderment too.

"I already told you, or tried to. Carstarfin made me an offer—your life and freedom, in return for my to staying with him. I agreed because I saw no other hope. After all, according to Jack Trimble, you were being held in the dungeons in the seventh level, which was supposed to be the worst. Even your friend Abraham had little hope of storming the gaol and rescuing you. What else could I do?" Maddie took a deep breath. "Carstarfin imposed another condition, too. He was afraid, you see, that you'd come back for me and he didn't want you to. To discourage you, I was to renounce my love for you and pretend to desire *him* instead. If I refused, or if I failed to convince you, I'd be led in chains to watch you hang.''

His eyes were hard as they remained fixed upon her. ''A pretty story,'' he said coldly, ''and quite clever of you, really, but I know how devoutly you worked to save my life. Tell me, was it your idea or his, to use me as quarry for the amusement of the Royal Navy?''

Maddie turned away with tears glistening in her eyes. ''How could I have known that his promises were all lies? In any case, what choice did I have? At least you had some small chance to get away, which happily you took. Tell me, Henri, how did you do it?'' For him to have survived seemed nothing less than a miracle to her.

''Do you really care, or are you merely taking note, to make sure it doesn't happen again?'' His voice spilled over with scorn.

Wearily, she sighed. ''You can believe anything you like, Henri, and as for me—do what you will. But spare my life at least until after the child is born, and a wet nurse can be found to replace me. Like it or not, the child is yours, conceived of our love in your fortress on Dominica.''

She turned from him now and walked to the door. With each step, she half-expected him to leap from the bunk and run a sword through her back, but he did not. With trembling hand, she reached for the latch. To her surprise, it opened easily. She stood in its frame and glanced one last time to him. Darkness had fallen to shroud him.

He did not speak. He did not move. After one long, last lingering moment, Maddie walked outside. The night was dark. Only a few stars lit the sky. Clad in his blanket, Maddie shivered as she stood, naked underneath. She stared outward at the sea below and sighed. The sea smelled especially fishy tonight. Water lapped with a tuneless gurgle against the wooden ribs of Henri's ship, and from deep below in the waters, she heard the songs of whales. Too restless to remain, Maddie walked away. For the rest of the night, she wandered the ship like a wraith, lost and alone to all time and love. Her heart ached for Henri. She craved the tenderness he alone could give her, but wishing did no good. Henri hated her now. Somehow, she would have to learn to live without him.

The following day, Maddie wandered outside on deck, dressed in one of her own loose-fitting gowns brought over from the *Dundee*. Work went on around her, and few even seemed to notice that she stood aimlessly by. Toward evening, she saw Peter again, passing by on his way somewhere else. She called out to him.

He moved toward her with an uneasy look on his face. "Maddie, are you all right?" He glanced around as if afraid to be seen with her. Afraid of Henri's wrath, he did not touch or embrace her, but stood carefully away.

Maddie shrugged. "As well as can be, I guess."

His face, peering into hers, revealed bewildered concern. "What on earth was all that about yesterday? I've never seen anything like it. Never have I seen Rohan lay into anyone the way he did to you—not even captured crewmen, and certainly not other woman."

"He thinks I did a horrible thing. I did not. I am innocent, but he was made to believe otherwise. He still accepts the lie our enemies handed him."

"Lie?" Peter stared, clearly bewildered.

"He believes I betrayed him, but it's not true," she explained to her friend from so long ago what had happened. When she had finished, she watched him shrug and shake his head. "I wish I could help. You did so much for me; I'd like to repay you, but in this case, I don't see how. Somehow you've got to convince him you're not what he thinks, but I don't know how...."

His voice trailed off.

Maddie sighed, seeing no way to do so. "I would give anything to start over, to be a girl again living in my father's house. I wish I could go home."

"Well, why don't you?"

Maddie shook her head, then turned away. For a second she stood without speaking, as thoughts and memories raced through her mind. What harm would it do to confide in him now? After all, she was so many miles and lifetimes away from Salem. Even Mathias had been left behind. With new resolve, Maddie turned back to her friend.

"Henri spoke of me as a witch. He was wrong, of course. I am no witch and he knows it." She explained about Andrew Mathias and his false accusation, and how she had fled home for her life.

"But that was over a year ago!" he protested. "I heard some men just a few weeks ago, talking in a tavern. New Englanders, they were, whalers following south into warmer waters. One of them mentioned Salem, and it got 'em all started. They've opened their jail, Maddie, and let the accused witches go. It turned out to be just a horrible mistake—all of it. Those girls had only *pretended*. No one bewitched them. It's turned into quite a scandal."

Maddie's eyes widened. A flush of indignation heated her. Forty-nine people had died, put to death by hanging on those girls' testimony. She herself would have died, too, if she hadn't fled.

"So you see," continued Peter, "you *can* go back."

"I'm not sure I want to!" Underneath her words, however, she felt a twinge of longing. She would give anything to see her father again. If he still lived, he must be mad with worry. Despite all the pain it had caused her, home seemed suddenly like a haven to her now—a refuge where she might take her baby and recover from all the psychic wounds inflicted upon her. However, the whole discussion seemed pointless. She was on a ship, headed she knew not where. "But where is all this talk getting me?" she asked, turning to him. "I can hardly jump off this ship and swim home."

"You won't have to," he replied. "We'll be docking in Trenton. It's a safe harbor and the governor is friendly, so long as we remember to give him his share."

"Trenton?" Maddie gasped aloud the name. New Jersey was close to home. From there, she could travel north to see her father again. Now that Henri so despised her, nothing remained for her here.

Maddie's thoughts turned inward upon the baby—Henri's child. Despite the men she had known, by consent or by rape, Maddie held no doubts as to who had fathered it. After all, a monthly cycle had come and gone between her encounter with Jed Hawkins and her reunion with Henri. Maddie smiled a secret maternal thrill of pleasure. The child had grown, and from the way it kicked against the inner walls of her belly, she knew it lived, and healthily. Even if she and Henri never saw one another again, the flesh of their child would link them together for all time, if it survived. In its offspring, she and Henri would pass together far into future generations, joined together forever in the river of life. She knew that their baby, now fully formed, would come soon, perhaps even on board its father's ship. Maddie hoped and prayed that the sight of it would melt Henri's heart.

In her loneliness, Maddie tried to console herself by thinking again of all the friends she had ever known, in all the places strange and whimsical fate had carried her. With a pang, she wondered if any of them still remembered her. Of those who did, how many spoke her name with affection? Just then, Maddie saw a movement out of the corner of her eye. She glanced up to Henri standing on a parapet. Their eyes met. He held hers locked in his own, with an angry question burning there. A sharp noise from below startled her. Unable to stop herself, she whirled. When she turned back, Henri had disappeared. Crying out his name, she ran toward where he had stood, but no traces lingering. With a sob, she turned away.

Gradually, she realized that things seemed to be lurching more than before. The waves underneath their ship swelled larger. The sky grayed and darkened. Black clouds billowed overhead blotting out the sun, which at best that day had shone only dim and haze-shrouded. The air felt and tasted damp. All sounds around her had magnified. Raw energy crackled in the atmosphere of impending storm.

The ship had moved farther north, into waters which even under sunshine stretched a cold gray-blue with white froth foaming upon its swells. As a chill wind blew around her now, Maddie clutched arms to her chest and shivered.

With faces tense, the crew shifted the lateens to catch a wind that would blow them farther out to sea, instead of crashing toward rocky shoreline. An hour passed, then another. The screaming wind tossed their ship far beyond sight of land.

The waves reached up to lick the sides of their ship. In those swells, the *Genvieve* bobbed and dropped like a cork, like driftwood tossed and flung at whim. With all her strength, Maddie clung to the rail as she stared around her with horrified fascination. She could not tear her eyes from watching men toil as if their very lives depended on it.

Henri passed by, glancing toward her as he drew close. Her own eyes widened in hope. Was he about to relent, perhaps even offering her a kind word, even if it were only a warning to be careful? "Henri!" she greeted him, in eager anticipation. At once, however, Maddie's heart sank. His eyes remained hard and cold, his face impassive.

"Get to your quarters." In a curt tone, he ordered her away. She saw, however, that she should obey. The storm had gotten dangerously rough. Each passing minute had brought increasing wind. Lightning sizzled ever closer in the sky overhead. Thunder deafened her. Reluctantly, Maddie inched her way across deck, clinging to whatever she could as she made her way to the steep and narrow steps leading to the higher level where she had lived since her capture.

She reached the rail and started to climb. She felt at once how wet the rain had turned those wooden steps, and how slippery. Suddenly the entire ship lurched. A horrible shudder ran through it from stem to stern.

Its force of movement threw Maddie off balance. Her body, cumbersome with child, twisted around midair, while her hands, already sliding on that slick rail surface, lost their grip.

On the storm-tossed ship, she hurtled through the air. She screamed as she fell, then landed belly-down on the deck below. Her entire universe convulsed into one huge seizure of pain.

Chapter Thirty-five

Pain lingered. It blotted out all other sensation. It obscured her awareness of everything else. From far away, as if it were someone else's, she heard her own voice screaming. The contractions came harder, faster. They felt like an iron glove reaching into her insides to clutch whatever it found. The horror of it intensified, then ebbed. Each time it returned, it seemed to worsen and last longer.

Hot salt tears streamed out of her eyes. She moaned, and from time to time felt a cloth wiping away the briny sweat that soaked her bedding and clothes.

The storm thundered on. Dimly she noticed the way their ship lurched and swirled under its cruel wind, but the pain of her insides spilling outward, of flesh tearing away from flesh, diminished it in her mind.

Finally, a great shuddering scream brought the end of it. Following the angry cry of a baby, her pain fell into a dull, throbbing ache. Voices and faces floated over her. One of them looked familiar, and with a surge of love, she called out to it, "Henri!" Her word quavered barely audible. Her voice sounded old. "Our baby—" One thought, one fear obsessed her. Had the fall injured their child?

"He's all right." Henri's voice was gentle now. "Your baby is all right. A fine little boy."

Maddie tried to sit up, but he pressed her back down. "He's *your* baby, too." Relief melted into dismay. One thought screamed through her mind. Henri must be made to see that it was *his* child as well. "He's *your* baby, not someone else's!"

"Rest now, Maddie, and we'll talk about it later." Intent upon soothing her, calming her, his voice crooned soft and low. "For now, just try to get your strength back."

"But the baby!" Her voice rose into a scream. She felt his hands clasp her shoulders, shaking now in hysterical sobbing.

"I'll take care of the baby. I promise."

With a dizzying spin, her surroundings melted into darkness.

When she opened her eyes again, her mind seemed far away. The colors in that room had heightened to unnatural brightness. She wondered dimly what was wrong with her. She had forgotten why she was here, lying in a bed of pain. Why did she feel so strange? From whence came that terrible heat? Maddie called out Henri's name again—the only word or thought in her mind. In her delirium, she babbled words of love.

They thought that she would die, but she surprised them. She was young and strong. In spite of everything, the strength came back to her. Consciousness returned, and she smiled often and lovingly upon the sturdy baby lying by her side. When he cried, she raised his little mouth to one nipple. Lovingly she held him close. Her entire body tingled with strange delight whenever he sucked into himself her milk.

He had come into the world with a thatch of golden hair. His newborn blue eyes soon turned to gray like his father's, and whenever Maddie looked upon his little face, she saw things about him that reminded her of Henri.

A few days passed in peace. Suddenly one morning Henri's cabin door crashed open. Maddie's eyes widened when she saw her husband standing there, looking grim and troubled, yet proud. "Henri!" Maddie smiled in hopeful eagerness as she whispered his name. He had changed during her sickness enough to give her hope. She prayed the caring would remain once she recovered.

"I came to speak to you." Maddie saw in his expression something that shattered her heart. "We'll be landing in Boston in a few days, a week at most. I'll find a wet nurse there, and leave the baby with her."

Maddie's jaw dropped. "But I have milk, Henri, plenty of it. Our baby needs no wet nurse."

"You will not be keeping your baby," he replied. "I consider you an unfit mother, and I will not have my son raised by you."

She felt as if the floor were falling out from

underneath her. To brace herself, she inhaled a deep breath. "Well, at least you admit he's yours," she said, speaking acidly.

"I knew it almost from the first."

"He's *my* son, too." Maddie clung to her baby. "I won't let you take him!" Her voice had risen hysterically. The child, alarmed, began to cry.

"Now you see what you've done!" Henri spoke impatiently. "You've upset him."

Maddie glared at him. Her own voice dropped cold and hard. "I'm surprised you don't tear him from my arms right now. It'd be just like you."

"I have no milk to feed him," replied Henri. "Otherwise I might."

"I'm amazed you'd ever let a little thing like your child's welfare stand in the way of your own blind hatred!" Her eyes burned angrily into his. "A child needs his mother, you know, but maybe you don't care. I suppose hurting me for what you imagine I did matters more to you than what he really needs." She glanced to the little boy. Secretly she had named him Henri, after his father. She had endured so much for his sake, and for his father's. To have him torn from her now was unthinkable. Tears flooded Maddie's eyes. She vowed she'd do what she could to prevent their separation.

"We'll talk about it later," Henri said coldly and started to leave.

"We'll talk about it now!" Maddie's voice broke. He paid no attention, however but instead turned on his heel and stalked out. Once alone Maddie fought back the urge to break into sobbing. Tears would serve no purpose. Instead, she put her hand down to her babe and let his tiny fingers curl around one of her own. "We'll find a way, darling," she whispered. "I promise you. I'll make sure they don't steal you from your mama."

She knew she'd need all her strength, so Maddie fought to recover. So little time remained. Within two days, she was up and about, carrying her baby when she went on board. As before, she hardly ever saw Henri, but sometimes when he thought she didn't notice, she'd see him standing somewhere just watching her. She tried not to let him know that she noticed. As she moved, eating or exercising to get her muscles in tone again, she wracked her brain to think of a plan—any means to spirit herself and the baby off the *Genvieve* before Henri took him from her.

One night a few days off Boston, she had left the baby Henri alone, sleeping in his cradle. Restless and unable to relax, Maddie decided to get up and take a walk. Maybe some fresh night air and exercise would tire her. While out, she overheard a whispered conversation. "It's already happening—just a matter of minutes. We'll get him while he sleeps. Once he's killed, his crew'll be no trouble at all. They're all afraid of him, they are, and with good cause. He's a tyrant, he is."

"Yes indeed, they'll probably thank us." Maddie recognized the half-whispered voice as belonging to one of the passengers captured along with her. Instead of locking them down in the hold, Henri had let them roam free aboard the *Genvieve*. Instead of thanking his mercy, however, the ingrates planned to foment mutiny. "In any case, we've got six of the crew with us already."

Maddie's eyes widened as she listened to their plans. Beyond doubt, Henri was in danger, immediate and deadly. He would have to be warned.

In her frenzy Maddie forgot how he had hurt her. She even pushed to the back of her mind how he had threatened to tear from her arms their baby. The man she still loved more than life itself was in danger, betrayed by passengers and mutinous crew. Her only thought now was to warn him.

She knew he had set up a cot in the navigation room. On her way running to him, she passed her friend Peter. "Maddie, you look terrible! What is it?" He stared at her in horror.

Maddie drew back. "What are you doing out here?" The hour was late, he should have been asleep. The horrible possibility that he was one of the mutineers slapped her hard.

"I just got off watch. Why?" He seemed clearly bewildered.

"Oh, thank God!" Maddie glanced around. When she saw no one nearby, she leaned to him and whispered in his ear. "Some of the crew are planning a mutiny. Go for help, while I warn Henri!" She had too little time to explain how she knew, or to build up to it.

In night's dim light, Peter visibly paled. "Mutiny?" Horrified, he stared at her. "But who?"

"That's right. Now go for help. I don't know who. The male passengers—all of them, I suppose—and six of the crew. Now go!"

Not waiting to hear what he had to say, Maddie whirled. She ran to his cabin in the navigation room raised, like his own quarters, above the main deck. Breathless, she took great gulps of air that seared her lungs, then climbed. Once she reached the top step and saw inside that tiny map-lined room, she found him not alone, but already captured by two of his crew, holding a knife at his throat.

Outside the door Maddie slipped off her shoes, then entered barefoot, so quietly they did not notice. Henri glanced to her, then quickly away. Whether friend or foe, he knew it would be safer not to acknowledge her presence until he knew. With wide eyes she saw that one of Henri's captors even now looped a rope around his wrists to tie his hands. "You think you rule the sea? Well, you can't. Not anymore. *Diable* is good as dead now, and *I'll* take your place."

"You?" Henri spoke with contempt. "You're nothing but a worm, Frazier!"

Maddie knew she had to act fast. Once those ropes were knotted around his wrists, he'd be helpless. Out of the corner of her eye she saw an unlit brass lamp attached by hook to the wall. Very carefully and quickly, she lifted it.

The lamp weighed more than she expected, but luckily she had braced herself well. Grimacing from her effort she raised it now and flung it at the men who would bind Henri and slit his throat.

Because she had not the strength to throw it far, the crash proved more distracting than damaging. It stole the mutineers' attention long enough, however, for Henri to kick free, shake off the bonds looped but not tied around his wrists, then raise both arms to fight the ones who had attacked him. As it hurtled through the air, Maddie screamed, loud and long, then again, praying her cries would summon aid, not more enemies.

The man nearest Maddie whirled and lunged at her. She screamed again. Her eyes darted around, searching for something to throw at him and saw a low, wooden bench. She lifted this up, jabbing at him to keep him away, but he tore it from her grasp and flung it away.

Out of the corner of her eye, she saw Henri grab one of his attackers by the collar. With a yell he hurtled the man who crashed headfirst into ship's wainscotting. Maddie, too desperate defending herself to pay much attention, hardly noticed how blood oozed from him now.

Other mutineers had come to the aid of their cronies. One of these grabbed Maddie from behind. She screamed, kicking in desperate terror as he held her. She writhed from him. Her heel hit his shinbone. A cry of pain, followed by a curse, told her she had found her target.

Beyond, in one corner Henri struggled with two others. Shadows from an oil lamp still mounted on the wall cast the entire scene in grotesque light and dark. Their faces all glowed lurid yellow from the whale-oil fire. Other voices joined those already there. Crewmen loyal to Henri poured in, with knives and swords drawn. Shouts and the clash of enemies fighting one another, mutineers against crew, filled the air with their conflict.

Suddenly searing pain stabbed through Maddie's shoulder. A blinding flash of light blotted out what went on around her. She crumpled to the floor in a rapidly fading haze.

Chapter Thirty-six

Maddie awakened to find herself in bed. When she moved, pain stabbed through her, holding her prisoner as no ropes had ever done. Henri sat by her side, his gray eyes tender as he met her gaze. "Henri?" she whispered.

"Maddie, I was so worried. That you should be wounded so soon after all you suffered during childbirth." At mention of it, her eyes widened. Suddenly alarmed, she struggled into sitting position. "My baby. Where is my baby?" At once, blinding pain forced her back down.

"Our baby is all right, but you have to save your strength. Whoever did it cut you awfully deep. A few inches over, and—" Henri shuddered.

"Never mind that." She stared at him now suddenly concerned. "What about *you*?" That terrible struggle in the navigation room burst with fresh intensity into her memory. "Those terrible men!"

"They're all gone now," he replied. "They were outnumbered, and they knew it. If they had killed me, their little plan might have succeeded, but thanks to you, Maddie, they failed."

Maddie's body went limp with relief. "Oh, thank God! But what will become of them?"

Henri shrugged. "Those men of my crew suffered the fate of mutineers everywhere. They were hanged this morning as a lesson to anyone else who might try what they did. As for the passengers involved, I've decided to show mercy. After all, they owed me no loyalty. We'll be putting into port soon. I'll let them go their own ways unharmed. But tell me—how did you know about it? How did you find out they planned that little uprising?"

To answer and reassure him, Maddie explained how she had overheard two of the conspirators deep in conversation planning it all. "Luckily, I realized I hadn't any time to waste," she said, concluding, "as it was, I got there none too soon."

With stunningly tender eyes, Henri gazed down at her. "What love you've shown! I wished I had deserved it." As he stroked her hair, a thrill tingled through Maddie's flesh. At his touch, her heart fluttered.

"Oh, Henri!" she whispered, "don't say that!" She wanted to forget those unhappy times.

"I treated you so badly." With pain in his eyes now, Henri shook his head. "I humiliated you publicly. I mistreated you. I even threatened to take away your baby. You should have stabbed me in the back, instead of saving me."

"I never blamed you." Tears blurred her vision. "It was all Andrew Mathias's doing. He's a devil, nothing more or less. *He* thought up the whole plan to trick me into denouncing you. He hoped to shatter you and rob all remaining hope and joy from your life, yet even that wasn't enough to satisfy him. He still planned all along that you'd die, and he wanted you to leave this earth believing that the woman you loved had betrayed you.''

Henri's jaw hardened. ''And I fell for it. If I ever see him again, I'll do for him, God willing, what I did for Carstarfin.''

Maddie closed her eyes in a sigh. ''I would rather not even be near him, or have you do it, either. Let him rot in Port Royal with his wretched wife, while we live our lives somewhere else.''

Henri smiled. He slipped from her view for a moment, then returned, carrying their child. Very gently, he laid the infant Henri in her arms. ''Our baby needs his mother,'' he said. ''He's hungry I think, so you'd better feed him. I want him strong and healthy when we take him to see his grandfather.''

Maddie let out a cry. ''His grandfather?'' You mean, we're—''

''Setting out for Salem as soon as I've finished my business in Trenton. We can travel over land if you like. It's not that far.''

''Oh, Henri!'' Tears of joy filled her eyes. As they swelled out to stream down her cheeks, her loving husband kissed them away.